Women of Futures Past:
Classic Stories

Women of Futures Past:
Classic Stories

Edited by
Kristine Kathryn Rusch

WOMEN OF FUTURES PAST

A Baen Books Original

Baen Publishing Enterprises
P.O. Box 1403
Riverdale, NY 10471
www.baen.com

ISBN: 978-1-4767-8161-7

Cover art by Christine Mitzuk

First Baen printing, September 2016

Distributed by Simon & Schuster
1230 Avenue of the Americas
New York, NY 10020

Printed in the United States of America

10 9 8 7 6 5 4 3 2 1

Table of Contents

✸

Acknowledgments

I owe a huge debt of gratitude to Toni Weisskopf, the publisher of Baen Books, for her willingness to take on this project. She's made it easy. I owe another big debt to Hank Davis for all the materials he sent, and all of the letters pointing me in the right direction. Thanks to everyone else at Baen Books for all they've done to help bring this project to fruition.

A large number of others have helped along the way. I'm sure I'm going to miss a few of you, and I'm sorry for that. Many thanks to Ann and Jeff VanderMeer for helping with a story and for . . . well, you know. Thanks to Stephen Haffner, Mike Resnick, Rick Katze, David G. Grubbs, Vaughne Hansen, Betsy Mitchell, Judy Cashner, and Allyson Longuiera for helping with the stories. Thanks to Jean Rabe, Keith West, Todd McCaffrey, and Eileen Gunn for answering questions I had quickly.

A big thanks to the visitors to the Women in Science Fiction website I started along with this project. I appreciate all of your suggestions and your support.

Folks, if you want to see a list of favorite women science fiction writers, with reader commentary as to why someone loved a particular author, go to womeninsciencefiction.com.

Women of Futures Past:
Classic Stories

Introduction:
Invisible Women

☉

by Kristine Kathryn Rusch

WHEN I PROPOSED THIS BOOK of classic science fiction stories by women to Toni Weisskopf, the publisher of Baen Books, she suggested a title for this introductory essay: "The Women Fen Don't See." It's a great title with a marvelous pun, which is very science fiction.

Let me explain why the title is great, and why I didn't use it.

Toni's title is a fannish in-joke.

One of the classic feminist stories of science fiction is James Tiptree Jr.'s "The Women That Men Don't See." (Tiptree, for those of you who don't know, was a woman. You can find the story in her collection, *Her Smoke Rose Up Forever.*)

Toni changed the word "men" for the word "fen." Hardcore science fiction people (like me) generally use the word "fen" as the plural of the word "fan" when referring to sf fans. Science fiction fandom is a separate community from general science fiction readers (those who have never attended a convention, for instance). Science fiction fandom rose in tandem with the genre of science fiction, and for a long time, science fiction fandom seemed so small that the worldwide fen could gather in a single hotel.

When looked at under a hard cold light, that last statement was not true. But like so many things in science fiction, it *felt* true.

1

Just like Toni's proposed title felt true as well. I went with it until I started the research for this anthology. And then I realized that fen do see their own history. They know about the women who have been part of the field from the beginning, and have consistently honored those women for decades.

It's actually people who have little history with the hardcore center of the science fiction field who believe that women have had no place in the genre. To those people (those non-fen), the women of science fiction have become invisible.

I was rather shocked when I realized that the women of science fiction had become invisible. Okay, no. I was *exceedingly* shocked when I realized it.

Because I have written and edited science fiction for more than thirty years, and never once had I had a story rejected because I was female. Nor was I turned away from any editing jobs that I wanted because of my gender.

For those of you who don't know, I'm a bestselling writer in multiple genres. My sf books have hit the *USA Today* bestseller list, the *Wall Street Journal* bestseller list, and the *Times* of London bestseller list, as well as other lists. I've been nominated for every award in the sf genre, and I've won quite a few of them, including the prestigious Hugo Award (which I won twice, once for editing and once for my writing).

My science fiction resume goes on for pages, just like the resumes of so many women authors in the science fiction field. And I have not been invisible to the fen.

I have been the guest of honor at many science fiction conventions, often co-guest of honor with other women, like Connie Willis or Lois McMaster Bujold. Women have always been on the programming items, and women have often planned and run the conventions, which are, in some cases, multimillion dollar enterprises.

The idea that women are discriminated against in science fiction is ludicrous to me.

Have I encountered boorish behavior at sf conventions? Hell, yes. Connie Willis and I were repeatedly called "little lady" on a panel at a Westercon by an outspoken male fan who wore (I kid you not) a propeller beanie. Everyone in the audience expected us to shout him down.

We didn't. I expected Connie to yell at him. She expected me to. So we both stared at the guy we later called "Beanie Boy" in gap-mouthed surprise.

Surprise because such behavior is rare at sf conventions.

Yeah, I got groped in the late 1980s and early 1990s, back when I was young and cute. I got groped outside of sf conventions as well. Sexual predators appear in all forms at sf conventions, just like they do in the real world, and those horrid people need to be reported no matter where you encounter them.

And when I became the editor of *The Magazine of Fantasy & Science Fiction* in 1991, I received a lot of weird responses in part because I was the first (and so far only) female editor of the magazine. When Edward L. Ferman, the publisher of *The Magazine of Fantasy & Science Fiction*, announced that I would replace him as editor, the reaction was generally positive. After all, women have edited science fiction since the genre's official beginnings in 1926.

After Ed's announcement, I got a lot of hate mail, including one memorable—and completely serious—signed handwritten letter, telling me that I couldn't edit because I didn't have a penis. I've often wondered about that: Is there some editing trick that male editors use their penises for? None of the male editors will tell me.

In all seriousness, though, those letters angered my husband more than they angered me. That marked the first time my husband (Dean Wesley Smith, an sf writer himself) had ever seen the kinds of disparaging and harassing comments that women in all businesses *still* receive on a regular basis.

Most women develop coping mechanisms.

Mine are pretty simple: a hard elbow to the gut of any man who pinches my ass, a report to the proper authority of any person who harasses me (sexually or otherwise), a sharp retort to a sexist idiot (with the singular exception of Beanie Boy, because he caught me off guard), and a good hard laugh at the some of the stupidity that bigots come up with—like the penis comment.

I also tend to look at the positives rather than the negatives. When Ed made that announcement twenty-five years ago, only about one-quarter of the response I received was negative. The positive responses warmed my heart. They included marvelous cards and letters from hundreds of people in the field. I also got a congratulatory phone call from Nobel Prize winning scientist Linus Pauling, who had subscribed to the magazine since its inception in 1949.

In my decades in science fiction, I have worked with hundreds of professional women—some behind the scenes and some out front. Women are some of the science fiction field's biggest bestsellers and its most decorated writers. Since 1968, not a year has gone by without women being nominated for the field's top awards.

In fact, science fiction's most award-winning writer is Connie Willis. *Wired Magazine* in an August 23, 2015, article about the Hugo Awards, called her the Meryl Streep of the genre.

Streep received her awards and nominations at the Academy Awards, where the awards are segregated by gender. The major science fiction awards don't segregate its categories by gender.

Connie isn't the most award-winning woman in the field in women-only categories. She's the most award-winning *person* in the field, period.

Full stop. End of story.

So, imagine my surprise when young writers who were trying to break into the field told me that women didn't write science fiction. And then when the young writers saw the look of complete surprise on my face, some of them had the grace to realize who they were talking to— the *woman* with whom they had come to study how to write science fiction—and they would say, "Present company excepted, of course."

Of course.

The first time I heard this, I wrote it off. The young writer who had mouthed this inanity wasn't the brightest bulb in the chandelier. I figured she just didn't know.

Then I heard it again, and again, and yet again. (Hell, I heard it just last week at my local professional writers' lunch from a young woman who had been born in the 1990s, and who knew I was working on this project. She had the grace to look embarrassed.)

I would answer these young writers by listing wonderful writers. I would say, "Of course, women get published in science fiction. What about Connie Willis? What about Nancy Kress? What about Ursula K. Le Guin, Anne McCaffrey, Andre Norton, Lois McMaster Bujold . . . ?"

The most common response I got was this: "They're exceptions," these young writers would say. "Just like you are."

But sometimes—okay, often—the response I got was: "Who? I've never heard of these writers."

Whenever I got the second response, I was stunned. Again, I figured ignorance on the part of the speaker—at first.

But then I encountered that "who?" response more often than the "exceptions" response.

Something else was at play here.

I'm a former journalist. I also received my B.A. in history. Those two disciplines taught me that a myth doesn't spring up overnight just because everyone chooses to believe something that's not true. A myth shows up because the evidence to counteract it is often hard to find.

About the time I was coming to realize that today's young female writers had no idea that they *weren't* storming the barricades—that there *were* no barricades and had never been any in sf—I taught a science fiction class for professional writers. That class, in June of 2013, was the first time I had ever taught science fiction to established writers.

I teach two craft workshops per year in person at the WMG Publishing offices. (I co-teach others online with Dean.) Those in-person craft workshops are always for writers who already have credentials, always with an eye toward continuing education. One trick I learned early was that the classes need to have a common fictional vocabulary, so I always assign a long reading list before the class begins. I always make sure the books and stories I choose are easy to purchase or are accessible online.

As I prepped the science fiction class's list, I discovered something shocking. I couldn't find most of the classic science fiction short stories by women. Those stories weren't in print. Worse, they'd rarely been anthologized.

The award-nominated stories, the award-*winning* stories, by women writers somehow rarely made it into the best science fiction of the year anthologies, especially the volumes that were compiled in the 1990s and the early 2000s.

When I was coming into the field, Isaac Asimov edited a volume of Hugo-nominated stories every year, but he died in 1992. Connie Willis edited the last volume of those stories ever published, in 1992. After that, the best stories of the year—as voted on by fen—rarely got anthologized.

The same thing happened with the stories that won readers awards at the top magazines of the genre. Even though women won those awards every year, those stories never got anthologized. That happens to men's stories as well, partly because of publishing schedules. The best-of volumes usually appear about the time the short lists for the various awards from the previous year get announced.

But the fact remains that the best stories of the year, chosen by *readers*, the people who give their hard-earned money to buy fiction, were rarely put in the best-of anthologies.

But timing isn't the only reason women got left off that list most of the time. There are year's best volumes—thick ones—with only a handful of female authors included, in years when women dominated the awards. For example, women received the majority of the fifteen short fiction nominations in the 1993 Hugo awards, winning two of those awards. A glance at the table of contents of the only science fiction best-of still in print from that year shows that of those eight short stories by women, only three of them appear in that volume— and only one of the winners. (There were twenty-four stories in that volume, and only seven of them were by women.)

Discrimination? Oh, probably not. Probably something called unconscious bias or second-generation discrimination. The person who has unconscious bias, unlike a hardcore bigot, will prefer someone who looks like him to someone who doesn't.

That unconscious bias will show up in editing by the stories that appeal to the editor. Editors often prefer stories that speak to their own experiences. Since the majority of editors of years-best collections in the past sixty years have been male, those editors often chose the stories that most reflected their own experiences.

There's a secondary bias at work as well. In the last half of the twentieth century, space opera was considered "inferior" to hard science fiction in the literary circles of science fiction publishing. Many of our best women writers became bestsellers by writing space opera.

And literati of science fiction also had one other surprising prejudice: they believed that bestselling books were inferior to other books. If a mass readership liked something, these people reasoned, then it was bad by definition.

This is the reason that science fiction as a publishing category nearly died off in the 1990s. Things have improved a lot in this century, but that doesn't help the *perception* that the writers who toiled in the successful, but less accepted, subgenres didn't exist at all.

I mention the literary part of the genre because it held its strongest sway in the short fiction categories. It's easier to maintain a magazine with literary pretensions than it is to maintain a book line with the same attitudes. A lot of sf book lines died in the late 1990s and early 2000s. Some magazines, including the one that I used to edit, lost a vast amount of readership when those literary attitudes I just mentioned took over at the turn of this century.

On the other hand, some of the sf magazines grew in circulation. For example, *Asimov's Science Fiction* grew in *overall* circulation after Sheila Williams became editor. She got rid of a lot of the slipstream fiction (the stuff you couldn't tell from realistic fiction) and purchased a lot of space opera and adventure fiction. Her company, Dell Magazines, also jumped into the digital revolution quickly and whole-heartedly, which upped their subscription base considerably. And, just a note: Dell Magazines employs three women editors at its four digest fiction magazines.

Science fiction with a sense of wonder, space opera, and adventurous science fiction rose in popularity in this century. But finding it at the short length—in anthologies—has been hard.

As I dug deeper and deeper into the recent past, looking for easy ways to give my students some of the best stories in the genre, I realized that for a variety of reasons, the best stories, the most memorable stories, have been lost.

The young writers, particularly young female writers, immediately assumed discrimination. Since I know most of the editors and publishers in the science fiction field, I never assumed discrimination. Many of the editors those young writers were accusing of discrimination were women. (Of course the young writers didn't know that: they had no idea who edited books and book lines.)

So the shouts of discrimination made no sense to me . . . until I went to Wikipedia one afternoon in 2014. I looked up "women in science fiction," and found no listing. Wikipedia suggested I try "women in speculative fiction," so I did—and immediately got mad.

The Wikipedia entry was all about how women were denied entry into sf (without citations, mostly). Then on that page, there was also a listing of the women who wrote sf. With a half dozen exceptions, the *only* women listed had been published in the twenty-first century.

None of those women listed were the most successful authors in the genre. No Anne McCaffrey, no C.J. Cherryh, no Elizabeth Moon, not a one. Yeah, Tiptree was there, and so was Le Guin, but Connie Willis, the Meryl Streep of Science Fiction? Not there.

(As I have reviewed the listing two years later in prep for this essay, I saw that the listing has been cleaned up considerably, but I've been complaining about it during that entire time, and I asked people to contribute to it. A lot of people have clearly stepped up. If you're one of them, thank you!)

After I looked for the award-winning stories and saw that Wikipedia list, I started to understand those young writers' point of view. To them, the women who came before them had faded into nothingness. We had become invisible, and therefore, to new writers, we did not exist.

I never thought of myself as invisible, even though I often got left off of lists of women who wrote science fiction. I'd been told repeatedly by a certain segment of the field that I didn't write stories of interest to women (!), hence I was never mentioned.

I found it irritating, but I ignored it, because I'm clearly doing well without being on any of those lists, just like other women writers who routinely get left off the lists of women sf writers. I honestly didn't give these things much thought.

Until January 14, 2015. That was the day that Charles Coleman Finlay's ascension to the editorship of *The Magazine of Fantasy & Science Fiction* was announced.

The science fiction field's oldest news magazine, *Locus*, reported Finlay's editorship and listed the previous editors of the *F&SF—all* of them, except me. In fact, *Locus* stated that my successor, Gordon Van Gelder, took over the editorship from Edward L. Ferman, wiping me out of existence entirely.

I have had to deal with incredible nastiness about my years as editor of *F&SF* for decades now. Comments about the way that I ruined the magazine with my choice of stories. Comments about my youth (even though I was the same age as both Gordon and Ed Ferman were when they took over), my appearance, and my female bent. The kinds of comments women have received in business for decades.

My tenure at *F&SF* was quite successful, including making the magazine competitive in the genre awards again, and presiding over the largest circulation the magazine held in the 1990s, circulation that has dropped off precipitously in the past fifteen years.

Much of that nastiness has been behind the scenes, although it creeps up in places like *The Encyclopedia of Science Fiction*, and Wikipedia again, where my contribution to the magazine is mentioned only once, in a list.

That January day, I had had enough. I posted on Facebook and other social media sites (in posts that are still there):

> *You want to know how women get ignored in the sf/f field? Read this from Locus Mag, theoretically the news magazine of the field. It says that Gordon Van Gelder took over the editing duties of F&SF from the previous editor, Ed Ferman. Hello! Gordon got the editing duties after ME. I was the previous editor of F&SF.*

At the same time, I called *Locus* and demanded that they fix this problem immediately. The editor-in-chief, Liza Groen Trombi, apologized. She claimed that the error came from *Locus* itself. She said that the writer and the copy editors of the piece hadn't seen the error. She immediately corrected the story—as she should have.

Honestly, I would much rather have had the oversight be an intentional slight. Because if Liza's statements are true, my editorship—as the first female editor of one of the genre's most important magazines—has become so marginalized that staff writers and copy editors at the oldest news magazine in the field had no idea I had ever been editor of *The Magazine of Fantasy & Science Fiction*.

I stand by my comments on Facebook that day. This is how women become invisible. We get left off official histories. When we are mentioned, there is no analysis. We're just a name on a page. We get ignored by the "premiere news magazine" of the field. We get marginalized.

After that, I started talking to other active women in the field, women who've been writing and publishing science fiction for decades, and discovered that they have had similar experiences. I also found out that just the mention of the fact that some writers were claiming there were no women in science fiction made the professional women writers I'd been talking to vibrate with anger. In fact, I discovered a reservoir of anger so deep that we could probably irrigate the Mojave Desert with it.

If you want to see but one example, go to multiple award-winning sf writer Eleanor Arnason's online essay at *Strange Horizons*, which she posted on April 13, 2015. Her title, "What Are We, Chopped Liver?" says it all.

Within the sf field itself—the critics and academics, the well-intentioned male editors feeling liberal guilt, the new women writers bravely storming barricades that were never there—we women do not exist.

The fen know that we're here. The fen know that we've always been there.

But that narrative in which there has been no female participation in sf, no women writing sf, in which women had to hide under pen names and initials because of being discriminated against . . . that narrative has triumphed over the truth.

That narrative is insulting. It's demeaning. And it's wrong.

I don't believe in bitching about things. I believe in taking action.

So I sat down with Toni Weisskopf, the *publisher* of Baen Books, at a conference in February of 2015. Toni has worked in the sf field for almost thirty years in an exceedingly influential capacity. We discussed our invisibility (hence the joke: "The Women Fen Don't See") and I pitched this anthology.

Toni thought it a good idea. She gave me a hundred-thousand words, which she wanted divided up as ninety-thousand words of fiction and a ten-thousand word essay.

To do the women of sf justice, I would need several *million* words of fiction. Women have written a lot of science fiction from the very beginning—whether you date sf as beginning with the Epic of Gilgamesh in 2400 B.C. (as the marvelous writer Jack Williamson used to do), Mary Shelly's *Frankenstein* in 1818 or with Hugo Gernsback's *Amazing Stories* in 1926.

For the purposes of this anthology, I'm going to define the beginning of science fiction in the modern era the way that science fiction fandom generally does, with the publication of *Amazing Stories* in 1926. That puts this anthology in line with two very good twenty-first century scholarly works, one by Justine Larbalestier and the other by Eric Leif Davin.

I'm relying in part on their research for the next section of this introduction. I've confirmed some of it with my own sources. My husband owns a complete sf digest collection (and we used to own a massive pulp collection). We have a great deal of research material at our fingertips. I've done spot checks on the quotes in both books, using our collection, and found that the books are accurate.

Davin, in particular, has done much of the work I initially planned to do, and so much more. His astonishingly well-researched *Partners in Wonder: Women and The Birth of Science Fiction 1926-1965*, published by Lexington Books in 2006, *begins* with a list of two hundred and three known women who published in U.S. science fiction magazines between 1926 and 1960. He adds an appendix with minibiographies of more than a hundred of them, which turned out to be the ones he could trace.

In addition, he lists twenty-six women who edited "science fiction, fantasy, and weird" magazines in the years between 1928 and 1960. His editorial listings start with Miriam Bourne, who acted as an associate editor and managing editor for *Amazing Stories*, beginning in 1928, its first year of publication. He also lists Marcia Nardi, an associate editor with *All-Story* in 1929, and Madeline Heath, who *edited All-Story* in 1929.

In other words, women not only published stories at the dawn of the modern science fiction era, they *edited* stories as well.

Pick up Davin's book for the bibliographic material alone. The amount of work he did here is astonishing and extremely valuable to the field—and so many people don't know it exists. Give it to anyone who tells you that women did not publish science fiction before the year 2000. (Or the year 1970—or whatever myth someone chooses to believe.)

Amazing Stories' first issue appeared in April of 1926. In the June 1927 issue, Clare Winger Harris became the first woman to publish a story in a science fiction magazine.

"It was the beginning of a popular and rewarding science fiction career for Harris," Davin writes, "(in) a field still so young that it was composed of only a single magazine. Nevertheless, she was there, almost from the beginning, *with her name splashed on future covers to attract readers.*" [Davin, page 29]

That latter emphasis is mine. I've been in publishing a very long time, and the rules now are the same as they were ninety years ago. You put the names of popular writers on the cover *to sell* your magazine. Clearly, Harris had a following. And Hugo Gernsback, rather than hiding the fact that he was publishing a woman, was investing in Harris—and her female byline.

Indeed, Gernsback was deeply aware that he had a female audience for his magazine. He wrote this in his editorial for the September 1926 issue:

"A totally unforeseen result of the name (*Amazing Stories*), strange to say, was that a great many women were already reading the new magazine. This is most encouraging." [quoted in *The Battle of The Sexes in Science Fiction*, Justine Larbalestier, Wesleyan University Press, 2002, page 23]

Indeed, the presence of women in the science fiction field, as writers, editors, fans and casual readers, is clearly there for anyone willing to look. Davin looked. He conducted what he calls "an archeological dig" into the archives of early twentieth century science fiction for *Partners in Wonder*. He builds on the groundwork that Justine Larbalestier lays in *The Battle of the Sexes in Science Fiction*, in which she does a textural analysis of gender relations from 1926 to the 1990s, with an emphasis on feminist thought.

Larbalestier states that "the period from 1926 to 1973 is absolutely crucial to the formation of contemporary feminist science fiction, and yet very little critical work has been undertaken on that period." [Larbalestier, page 2]

Davin took that statement as a clear challenge to explore the history of women in the science fiction field. Exploring the history of women in the field is *different* than examining feminist science fiction.

Not every feminist is a woman and not every woman is a feminist. Feminism brings a particular political point of view to the research. That point of view is generally seeks to explore issues of gender, sometimes following a corrective impulse and sometimes to inform readers about the differences between the past and present (if there are any).

For the purposes of this volume, I prefer Davin's purely factual data-driven account. And before some critics accuse me of anti-feminist leanings, let me set the record straight.

I am a feminist of longstanding. I studied women's history and gender studies from some of the pioneering women in both disciplines, including the renown Gerda Lerner. I use a lot of my experiences in my fiction, particularly my mystery fiction. It would be a lie to tell you that my feminist leanings have nothing to do with this book.

This book comes directly from my training and my point of view, but in a very different way than most feminists approach things. When I worked at rape crisis centers and suicide hotlines in the 1970s and 1980s, I learned the dangers of silence, secrets, and hidden information. I learned to speak up and speak the truth, even when the truth was hurtful.

It is that impulse (yes, a corrective impulse) which informs this book.

I'm leaning on Davin because, unlike so many historians and writers of gender studies before him, Davin isn't out to prove a feminist theory with his book. He wants to prove that the accepted story of women in the sf field is incorrect. So he wrote a more general book about the early years of twentieth century science fiction than Larbalestier did.

Davin's phrase "archeological dig" is an accurate one: he examined "*every* issue of *every* science fiction magazine published in the United States in [the years 1926 to 1965] . . ." He looked for "stories written under both female names and pseudonyms of known women . . . Pertinent editorial comments and readers' letters were also examined . . . one of the results of this research has been the assembly of the most complete bibliography of female authors in the science fiction magazines."

He notes, "This bibliography reveals a fascinating form of 'invisibility'—scores of female authors and hundreds of their stories 'hiding in plain sight.'" [Davin, page 20]

Indeed, Davin discovered "at least" two hundred thirty-three women writers who published a total of 1,055 stories in the science fiction magazines between 1926 and 1965.

He writes, "These stories represent an entire school of literature, with its own themes and concerns. It is an impressive body of work— a thousand and one tales of Scheherazade, existing like some secret female script, unknown to the larger world. Unacknowledged and trivialized they may be, yet the authors and their stories are there. They represent a female counter-culture flourishing in the midst of the larger male body of work which historians of both genders have wrongly assumed characterized the entire genres in those years." [Davin, page 313]

Why did "historians of both genders" assume that science fiction is a male-only literature? For the same reason the young writers I've been talking to assumed that almost no women wrote science fiction before them.

For the entire history of modern science fiction, the stories by women weren't anthologized as much as the stories by men.

The science fiction anthologies mostly came into being in the 1950s. Publishing changed in those years for a variety of reasons that are out of our purview here. One of the changes (pioneered by a woman, Betty Ballantine, in collaboration with her husband Ian) was the rise of mass market paperback books. Those books made it possible for the first time to easily anthologize genre stories (as opposed to literary stories, which were often anthologized in hardcover).

Historians of the science fiction field, looking at important works of the field in a particular decade, will often begin with compilation anthologies and those give a partial (and often misleading) view of the past.

Again, Davin's research comes in handy. He writes that most anthology editors overlooked the work of early women writers. Those editors "have followed the lead of Damon Knight in his influential *Science Fiction of the Thirties* (1975). Knight chose eighteen stories (by nineteen authors) to represent the 1930s. Not one of them was by a woman. Likewise, Martin Harry Greenberg and Joseph Olander, in their *Science Fiction of the Fifties*, also slighted the role of women. Out of twenty-one stories they picked to represent the 1950s, only two were by women. . . . Similarly, in his 1996 unearthing of the 'greatest stories of the decade,' Robert Silverberg found eighteen stories from the Fifties worth noting. Only one was by a woman. And in *The End of Summer: Science Fiction of the Fifties*, edited by Barry N. Malzberg and Bill Pronzini, we find ten stories they claim to be representative of the decade. Not even one is by a woman."

Davin adds a personal note to all of this information.

"Had I relied on such works," he writes, "I would have had as skewed a vision of the past as have most others in the field, and there would have been little to write about." [Davin, page 246]

In an essay, "The Women that SF Doesn't See," (note the title) for *Asimov's* in October of 1992, Connie Willis points out that women *did* exist in large numbers in the sf genre before 1960. She writes:

> *The field didn't just have women writers—it had really good women writers. These were wonderful stories, and I don't believe they were overlooked at the time, because when I read them, they were all in Year's Best collections.*

I've only done a spot-check, but it seems that the year's best collections which Connie saw as a young girl were edited by a woman, Judith Merril. The Merril anthologies carry all of the women writers that Connie mentions in her essay and more.

It doesn't help, however, because the compilation anthologies—the best of the decade anthologies—never included those stories by women.

I find it particularly sad to see Damon Knight listed as the leader of this awful trend. Damon, also a mentor and teacher of mine, was married to Kate Wilhelm, one of the best science fiction writers in the field. She's also one of the field's most influential women. (And no, I couldn't squeeze a story of hers here. Her "Forever Yours, Anna" [and two other award-nominated stories] ended up on my editing equivalent of the cutting room floor.)

Kate influenced generations of science fiction writers through her writings. She also influenced generations, in partnership with Damon, at the Clarion Writers Workshops, which they founded with Robin Scott Wilson. She was one of the founders of the Science Fiction Writers of America in 1965 and designed the template for the Nebula Award, the actual physical award.

A side note: I looked up her history online so that I could cite some of these things, several of which she told me in person. She's not mentioned, even in connection with the founding of Clarion, or if she is, she's mentioned in passing, as if she had nothing to do with these things. Again, a woman's contribution disappears.

Although, to be fair, Kate's prodigious writing output, which spans from the 1950s to now, is front and center in her biography—as it should be.

Kate's marginalization on her activities with Damon points out another way that women get marginalized. Women who are married to a man in the same (or a similar) field often get ignored while the man receives credit for things they have both done.

One of the many research books I've used to prepare this essay repeatedly quotes and honors Lester Del Rey as the brains behind the imprint Del Rey books, but neglects to mention his wife, Judy-Lynn Del Rey, whose editing work helped create the modern fantasy genre. Judy-Lynn Del Rey was the brains behind Del Rey books, the person who upended the entire fantasy genre and put writers who are now famous on the map.

(Her work in the fantasy genre—in fact, the *entire* fantasy genre—is outside the purview of this essay as well, but I hope to get to that in another book.)

The same thing happens in these research books to Betty Ballantine. She founded Ballantine Books with her husband Ian, and in many histories of publishing, gets little or no credit. Fortunately, the fen have come to the rescue again. She and Ian were inducted into the Science Fiction Hall of Fame in a joint citation.

Sometimes marginalization happens when writers collaborate. C.L. Moore collaborated with her husband, Henry Kuttner, throughout their marriage, and early writings about them gives Kuttner more credit than Moore for those stories. (In recent years, Moore has received a lot more credit for her work with Kuttner.)

When I first heard of Moore, I'd been given to understand that she owed her career to Kuttner, when it couldn't be further from the truth. They hadn't met when she published her first stories. They met after *he* wrote *her* a fan letter.

But it wasn't just the presence of men in a woman's life that got her dismissed or the fact that an anthology editor didn't notice her. An anthology editor might have liked a woman's writing, but her subject matter might have prevented her inclusion in the anthologies of the mid-twentieth century.

Many of the writers (not just women) who wrote in the pre-space flight era of the 1930s to 1960 (or so) wrote stories with science that became outdated by the time Damon published his *Science Fiction of the 1930s* volume. The 1970s and 1980s were a particularly combative time period in science fiction history, in which many of the literary critics (including Damon) and the editors at major publishing houses dismissed space opera entirely.

These same folks fought the influence of *Star Trek* and *Star Wars* on science fiction of the day. Clearly, the editors and critics of that period lost their battle against popularity.

But not without damaging some of our best writers along the way. One of those writers was Leigh Brackett. In *The Best of Leigh Brackett*, a collection of short stories by Brackett published shortly before her death in 1977, her husband, science fiction writer Edmond Hamilton, wrote a somewhat defensive introduction to the stories that included this paragraph, aimed at critics like Damon:

> *Those were the days when we were all writing, in accordance with the latest guesses of astronomers and scientists, about a Mercury that kept one face always to the sun and the other to space and had a Twilight Belt between these extremes of savage heat and bitter cold, where there were alternate sunsets and sunrises due to the rocking of the planet, and where life might conceivably exist. Today those concepts have been shot down by better data from probes and more advanced scientific methods. But in those days they were valid....* [*The Best of Leigh Brackett*, edited by Edmond Hamilton, Nelson Doubleday, Inc., 1977, page ix]

The best-of-the-decade anthologies, published after space probes and "more advanced scientific methods" didn't just leave out Brackett's Mars, but also C.L. Moore's Northwest Smith stories and Ray Bradbury's classic Martian tales. They were considered unworthy, disproven by science, just as *Star Wars* was considered unworthy and more of a fantasy. (To see the *Star Wars* arguments, which have continued into the twenty-first century, see *Star Wars on Trial*, edited by David Brin.)

A lot of very good fiction has been dismissed by literary critics and anthologists. Sometimes, the fiction was dismissed when it came out. In the 1950s, science fiction by women got dismissed if it revolved around hearth and home.

Writer and critic James Blish, using his William Atheling, Jr., pen name, wrote this about Rosel George Brown:

> *Mrs. Brown is just about the only one of F&SF's former gaggle of housewives who doesn't strike me as verging on the*

feebleminded: in fact I think her work has attracted less attention than it deserves. [Larbalestier, page 173]

By the time Blish wrote that, in 1964, Brown had been nominated for Best New Author Hugo in 1958. (Yes, there was once a Best New Author Hugo.) She was receiving quite a bit of attention. (And no, unfortunately, she's not in this volume either, although her very creepy story, "Car Pool" came close. You can find it reprinted in *Earthblood and Other Stories*, by Keith Laumer and Rosel George Brown, also from Baen.)

And the other writers that Blish dismissed as a gaggle of feebleminded housewives? They include Mildred Clingerman, Zenna Henderson, Evelyn E. Smith, Judith Merril, Margaret St. Clair, Kit Reed and Shirley Jackson. Yes, so they wrote about hearth and home—often funny, scary or deeply satirical stories about a very claustrophobic period of time.

So did Leigh Brackett, even though Larbalestier quotes her as dismissing the genre, ignoring the fact that Brackett wrote stories like the very creepy "The Tweener" and the equally upsetting "The Queer Ones."

Men also wrote hearth-and-home stories in the 1950s—Ray Bradbury is a case in point—but those stories weren't dismissed. In fact, they were often seen for what they were: social commentary often of the *Twilight Zone* variety.

But hearth-and-home stories didn't just get dismissed by male critics. Female critics dismissed them, too, as unworthy subjects for fiction. In the 1970s, Joanna Russ doubly dismissed hearth-and-home stories in her analysis of the kinds of science fiction women tend to write. She called hearth-and-home stories either "galactic suburbia" stories or "ladies magazine fiction," which she defined as stories "in which the sweet, gentle, intuitive heroine solves an interstellar crisis by mending her slip or doing something equally domestic after her big heroic husband has failed." [Larbalestier, page 173]

Sadly for women, the other two categories that Russ said women wrote were space opera (which was already on its way out) and avant-garde fiction, which was never very popular.

Russ, as with many critics, often couldn't see the forest for the trees. Clingerman's fiction, for example, is extremely subversive and biting. Yes, her intuitive heroines solve problems in untraditional not-always-heroic ways *and that is the point.* Clingerman, Jackson, early Kit Reed, all focused on powerless people who managed the world much better than the powerful.

Writers are constantly being told what they can and cannot write. Or, perhaps I should amend that to, what they *should* and *should not* write. Even now, it seems that the only "important" stories women should tell are about gender issues.

I've been told repeatedly by women in the sf field that I don't write stories of interest to women. I always thought that comment was just something people said to me, not to other women. So, imagine my surprise when I read Connie Willis's afterword to her story "Even The Queen," in *The Best of Connie Willis.* For those of you who have never read the story, "Even The Queen" (which won the Hugo for best short story in 1993) examines a world in which menstrual cycles are optional.

About the story, Connie wrote:

> *. . . the episode that really convinced me I needed to write about this came when I was on a panel at a certain feminist science-fiction convention that shall remain nameless. (You know who you are.) I don't remember what the panel was about, but I do remember that one of the panel members said that women only thought of their menstrual cycles as a "curse" because the male-dominated patriarchy had taught them to, and that left on their own, women would welcome and embrace their menses.*
>
> *I thought then (and think now) that this was one of the most idiotic things I had ever heard. . . . After the panel, I did some research and found out that this theory was not just the ravings of one lunatic but actually pretty common in feminist circles, and then I talked to every young woman I could find (just in case attitudes had changed), and they were all as outraged and/or gobsmaked as I had been. . . .*
>
> *Plus, some of my fellow women science-fiction writers had been on my case because I wrote stories about time-travelers and old moves and the end of the world instead of writing stories about 'women's issues.'*
>
> *So I decided to write one.* [*The Best of Connie Willis*, Bantam Books, 2013, page 252]

When I pitched this anthology to Toni, I had "Even The Queen" as the story I would pick from Connie Willis. I included "The Women Men Don't See" as the story I would pick from James Tiptree, Jr. I also thought about including the Hugo-Award-winning "Boobs," by Suzy McKee Charnas.

And then I realized I was falling into the women-must-write-about-women's-issues trap, which is expressly what I wanted to avoid for this anthology.

I call this a trap, because it seems like a large part of the science fiction literary community read Pamela Sargent's groundbreaking *Women of Wonder* anthologies as prescriptive rather than corrective. The first volume, *Women of Wonder*, appeared from Vintage in 1975, the very same year that Damon Knight published *Science Fiction of the Thirties* and did not include a single woman.

Pam Sargent was correcting similar problems to the ones that I'm trying to correct now, only for a different generation, a generation for whom calling women writers "feebleminded housewives" in a respected literary journal was acceptable behavior. In addition to fighting the perception that women didn't write science fiction, Pam was also fighting something that Justine Larbalestier calls the love interest problem: there was a perception among science fiction writers and critics that female *characters* only existed in science fiction as the yes-honey girl, the love interest for the hero.

Pam reprinted old stories in *Women of Wonder* and *More Women of Wonder* to show that female characters weren't just the love interest *and* that women wrote science fiction throughout the history of science fiction. She says this in her introduction to the first volume:

> *My primary concern was to present entertaining, thoughtful, and well-written science fiction stories by women,* in which women characters play important roles. (KKR: Emphasis mine) [*Women of Wonder,* page xiii]

Pam's book was groundbreaking, one of the most important anthologies of its time, leading to *More Women of Wonder* in 1976 and *Women of Wonder: The Contemporary Years* in 1995. Since then, there have been other women-only anthologies, including last year's *Sisters of the Revolution*, edited by Ann and Jeff VanderMeer, anthologies which acknowledge their debt to *Women of Wonder*. In fact, Ann and Jeff, in their introduction, state that their volume is "a contribution to an ongoing conversation" about "feminist speculative fiction." [*Sisters of the Revolution*, edited by Ann and Jeff VanderMeer, PM Press, 2015, page 1]

Ann and Jeff are right about the ongoing conversation about feminist speculative fiction. That conversation has dominated the discussion of women in science fiction since the James Tiptree Memorial Award began in 1991. That award does *not* reward the best women writing in sf, as some assume. Instead, the aim of the award is, as the website for the award states, "*not* to look for work that falls into some narrow definition of political correctness, but rather to seek out work that is thought-provoking, imaginative, and perhaps even infuriating. The Tiptree Award is intended to reward those women *and men* who are bold enough to contemplate shifts and changes in gender roles, a fundamental aspect of any society."

Because the ongoing conversation has focused on gender and that focus has merged with the discussion of women in science fiction in general, anthology after anthology has had the same narrow focus as Pam Sargent's necessary and groundbreaking works from forty years ago.

And we women who wrote about things other than women's issues or who dared to have male protagonists instead of female ones in our stories were often told we don't write for women or that we really aren't women science fiction writers.

(Whenever I was told this [and I was told it more than once], I put it in a little box with the idea that male editors edit with their penises. I find myself exploring these concepts on occasion. How can I, a woman who writes science fiction, be anything other than a woman science fiction writer?)

It's a shame that so many editors and anthologists have viewed Pam Sargent's work as a blueprint rather than as a door thrown open on that impressive body of work that Davin writes about. By looking at Pam Sargent's work as a blueprint, so many anthologies have reprinted the same stories by the same women, as if those women wrote nothing else. The anthologies also left out work by women who have a larger following than the women of the so-called canon.

There are a variety of ways to measure success in publishing. Some measure success by reviews in the right places or by being accepted by the literary powers that be, whoever they are at a certain moment in time. Others measure success by awards and award nominations. Still others measure success by the number of books sold—the more the better.

Science fiction turned its back on sales long ago. In fact, Damon Knight (again, Damon!) famously and mistakenly said, "Science fiction will never be popular. It can't stand the suppression." As if popularity was something to be avoided rather than achieved. [Quoted in "Science Fiction and Fantasy: Describing our Field" by Rob Chilson, *Locus*, November 1998.]

Unfortunately for that point of view, the works which survive hundreds of years are, for the most part, the most popular works of their day. No matter what the important critics say or what award a certain piece of fiction received was, the fiction in question wouldn't survive past a generation or two if only a handful of people liked it. The books we pass to our children and friends are the books that will form the literature of the future.

It has long bothered me that the popular authors in science fiction—male and female—were dismissed by the literary establishment (critics, academics, and some publishers). Somehow, that establishment missed the forest for the trees.

Whenever I look at modern anthologies that continue the "ongoing conversation," they don't have a very wide scope. In fact, they ignore much of what the most successful people in the genre write. They really ignore the successful women in the genre, partly because they write space opera or about the end of the world.

As I put together this anthology, I slowly came to realize that I did not want to reprint the same old stories that everyone else has reprinted. I didn't want a feminist anthology.

I wanted to show the young writers of the field that women write science fiction—of all kinds. Not just space opera, avant-garde, and galactic suburbia stories. Not just stories about women. But stories. Excellent stories, about anything the writer damn well pleased.

In making my final choices for this volume, I decided to include as many of the bestselling and most influential authors in the genre as I could. When possible, I chose work that represented what the writer was best known for, be it a series character or a type of story. I was constrained, as all anthology editors are, by a word limit. I also set some of my own constraints.

I wanted stories that entertained as much now as they had when they were published. Sometimes I did not choose good stories with language that would be offensive to a modern audience, although there is a little archaic language in some of the older stories. (Just deal with it.) I also wanted stories that had an impact on other writers in the field—not just female writers, but male writers as well.

Finally, I did not want the stories in this volume to have a particular political slant. This introduction and the introduction to the stories have a slant, because I'm trying to introduce the important women writers of science fiction to a generation who does not know they exist.

But that's as far as the politics go here. The stories themselves are politically all over the map. They're also all over the subgenre map. I've made sure that we have hearth-and-home stories, space opera, alien-among-us stories, hard science fiction, post-apocalyptic fiction, alternate history and time travel.

Yes, there are some gender-bending stories and some stories with strong feminist themes in this anthology. But there are also stories that feature male protagonists in a traditional role.

Are there things missing from this volume? Oh, my goodness, yes. For every writer I've included there are dozens of other worthy candidates. For every story I've included by these major writers, there are several more by the same writers that should be in here.

So, what is glaringly, obviously missing from this volume? Writers of color. Writers from countries outside of the United States. Writers whose work is best at the novella length. Writers who write only novels. Writers who wrote their best stories in collaboration with someone else. Humor. A list of all the women writers who ever wrote sf. A list of women editors. A list of women publishers. A list of the most influential women of all time in science fiction. A list of the awards won by women. A list of the awards named for women. A recommended reading list. And on and on.

Some of the reasons for the big gaps, like a lack of writers of color or writers from other countries, comes from the fact that I've limited this volume to works published before the year 2000. While science fiction published in the United States had a lot of female writers in the years between 1926 and 2000, it had very few writers of color who self-identified as non-white. It also had very few writers from countries outside of the U.S. Those who did appear in the U.S. were often British. The growth of other voices in translation or writing from cultural backgrounds different than Anglo-whatever is more of a late twentieth century and early twenty-first century phenomenon.

Then there are the writers whom I deemed absolutely essential to this volume whose work I was unable to secure permission to use. (If I were to tell you the saga of my permissions adventures on this one volume alone, it would take another fifteen thousand words.)

The most heartbreaking for me personally is Octavia Butler. Her work is missing from these pages. Octavia wrote one of my very favorite novels, *Kindred,* a novel that influenced my own writing more than I can say.

I subsequently read everything she ever wrote. We became friendly over the years, which I valued. She died much too young, but she left a body of marvelous writing that includes only a handful of short stories.

As I put this volume together in the summer of 2015, I ran into the man who handled the permissions for Octavia's estate. (This man was not Octavia's agent; he belonged to another entity altogether.) He refused to license her work for this volume, upping the price of using a single story each time I tried to negotiate with him. His final ask for the use of one of her stories was double my entire advance for this book.

I finally quit trying to negotiate with him in disgust, and later discovered that other editors have had the same problems in dealing with him. Unlike all but one of those other editors, I informed the agent for Octavia's estate that this man was unreasonable. The agent has promised to get him out of the loop. Whether or not that happens remains to be seen.

If he does not get out of the loop, one of the greatest voices in the science fiction field will be slowly lost—at least on the short fiction side. So for the record, the story of Octavia's that I wanted to use here was "Speech Sounds." You can find it in her collection, *Blood Child and Other Stories.* I encourage you to do so. I would have slotted it near C.J. Cherryh's story in this volume, so if you're reading in order, take a break, find and read Octavia's story, and then continue reading this book. I love how upbeat the ending of that story is, and I also love what the story has to say about silence, communication, and relationships.

Writers get lost. They get ignored. They vanish. Sometimes this happens because of estate issues, as in the case of Octavia. But often, they disappear because the easily available sources do not include them. Davin had to dig through dusty old magazines to find 933 stories by 203 women because, as he says, the anthologists of the time did not include them.

I was born in the mid-twentieth century. I know how hard it was to be taken seriously as a woman in those years. The fact that male anthologists often left women writers and a female point of view out of those anthologies does not surprise me.

What does surprise me is that many anthologists of the "important" volumes of science fiction from the past twenty years have done the same thing.

It is no wonder that young female writers believe that they are knocking down barriers to a male-dominated science fiction field. The easily accessible volumes from the recent past make it seem that way. These writers would have to examine dusty old magazines to see the preponderance of female names. They would have to actually look at the awards ballots from the 1990s to see that women dominated the short fiction categories for *years*.

This anthology is but one corrective. Since I announced this project on a website titled women in science fiction, others have taken up the fight to retrieve the history of the field. I say more power to them. We need to revive good stories by great writers—not just the women of the field, but the men as well.

Thank you for picking up the anthology. If you enjoy the stories you find here as much as I did, please share this book with another reader. That's how fiction survives. That's how invisible writers become visible again.

That's how stories live.

—Kristine Kathryn Rusch
Lincoln City, Oregon
September 12, 2015

The Indelible Kind

by Zenna Henderson

As so many readers have done before us, we start with Zenna Henderson. Zenna Henderson opened a door to the science fiction field for many sf writers. I first learned of her from award-winning fantasy and science fiction author Nina Kiriki Hoffman, who listed Henderson as a major influence. Hoffman isn't the only person to be influenced by Henderson. When I mentioned that I was putting this anthology together, writer after writer who got started in the 1980s recalled reading Henderson as a child.

So did a lot of science fiction fans. Priscilla Olson, a major sf fan who has run Worldcons, started APAs (small journals of fan writing), and helped NESFA Press bring neglected sf authors back into print, co-edited Ingathering: The Complete People Stories of Zenna Henderson *with her husband Mark Olson. In her introduction to that invaluable collection, Priscilla Olson writes about how essential Zenna Henderson was to young readers:*

> Like so many others, I started reading science fiction as an adolescent, and discovered Zenna Henderson then. Adolescence isn't easy, but the People helped some of us make it through. . . . [Ingathering, page ix]

The People stories fall into a traditional science fiction subgenre, the alien among us. They also examine the fate of the Other in modern society—whatever the other might be.

Zenna Chlarson Henderson was an expert at being an outsider herself. Born in Tucson, Arizona, in 1917 to a family of Mormon pioneers, Henderson experienced the tightness of a Mormon community only to lose touch with that community when she divorced her husband in 1944. By that time, she had her teaching certificate, along with a B.A. in literature and languages from Arizona State University, back when its name was Arizona Teacher's College.

She spent the World War II years teaching children in Sacaton, one of the Japanese internment camps in Arizona. There, Henderson saw discrimination firsthand. She saw it later in her career as well, when she taught Mexican-American students in the Tucson school district.

Unsurprisingly, racism, hatred, and discrimination factor into most of her stories in one way or another. She views the outsider with great compassion and understanding, and her work does what the best science fiction does: it presents a modern problem in an imaginary context, so that readers will live the story along with the protagonist.

Henderson often writes about teachers and students who don't fit, which is probably why young science fiction readers of all genders and races identified with her stories.

Henderson was best known for her short fiction. She published four books during her lifetime. (She died in 1983.) By the mid-1990s when Ingathering *appeared, her works were all out of print. The short stories she was known for, including the Hugo-nominated novelette, "Captivity," were equally hard to find. The NESFA Press collection, which is still available, has reprinted Henderson's The People stories, but many of her other works are no longer in print.*

The story that follows, "The Indelible Kind," is particular favorite of mine. Compassionate and compelling, "The Indelible Kind" is impossible to put down. It also provides an excellent introduction to the People.

❀ ❀ ❀

I'VE ALWAYS BEEN a down-to-earth sort of person. On re-reading that sentence, my mouth corners lift. It reads differently now. Anyway, matter-of-fact and just a trifle sceptical—that's a further description of me. I've enjoyed—perhaps a little wistfully—other people's ghosts, and breath-taking coincidences, and flying saucer sightings, and table tiltings and prophetic dreams, but I've never had any of my own. I suppose it takes a very determined, or very childlike—not childish—person to keep illusion and wonder alive in a lifetime of teaching. "Lifetime" sounds awfully elderly making, doesn't it? But more and more I feel that I fit the role of observer more than that of participant. Perhaps that explains a little of my unexcitement when I did participate. It was mostly in the role of spectator. But what a participation! What a spectacular!

But, back to the schoolroom. Faces and names have a habit of repeating and repeating in your classes over the years. Once in a while, though, along comes one of the indelible kind—and they mark you, happily or unhappily beyond erasing. But, true to my nature, I didn't even have a twinge or premonition.

The new boy came alone. He was small, slight, and had a smooth cap of dark hair. He had the assurance of a child who had registered many times by himself, not particularly comfortable or uncomfortable at being in a new school. He had brought a say-nothing report card, which, I noted in passing, gave him a low grade in Group Activity Participation and a high one in Adjustment to Redirective Counseling—by which I gathered that he was a loner but minded when spoken to, which didn't help much in placing him academically.

"What book were you reading?" I asked, fishing on the shelf behind me for various readers in case he didn't know a specific name. Sometimes we get those whose faces overspread with astonishment and they say, "Reading?"

"In which of those series?" he asked. "Look-and-say, ITA, or phonics?" He frowned a little. "We've moved so much and it seems as though every place we go is different. It does confuse me sometimes." He caught my surprised eye and flushed. "I'm really not very good by any method, even if I do know their names," he admitted. "I'm functioning only on about a second-grade level."

"Your vocabulary certainly isn't second grade," I said, pausing over the enrollment form.

"No, but my reading is," he admitted. "I'm afraid—"

"According to your age, you should be third grade." I traced over his birthdate. This carbon wasn't the best in the world.

"Yes, and I suppose that counting everything, I'd average out about third grade, but my reading is poor."

"Why?" Maybe knowing as much as he did about his academic standing, he'd know the answer to this question.

"I have a block," he said, "I'm afraid—"

"Do you know what your block is?" I pursued, automatically probing for the point where communication would end.

"I—" his eyes dropped. "I'm not very good in reading," he said. I felt him folding himself away from me. End of communication.

"Well, here at Rinconcillo, you'll be on a number of levels. We have only one room and fifteen students, so we all begin our subjects at the level where we function best—" I looked at him sharply. "And work like mad!"

"Yes, ma'am." We exchanged one understanding glance; then his eyes became eight-year-old eyes and mine, I knew, teacher eyes. I dismissed him to the playground and turned to the paper work.

Kroginold, Vincent Lorma, I penciled into my notebook. A lumpy sort of name, I thought, to match a lumpy sort of student— scholastically speaking.

Let me explain Rinconcillo. Here in the mountainous West, small towns, exploding into large cities, gulp down all sorts of odd terrain in expanding their city limits. Here at Winter Wells, city growth has followed the three intersecting highways for miles out, forming a spidery, six-legged sort of city. The city limits have followed the growth in swatches about four blocks wide, which leaves long ridges, and truly ridges—mountainous ones—of non-city projecting into the city. Consequently, here is Rinconcillo, a one-roomed school with only 15 students, and only about half a mile from a school system with eight schools and 4800 students. The only reason this school exists is the cluster of family units around the MEL (Mathematics Experimental Laboratory) facilities, and a half-dozen fiercely independent ranchers who stubbornly refuse to be urbanized and cut up into real estate developments or be city-limited and absorbed into the Winter Wells school system.

As for me—this was my fourth year at Rinconcillo, and I don't know whether it's being fiercely independent or just stubborn, but I come back each year to my "little inside corner" tucked quite literally under the curve of a towering sandstone cliff at the end of a box canyon. The violently pursuing and pursued traffic, on the two highways sandwiching us, never even suspects we exist. When I look out into the silence of an early school morning, I still can't believe that civilization could be anywhere within a hundred miles. Long shadows under the twisted, ragged oak trees mark the orangy gold of the sand in the wash that flows—dryly mostly, wetly tumultuous seldomly—down the middle of our canyon. Manzanitas tangle the hillside until the walls become too steep and sterile to support them. And yet, a twenty-minute drive—ten minutes out of here and ten minutes into there—parks you right in front of the MONSTER MERCANTILE, EVERYTHING CHEAPER. I seldom drive that way.

Back to Kroginold, Vincent Lorma—I was used to unusual children at my school. The lab attracted brilliant and erratic personnel. The majority of the men there were good, solid citizens and no more eccentric than a like number of any professionals, but we do get our share of kooks, and their sometimes twisted children. Besides the size and situation being an ideal set-up for ungraded teaching, the uneven development for some of the children made it almost mandatory. As, for instance, Vincent, almost nine, reading, so he said, on second-grade level, averaging out to third grade, which implied above-age excellence in something. Where to put him? Why, second grade (or maybe first) and fourth (or maybe fifth) and third—of course! Perhaps a conference with his mother would throw some light on his "block." Well, difficult. According to the enrollment blank, both parents worked at MEL.

By any method we tried, Vincent *was* second grade—or less—in reading.

"I'm sorry." He stacked his hands on the middle page of *Through Happy Hours,* through which he had stumbled most woefully. "And reading is so basic, isn't it?"

"It is," I said, fingering his math paper—above age-level. And the vocabulary check test—"If it's just words, I'll define them," he had said. And he had. Third year of high school worth. "I suppose your math ability comes from your parents," I suggested.

"Oh, no!" he said, "I have nothing like their gift for math. It's—it's—I like it. You can always get out. You're never caught—"

"Caught?" I frowned.

"Yes—look!" Eagerly he seized a pencil. "See! One plus one equals two. Of course it does, but it doesn't stop there. If you want to, you can back right out. Two equals one plus one. And there you are—out! The doors swing both ways!"

"Well, yes," I said, teased by an almost grasping of what he meant. "But math traps me. One plus one equals two whether I want it to or not. Sometimes I want it to be one and a half or two and three-fourths and it won't—ever!"

"No, it won't." His face was troubled. "Does it bother you all the time?"

"Heavens, no, child!" I laughed. "It hasn't warped my life!"

"No," he said, his eyes widely on mine. "But that's why—" His voice died as he looked longingly out the window at the recess-roaring playground, and I released him to go stand against the wall of the school, wistfully watching our eight other boys manage to be sixteen or even twenty-four in their wild gyrations.

So that's why? I doodled absently on the workbook cover. I didn't like a big school system because its one-plus-one was my one and one-half—or two and three-fourths? Could be—could be. Honestly! What kids don't come up with! I turned to the work sheet I was preparing for consonant blends for my this-year's beginners—all both of them—and one for Vincent.

My records on Vincent over the next month or so were an odd patchwork. I found that he could read some of the articles in the encyclopedia, but couldn't read *Billy Goats Gruff.* That he could read *What Is So Rare as a Day in June,* but couldn't read *Peter, Peter, Pumpkin Eater.* It was beginning to look as though he could read what he wanted to and that was all. I don't mean a capricious wanting-to, but that he shied away from certain readings and actually *couldn't* read them. As yet I could find no pattern to his un-readings; so I let him choose the things he wanted and he read—oh, how he read! He gulped down the material so avidly that it worried me. But he did his gulping silently. Orally, he wore us both out with his stumbling struggles.

He seemed to like school, but seldom mingled. He was shyly pleasant when the other children invited him to join them, and played quite competently—which isn't the kind of play you expect from an eight-year-old.

And there matters stood until the day that Kipper—our eighth grade—dragged Vincent in, bloody and battered.

"This guy's nearly killed Gene," Kipper said. "Ruth's out there trying to bring him to. First aid says don't move him until we know."

"Wait here," I snapped at Vincent as I headed for the door. "Get tissues for your face!" And I rushed out after Kipper.

We found Gene crumpled in the middle of a horrified group gathered at the base of the canyon wall. Ruth was crying as she mopped his muddy forehead with a soggy tissue. I checked him over quickly. No obvious bleeding. I breathed a little easier as he moaned, moved, and opened his eyes. He struggled to a sitting position and tenderly explored the side of his head.

"Ow! That dang rock!" He blinked tears as I parted his hair to see if he had any damage besides the egg-sized lump. He hadn't. "He hit me with that big rock!"

"My!" I giggled, foolish with relief. "He must have addled your brains at the same time. Look at the size of that rock!" The group separated to let Gene look, and Pete scrambled down from where he had perched on the rock for a better look at the excitement.

"Well." Gene rubbed his head tenderly. "Anyway, he did!"

"Come on inside," I said, helping him up. "Do you want Kipper to carry you?"

"Heck no!" Gene pulled away from my hands. "I ain't hurt. G'wan—noseys!" He turned his back on the staring children.

"You children stay out here." I herded Gene ahead of me. "We have things to settle inside."

Vincent was waiting quietly in his seat. He had mopped himself fairly clean, though he still dabbled with a tissue at a cut over his left eye. Two long scratches oozed redly down his cheek. I spent the next few minutes rendering first aid. Vincent was certainly the more damaged of the two, and I could feel the drumming leap of his still-racing heart against me as I turned his docile body around, tucking in his shirt during the final tidying up.

"Now." I sat, sternly teacher, at my desk and surveyed the two before me. "Gene, you first."

"Well." he ruffed his hair up and paused to finger, half proudly, the knot under his hair. "He said let my ground squirrel go and I said no. What the heck! It was mine. And he said let it go and I said no and he took the cage and busted it and—" Indignation in his eyes faded into defensiveness. "—and I busted him one and—and— Well, then he hit me with that rock! Gosh! I was knocked out, wasn't I?"

"You were," I said, grimly. "Vincent?"

"He's right." His voice was husky, his eyes on the tape on the back of one hand. Then he looked up with a tentative lift of his mouth corners. "Except that I hit the rock with him."

"Hit the rock with him?" I asked. "You mean like judo or something? You pushed him against the rock hard enough to knock him out?"

"If you like," he shrugged.

"It's not what I like," I said. "It's—what happened?"

"I hit the rock with him," Vincent repeated.

"And why?" I asked, ignoring his foolish insistence.

"We were having a fight. He told you."

"You busted my cage!" Gene flushed indignantly.

"Gene," I reminded. "You had your turn. Vincent?"

"I had to let it go," he said, his eyes hopefully on mine. "He wouldn't, and it—it wanted to get out—the ground squirrel." His eyes lost their hopefulness before mine.

"It wasn't yours," I reminded.

"It wasn't *his* either!" His eyes blazed. "It belonged to itself! He had no right—!"

"I caught it!" Gene blazed back

"Gene! Be still or I'll send you outside!"

Gene subsided, muttering.

"You didn't object to Ruth's hamster being in a cage." "Cage" and "math" seemed trying to equate in my mind.

"That's because it was a cage beast!" he said, fingering the taped hand again. "It didn't know any better. It didn't care." His voice tightened. "The ground squirrel did. It would have killed itself to get out. I—I just *had* to—"

To my astonishment, I saw tears slide down his cheek as he turned his face away from me. Wordlessly I handed him a tissue from the box on my desk. He wiped his face, his fingers trembling.

"Gene?" I turned to him. "Anything more?"

"Well, gollee! It was mine! And I liked it! It—it was *mine!*"

"I'll trade you," said Vincent. "I'll trade you a white rat in a real neat aluminum cage. A pregnant one, if you like. It'll have four or five babies in about a week."

"Gollee! Honest?" Gene's eyes were shining.

"Vincent?" I questioned him.

"We have some at home," he said. "Mr. Wellerk at MEL gave me some when we came. They were surplus. Mother says I may trade if his mother says okay."

"She won't care!" cried Gene. "Us kids have part of the barn for our pets, and if we take care of them, she doesn't care what we have. She don't even ever come out there! Dad checks once in a while to be sure we're doing a decent job. They won't care."

"Well, you have your mother write a note saying you may have the rat, and Vincent, if you're sure you want to trade, bring the rat tomorrow and we'll consider the affair ended." I reached for my hand bell. "Well, scoot, you two. Drinks and rest room, if necessary. It's past bell time now."

Gene scooted and I could hear him yelling, "Hey! I getta white rat—"

Vincent was at the door when I stopped him with a question. "Vincent, did your mother know before you came to school that you were going to let the ground squirrel go?"

"No, ma'am. I didn't even know Gene had it."

"Then she didn't suggest you trade with Gene."

"Yes, ma'am, she did," he said reluctantly.

"When?" I asked, wondering if he was going to turn out to be a twisted child after all.

"When you were out getting Gene. I called her and told her." He smiled his tentative lip-smile. "She gave me fits for fighting and suggested Gene might like the rat. I like it, too, but I have to make up for the ground squirrel." He hesitated. I said nothing. He left.

"Well!" I exploded my held breath out. "Ananias K. Munchausen! Called his mother, did he? And no phone closer than MONSTER MERCANTILE! But still—" I was puzzled. "It didn't feel like a lie!"

Next afternoon after dismissal time I sighed silently. I was staring moodily out the window where the lonely creaking of one swing signified that Vincent, as well as I, was waiting for his mother to appear. Well, inevitable, I guess. Send a taped-up child home, you're almost sure to get an irate parent back. And Vincent had been taped up! Still was, for that matter.

I hadn't heard the car. The creaking of the swing stopped abruptly, and I heard Vincent's happy calling voice. I watched the two of them come up onto the porch, Vincent happily clinging.

"My mother, Teacher," he said, "Mrs. Kroginold."

"Good afternoon, Miss Murcer." Mrs. Kroginold was small, dark haired and bright eyed. "You wait outside, erring man-child!" She dismissed him with a spat on his bottom. "This is adult talk." He left, his small smile slanting back over his shoulder a little anxiously.

Mrs. Kroginold settled comfortably in the visitor's chair I had already pulled up beside my desk.

"Prepared, I see," she sighed. "I suppose I should have come sooner and explained Vincent."

"He is a little unusual," I offered cautiously. "But he didn't impress me as the fighting kind."

"He isn't," said Mrs. Kroginold. "No, he's—um—unusual in plenty of other ways, but he comes by it naturally. It runs in the family. We've moved around so much since Vincent's been in school that this is the first time I've really felt I should explain him. Of course, this is also the first time he ever knocked anyone out. His father could hardly believe him. Well, anyway, he's so happy here and making such progress in school that I don't want anything to tarnish it for him, so—" she sighed and smiled. "He says you asked him about his trading the rat—"

"The pregnant rat," I nodded.

"He *did* ask me," she said. "Our family uses a sort of telepathy in emergencies."

"A *sort* of telepathy—!" My jaw sagged, then tightened. Well, I could play the game, too. "How interesting!"

Her eyes gleamed. "Interesting aberration, isn't it?" I flushed and she added hastily, "I'm sorry. I didn't mean to—to put interpretations into your mouth. But Vincent did hear—well, maybe 'feel' is a better word—the ground squirrel crying out against being caged. It caught him right where he lives. I think the block he has in reading is against anything that implies unwilling compulsion—you know, being held against your will—or prevented—"

Put her in a pumpkin shell, my memory chanted. *The three Billy Goats Gruff were afraid to cross the bridge because—*

"The other schools," she went on, "have restricted him to the reading materials provided for his grade level, and you'd be surprised how many of the stories—

"And he *did* hit the rock with Gene." She smiled ruefully. "Lifted him bodily and threw him. A rather liberal interpretation of our family rules. He's been forbidden to lift any large objects in anger. He considered Gene the lesser of the two objects.

"You see, Miss Murcer, we do have family characteristics that aren't exactly—mmm—usual, but Vincent is still just a school child, and we're just parents, and he likes you much and we do, too. Accept us?"

"I—" I said, trying to blink away my confusion "I—I—"

"Ay! Ay!" Mrs. Kroginold sighed and, smiling, stood up. "Thank you for not being loudly insulted by what I've told you. Once a neighbor of ours that I talked a little too freely to, threatened to sue— so I appreciate. You are so good for Vincent. Thanks."

She was gone before I could get my wits collected. It had been a little like being caught in a dustless dust-devil. I hadn't heard the car leave, but when I looked out, there was one swing still stirring lazily between the motionless ones, and no one at all in sight on the school grounds.

I closed up the schoolroom and went into the tiny two-roomed teacherage extension on the back of the school to get my coat and purse. I had lived in those two tiny rooms for the first two years of my stay at Rinconcillo before I began to feel the need of more space and more freedom from school. Occasionally, even now, when I felt too tired to plunge out into the roar of Winter Wells, I would spend a night on my old narrow bed in the quiet of the canyon.

I wondered again about not hearing the car when I dipped down into the last sand wash before the highway. I steered carefully back across the packed narrowness of my morning tracks. Mine were the only ones, coming or going. I laid the odd discovery aside because I was immediately gulped up by the highway traffic. After I had been honked at and muttered at by two Coast drivers and had muttered at (I don't like to honk) and swerved around two Midwest tourist types roaring along at twenty-five miles an hour in the center lane admiring the scenery, I suddenly laughed. After all, there was nothing mysterious about my lonely tire tracks. I was just slightly disoriented. MEL was less than a mile away from the school, up over the ridge, though it was a good half hour by road. Mrs. Kroginold had hiked over for the conference and the two of them had hiked back together. My imagination boggled a little at the memory of Mrs. Kroginold's strap'n'heel sandals and the hillsides, but then, not everyone insists on flats to walk in.

Well, the white rat achieved six offspring, which cemented the friendship between Gene and Vincent forever, and school rocked along more or less serenely.

Then suddenly, as though at a signal, the pace of space exploration was stepped up in every country that had ever tried launching anything; so the school started a space unit. We went through our regular systematic lessons at a dizzying pace, and each child, after he had finished his assignment, plunged into his own chosen activity—all unrealizing of the fact that he was immediately putting into practice what he had been studying so reluctantly.

My primary group was busy working out a moonscape in the sand table. It was to be complete with clay moon-people—"They don't *have* to have any noses!" That was Ginny, tender to critical comment. "They're different! They don't breathe. No air!" And moon-dogs and cats and cars and flowers; and even a moon-bird. "It can't fly in the sky 'cause there ain't—isn't any air so it flies in the dirt!" That was Justin. "It likes bottoms of craters 'cause there's more dirt there!"

I caught Vincent's amused eyes as he listened to the small ones. "Little kids are funny!" he murmured. "Animals on the moon! My dad, when he was there, all he saw—" His eyes widened and he became very busy choosing the right-sized nails from the rusty coffee can.

"Middle-sized kids are funny, too," I said. "Moon, indeed! There aren't any dads on the moon, either!"

"I guess not." He picked up the hammer and, as he moved away, I heard him whisper, "Not now!"

My intermediates were in the midst of a huge argument. I umpired for a while. If you use a BB shot to represent the Earth, would there be room in the schoolroom to make a scale mobile of the planetary system? I extinguished some of the fire bred of ignorance, by suggesting an encyclopedia and some math, and moved on through the room.

Gene and Vincent, not caring for such intellectual pursuits, were working on our model space capsule, which was patterned after the very latest in U.S. spacecraft, modified to include different aspects of the latest in flying saucers. I was watching Vincent leaning through a window, fitting a tin can altitude gauge—or some such—into the control panel. Gene was painting purple a row of cans around the middle of the craft. Purple was currently popular for flying saucer lights.

"I wonder if astronauts ever develop claustrophobia?" I said idly. "I get a twinge sometimes in elevators or mines."

"I suppose susceptible ones would be eliminated long before they ever got to be astronauts," grunted Vincent as he pushed on the tin can. "They go through all sorts of tests."

"I know," I said. "But people change. Just supposing—"

"Gollee!" said Gene, his poised paint brush dribbling purple down his arm and off his elbow. "Imagine! Way up there! No way out! Can't get down! And claustrophobia!" He brought out the five syllables proudly. The school had defined and discussed the word when we first started the unit.

The tin can slipped and Vincent staggered sideways, falling against me.

"Oh!" said Vincent, his shaking hands lifting, his right arm curling up over his head. "I—"

I took one look at his twisted face, the cold sweat beading his hairline, and, circling his shoulders, steered him over to the reading bench near my desk. "Sit," I said.

"Whatsa matter with him?" Now the paint was dripping on one leg of Gene's Levi's.

"Just slightly wampsy," I said. "Watch that paint. You're making a mess of your clothes."

"Gollee!" He smeared his hand down his pants from hip to knee. "Mom'll kill me!"

I lifted my voice. "It's put-away time. Kipper, will you monitor today?"

The children were swept into organized confusion. I turned back to Vincent. "Better?"

"I'm sorry." Color hadn't come back to his face yet, but it was plumping up from its stricken drawnness. "Sometimes it gets through too sharply—"

"Don't worry about it," I said, pushing his front hair up out of his eyes. "You could drive yourself crazy—"

"Mom says my imagination is a little too vivid—" His mouth corners lifted.

"So 'tis," I smiled at him, "if it must seize upon my imaginary astronaut. There's no point to your harrowing up your soul with what might happen. Problems we have always with us. No need to borrow any."

"I'm not exactly borrowing," he whispered, his shoulder hunching up towards his wincing head. "He never did want to, anyway, and now that they're orbiting, he's still scared. What if—" He straightened resolutely. "I'll help Gene." He slid away before I could stop him.

"Vincent," I called. "*Who's* orbiting—" And just then Justin dumped over the whole stack of jigsaw puzzles, upside down. That ended any further questions I might have had.

That evening I pushed the newspaper aside and thoughtfully lifted my coffee cup. I stared past its rim and out into the gathering darkness. This was the local newspaper, which was still struggling to become a big metropolitan daily after half a century of being a four-page county weekly. Sometimes its reach exceeded its grasp, and it had to bolster short columns with little folksy-type squibs. I re-read the one that had caught my eye. Morris was usually good for an item or two. I watched for them since he had had a conversation with a friend of mine I'd lost track of.

Local ham operator, Morris Staviski, says the Russians have a new manned sputnik in orbit. He says he has monitored radio signals from the capsule. He can't tell what they're saying, but he says they're talking Russian. He knows what Russian sounds like because his grandmother was Russian.

"Hmm," I thought. "I wonder. Maybe Vincent knows Morris. Maybe that's where he got this orbiting bit."

So the next day I asked him.

"Staviski?" He frowned a little. "No, ma'am, I don't know anyone named Staviski. At least I don't remember the name. Should I?"

"Not necessarily," I said. "I just wondered. He's a ham radio operator—"

"Oh!" His face flushed happily. "I'm working on the code now so I can take the test next time it's given in Winter Wells! Maybe I'll get to talk to him sometimes!"

"Me, too!" said Gene. "I'm learning the code, too!"

"He's a little handicapped, though," Vincent smiled. "He can't tell a *dit* from a *dah* yet!"

The next morning Vincent crept into school with all the sun gone out. He moved like someone in a dream and got farther and farther away. Before morning recess came, I took his temperature. It was normal. But he certainly wasn't. At recess the rapid outflow of children left him stranded in his seat, his pinched face turned to the window, his unfinished work in front of him, his idle pencil in the hand that curved up over the side of his head.

"Vincent!" I called, but there was no sign he even heard me. "Vincent!"

He drew a sobbing breath and focused his eyes on me slowly. "Yes, ma'am?" He wet his dry lips.

"What *is* the matter?" I asked. "Where do you feel bad?"

"Bad?" His eyes unfocused again and his face slowly distorted into a crying mask. With an effort he smoothed it out again. "I'm not the one. It's—it's—" He leaned his shaking chin in the palm of his hand and steadied his elbow on the top of his desk. His knuckles whitened as he clenched his fingers against his mouth.

"Vincent!" I went to him and touched his head lightly. With a little shudder and a sob, he turned and buried his face against me.

"Oh, Teacher! Teacher!"

A quick look out the window showed me that all the students were down in the creek bed building sand forts. Eight-year-old pride is easily bruised. I led Vincent up to my desk and took him onto my lap. For a while we sat there, my cheek pressed to his head as I rocked silently. His hair was spiky against my face and smelled a little like a baby chick's feathers.

"He's afraid! He's afraid!" he finally whispered, his eyes tight shut. "The other one is dead. It's broken so it can't come back. He's afraid! And the dead one keeps looking at him with blood on his mouth! And he can't come down! His hands are bleeding! He hit the walls wanting to get out. But there's no air outside!"

"Vincent," I went on rocking, "have you been telling yourself stories until you believe them?"

"No!" He buried his face against my shoulder, his body tense. "I know! I know! I can hear him! He screamed at first, but now he's too scared. Now he—" Vincent stilled on my lap. He lifted his face—listening. The anguish slowly smoothed away. "It's gone again! He must go to sleep. Or unconscious. I don't hear him all the time."

"What was he saying?" I asked, caught up in his—well, whatever it was.

"I don't know." Vincent slid from my lap, his face still wary. "I don't know his language."

"But you said—" I protested. "How do you know what he's feeling if you don't even know—"

He smiled his little lip-lift. "When you look at one of us kids without a word and your left eyebrow goes up—what do you mean?"

"Well, that depends on what who's doing," I flushed.

"If it's for me, I *know* what you mean. And I stop it. So do the other kids about themselves. That's the way I know this." He started back to his desk. "I'd better get my spelling done."

"Is that the one that's orbiting?" I asked hopefully, wanting to tie something to something.

"Orbiting?" Vincent was busily writing. "That's the sixth word. I'm only on the fourth."

That afternoon I finally put aside the unit tests I'd been checking and looked at the clock. Five o'clock. And at my hands. Filthy. And assessed the ache across my shoulders, the hollow in my stomach, and decided to spend the night right where I was. I didn't even straighten my desk, but turned my weary back on it and unlocked the door to the teacherage.

I kicked off my shoes, flipped on the floor lamp, and turned up the thermostat to take the dank chill out of the small apartment. The cupboards yielded enough supplies to make an entirely satisfying meal. Afterwards, I turned the lights low and sat curled up at one end of the couch listening to one of my Acker Bilke records while I drank my coffee. I flexed my toes in blissful comfort as I let the clear, concise, tidy notes of the clarinet clear away my cobwebs of fatigue. Instead of purring, I composed another strophe to my Praise Song:

Praise God for Fedness—and Warmness—and Shelteredness—and Darkness—and Lightness—and Cleanness—and Quietness—and Unharriedness—

※ ※ ※

I dozed then for a while and woke to stillness. The stereo had turned itself off, and it was so still I could hear the wind in the oak trees and the far, unmusical blat of a diesel train. And I also could hear a repetition of the sound that had wakened me.

Someone was in the schoolroom.

I felt a throb of fright and wondered if I had locked the teacherage door. But I *knew* I had locked the school door just after four o'clock. Of course, a bent bobby pin and your tongue in the correct corner of your mouth and you could open the old lock. But what—who would want to? What was in there? The stealthy noises went on. I heard the creak of the loose board in the back of the room. I heard the *yaaaawn* of the double front door hinges and a thud and clatter on the front porch.

Half paralyzed with fright, I crept to the little window that looked out onto the porch. Cautiously I separated two of the slats of the blind and peered out into the thin slice of moonlight. I gasped and let the slats fall.

A flying saucer! With purple lights! On the porch!

Then I gave a half grunt of laughter. Flying saucers, indeed! There was something familiar about that row of purple lights—unglowing—around its middle. I knew they were purple—even by the dim light—because that was *our* space capsule! Who was trying to steal our cardboard-tincan-poster-painted capsule?

Then I hastily shoved the blind aside and pressed my nose to the dusty screen. The blind retaliated by swinging back and whacking me heavily on the ear, but that wasn't what was dizzying me.

Our capsule was taking off!

"It can't!" I gasped as it slid up past the edge of the porch roof. "Not that storage barrel and all those tin cans! It can't!" And, sure enough, it couldn't. It crash-landed just beyond the flagpole. But it staggered up again, spilling several cans noisily, and skimmed over the swings, only to smash against the boulder at the base of the wall.

I was out of the teacherage, through the dark schoolroom, and down the porch steps before the echo of the smash stopped bouncing from surface to surface around the canyon. I was halfway to the capsule before my toes curled and made me conscious of the fact that I was barefooted. Rather delicately I walked the rest of the way to the crumpled wreckage. What on earth had possessed it—?

In the shadows I found what had possessed it. It was Vincent, his arms wrapped tightly over his ears and across his head. He was writhing silently, his face distorted and gasping.

"Good Lord!" I gasped and fell to my knees beside him. "Vincent! What on earth!" I gathered him up as best I could with his body twisting and his legs flailing, and moved him out into the moonlight.

"I have to! I have to! I have to!" he moaned, struggling away from me. "I hear him! I hear him!"

"Hear whom?" I asked. "Vincent!" I shook him. "Make sense! What are you doing here?"

Vincent stilled in my arms for a frozen second. Then his eyes opened and he blinked in astonishment. "Teacher! What are *you* doing here?"

"I asked first," I said. "What *are* you doing here, and what is this capsule bit?"

"The capsule?" He peered at the pile of wreckage and tears flooded down his cheeks. "Now I can't go and I have to! I have to!"

"Come on inside," I said. "Let's get this thing straightened out once and for all." He dragged behind me, his feet scuffling, his sobs and sniffles jerking to the jolting movement of his steps. But he dug in at the porch and pulled me to a halt.

"Not inside!" he said. "Oh, not inside!"

"Well, okay," I said. "We'll sit here for now."

He sat on the step below me and looked up, his face wet and shining in the moonlight. I fished in the pocket of my robe for a tissue and swabbed his eyes. Then I gave him another. "Blow," I said. He did. "Now, from the beginning."

"I—" He had recourse to the tissue again. "I came to get the capsule. It was the only way I could think of to get the man."

Silence crept around his flat statement until I said, "*That's* the beginning?"

Tears started again. I handed him another tissue. "Now look, Vincent, something's been bothering you for several days. Have you talked it over with your parents?"

"No," he hiccoughed. "I'm not supp-upposed to listen in on people. It isn't fair. But I didn't really. He came in first and I can't shut him out now because I know he's in trouble, and you can't *not* help if you know about someone's need—"

Maybe, I thought hopefully, maybe this is still my nap that I'll soon wake from—but I sighed. "Who is this man? The one that's orbiting?"

"Yes," he said, and cut the last hope for good solid sense from under my feet. "He's up in a capsule and its retro-rockets won't fire. Even if he could live until the orbital decay dropped him back into the atmosphere, the re-entry would burn him up. And he's so afraid! He's trapped! He can't get out!"

I took hold of both of his shaking shoulders. "Calm down," I said. "You can't help him like this." He buried his face against the skirt of my robe. I slid one of my hands over to his neck and patted him for a moment.

"How did you make the capsule move?" I asked. "It *did* move, didn't it?"

"Yes," he said. "I lifted it. We can, you know—lift things. My People can. But I'm not big enough. I'm not supposed to anyway, and I can't sustain the lift. And if I can't even get it out of this canyon, how can I lift clear out of the atmosphere? And he'll die—scared!"

"You can make things fly?" I asked.

"Yes, all of us can. And ourselves, too. See?"

And there he was, floating! His knees level with my head! His shoe laces drooped forlornly down, and one used tissue tumbled to the steps below him.

"Come down," I said, swallowing a vast lump of some kind. He did. "But you know there's no air in space, and our capsule—*Good Lord! Our* capsule? In *space?*—wasn't airtight. How did you expect to breathe?"

"We have a shield," he said. "See?" And there he sat, a glint of something about him. I reached out a hand and drew back my stubbed fingers. The glint was gone. "It keeps out the cold and keeps in the air," he said.

"Let's—let's analyze this a little," I suggested weakly, nursing my fingers unnecessarily. "You say there's a man orbiting in a disabled capsule, and you planned to go up in our capsule with only the air you could take with you and rescue him?" He nodded wordlessly. "Oh, child! Child!" I cried. "You couldn't possibly!"

"Then he'll die." Desolation flattened his voice and he sagged forlornly.

Well, what comfort could I offer him? I sagged, too. Lucky, I thought then, that it's moonlight tonight. People traditionally believe all kinds of arrant nonsense by moonlight. So. I straightened. Let's believe a little—or at least act as if.

"Vincent?"

"Yes, ma am." His face was shadowed by his hunched shoulders.

"If you can lift our capsule this far, how far could your daddy lift it?"

"Oh, *lots* farther!" he cried. "My daddy was studying to be a regular Motiver when he went to the New Home, but he stopped when he came back across space to Earth again because Outsiders don't accept—oh!" His eyes rounded and he pressed his hands to his mouth. "Oh, I forgot!" His voice came muffled. "I forgot! You're an Outsider! We're forbidden to tell—to show—Outsiders don't—"

"Nonsense," I said. "I'm not an Outsider. I'm a teacher. Can you call your mother tonight the way you did the day you and Gene had that fight?"

"A fight? Me and Gene?" The fight was obviously an event of the neolithic period for Vincent. "Oh, yes, I remember. Yes, I guess I could, but she'll be mad because I left—and I told—and—and—" Weeping was close again.

"You'll have to choose," I pointed out, glad to the bones that it wasn't my choice to make, "between letting the man die or having her mad at you. You should have told them when you first knew about him."

"I didn't want to tell that I'd listened to the man—"

"Is he Russian?" I asked, just for curiosity's sake.

"I don't know," he said. "His words are strange. Now he keeps saying something like *Hospodi pomelui.* I think he's talking to God."

"Call your mother," I said, no linguist I. "She's probably worried to death by now."

Obediently, he closed his eyes and sat silent for a while on the step below me. Then he opened his eyes. "She'd just found out I wasn't in bed," he said. "They're coming." He shivered a little. "Daddy gets so mad sometimes. He hasn't the most equitable of temperaments?"

"Oh, Vincent!" I laughed. "What an odd mixture you are!"

"No, I'm not," he said. "Both my mother and daddy are of the People. Remy is a mixture 'cause his grampa was of the Earth, but mine came from the Home. You know—when it was destroyed. I wish I could have seen the ship our People came to Earth in. Daddy says when he was little, they used to dig up pieces of it from the walls and floors of the canyon where it crashed. But they still had a life ship in a shed behind their house and they'd play they were escaping again from the big ship." Vincent shivered. "But some didn't escape. Some died in the sky and some died because Earth people were scared of them."

I shivered too and rubbed my cold ankles with both hands. I wondered wistfully if this wasn't asking just a trifle too much of my ability to believe, even in the name of moonlight.

Vincent brought me back abruptly to my particular Earth. "Look! Here they are already! Gollee! That was fast. They sure must be mad!" And he trailed out onto the playground.

I looked expectantly toward the road and only whirled the other way when I heard the thud of feet. And there they stood, both Mr. and Mrs. Kroginold. And he *did* look mad! His—well—rough-hewn is about the kindest description—face frowning in the moonlight. Mrs. Kroginold surged toward Vincent and Mr. Kroginold swelled preliminary to a vocal blast—or so I feared—so I stepped quickly into the silence.

"There's our school capsule," I said, motioning towards the crushed clutter at the base of the boulder. "That's what he was planning to go up in to rescue a man in a disabled sputnik. He thought the air inside that shiny whatever he put around himself would suffice for the trip. He says a man is dying up there, and he's been carrying that agony around with him, all alone, because he was afraid to tell you."

I stopped for a breath and Mr. Kroginold deflated and— amazingly—grinned a wide, attractive grin, half silver, half shadow.

"Why the gutsy little devil!" he said admiringly. "And I've been fearing the stock was running out! When I was a boy in the canyon—" But he sobered suddenly and turned to Vincent. "Vince! If there's need, let's get with it. What's the deal?" He gathered Vincent into the curve of his arm, and we all went back to the porch. "Now. Details." We all sat.

Vincent, his eyes intent on his father's face and his hand firmly holding his mother's, detailed.

"There are two men orbiting up there. The capsule won't function properly. One man is dead. I never did hear him. The other one is crying for help." Vincent's face tightened anxiously. "He—he feels so bad that it nearly kills me. Only sometimes I guess he passes out because the feeling goes away—like now. Then it comes back worse—"

"He's orbiting," said Mr. Kroginold, his eyes intent on Vincent's face.

"Oh," said Vincent weakly, "of course! I didn't think of that! Oh, Dad! I'm so stupid!" And he flung himself on Mr. Kroginold.

"No," said Mr. Kroginold, wrapping him around with the dark strength of his arms. "Just young. You'll learn. But first learn to bring your problems to your mother and me. That's what we're for!"

"But," said Vincent, "I'm not supposed to listen in—"

"Did you seek him out?" asked Mr. Kroginold. "Did you know about the capsule?"

"No," said Vincent. "He just came in to me—"

"See?" Mr. Kroginold set Vincent back on the step. "You weren't listening in. You were invaded. You just happened to be the right receptivity. Now, what were your plans?"

"They were probably stupid, too," admitted Vincent. "But I was going to lift our capsule—I had to have something to put him in—and try to intercept the orbit of the other one. Then I was going to get the man out—I don't know how—and bring him back to Earth and put him down at the FBI building in Washington. They'd know how to get him home again."

"Well." Mr. Kroginold smiled faintly. "Your plan has the virtue of simplicity, anyway. Just nit-picking, though, I can see one slight problem. How would the FBI ever convince the authorities in his country that we hadn't impounded the capsule for our own nefarious purposes?" Then he became very business-like.

"Lizbeth, will you get in touch with Ron? I think he's in Kerry tonight. Lucky our best Motiver is This End right now. I'll see if Jemmy is up-canyon. We'll get his okay on Remy's craft at the Selkirk. If this has been going on for very long, time is what we've got little of."

It was rather anti-climactic after all those efficient rattlings-out of directions to see the three of them just sit quietly there on the step, hands clasped, their faces lifted a little in the moonlight, their eyes closed. My left foot was beginning to go to sleep when Vincent's chin finally dropped, and he pulled one hand free from his mother's grasp to curl his arm up over his head. Mrs. Kroginold's eyes flipped open. "Vincent?" Her voice was anxious.

"It's coming again," I said. "That distress—whatever it is."

"Ron's heading for the Selkirk now," she said, gathering Vincent to her. "Jake, Vincent's receiving again."

Mr. Kroginold said hastily to the eaves of the porch, "—as soon as possible. Hang on. Vincent's got him again. Wait, I'll relay. Vince, where can I reach him? Show me."

And damned if they didn't all sit there again—with Vincent's face shining with sweat and his mother trying to cradle his twisting body. Then Mr. Kroginold gave a grunt, and Vincent relaxed with a sob. His father took him from his mother.

"Already?" I asked. "That was a short one."

Mrs. Kroginold fished for a tissue in her pocket and wiped Vincent's face. "It isn't over yet," she said. "It won't be until the capsule swings behind the Earth again, but he's channeling the distress to his father, and he's relaying it to Jemmy up-canyon. Jemmy is our Old One. He'll help us handle it from here on out. But Vincent will have to be our receptor—"

" 'A sort of telepathy,' " I quoted, dizzy with trying to follow a road I couldn't even imagine.

"A sort of telepathy." Mrs. Kroginold laughed and sighed, her finger tracing Vincent's cheek lovingly. "You've had quite a mish-mash dumped in your lap, haven't you? And no time for us to be subtle."

"It *is* bewildering," I said. "I've been adding two and two and getting the oddest fours!"

"Like?" she asked.

"Like maybe Vincent's forefathers didn't come over in the *Mayflower*, but maybe a spaceship?"

"But not quite *Mayflower* years ago," she smiled. "And?"

"And maybe Vincent's dad *has* seen no life on the moon?"

"Not so very long ago," she said. "And?"

"And maybe there *is* a man in distress up there and you *are* going to try to rescue him?"

"Well," said Mrs. Kroginold. "Those fours look all right to me."

"They *do?*" I goggled. Then I sighed, "Ah well, this modern math! I knew it would be the end of me!"

Mr. Kroginold brought his eyes back to us. "Well, it's all set in motion. Ron's gone for the craft. He'll be here to pick us up as soon as he can make it. Jemmy's taking readings on the capsule so we'll be able to attempt rendezvous. Then, the Power being willing, we'll be able to bring the fellow back."

"I—I—" I stood up. This was suddenly too much. "I think maybe I'd better go back in the house." I brushed the sand off the back of my robe. "One thing bothers me still, though."

"Yes?" Mrs. Kroginold smiled.

"How *is* the FBI going to convince the authorities of the other country?"

"Ay!" she said, sobering. "Jake—"

And I gathered my skirts up and left the family there on the school porch. As I closed the teacherage door behind me, I leaned against it. It was so dark—in here. And there was such light out there! Why, they had jumped into helping without asking one single question! Then I wondered what questions I had expected—Was the man a nice man? Was he worth saving? Was he an important personage? What kind of reward? *Is there a need?* That's all they needed to know!

I looked at the sleepcoat I hadn't worn yet, but I felt too morning to undress and go to bed properly, so I slid out of my robe and put my dress back on. And my shoes. And a sweater. And stood irresolutely in the middle of the floor. After all! What is the etiquette for when your guests are about to go into orbit from your front porch?

Then there was a thud at the door and the knob rattled. I heard Mrs. Kroginold call softly, "But Vincent! An Outsider?"

"But she isn't!" said Vincent, fumbling again at the door. "She said she isn't—she's a teacher. And I know she'd like—" The door swung open suddenly and tumbled Vincent to the schoolroom floor. Mrs. Kroginold was just outside the outer door on the porch.

"Sorry," she said. "Vincent thinks maybe you'd like to see the craft arrive—but—"

"You're afraid I might tell," I said for her. "And it should be kept in the family. I've been repository for odd family stories before. Well, maybe not *quite*—"

Vincent scrambled for the porch. "Here it comes!" he cried.

I was beside Mrs. Kroginold in a split second and, grasping hands, we raced after Vincent. Mr. Kroginold had been standing in the middle of the playground, but he drifted back to us as a huge—well, a huge *nothing* came down through the moonlight.

"It—where is it?" I wondered if some dimension I didn't know was involved.

"Oh," said Mrs. Kroginold. "It has the unlight over it. Jake! Ask Ron—"

Mr. Kroginold turned his face to the huge nothing. And there it was! A slender silver something, its nose arcing down from a rocket position to rest on the tawny sands of the playground.

"The unlight's so no one will see us," said Mrs. Kroginold, "and we flow it so it won't bother radar and things like that." She laughed. "We're not the right shape for this year's flying saucers, anyway. I'm glad we're not. Who wants to look like a frosted cupcake on a purple lighted plate? That's what's so In now."

"Is it really a spaceship?" I asked, struck by how clean the lovely gleaming craft was that had come so silently to dent our playground.

"Sure it is!" cried Vincent. "The Old Man had it and they took him to the moon in it to bury him and Bethie too and Remy went with their dad and mom and—"

"A little reticence, Son," said Mr. Kroginold, catching Vincent's hand. "It isn't necessary to go into all that history."

"She—she realizes," said Mrs. Kroginold. "It's not as if she were a stranger."

"We shouldn't be gone too long," said Mr. Kroginold. "I'll pick you up here as soon—"

"Pick us up! I'm going with you!" cried Mrs. Kroginold. "Jake Kroginold! If you think you're going to do me out of a thing as wild and wonderful as this—"

"Let her go with us, Dad," begged Vincent.

"With *us?*" Mr. Kroginold raked his fingers back through his hair. "You, too?"

"Of course!" Vincent's eyes were wide with astonishment. "It's *my* man!"

"Well, *adonday veeah* in cards and spades!" said Mr. Kroginold. He grinned over at me. "Family!" he said.

I studiously didn't meet his eyes. I felt a deep wave of color move up my face as I kept my mouth clamped shut. I *wouldn't* say anything! I couldn't ask! I had no right to expect—

"And Teacher, too!" cried Vincent. "Teacher, too!"

Mr. Kroginold considered me for a long moment. My wanting must have been a flaring thing because he finally shrugged an eyebrow and echoed, "And Teacher, too."

Then I nearly died! It *was* so wild and wonderful and impossible and I'm scared to death of heights! We scurried about getting me a jacket. Getting Kipper's forgotten jacket out of the cloak room for Vincent, who had come off without his. Taking one of my blankets, just in case. I paused a moment in the mad scramble, hand poised over my Russian-English, English-Russian pocket dictionary. Then left it. The man might not be Russian at all. And even if he was, people like Vincent's seemed to have little need for such aids to communication.

A door opened in the craft. I looked at it, thinking blankly, Ohmy! Ohmy! We had started across the yard toward the craft when I gasped, "The—the door! I have to lock the door!"

I dashed back to the schoolhouse and into the darkness of the teacherage. And foolishly, childishly, there in the dark, I got awfully hungry! I yanked a cupboard door open and scrabbled briefly. Peanut butter—slippery, glassy cylinder—crackers—square-cornered, waxy carton. I slammed the cupboard shut, snatched up my purse as though I were on the way to the MONSTER MERCANTILE, staggered out of the door, and juggled my burdens until I could manipulate the key. Then I hesitated on the porch, one foot lifting, all ready to go to the craft, and silently gasped my travel prayer. "Dear God, go with me to my destination. Don't let me imperil anyone or be imperiled by anyone. Amen." I started down the steps, paused, and cried softly, "To my destination *and back!* Oh, please! And back!"

Have you, oh, have you ever watched space reach down to surround you as your hands would reach down to surround a minnow? Have you ever seen Earth, a separate thing, apart from you, and see-almost-all-able? Have you ever watched color deepen and run until it blared into blaze and blackness? Have you ever stepped out of the context in which your identity is established and floated un-anyone beyond the steady pulse of night and day and accustomed being? Have you ever, for even a fleeting second, shared God's eyes? I have! *I have!*

And Mrs. Kroginold and Vincent were with me in all the awesome wonder of our going. You couldn't have seen us go even if you had known where to look. We were wrapped in unlight again, and the craft was flowed again to make it a nothing to any detection device.

"I wish I could space walk!" said Vincent, finally, turning his shoulders but not his eyes away from the window. "Daddy—"

"No." Mr. Kroginold's tone left no loophole for further argument.

"Well, it would be fun," Vincent sighed. Then he said in a very small voice, "Mother, I'm hungry."

"So sorry!" Mrs. Kroginold hugged him to her briefly. "Nearest hamburger joint's a far piece down the road!"

"Here—" I found, after two abortive attempts, that I still had a voice. I slithered cautiously to my knees on the bare floor—no luxury liner, this—and sat back. "Peanut butter." The jar clicked down. "And crackers." The carton thumped—and my elbow creaked almost audibly as I straightened it out from its spasmed clutch.

"Gollee! Real deal!" Vincent plumped down beside me and began working on the lid of the jar. "What'll we spread it with?"

"Oh!" I blankly considered the problem. "Oh, I have a nail file here in my purse." I was fishing for it amid the usual clutter when I caught Mrs. Kroginold's surprised look. I grinned sheepishly. "I thought I was hungry. But I guess that wasn't what was wrong with my stomach!"

Shortly after the jar was opened and the roasty smell of peanuts spread, Mr. Kroginold and another fellow drifted casually over to us. I preferred to ignore the fact that they actually drifted—no steps on the floor. The other fellow was introduced as Jemmy. The Old One? Not so old, it seemed to me. But then "old" might mean "wise" to these people. And on that score he could qualify. He had none of the loose ends that I can often sense in people. He was—whole.

"Ron is lifting," said Mr. Kroginold through a mouthful of peanut butter and crackers. He nodded at the center of the room, where another fellow sat looking intently at a square, boxy-looking thing.

"That's the amplifier," Jemmy said, as though that explained anything. "It makes it possible for one man to manage the craft."

Something buzzed on a panel across the room. "There!" Mr. Kroginold was at the window, staring intently. "There it is! Good work, Ron!"

At that moment Vincent cried out, his arms going up in their protesting posture. Mrs. Kroginold pushed him over to his father, who drew him in the curve of his shoulder to the window, coaxing down the tense arms.

"See? There's the craft! It looks odd. Something's not right about it."

"Can—can we take off the unlight now?" asked Vincent, jerkily. "So he can see us? Then maybe he won't feel so bad—"

"Jemmy?" Mr. Kroginold called across the craft. "What do you think? Would the shock of our appearance be too much?"

"It could hardly be worse than the hell he's in now," said Jemmy. "So—"

"Oh!" cried Vincent. "He thinks he just now died. He thinks we're the Golden Gates!"

"Rather a loose translation." Jemmy flung a smiling glance at us. "But he is wondering if we are the entrance to the afterworld. Ron, can we dock?"

Moments later, there was a faint metallic click and a slight vibration through our craft. Then we three extras stood pressed to the window and watched Mr. Kroginold and Jemmy leave our craft. They were surrounded, it's true, by their shields that caught light and slid it rapidly around, but they did look so unguarded—no, they didn't! They looked right at home and intent on their rescue mission. They disappeared from the sight of our windows. We waited and waited, not saying anything—not aloud, anyway. I could feel a clanking through the floor under me. And a scraping. Then a long nothing again.

Finally they came back in sight, the light from our window glinting across a mutual protective bubble that enclosed the two of them and a third inert figure between them.

"He still thinks he's dead," said Vincent soberly. "He's wondering if he ought to try to pray. He wasn't expecting people after he died. But mostly he's trying not to think."

They brought him in and laid him on the floor. They eased him out of his suit and wrapped him in my blanket. We three gathered around him looking at his quiet, tight face. *So young!* I thought. *So young!* Unexpectedly his eyes opened, and he took us in, one by one. At the sight of Vincent, his mouth dropped open and his eyes fled shut again.

"What'd he do that for?" asked Vincent, a trifle hurt.

"Angels," said his mother firmly, "are not supposed to have peanut butter around the mouth!"

The three men consulted briefly. Then Mr. Kroginold prepared to leave our craft again. This time he took a blanket from the Rescue Pack they had brought in the craft.

"He can manage the body alone," said Jemmy, being our intercom. A little later— "He has the body out, but he's gone back—" His forehead creased, then cleared. "Oh, the tapes and instrument packets," he explained to our questioning glances. "He thinks maybe they can study them and prevent this happening again."

He turned to Mrs. Kroginold. "Well, Lizbeth, back when all of you were in school together in the canyon, I wouldn't have given a sandwiched quarter for the chances of any Kroginold ever turning out well. I sprinkle repentant ashes on my bowed head. Some good *can* come from Kroginolds!"

And Vincent screamed!

Before we could look his way, there was a blinding flash that exploded through every window as though we had suddenly been stabbed through and through. Then we were all tumbled in blinded confusion from one wall of our craft to another until, almost as suddenly, we floated in a soundless blackness. "Jake! Oh, Jake!" I heard Mrs. Kroginold's whispering gasp. Then she cried out, "Jemmy! Jemmy! What happened? Where's Jake?"

Light came back. From where, I never did know. I hadn't known its source even before.

"The retro-rockets—" I felt more of his answer than I heard. "Maybe they finally fired. Or maybe the whole capsule just blew up. Ron?"

"Might have holed us." A voice I hadn't heard before answered. "Didn't. Capsule's gone."

"But—but—" The enormity of what had happened slowed our thoughts. "Jake!" Mrs. Kroginold screamed. "Jemmy! Ron! Jake's out there!"

And, as suddenly as the outcry came, it was cut off. In terror I crouched on the floor, my arms up defensively, not to my ears as Vincent's had gone—there was nothing to hear—but against the soundless, aimless tumbling of bodies above me. Jemmy and Vincent and Mrs. Kroginold were like corpses afloat in some invisible sea. And Vincent, burrowed into a corner, was a small, silent, humped-up bundle.

I think I would have gone mad in the incomprehensible silence if a hand hadn't clutched mine. Startled, I snatched my hand away, but gave it back, with a sob, to our shipwrecked stranger. He accepted it with both of his. We huddled together, taking comfort in having someone to cling to.

Then I shook with hysterical laughter as I suddenly realized. " 'A sort of telepathy'!" I giggled. "They are not dead, but speak. Words are slow, you know." I caught the young man's puzzled eyes. "And of very little use in a situation like this."

I called to Ron where he crouched near the amplifier box, "They are all right, aren't they?"

"They?" His head jerked upward. "Of course. Communicating."

"Where's Mr. Kroginold?" I asked. "How can we ever hope to find him out there?"

"Trying to reach him," said Ron, his chin flipping upward again. "Don't feel him dead. Probably knocked out. Can't find him unconscious."

"Oh." The stranger's fingers tightened on mine. I looked at him. He was struggling to get up. I let go of him and shakily, on hands and knees, we crawled to the window, his knees catching on the blanket. For a long moment, the two of us stared out into the darkness. I watched the lights wheel slowly past until I reoriented, and we were the ones wheeling. But as soon as I relaxed, again it was the lights wheeling slowly past. I didn't know what we were looking for. I couldn't get any kind of perspective on anything outside our craft. Any given point of light could have been a dozen light-years away—or could have been a glint inside the glass—or was it glass?—against which I had my nose pressed.

But the stranger seemed to know what he was looking for. Suddenly I cried out and twisted my crushed fingers to free them. He let go and gestured toward the darkness, saying something tentative and hopeful.

"Ron!" I called, trying to see what the man was seeing. "Maybe— maybe he sees something." There was a stir above me and Jemmy slid down to the floor beside me.

"A visual sighting?" he whispered tensely.

"I don't know," I whispered back. "Maybe he—"

Jemmy laid his hand on the man's wrist, and then concentrated on whatever it was out in the void that had caught the stranger's attention.

"Ron—" Jemmy gestured out the window and—well, I guess Ron

gestured with our craft—because things outside swam a different way until I caught a flick or a gleam or a movement.

"There, there, there," crooned Jemmy, almost as though soothing an anxious child. "There, there, there. Lizbeth!"

And all of us except Ron were crowded against the window, watching a bundle of some sort tumbling toward us. "Shield intact," whispered Jenny. "Praise the Power!"

"Oh, Daddy, Daddy!" choked Vincent against his whitened knuckles. Mrs. Kroginold clung to him wordlessly.

Then Jemmy was gone, streaking through our craft, away outside from us. I saw the glint of his shield as he rounded our craft. I saw him gather the tumbling bundle up and disappear with it. Then he was back in the craft again, kneeling—unglinted—beside Mr. Kroginold as he lay on the floor. Mrs. Kroginold and Vincent launched themselves toward them.

Our stranger tugged at his half-shed blanket. I shuffled my knees off it and he shivered himself back into it.

They had to peel Mr. Kroginold's arms from around the instrument packet before they could work on him—in their odd, undoing way of working. And the stranger and I exchanged wavery smiles of congratulations when Mr. Kroginold finally opened his eyes.

So that was it. After it was all over, I got the deep, breath-drawing feeling I get when I have finished a most engrossing book, and a sort of last-page-flipping—feeling, wistfully wishing there were more—just a little more!

Oh, the loose ends? I guess there were a few. They tied themselves quite casually and briskly in the next few days.

It was only a matter of moments after Mr. Kroginold had sat up and smiled a craggy smile of satisfaction at the packet he had brought back with him that Ron said, "Convenient." And we spiraled down— or so it felt to me—to the Earth beneath while Jemmy, fingers to our stranger's wrist, communicated to him in such a way that the stranger's eyes got very large and astonished and he looked at me—at *me!*— questioningly. I nodded. Well, what else could I do? He was asking something, and, so far, every question around these People seemed to have a positive answer!

So it was that we delivered him, not to the FBI in Washington, but to his own doorstep at a launching base somewhere deep in his own country. We waited, hovering under our unlight and well flowed, until the door swung open and gulped him in, instrument packet, my blanket, and all.

Imagination boggles at the reception there must have been for him! They surely knew the capsule had been destroyed in orbit. And to have him walk in—!

And Mr. Kroginold struggled for a couple of days with "Virus X" without benefit of the company doctor, then went back to work.

A couple of weeks later they moved away to another lab, half across the country, where Mr. Kroginold could go on pursuing whatever it is he is pursuing.

And a couple of days before they left, I quite unexpectedly gave Vincent a going-away gift.

That morning Vincent firmed his lips, his cheeks coloring, and shook his head. "I can't read it," he said, and began to close the book.

"*That* I don't believe," I said firmly, my flare of exasperation igniting into sudden inspiration. Vincent looked at me, startled. He was so used to my acceptance of his reading block that he was shaken a bit.

"But I *can't*," he said patiently.

"Why not?" I asked bluntly.

"I have a block," he said as flatly.

"What triggers it?" I probed.

"Why—why, Mother says anything that suggests unhappy compulsion—"

"How do you know this story has any such thing in it?" I asked. "All it says in the title is a name—*Stickeen*."

"But I *know*," he said miserably, his head bent as he flicked the pages of the story with his thumb.

"I'll tell you how you know," I said. "You know because you've read the story already."

"But I haven't!" Vincent's face puckered. "You only brought this book today!"

"That's true," I said. "And you turned the pages to see how long the story was. Only then did you decide you *wouldn't* read it—again!"

"I don't understand—" Wonder was stirring in his eyes.

"Vincent," I said, "you read this whole story in the time it took you to turn the pages. You gulped it page by page and that's how you know there's unhappy compulsion in it. So, you refuse to read it—again."

"Do—do you really think so?" asked Vincent in a hopeful half whisper. "Oh, Teacher, can I really read after all? I've been so ashamed! One of the People, and not able to read!"

"Let's check," I said, excited, too. "Give me the book. I'll ask you questions—" And I did. And he answered every single one of them!

"I can read!" He snatched the book from me and hugged it to him with both arms. "Hey! Gene! I can read!"

"Big deal!" said Gene, glancing up from his labor on the butcher paper spread on the floor. He was executing a fanciful rendition, in tempera, of the Indians greeting Columbus in a chartreuse, magenta, and shriek-pink jungle. "I learned to read in the first grade. Which way do a crocodile's knees bend?"

"All you have to remember," I said to a slightly dashed Vincent, "is to slow down a bit and be a little less empathetic." I was as pleased as he was. "And to think of the time I wasted for both of us, making you sound out your words—"

"But I need it," he said. "I still can't spell for sour apples!"

Vincent gave me a going-away present the Friday night that the Kroginolds came to say goodby. We were sitting in the twilight on the school porch. Vincent, shaken by having to leave Rinconcillo and Gene, and still thrilling to knowing he could read, gave me one of his treasures. It was a small rock, an odd crystalline formation that contrived at the same time to be betryoidal. In the curve of my palm it even had a strange feeling of resilience, though there was no yielding in it when I pressed my thumb to it.

"Daddy brought it to me from the moon," he told me, and deftly fielded it as my astonishment let it fall. "I'll probably get another one, someday," he said as he gave it back to me. "But even if I don't, I want you to have it."

Mr. and Mrs. Kroginold and I talked quietly for a while with no reference to parting. I shook them a little with, "Why do you suppose that stranger could send his thoughts to Vincent? I mean, he doesn't pick up distress from everyone, very apparently. Do you suppose that man might be from People like you? *Are* there People like you in that part of the world?"

They looked at each other, startled. "We really don't know!" said Mr. Kroginold. "Many of our People were unaccounted for when we arrived on Earth, but we just assumed that all of them were dead except for the groups around here—"

"I wonder if it ever occurred to Jemmy," said Mrs. Kroginold thoughtfully.

After they left, disappearing into the shadows of the hillside toward MEL, I sat for a while longer, turning the moon-pebble in my hands. What an odd episode! In a month or so it would probably seem like a distant dream, melting into my teaching years along with all the other things past. But it still didn't seem quite finished to me. Meeting people like the Kroginolds and the others, makes an indelible impression on a person. Look what it did for that stranger—

What *about* that stranger? How was he explaining? Were they giving him a hard time? Then I gulped. I had just remembered. My name and address were on a tape on the corner of that blanket of mine he had been wrapped in. If he had discovered it—! And if things got too thick for him—

Oh, gollee! What if some day there comes a knock on my door and there—!

The Smallest Dragonboy

by Anne McCaffrey

When the marvelous Anne McCaffrey died at the age of 85 in 2011, she left a huge hole in the science fiction field. Fortunately, she gave us hundreds of novels, essays, and short stories to help fill some of that hole, although new readers will never get the chance to see her in person, which was always a treat.

Anne McCaffrey is one of science fiction's most popular authors. After her novel, The White Dragon (1978), became one of the first science fiction novels to ever hit The New York Times bestseller list, Anne's work remained a staple of bestseller lists for decades.

Most non-readers of McCaffrey associate her with the Dragonriders of Pern series and, because the series has "dragon" in the title, erroneously believe the series is fantasy. Instead, it examines human history on a planet called Pern. Science fiction tropes abound—a planet with an odd orbit, spaceships, telepathy, lost (but useful) technology, as well as the existence of the Other on two levels—the dragons themselves and the dragonriders, who bond with those dragons.

If Pern were the only thing Anne McCaffrey ever wrote, it would cement her place in science fiction forever. But it's not. She also wrote the Brain & Brawn Ship series, which features such classic tales as The Ship Who Sang, the Catteni series, the Talents universe, and more series than I can name in this brief introduction.

McCaffrey's importance to the field cannot be understated. She is the first woman to win a Hugo for fiction. (The first woman to win a Hugo period was Elinor Busby who, along with F. M. Busby, Burnett Toskey, and Wally Weber, won the Best Fanzine award in 1960.) McCaffrey was also the first woman to win the Nebula Award, winning it in the fourth year the award was given out.

Her awards are too numerous to list here, but they include the Science Fiction Writers of America Grand Master award, several lifetime achievement awards, and the Golden Pen award, which is given by children to their favorite author.

With such a vast array of excellent fiction to choose from, I found it hard to pick the best story for this volume. McCaffrey excels at the novella length, and my favorites of hers are the longer pieces. Because of my word-length constraints for this volume, I spent a lot of happy hours reading her shorter stories.

And then I came across "The Smallest Dragonboy," which I had not read before. It does everything I wanted in the perfect McCaffrey story. It's entertaining, touching, and compelling. And it's in her best known series.

If you've never read any of Anne McCaffrey's work, this story will open doors for you that will keep you reading her excellent fiction for decades to come.

🐢 🐢 🐢

ALTHOUGH KEEVAN lengthened his walking stride as far as his legs would stretch, he couldn't quite keep up with the other candidates. He knew he would be teased again.

Just as he knew many other things that his foster mother told him he ought not to know, Keevan knew that Beterli, the most senior of the boys, set that spanking pace just to embarrass him, the smallest dragonboy. Keevan would arrive, tail fork-end of the group, breathless, chest heaving, and maybe get a stem look from the instructing wing-second.

Dragonriders, even if they were still only hopeful candidates for the glowing eggs which were hardening on the hot sands of the Hatching Ground cavern, were expected to be punctual and prepared. Sloth was not tolerated by the Weyrleader of Benden Weyr. A good record was especially important now. It was very near hatching time, when the baby dragons would crack their mottled shells, and stagger forth to choose their lifetime companions. The very thought of that glorious moment made Keevan's breath catch in his throat. To be chosen—to be a dragonrider! To sit astride the neck of a winged beast with jeweled eyes: to be his friend, in telepathic communion with him for life; to be his companion in good times and fighting extremes; to fly effortlessly over the lands of Pern! Or, thrillingly, *between* to any point anywhere on the world! Flying *between* was done on dragonback or not at all, and it was dangerous.

Keevan glanced upward, past the black mouths of the weyr caves in which grown dragons and their chosen riders lived, toward the Star Stones that crowned the ridge of the old volcano that was Benden Weyr. On the height, the blue watch dragon, his rider mounted on his neck, stretched the great transparent pinions that carried him on the winds of Pern to fight the evil Thread that fell at certain times from the skies. The many-faceted rainbow jewels of his eyes glistened fleetingly in the greeny sun. He folded his great wings to his back, and the watch pair resumed their statuelike pose of alertness.

Then the enticing view was obscured as Keevan passed into the Hatching Ground cavern. The sands underfoot were hot, even through heavy wher-hide boots. How the bootmaker had protested having to sew so small! Keeven was forced to wonder why being small was reprehensible. People were always calling him "babe" and shooing him away as being "too small" or "too young" for this or that. Keevan was constantly working, twice as hard as any other boy his age, to prove himself capable. What if his muscles weren't as big as Beterli's? They were just as hard. And if he couldn't overpower anyone in a wrestling match, he could outdistance everyone in a footrace.

"Maybe if you run fast enough," Beterli had jeered on the occasion when Keevan had been goaded to boast of his swiftness, "you could catch a dragon. That's the only way you'll make a dragonrider!"

"You just wait and see, Beterli, you just wait," Keevan had replied. He would have liked to wipe the contemptuous smile from Beterli's face, but the guy didn't fight fair even when a wingsecond was watching. "No one knows what Impresses a dragon!"

"They've got to be able to *find* you first, babe!"

Yes, being the smallest candidate was not an enviable position. It was therefore imperative that Keevan Impress a dragon in his first hatching. That would wipe the smile off every face in the cavern, and accord him the respect due any dragonrider, even the smallest one.

Besides, no one knew exactly what Impressed the baby dragons as they struggled from their shells in search of their lifetime partners.

"I like to believe that dragons see into a man's heart," Keevan's foster mother, Mende, told him. "If they find goodness, honesty, a flexible mind, patience, courage—and you've got that in quantity, dear Keevan—that's what dragons look for. I've seen many a well-grown lad left standing on the sands., Hatching Day, in favor of someone not so strong or tall or handsome. And if my memory serves me"—which it usually did: Mende knew every word of every Harper's tale worth telling, although Keevan did not interrupt her to say so—"I don't believe that F'lar, our Weyrleader, was all that tall when bronze Mnementh chose him. And Mnementh was the only bronze dragon of that hatching."

Dreams of Impressing a bronze were beyond Keevan's boldest reflections, although that goal dominated the thoughts of every other hopeful candidate. Green dragons were small and fast and more numerous. There was more prestige to Impressing a blue or brown than a green. Being practical, Keevan seldom dreamed as high as a big fighting brown, like Canth, F'nor's fine fellow, the biggest brown on all Pern. But to fly a bronze? Bronzes were almost as big as the queen, and only they took the air when a queen flew at mating time. A bronze rider could aspire to become Weyrleader! Well, Keevan would console himself, brown riders could aspire to become wingseconds, and that wasn't bad. He'd even settle for a green dragon: they were small, but so was he. No matter! He simply had to Impress a dragon his first time in the Hatching Ground. Then no one in the Weyr would taunt him anymore for being so small.

Shells, Keevan thought now, but the sands are hot!

"Impression time is imminent, candidates," the wingsecond was saying as everyone crowded respectfully close to him. "See the extent of the striations on this promising egg." The stretch marks *were* larger than yesterday.

Everyone leaned forward and nodded thoughtfully. That particular egg was the one Beterli had marked as his own, and no other candidate dared, on pain of being beaten by Beterli at his first opportunity, to approach it. The egg was marked by a large yellowish splotch in the shape of a dragon backwinging to land, talons outstretched to grasp rock. Everyone knew that bronze eggs bore distinctive markings. And naturally, Beterli, who'd been presented at eight Impressions already and was the biggest of the candidates, had chosen it.

"I'd say that the great opening day is almost upon us," the wingsecond went on, and then his face assumed a grave expression. "As we well know, there are only forty eggs and seventy-two candidates. Some of you may be disappointed on the great day. That doesn't necessarily mean you aren't dragonrider material, just that *the* dragon for you hasn't been shelled. You'll have other hatchings, and it's no disgrace to be left behind an Impression or two. Or more."

Keevan was positive that the wingsecond's eyes rested on Beterli, who'd been stood off at so many Impressions already. Keevan tried to squinch down so the wingsecond wouldn't notice him. Keevan had been reminded too often that he was eligible to be a candidate by one day only. He, of all the hopefuls, was most likely to be left standing on the great day. One more reason why he simply had to Impress at his first hatching.

"Now move about among the eggs," the wingsecond said. "Touch them. We don't know that it does any good, but it certainly doesn't do any harm."

Some of the boys laughed nervously, but everyone immediately began to circulate among the eggs. Berterli stepped up officiously to "his" egg, daring anyone to come near it. Keevan smiled, because he had already touched it—every inspection day, when the others were leaving the Hatching Ground and no one could see him crouch to stroke it.

Keevan had an egg he concentrated on, too, one drawn slightly to the far side of the others. The shell had a soft greenish-blue tinge with a faint creamy swirl design. The consensus was that this egg contained a mere green, so Keevan was rarely bothered by rivals. He was somewhat perturbed then to see Beterli wandering over to him.

"I don't know why you're allowed in this Impression, Keevan. There are enough of us without a babe," Beterli said, shaking his head.

"I'm of age." Keevan kept his voice level, telling himself not to be bothered by mere words.

"Yah!" Beterli made a show of standing in his toetips. "You can't even see over an egg; Hatching Day, you better get in front or the dragons won't see you at all. 'Course, you could get run down that way in the mad scramble. Oh, I forget, you can run fast, can't you?"

"You'd better make sure a dragon sees *you*, this time, Beterli," Keevan replied. "You're almost overage, aren't you?"

Beterli flushed and took a step forward, hand half-raised. Keevan stood his ground, but if Beterli advanced one more step, he would call the wingsecond. No one fought on the Hatching Ground. Surely Beterli knew that much.

Fortunately, at that moment, the wingsecond called the boys together and led them from the Hatching Ground to start on evening chores. There were "glows" to be replenished in the main kitchen caverns and sleeping cubicles, the major hallways, and the queen's apartment. Firestone sacks had to be filled against Thread attack, and black rock brought to the kitchen hearths. The boys fell to their chores, tantalized by the odors of roasting meat. The population of the Weyr began to assemble for the evening meal, and the dragonriders came in from the Feeding Ground on their sweep checks.

It was the time of day Keevan liked best: once the chores were done but before dinner was served, a fellow could often get close enough to the dragonriders to hear their talk. Tonight, Keevan's father, K'last, was at the main dragonrider table. It puzzled Keevan how his father, a brown rider and a tall man, could be his father—because he, Keevan, was so small. It obviously puzzled K'last, too, when he deigned to notice his small son: "In a few more Turns, you'll be as tall as I am— or taller!"

K'last was pouring Benden wine all around the table. The dragonriders were relaxing. There'd be no Thread attack for three more days, and they'd be in the mood to tell tall tales, better than Harper yarns, about impossible maneuvers they'd done a-dragonback. When Thread attack was closer, their talk would change to a discussion of tactics of evasion, of going *between*, how long to suspend there until the burning but fragile Thread would freeze and crack and fall harmlessly off dragon and man. They would dispute the exact moment to feed firestone to the dragon so he'd have the best flame ready to sear Thread midair and render it harmless to ground—and man—below. There was such a lot to know and understand about being a dragonrider that sometimes Keevan was overwhelmed. How would he ever be able to remember everything he ought to know at the right moment? He couldn't dare ask such a question; this would only have given additional weight to the notion that he was too young yet to be a dragonrider.

"Having older candidates makes good sense," L'vel was saying, as Keevan settled down near the table. "Why waste four to five years of a dragon's fighting prime until his rider grows up enough to stand the rigors?" L'vel had Impressed a blue of Ramoth's first clutch. Most of the candidates thought L'vel was marvelous because he spoke up in front of the older riders, who awed them. "That was well enough in the Interval when you didn't need to mount the full Weyr complement to fight Thread. But not now. Not with more eligible candidates than ever. Let the babes wait."

"Any boy who is over twelve Turns has the right to stand in the Hatching Ground," K'last replied, a slight smile on his face. He never argued or got angry. Keevan wished he were more like his father. And oh, how he wished he were a brown rider! "Only a dragon—each particular dragon—knows what he wants in a rider. We certainly can't tell. Time and again the theorists," K'last's smile deepened as his eyes swept those at the table, "are surprised by dragon choice. They never seem to make mistakes, however."

"Now, K'last, just look at the roster this Impression. Seventy-two boys and only forty eggs. Drop off the twelve youngest, and there's still a good field for the hatchlings to choose from. Shells! There are a couple of weyrlings unable to see over a wher egg much less a dragon! And years before they can ride Thread."

"True enough, but the Weyr is scarcely under fighting strength, and if the youngest Impress, they'll be old enough to fight when the oldest of our current dragons go *between* from senility."

"Half the Weyr-bred lads have already been through several Impressions," one of the bronze riders said then. "I'd say drop some of *them* off this time. Give the untried a chance."

"There's nothing wrong in presenting a clutch with as wide a choice as possible," said the Weyrleader, who had joined the table with Lessa, the Weyrwoman.

"Has there ever been a case," she said, smiling in her odd way at the riders, "where a hatchling didn't choose?"

Her suggestion was almost heretical and drew astonished gasps from everyone, including the boys.

F'lar laughed. "You say the most outrageous things, Lessa."

"Well, *has* there ever been a case where a dragon didn't choose?"

"Can't say as I recall one," K'last replied.

"Then we continue in this tradition," Lessa said firmly, as if that ended the matter.

But it didn't. The argument ranged from one table to the other all through dinner, with some favoring a weeding out of the candidates to the most likely, lopping off those who were very young or who had had multiple opportunities to Impress. All the candidates were in a swivet, though such a departure from tradition would be to the advantage of many. As the evening progressed, more riders were favoring eliminating the youngest and those who'd passed four or more Impressions unchosen. Keevan felt he could bear such a dictum only if Beterli were also eliminated. But this seemed less likely than that Keevan would be turfed out, since the Weyr's need was for fighting dragons and riders.

By the time the evening meal was over, no decision had been reached, although the Weyrleader had promised to give the matter due consideration.

He might have slept on the problem, but few of the candidates did. Tempers were uncertain in the sleeping caverns next morning as the boys were routed out of their beds to carry water and black rock and cover the "glows." Twice Mende had to call Keevan to order for clumsiness.

"Whatever is the matter with you, boy?" she demanded in exasperation when he tipped blackrock short of the bin and sooted up the hearth.

"They're going to keep me from this Impression."

"What?" Mende stared at him. "Who?"

"You heard them talking at dinner last night. They're going to turf the babes from the hatching."

Mende regarded him a moment longer before touching his arm gently. "There's lots of talk around a supper table, Keevan. And it cools as soon as the supper. I've heard the same nonsense before every hatching, but nothing is ever changed."

"There's always a first time," Keevan answered, copying one of her own phrases.

"That'll be enough of that, Keevan. Finish your job. If the clutch does hatch today, we'll need full rock bins for the feast, and you won't be around to do the filling. All my fosterlings make dragonriders."

"The first time?" Keevan was bold enough to ask as he scooted off with the rockbarrow.

Perhaps, Keevan thought later, if he hadn't been on that chore just when Beterli was also fetching black rock, things might have turned out differently. But he had dutifully trundled the barrow to the outdoor bunker for another load just as Beterli arrived on a similar errand.

"Heard the news, babe?" Beterli asked. He was grinning from ear to ear, and he put an unnecessary emphasis on the final insulting word.

"The eggs are cracking?" Keevan all but dropped the loaded shovel. Several anxieties flicked through his mind then: he was black with rock dust—would he have time to wash before donning the white tunic of candidacy? And if the eggs were hatching, why hadn't the candidates been recalled by the wingsecond?

"Naw! Guess again!" Beterli was much too pleased with himself.

With a sinking heart, Keevan knew what the news must be, and he could only stare with intense desolation at the older boy.

"C'mon! Guess, babe!"

"I've no time for guessing games," Keevan managed to say with indifference. He began to shovel black rock into the barrow as fast as he could.

"I said, guess." Beterli grabbed the shovel.

"And I said I have no time for guessing games."

Beterli wrenched the shovel from Keevan's hands. "Guess!"

"I'll have that shovel back, Beterli." Keevan straightened up, but he didn't come to Beterli's bulky shoulder. From somewhere, other boys appeared, some with barrows, some mysteriously alerted to the prospect of a confrontation among their numbers.

"Babes don't give orders to candidates around here, babe!"

Someone sniggered and Keevan, incredulous, knew that he must've been dropped from the candidacy.

He yanked the shovel from Beterli's loosened grasp. Snarling, the older boy tried to regain possession, but Keevan clung with all his strength to the handle, dragged back and forth as the stronger boy jerked the shovel about.

With a sudden, unexpected movement, Beterli rammed the handle into Keevan's chest, knocking him over the barrow handles. Keevan felt a sharp, painful jab behind his left ear, an unbearable pain in his left shin, and then a painless nothingness.

Mende's angry voice roused him, and startled, he tried to throw back the covers, thinking he'd overslept. But he couldn't move, so firmly was he tucked into his bed. And then the constriction of a bandage on his head and the dull sickishness in his leg brought back recent occurrences.

"Hatching?" he cried.

"No, lovey," Mende said in a kind voice. Her hand was cool and gentle on his forehead. "Though there's some as won't be at any hatching again." Her voice took on a stern edge.

Keevan looked beyond her to see the Weyrwoman, who was frowning with irritation.

"Keevan, will you tell me what occurred at the black-rock bunker?" asked Lessa in an even voice.

He remembered Beterli now and the quarrel over the shovel and . . . what had Mende said about some not being at any hatching? Much as he hated Beterli, he couldn't bring himself to tattle on Beterli and force him out of candidacy.

"Come, lad," and a note of impatience crept into the Weyrwoman's voice. "I merely want to know what happened from you, too. Mende said she sent you for black rock. Beterli—and every Weyrling in the cavern—seems to have been on the same errand. What happened?"

"Beterli took my shovel. I hadn't finished with it."

"There's more than one shovel. What did he *say* to you?"

"He'd heard the news."

"What news?" The Weyrwoman was suddenly amused.

"That . . . that . . . there'd been changes."

"Is that what he said?"

"Not exactly"

"What did he say? C'mon, lad, I've heard from everyone else, you know."

"He said for me to guess the news."

"And you fell for that old gag?" The Weyrwoman's irritation returned.

"Consider all the talk last night at supper, Lessa," Mende said. "Of course the boy would think he'd been eliminated."

"In effect, he is, with a broken skull and leg." Lessa touched his arm in a rare gesture of sympathy. "Be that as it may, Keevan, you'll have other Impressions. Beterli will not. There are certain rules that must be observed by all candidates, and his conduct proves him unacceptable to the Weyr."

She smiled at Mende and then left.

"I'm still a candidate?" Keevan asked urgently.

"Well, you are and you aren't, lovey," his foster mother said. "Is the numbweed working?" she asked, and when he nodded, she said, "You just rest. I'll bring you some nice broth."

At any other time in his life, Keevan would have relished such cosseting, but now he just lay there worrying. Beterli had been dismissed. Would the others think it was his fault? But everyone was there! Beterli provoked that fight. His worry increased, because although he heard excited comings and goings in the passageway, no one tweaked back the curtain across the sleeping alcove he shared with five other boys. Surely one of them would have to come in sometime. No, they were all avoiding him. And something else was wrong. Only he didn't know what.

Mende returned with broth and beachberry bread. "Why doesn't anyone come see me, Mende? I haven't done anything wrong, have I? I didn't ask to have Beterli turfed out."

Mende soothed him, saying everyone was busy with noontime chores and no one was angry with him. They were giving him a chance to rest in quiet. The numbweed made him drowsy, and her words were fair enough. He permitted his fears to dissipate. Until he heard a hum. Actually, he felt it first, in the broken shin bone and his sore head. The hum began to grow. Two things registered suddenly in Keevan's groggy mind: the only white candidate's robe still on the pegs in the chamber was his; and the dragons hummed when a clutch was being laid or being hatched. Impression! And he was flat abed.

Bitter, bitter disappointment turned the warm broth sour in his belly. Even the small voice telling him that he'd have other opportunities failed to alleviate his crushing depression. *This* was the Impression that mattered! This was his chance to show *everyone*, from Mende to K'last to L'vel and even the Weyrleader that he, Keevan, was worthy of being a dragonrider.

He twisted in bed, fighting against the tears that threatened to choke him. Dragonmen don't cry! Dragonmen learn to live with pain.

Pain? The leg didn't actually pain him as he rolled about on his bedding. His head felt sort of stiff from the tightness of the bandage. He sat up, an effort in itself since the numbweed made exertion difficult. He touched the splinted leg; the knee was unhampered. He had no feeling in his bone, really. He swung himself carefully to the side of his bed and stood slowly. The room wanted to swim about him. He closed his eyes, which made the dizziness worse, and he had to clutch the wall.

Gingerly, he took a step. The broken leg dragged. It hurt in spite of the numbweed, but what was pain to a dragonman?

No one had said he couldn't go to the Impression. "You are and you aren't," were Mende's exact words.

Clinging to the wall, he jerked off his bedshirt. Stretching his arm to the utmost, he jerked his white candidate's tunic from the peg. Jamming first one arm and then the other into the holes, he pulled it over his head. Too bad about the belt. He couldn't wait. He hobbled to the door, hung on to the curtain to steady himself. The weight on his leg was unwieldy. He wouldn't get very far without something to lean on. Down by the bathing pool was one of the long crooknecked poles used to retrieve clothes from the hot washing troughs. But it was down there, and he was on the level above. And there was no one nearby to come to his aid: everyone would be in the Hatching Ground right now, eagerly waiting for the first egg to crack.

The humming increased in volume and tempo, an urgency to which Keevan responded, knowing that his time was all too limited if he was to join the ranks of the hopeful boys standing around the cracking eggs. But if he hurried down the ramp, he'd fall flat on his face.

He could, of course, go flat on his rear end, the way crawling children did. He sat down, sending a jarring stab of pain through his leg and up to the wound on the back of his head. Gritting his teeth and blinking away tears, Keevan scrabbled down the ramp. He had to wait a moment at the bottom to catch his breath. He got to one knee, the injured leg straight out in front of him. Somehow, he managed to push himself erect, though the room seemed about to tip over his ears. It wasn't far to the crooked stick, but it seemed an age before he had it in his hand.

Then the humming stopped!

Keevan cried out and began to hobble frantically across the cavern, out to the bowl of the Weyr. Never had the distance between living caverns and the Hatching Ground seemed so great. Never had the Weyr been so breathlessly silent. It was as if the multitude of people and dragons watching the hatching held every breath in suspense. Not even the wind muttered down the steep sides of the bowl. The only sounds to break the stillness were Keevan's ragged gasps and the thump-thud of his stick on the hard-packed ground. Sometimes he had to hop twice on his good leg to maintain his balance. Twice he fell into the sand and had to pull himself up on the stick, his white tunic no longer spotless. Once he jarred himself so badly he couldn't get up immediately.

Then he heard the first exhalation of the crowd, the oohs, the muted cheer, the susurrus of excited whispers. An egg had cracked, and the dragon had chosen his rider. Desperation increased Keevan's hobble. Would he never reach the arching mouth of the Hatching Ground?

Another cheer and an excited spate of applause spurred Keevan to greater effort. If he didn't get there in moments, there'd be no unpaired hatchling left. Then he was actually staggering into the Hatchling Ground, the sands hot on his bare feet.

No one noticed his entrance or his halting progress. And Keevan could see nothing but the backs of the white-robed candidates, seventy of them ringing the area around the eggs. Then one side would surge forward or back and there'd be a cheer. Another dragon had been Impressed. Suddenly a large gap appeared in the white human wall, and Keevan had his first sight of the eggs. There didn't seem to be *any* left uncracked, and he could see the lucky boys standing beside wobble-legged dragons. He could hear the unmistakable plaintive crooning of hatchlings and their squawks of protest as they'd fall awkwardly in the sand.

Suddenly he wished that he hadn't left his bed, that he'd stayed away from the Hatching Ground. Now everyone would see his ignominious failure. So he scrambled as desperately to reach the shadowy walls of the Hatching Ground as he had struggled to cross the bowl. He mustn't be seen.

He didn't notice, therefore, that the shifting group of boys remaining had begun to drift in his direction. The hard pace he had set himself and his cruel disappointment took their double toll of Keevan. He tripped and collapsed sobbing to the warm sands. He didn't see the consternation in the watching Weyrfolk above the Hatching Ground, nor did he hear the excited whispers of speculation. He didn't know that the Weyrleader and Weyrwoman had dropped to the arena and were making their way toward the knot of boys slowly moving in the direction of the entrance.

"Never seen anything like it," the Weyrleader was saying. "Only thirty-nine riders chosen. And the bronze trying to leave the Hatching Ground without making Impression."

"A case in point of what I said last night," the Weyrwoman replied, "where a hatchling makes no choice because the right boy isn't there."

"There's only Beterli and K'last's young one missing. And there's a full wing of likely boys to choose from. . ."

"None acceptable, apparently. Where is the creature going? He's not heading for the entrance after all. Oh, what have we there, in the shadows?"

Keevan heard with dismay the sound of voices nearing him. He tried to burrow into the sand. The mere thought of how he would be teased and taunted now was unbearable.

Don't worry! Please don't worry! The thought was urgent, but not his own.

Someone kicked sand over Keevan and butted roughly against him.

"Go away. Leave me alone!" he cried.

Why? was the injured-sounding question inserted into his mind. There was no voice, no tone, but the question was there, perfectly clear, in his head.

Incredulous, Keevan lifted his head and stared into the glowing jeweled eyes of a small bronze dragon. His wings were wet, the tips drooping in the sand. And he sagged in the middle on his unsteady legs, although he was making a great effort to keep erect.

Keevan dragged himself to his knees, oblivious of the pain in his leg. He wasn't even aware that he was ringed by the boys passed over, while thirty-one pairs of resentful eyes watched him Impress the dragon. The Weyrmen looked on, amused, and surprised at the draconic choice, which could not be forced. Could not be questioned. Could not be changed.

Why? asked the dragon again. *Don't you like me?* His eyes whirled with anxiety, and his tone was so piteous that Keevan staggered forward and threw his arms around the dragon's neck, stroking his eye ridges, patting the damp, soft hide, opening the fragile-looking wings to dry them, and wordlessly assuring the hatchling over and over again that he was the most perfect, most beautiful, most beloved dragon in the Weyr, in all the Weyrs of Pern.

"What's his name, K'van?" asked Lessa, smiling warmly at the new dragonrider. K'van stared up at her for a long moment. Lessa would know as soon as he did. Lessa was the only person who could "receive" from all dragons, not only her own Ramoth. Then he gave her a radiant smile, recognizing the traditional shortening of his name that raised him forever to the rank of dragonrider.

My name is Heth, the dragon thought mildly, then hiccuped in sudden urgency. *I'm hungry.*

"Dragons are born hungry," said Lessa, laughing. "F'lar, give the boy a hand. He can barely manage his own legs, much less a dragon's."

K'van remembered his stick and drew himself up. "We'll be Just fine, thank you."

"You may be the smallest dragonrider ever, young K'van," Flar said, "but you're one of the bravest!"

And Heth agreed! Pride and joy so leaped in both chests that K'van wondered if his heart would burst right out of his body. He looped an arm around Heth's neck and the pair, the smallest dragonboy and the hatchling who wouldn't choose anybody else, walked out of the Hatching Ground together forever.

Out of All Them Bright Stars

※

by Nancy Kress

Like the other six living authors who've contributed to this anthology, Nancy Kress's best work in the field of science fiction might still be ahead of her. She published her first short story in 1976 and continues to produce high-quality, award-winning work to this day.

To date, she has published twenty-seven novels, three books on writing, four short story collections, and more than a hundred short stories. Her latest book, titled The Best of Nancy Kress, *appeared from Subterranean Press in late 2015.*

I feel it essential to include Nancy in a volume of stories on women in science fiction. Her short fiction has represented the best in the genre since she won her first Nebula in 1986. She has gone on to win five more Nebulas in every decade since, two Hugo Awards, a Theodore Sturgeon award, and a John W. Campbell Memorial Award.

Her work continues to be cutting edge. She mostly writes hard science fiction these days, often focusing on genetic engineering, and like so many authors in this anthology, has done much of her best work at the novella length. If I had an infinite number of pages, I would have chosen my personal favorite of hers, the novella "Beggars in Spain," which you can find in The Best of Nancy Kress.

Instead, I bring you the short story that really announced her presence to the field (even though she'd been writing for ten years before this story saw print). "Out of All Them Bright Stars" is the story that won the Best Short Story Nebula in 1986, starting Nancy on this long and important— and as yet unfinished—run.

※ ※ ※

SO I'M FILLING the catsup bottles at the end of the night, and I'm listening to the radio Charlie has stuck up on top of a movable panel in the ceiling, when the door opens and one of them walks in. I know right away it's one of them—no chance to make a mistake about that— even though it's got on a nice suit and a brim hat like Humphrey Bogart used to wear in *Casablanca*. But there's nobody with it, no professor or government men like on the TV show or even any students. It's all alone. And we're a long way out on the highway from the college.

It stands in the doorway, blinking a little, with rain dripping off its hat. Kathy, who's supposed to be cleaning the coffee machine behind the counter, freezes and stares with one hand holding the filter up in the air like she's never going to move again. Just then Charlie calls out from the kitchen, "Hey, Kathy, you ask anybody who won the Trifecta?" and she doesn't even answer him. Just goes on staring with her mouth open like she's thinking of screaming but forgot how. And the old couple in the corner booth, the only ones left from the crowd when the movie got out, stop chewing their chocolate cream pie and stare too. Kathy closes her mouth and opens it again and a noise comes out like "Uh—errrgh . . . "

Well, that got me annoyed. Maybe she tried to say "ugh" and maybe she didn't, but here it is standing in the doorway with rain falling around it in little drops and we're staring at it like it's a clothes dummy and not a customer. So I think that's not right and maybe we're even making it feel a little bad, I wouldn't like Kathy staring at me like that, and I dry my hands on my towel and go over.

"Yes, sir, can I help you?" I say.

"Table for one," it says, like Charlie's is some nice steak house in town. But I suppose that's the kind of place the government men mostly take them to. And besides, its voice is polite and easy to understand, with a sort of accent but not as bad as some we get from the college. I can tell what it's saying. I lead him to a booth in the corner opposite the old couple, who come in every Friday night and haven't left a tip yet.

He sits down slowly. I notice he keeps his hands on his lap, but I can't tell if that's because he doesn't know what to do with them or because he thinks I won't want to see them. But I've seen the close-ups on TV—they don't look so weird to me like they do to some. Charlie says they make his stomach turn, but I can't see it. You think he'd of seen worse meat in Vietnam. He talks enough like he did, on and on, and sometimes we even believe him.

I say, "Coffee, sir?"

He makes a kind of movement with his eyes. I can't tell what the movement means, but he says in that polite voice, "No, thank you. I am unable to drink coffee," and I think that's a good thing because I suddenly remember Kathy's got the filter out. But then he says, "May I have a green salad, please? With no dressing, please?"

The rain is still dripping off his hat. I figure the government people never told him to take off his hat in a restaurant, and for some reason that tickles me and makes me feel real bold. This polite blue guy isn't going to bother nobody, and that fool Charlie was just spouting off his mouth again.

"The salad's not too fresh, sir," I say, experimental-like, just to see what he'll say next. And it's the truth—the salad is left over from yesterday. But the guy answers like I asked something else.

"What is your name?" he says, so polite I know he's really curious and not trying to start anything. And what could he start anyway, blue and with those hands? Still, you never know.

"Sally," I say, "Sally Gourley."

"I am John," he says, and makes that movement again with his eyes. All of a sudden it tickles me—"John!" For this blue guy! So I laugh, and right away I feel sorry, like I might have hurt his feelings or something. How could you tell?

"Hey, I'm sorry," I say, and he takes off his hat. He does it real slow, like taking off the hat is important and means something, but all there is underneath is a bald blue head. Nothing weird like with the hands.

"Do not apologize," John says. "I have another name, of course, but in my own language."

"What is it?" I say, bold as brass, because all of a sudden I picture myself telling all this to my sister Mary Ellen and her listening real hard.

John makes some noises with his mouth, and I feel my own mouth open because it's not a word he says at all, it's a beautiful sound, like a bird call only sadder. It's just that I wasn't expecting it, that beautiful sound right here in Charlie's diner. It surprised me, coming out of that bald blue head. That's all it was: surprise.

I don't say anything. John looks at me and says, "It has a meaning that can be translated. It means—" but before he can say what it means Charlie comes charging out of the kitchen, Kathy right behind him. He's still got the racing form in one hand, like he's been studying the Trifecta, and he pushes right up against the booth and looks red and furious. Then I see the old couple scuttling out the door, their jackets clutched to their fronts, and the chocolate pie half-eaten on their plates. I see they're going to stiff me for the check, but before I can stop them Charlie grabs my arm and squeezes so hard his nails slice into my skin.

"What the hell do you think you're doing?" he says right to me. Not so much as a look at John, but Kathy can't stop looking and her fist is pushed up to her mouth.

I drag my arm away and rub it. Once I saw Charlie push his wife so hard she went down and hit her head and had to have four stitches. It was me that drove her to the emergency room.

Charlie says, "What the hell do you think you're doing?"

"I'm serving my table. He wants a salad. Large." I can't remember if John said a large or a small salad, but I figure a large order would make Charlie feel better. But Charlie don't want to feel better.

"You get him out of here," Charlie hisses. He still doesn't look at John. "You hear me, Sally? You get him out. The government says I gotta serve spics and niggers but it don't say I gotta serve him!"

I look at John. He's putting on his hat, ramming it onto his bald head, and half standing in the booth. He can't get out because Charlie and me are both in the way. I expect John to look mad or upset, but except that he's holding the muscles of his face in some different way I can't see any change of expression. But I figure he's got to feel something bad, and all of a sudden I'm mad at Charlie, who's a bully and who's got the feelings of a scumbag. I open my mouth to tell him so, plus one or two other little things I been saving up, when the door flies open and in burst four men, and damn if they aren't all wearing hats like Humphrey Bogart in *Casablanca*. As soon as the first guy sees John, his walk changes and he comes over slower but more purposeful-like, and then he's talking to John and Charlie in a sincere voice like a TV anchorman giving out the news.

I see the situation now belongs to him, so I go back to the catsup bottles. I'm still plenty burned though, about Charlie manhandling me and about Kathy rushing into the kitchen to get Charlie. She's a flake and always has been.

Charlie is scowling and nodding. The harder he scowls, the nicer the government guy's voice gets. Pretty soon the government guy is smiling sweet as pie. Charlie slinks back into the kitchen, and the four men move toward the door with John in the middle of them like some high school football huddle. Next to the real men he looks stranger than he did before, and I see how really flat his face is. But then when the huddle's right opposite my table with the catsup bottles, John breaks away and comes over to me.

"I am sorry, Sally Gourley," he says. And then, "I seldom have the chance to show our friendliness to an ordinary Earth person. I make so little difference!"

Well, that throws me. His voice sounds so sad, and besides I never thought of myself as an ordinary Earth person. Who would? So I just shrug and wipe off a catsup bottle with my towel. But then John does a weird thing. He just touches my arm where Charlie squeezed it, just touches it with the palm of one of those hands. And the palm's not slimy at all—dry, and sort of cool, and I don't jump or anything. Instead I remember that beautiful noise when he said his other name. Then he goes out with three of the men and the door bangs behind them on a gust of rain because Charlie never fixed the air-stop from when some kids horsing around broke it last spring.

The fourth man stays and questions me: what did the alien say, what did I say? I tell him, but then he starts asking the exact same questions all over again, like he didn't believe me the first time, and that gets me mad. Also he has this snotty voice, and I see how his eyebrows move when I slip once and say, "He don't." I might not know what John's muscles mean but I sure as hell can read those eyebrows. So I get miffed and pretty soon he leaves and the door bangs behind him.

I finish the catsup and mustard bottles and Kathy finishes the coffee machine. The radio in the ceiling plays something instrumental, no words, real sad. Kathy and me start to wash down the booths with disinfectant, and because we're doing the same work together and nobody comes in, I finally say to her, "It's funny."

She says, "What's funny?"

"Charlie called that guy 'him' right off. 'I don't got to serve him,' he said. And I thought of him as 'it' at first, leastways until I had a name to use. But Charlie's the one who threw him out."

Kathy swipes at the back of her booth. "And Charlie's right. That thing scared me half to death, coming in here like that. And where there's food being served, too." She snorts and sprays on more disinfectant.

Well, she's a flake. Always has been.

"The *National Enquirer*," Kathy goes on, "told how they have all this firepower up in the big ship that hasn't landed yet. My husband says they could blow us all to smithereens, they're so powerful. I don't know why they even came here. We don't want them. I don't even know why they came, all that way."

"They want to make a difference," I say, but Kathy barrels on ahead, not listening.

"The Pentagon will hold them off, it doesn't matter how much firepower they got up there or how much they insist on seeing about our defenses, the Pentagon won't let them get any toeholds on Earth. That's what my husband says. Blue bastards."

I say, "Will you please shut up?"

She gives me a dirty look and flounces off. I don't care. None of it is anything to me. Only, standing there with the disinfectant in my hand, looking at the dark windows and listening to the music wordless and slow on the radio, I remember that touch on my arm. And I think, they didn't come here with any firepower to blow us all to smithereens. I just don't believe it. So why did they come? Why come all that way from another star to walk into Charlie's diner and order a green salad with no dressing from an ordinary Earth person?

Charlie comes out with his keys to unlock the cash register and go over the tapes. I remember the old couple who stiffed me and I curse to myself. Only pie and coffee, but it still comes off my salary. The radio starts playing something else, not the sad song, but nothing snappy neither. It's a love song, about some guy giving and giving and getting treated like dirt. I don't like it much.

"Charlie," I say, "what did those government men say to you?"

He looks up from his tapes and scowls. "What do you care?"

"I just want to know."

"And maybe I don't want you to know," he says, and smiles nasty-like. Me asking has put him in a better mood, the creep. All of a sudden I remember what his wife said when she got the stitches: "The only way to get something from Charlie is to let him smack me around a little, and then ask him when I'm down. He'll give me anything when I'm down. He gives me shit if he thinks I'm on top."

I think again about the blue guy. John.

I do the rest of the clean-up without saying anything. Charlie swears at the night's take—I know from my tips that it's not much. Kathy teases her hair in front of the mirror behind doughnuts and pies, and I put down the breakfast menus. But all the time I'm thinking, and I don't much like my thoughts.

Charlie locks up and we all leave. Outside it's stopped raining but it's still misty and soft, real pretty but too cold. I pull my sweater around myself and in the parking lot, after Kathy's gone, I say, "Charlie."

He stops walking toward his truck. "Yeah?"

I lick my lips. They're all of a sudden dry. It's an experiment, like, what I'm going to say. It's an experiment.

"Charlie. What if those government men hadn't come just then and the . . . the blue guy hadn't been willing to leave? What would you have done?"

"What do you care?"

I shrug. "I don't. Just curious. It's your place."

"Damn straight it's my place!" Through the mist I can see him scowl. "I'd of squashed him flat!"

"And then what? After you squashed him flat, what if the men came then and made a stink?"

"Too bad. It'd be too late by then, huh?" He laughs and I can see how he's seeing it: the blue guy bleeding on the linoleum and Charlie standing over him, dusting his hands together.

Charlie laughs again and goes off to his truck, whistling. He has a little bounce in his step. He's still seeing it, almost like it really had happened. Over his shoulder he calls to me, "They're built like wimps. Or girls. All bone, no muscle. Even you must of seen that," and his voice is cheerful. It doesn't have any more anger in it, or hatred, or anything but a kind of friendliness. I hear him whistle some more, until the truck engine starts up and he peels out of the parking lot, laying rubber like a kid.

I unlock my Chevy. But before I get in, I look up at the sky. Which is really stupid because of course I can't see anything, with all the mist and clouds. No stars.

Maybe Kathy's husband is right. Maybe they do want to blow us all to smithereens. I don't think so, but what the hell difference does it ever make what I think? And all at once I'm furious at John, furious mad, as mad as I've ever been in my life.

Why does he have to come here, with his bird calls and his politeness? Why can't they all go someplace else besides here? There must be lots of other places they can go, out of all them bright stars up there behind the clouds. They don't need to come here, here where I need this job and so that means I need Charlie. He's a bully, but I want to look at him and see nothing else but a bully. Nothing else but that. That's all I want to see in Charlie, in the government men—just small-time bullies, nothing special, not a mirror of anything, not a future of anything. Just Charlie. That's all. I won't see nothing else.

I won't.

"I make so little difference," he says.

Yeah. Sure.

Angel

❦

by Pat Cadigan

Whenever Pat Cadigan does as much as lift a finger, she attracts attention. Wired labeled her a "sci-fi maverick," which probably describes her best. She always seems to be on the cutting edge.

Pat dates her first appearance in science fiction from her publication in New Dimensions 11 in 1980, but her fiction appeared before that in smaller press publications. The science fiction community already knew her in 1980 as the editor of World Fantasy award-winning magazine Shayol, which published some of the earliest fiction by an entire generation of writers. She still occasionally dabbles in editing, most notably with The Ultimate Cyberpunk (2002), which looks at the cyberpunk movement from its roots in early sf to the twenty-first century.

Pat is closely associated with the cyberpunk movement, often listed as its only female contributor (even though that's not true). Her novels Mindplayer, Synners, and Fools were incredibly influential in that subgenre as well as in science fiction as a whole. Both Synners and Fools won the prestigious Arthur C. Clarke Award for best sf novel. Many of Pat's fifteen books, which went out of print in the early part of this century, are available again in ebook editions, including the novels I just mentioned.

Throughout the last two decades of the twentieth century, she was nominated for a variety of awards. She was nominated for the Hugo four times in that period, but she didn't win a Hugo until 2013, for her story "The Girl-Thing Who Went Out for Sushi."

Her first Hugo nomination came for the story that follows. "Angel"
was also nominated for a Nebula, and a World Fantasy Award. The
story won the Locus *Award for best short story. Even though "Angel"*
was published in 1987, its themes and feel are disturbingly modern.
With only a handful of changes, the story could have been published
this year.

In this century, she has concentrated on her first love, short fiction,
more than on novels. "Angel" will show you one reason why.

❁ ❁ ❁

STAND WITH ME AWHILE, Angel, I said and Angel said he'd do
that. Angel was good to me that way, good to have with you on a cold
night and nowhere to go. We stood on the street corner together and
watched the cars going by and people and all. The streets were lit
unlike Christmas, streetlights, store lights, marquees over the all-night
movie houses and bookstores blinking and flashing; shank of the
evening in east midtown. Angel was getting used to things here and
getting used to how I did, nights. Standing outside, because what else
are you going to do. He was my Angel now, had been since that other
cold night when I'd been going home, because where are you going to
go, and I'd found him and took him with me. It's good to have someone
to take with you, someone to look after. Angel knew that. He started
looking after me, too.

Like now. We were standing there awhile and I was looking around
at nothing and everything, the cars cruising past, some of them
stopping now and again for the hookers posing by the curb, and then
I saw it, out of the corner of my eye. Stuff coming out of the Angel,
shiny like sparks but flowing like liquid. Silver fireworks. I turned and
looked all the way at him and it was gone. And he turned and gave a
little grin like he was embarrassed I'd seen. Nobody else saw it, though;
not the short guy who paused next to the Angel before crossing the
street against the light, not the skinny hype looking to sell the boom-
box he was carrying on his shoulder, not the homeboy strutting past
us with both his girlfriends on his arms, nobody but me.

The Angel said, Hungry?

Sure, I said. I'm hungry.

Angel looked past me. Okay, he said. I looked, too, and here they came, three leather boys, visor caps, belts, boots, keyrings. On the cruise together. Scary stuff, even though you know it's not looking for you.

I said, them? *Them?*

Angel didn't answer. One went by, then the second, and the Angel stopped the third by taking hold of his arm.

Hi.

The guy nodded. His head was shaved. I could see a little grey-black stubble under his cap. No eyebrows, disinterested eyes. The eyes were because of the Angel.

I could use a little money, the Angel said. My friend and I are hungry.

The guy put his hand in his pocket and wiggled out some bills, offering them to the Angel. The Angel selected a twenty and closed the guy's hand around the rest.

This will be enough, thank you.

The guy put his money away and waited.

I hope you have a good night, said the Angel.

The guy nodded and walked on, going across the street to where his two friends were waiting on the next corner. Nobody found anything weird about it.

Angel was grinning at me. Sometimes he was the Angel, when he was doing something, sometimes he was Angel, when he was just with me. Now he was Angel again. We went up the street to the luncheonette and got a seat by the front window so we could still watch the street while we ate.

Cheeseburger and fries, I said without bothering to look at the plastic-covered menus lying on top of the napkin holder. The Angel nodded.

Thought so, he said. I'll have the same, then.

The waitress came over with a little tiny pad to take our order. I cleared my throat. It seemed like I hadn't used my voice in a hundred years. "Two cheeseburgers and two fries," I said, "and two cups of—" I looked up at her and froze. She had no face. Like, nothing, blank from hairline to chin, soft little dents where the eyes and nose and mouth would have been. Under the table, the Angel kicked me, but gentle.

"And two cups of coffee," I said.

She didn't say anything—how could she?—as she wrote down the order and then walked away again. All shaken up, I looked at the Angel but he was calm like always.

She's a new arrival, Angel told me and leaned back in his chair. Not enough time to grow a face.

But how can she breathe? I said.

Through her pores. She doesn't need much air yet.

Yah, but what about—like, I mean, don't other people notice that's she's got nothing there?

No. It's not such an extraordinary condition. The only reason you notice is because you're with me. Certain things have rubbed off on you. But no one else notices. When they look at her, they see whatever face they expect someone like her to have. And eventually, she'll have it.

But you have a face, I said. You've always had a face. I'm different, said the Angel.

You sure are, I thought, looking at him. Angel had a beautiful face. That wasn't why I took him home that night, just because he had a beautiful face—I left all that behind a long time ago—but it was there, his beauty. The way you think of a man being beautiful, good clean lines, deep-set eyes, ageless. About the only way you could describe him—look away and you'd forget everything except that he was beautiful. But he did have a face. He did.

Angel shifted in the chair—these were like somebody's old kitchen chairs, you couldn't get too comfortable in them—and shook his head, because he knew I was thinking troubled thoughts. Sometimes you could think something and it wouldn't be troubled and later you'd think the same thing and it would be troubled. The Angel didn't like me to be troubled about him.

Do you have a cigarette? he asked.

I think so.

I patted my jacket and came up with most of a pack that I handed over to him. The Angel lit up and amused us both by having the smoke come out his ears and trickle out of his eyes like ghostly tears. I felt my own eyes watering for his; I wiped them and there was that stuff again, but from me now. I was crying silver fireworks. I flicked them on the table and watched them puff out and vanish.

Does this mean I'm getting to be you, now? I asked.

Angel shook his head. Smoke wafted out of his hair. Just things rubbing off on you. Because we've been together and you're—susceptible. But they're different for you.

Then the waitress brought our food and we went on to another sequence, as the Angel would say. She still had no face but I guess she could see well enough because she put all the plates down just where you'd think they were supposed to go and left the tiny little check in the middle of the table.

Is she—I mean, did you know her, from where you—Angel gave his head a brief little shake. No. She's from somewhere else. Not one of my—people. He pushed the cheeseburger and fries in front of him over to my side of the table. That was the way it was done; I did all the eating and somehow it worked out.

I picked up my cheeseburger and I was bringing it up to my mouth when my eyes got all funny and I saw it coming up like a whole series of cheeseburgers, whoom-whoom-whoom, trick photography, only for real. I closed my eyes and jammed the cheeseburger into my mouth, holding it there, waiting for all the other cheeseburgers to catch up with it.

You'll be okay, said the Angel. Steady, now. I said with my mouth full. That was—that was weird. Will I ever get used to this?

I doubt it. But I'll do what I can to help you. Yah, well, the Angel *would* know. Stuff rubbing off on me, he could feel it better than I could. He was the one it was rubbing off from. I had put away my cheeseburger and half of Angel's and was working on the french fries for both of us when I noticed he was looking out the window with this hard, tight expression on his face. Something? I asked him. Keep eating, he said.

I kept eating but I kept watching, too. The Angel was staring at a big blue car parked at the curb right outside the diner. It was silvery blue, one of those lots-of-money models and there was a woman kind of leaning across from the driver's side to look out the passenger window. She was beautiful in that lots-of-money way, tawny hair swept back from her face and even from here I could see she had turquoise eyes. Really beautiful woman. I almost felt like crying. I mean, jeez, how did people get that way and me too harmless to live.

But the Angel wasn't one bit glad to see her. I knew he didn't want me to say anything, but I couldn't help it.

Who is she?

Keep eating, Angel said. We need the protein, what little there is.

I ate and watched the woman and the Angel watch each other and it was getting very—I don't know, very *something* between them, even through the glass. Then a cop car pulled up next to her and I knew they were telling her to move it along. She moved it along.

Angel sagged against the back of his chair and lit another cigarette, smoking it in the regular, unremarkable way.

What are we going to do tonight? I asked the Angel as we left the restaurant.

Keep out of harm's way, Angel said, which was a new answer. Most nights we spent just kind of going around soaking everything up. The Angel soaked it up, mostly. I got some of it along with him, but not the same way he did. It was different for him. Sometimes he would use me like a kind of filter. Other times he took it direct. There'd been the big car accident one night, right at my usual corner, a big old Buick running a red light smack into somebody's nice Lincoln. The Angel had had to take it direct because I couldn't handle that kind of stuff. I didn't know how the Angel could take it but he could. It carried him for days afterwards, too. I only had to eat for myself.

It's the intensity, little friend, he'd told me, as though that were supposed to explain it.

It's the intensity, not whether it's good or bad. The universe doesn't know good or bad, only less or more. Most of you have a bad time reconciling this. *You* have a bad time with it, little friend, but you get through better than other people. Maybe because of the way you are. You got squeezed out of a lot, you haven't had much of a chance at life. You're as much an exile as I am, only in your own land.

That may have been true, but at least I belonged here, so that part was easier for me. But I didn't say that to the Angel. I think he liked to think he could do as well or better than me at living—I mean, I couldn't just look at some leather boy and get him to cough up a twenty dollar bill. Cough up a fist in the face or worse, was more like it.

Tonight, though, he wasn't doing so good and it was that woman in the car. She'd thrown him out of step, kind of.

Don't think about her, the Angel said, just out of nowhere. Don't think about her any more.

Okay, I said, feeling creepy because it was creepy when the Angel got a glimpse of my head. And then, of course, I couldn't think about anything else hardly.

Do you want to go home? I asked him.

No. I can't stay in now. We'll do the best we can tonight but I'll have to be very careful about the tricks. They take so much out of me and if we're keeping out of harm's way, I might not be able to make up for a lot of it.

It's okay, I said. I ate. I don't need anything else tonight, you don't have to do any more.

Angel got that look on his face, the one where I knew he wanted to give me things, like feelings I couldn't have any more. Generous, the Angel was. But I didn't need those feelings, not like other people seem to. For awhile, it was like, the Angel didn't understand that but he let me be.

Little friend, he said, and almost touched me. The Angel didn't touch a lot. I could touch him and that would be okay but if he touched somebody, he couldn't help doing something to them, like the trade that had given us the money. That had been deliberate. If the trade had touched the Angel first, it would have been different, nothing would have happened unless the Angel touched him back. All touch meant something to the Angel that I didn't understand. There was touching without touching, too. Like things rubbing off on me. And sometimes, when I did touch the Angel, I'd get the feeling that it was maybe more his idea than mine, but I didn't mind that. How many people were going their whole lives never being able to touch an Angel?

We walked together and all around us the street was really coming to life. It was getting colder, too. I tried to make my jacket cover more. The Angel wasn't feeling it. Most of the time hot and cold didn't mean much to him. We saw the three rough trade guys again. The one Angel had gotten the money from was getting into a car. The other two watched it drive away and then walked on. I looked over at the Angel.

Because we took his twenty, I said.

Even if we hadn't, Angel said.

So we went along, the Angel and me, and I could feel how different it was tonight than it was all the other nights we'd walked or stood together. The Angel was kind of pulled back into himself and it seemed to be keeping a check on me, pushing us closer together. I was getting more of those fireworks out of the corners of my eyes but when I'd turn my head to look, they'd vanish. It reminded me of the night I'd found the Angel standing on my corner all by himself in pain. The Angel told me later that was real talent, knowing he was in pain. I never thought of myself as any too talented but the way everyone else had been just ignoring him, I guess I must have had something to see him after all.

The Angel stopped us several feet down from an all-night bookstore. Don't look, he said. Watch the traffic or stare at your feet, but don't look or it won't happen.

There wasn't anything to see right then but I didn't look anyway. That was the way it was sometimes, the Angel telling me it made a difference whether I was watching something or not, something about the other people being conscious of me being conscious of them. I didn't understand but I knew Angel was usually right. So I was watching traffic when the guy came out of the bookstore and got his head punched.

I could almost see it out of the corner of my eye. A lot of movement, arms and legs flying and grunty noises. Other people stopped to look but I kept my eyes on the traffic, some of which was slowing up so they could check out the fight. Next to me, the Angel was stiff all over. Taking it in, what he called the expenditure of emotional kinetic energy. No right, no wrong, little friend, he'd told me. Just energy, like the rest of the universe.

So he took it in and I felt him taking it in and while I was feeling it, a kind of silver fog started creeping around my eyeballs and I was in two places at once. I was watching the traffic and I was in the Angel watching the fight and feeling him charge up like a big battery.

It felt like nothing I'd ever felt before. These two guys slugging it out—well, one guy doing all the slugging and the other skittering around trying to get out from under the fists and having his head punched but good and the Angel drinking it like he was sipping at an empty cup and somehow getting it to have something in it after all. Deep inside him, whatever made the Angel go was getting a little stronger.

I kind of swung back and forth between him and me, or swayed might be more like it was. I wondered about it, because the Angel wasn't touching me. I really was getting to be him, I thought; Angel picked that up and put the thought away to answer later. It was like I was traveling by the fog, being one of us and then the other, for a long time, it seemed, and then after awhile I was more me than him again and some of the fog cleared away.

And there was that car, pointed the other way this time and the woman was climbing out of it with this big weird smile on her face, as though she'd won something. She waved at the Angel to come to her.

Bang went the connection between us dead and the Angel shot past me, running away from the car. I went after him. I caught a glimpse of her jumping back into the car and yanking at the gear shift.

Angel wasn't much of a runner. Something funny about his knees. We'd gone maybe a hundred feet when he started wobbling and I could hear him pant. He cut across a Park & Lock that was dark and mostly empty. It was back-to-back with some kind of private parking lot and the fences for each one tried to mark off the same narrow strip of lumpy pavement. They were easy to climb but Angel was too panicked. He just *went* through them before he even thought about it; I knew that because if he'd been thinking, he'd have wanted to save what he'd just charged up for when he really needed out bad enough.

I had to haul myself over the fences in the usual way and when he heard me rattling on the saggy chainlink, he stopped and looked back.

Go, I told him. Don't wait on me!

He shook his head sadly. Little friend, I'm a fool. I could stand to learn from you a little more.

Don't stand, run! I got over the fences and caught up with him. Let's go! I yanked his sleeve as I slogged past and he followed at a clumsy trot.

Have to hide somewhere, he said, camouflage ourselves with people.

I shook my head, thinking we could just run maybe four more blocks and we'd be at the freeway overpass. Below it were the butt-ends of old roads closed off when the freeway had been built. You could hide there the rest of your life and no one would find you. But Angel made me turn right and go down a block to this rundown crack-in-the-wall called Stan's Jigger. I'd never been in there—I'd never made it a practice to go into bars—but the Angel was pushing too hard to argue.

Inside it was smelly and dark and not too happy. The Angel and I went down to the end of the bar and stood under a blood-red light while he searched his pockets for money.

Enough for one drink apiece, he said.

I don't want anything.

You can have soda or something.

The Angel ordered from the bartender, who was suspicious. This was a place for regulars and nobody else, and certainly nobody else like me or the Angel. The Angel knew that even stronger than I did but he just stood and pretended to sip his drink without looking at me. He was all pulled into himself and I was hovering around the edges. I knew he was still pretty panicked and trying to figure out what he could do next. As close as I was, if he had to get real far away, he was going to have a problem and so was I. He'd have to tow me along with him and that wasn't the most practical thing to do.

Maybe he was sorry now he'd let me take him home. He'd been so weak then and now what with all the filtering and stuff I'd done, he couldn't just cut me off without a lot of pain.

I was trying to figure out what I could do for him when the bartender came back and gave us a look that meant order or get out and he'd have liked it better if we got out. So would everyone else there. The few other people standing at the bar weren't looking at us but they knew right where we were, like a sore spot. It wasn't hard to figure out what they thought about us, either, maybe because of me or because of the Angel's beautiful face.

We got to leave, I said to the Angel but he had it in his head this was good camouflage. There wasn't enough money for two more drinks so he smiled at the bartender and slid his hand across the bar and put it on top of the bartender's. It was tricky doing it this way; bartenders and waitresses took more persuading because it wasn't normal for them just to give you something.

The bartender looked at the Angel with his eyes half-closed. He seemed to be thinking it over. But the Angel had just blown a lot going through the fence instead of climbing over it and the fear was scuttling his concentration and I just knew that it wouldn't work. And may be my knowing that didn't help, either.

The bartender's free hand dipped down below the bar and came up with a small club. "*Faggot!*" he roared and caught Angel just over the ear. Angel slammed into me and we both crashed to the floor.

Plenty of emotional kinetic energy in here, I thought dimly as the guys standing at the bar fell on us and I didn't think anything more as I curled up into a ball under their fists and boots.

We were lucky they didn't much feel like killing anyone. Angel went out the door first and they tossed me out on top of him. As soon as I landed on him, I knew we were both in trouble; something was broken inside him. So much for keeping out of harm's way. I rolled off him and lay on the pavement, staring at the sky and trying to catch my breath. There was blood in my mouth and my nose and my back was on fire.

Angel? I said, after a bit.

He didn't answer. I felt my mind get kind of all loose and runny, like my brains were leaking out my ears. I thought about the trade we'd taken the money from and how I'd been scared of him and his friends and how silly that had been. But then, I was too harmless to live.

The stars were raining silver fireworks down on me. It didn't help.

Angel? I said again.

I rolled over onto my side to reach for him and there she was. The car was parked at the curb and she had Angel under the armpits, dragging him toward the open passenger door. I couldn't tell if he was conscious or not and that scared me. I sat up.

She paused, still holding the Angel. We looked into each other's eyes and I started to understand.

"Help me get him into the car," she said at last. Her voice sounded hard and flat and unnatural. "Then you can get in, too. In the *back* seat."

I was in no shape to take her out. It couldn't have been better for her than if she'd set it up herself. I got up, the pain flaring in me so bad that I almost fell down again and sort of took the Angel's ankles. His ankles were so delicate, almost like a woman's, like hers. I didn't really help much except to guide his feet in as she sat him on the seat and strapped him in with the shoulder harness. I got in the back as she ran around to the other side of the car, her steps real light and peppy, like she'd found a million dollars lying there on the sidewalk.

We were out on the freeway before the Angel stirred in the shoulder harness. His head lolled from side to side on the back of the seat. I reached up and touched his hair lightly, hoping she couldn't see me do it.

Where are you taking me, the Angel said.

"For a ride," said the woman. "For the moment."

Why does she talk out loud like that? I asked the Angel.

Because she knows it bothers me.

"You know I can focus my thoughts better if I say things out loud," she said. "I'm not like one of your little pushovers." She glanced at me in the rear-view mirror. "Just what have you gotten yourself into since you left, darling? Is that a boy or a girl?"

I pretended I didn't care about what she said or that I was too harmless to live or any of that stuff but the way she said it, she meant it to sting.

Friends can be either, Angel said. It doesn't matter which. Where are you taking us?

Now it was *us.* In spite of everything, I almost could have smiled.

"Us? You mean, you and me? Or are you really referring to your little pet back there?"

My friend and I are together. You and I are *not.*

The way the Angel said it made me think he meant more than not together; like he'd been with her once the way he was with me now The Angel let me know I was right. Silver fireworks started flowing slowly off his head down the back of the seat and I knew there was something wrong about it. There was too much all at once.

"Why can't you talk out loud to me, darling?" the woman said with fakey-sounding petulance. "Just say a few words and make me happy. You have a lovely voice when you use it."

That was true, but the Angel never spoke out loud unless he couldn't get out of it, like when he'd ordered from the bartender. Which had probably helped the bartender decide about what he thought we were, but it was useless to think about that.

"All right," said Angel, and I knew the strain was awful for him. "I've said a few words. Are you happy?" He sagged in the shoulder harness.

"Ecstatic. But it won't make me let you go. I'll drop your pet at the nearest hospital and then we'll go home." She glanced at the Angel as she drove. "I've missed you so much. I can't stand it without you, without you making things happen. Doing your little miracles. You knew I'd get addicted to it, all the things you could do to people. And then you just took off, I didn't know what had happened to you. And it *hurt*." Her voice turned kind of pitiful, like a little kid's. "I was in *real* pain. You must have been, too. Weren't you? Well, *weren't* you?"

Yes, the Angel said. I was in pain, too.

I remembered him standing on my corner where I'd hung out all that time by myself until he came. Standing there in pain. I didn't know why or from what then, I just took him home and after a little while, the pain went away. When he decided we were together, I guess.

The silvery flow over the back of the car seat thickened. I cupped my hands under it and it was like my brain was lighting up with pictures. I saw the Angel before he was my Angel in this really nice house, the woman's house, and how she'd take him places, restaurants or stores or parties, thinking at him real hard so that he was all filled up with her and had to do what she wanted him to. Steal sometimes; other times, weird stuff, make people do silly things like suddenly start singing or taking their clothes off. That was mostly at the parties, though she made a waiter she didn't like burn himself with a pot of coffee. She'd get men, too, through the Angel, and they'd think it was the greatest idea in the world to go to bed with her. Then she'd make the Angel show her the others, the ones that had been sent here the way he had for crimes nobody could have understood, like the waitress with no face. She'd look at them, sometimes try to do things to them to make them uncomfortable or unhappy. But mostly she'd just stare.

It wasn't like that in the very beginning, the Angel said weakly and I knew he was ashamed.

It's okay, I told him. People can be nice at first, I know that. Then they find out about you.

The woman laughed. "You two are so sweet and pathetic. Like a couple of little children. I guess that's what you were looking for, wasn't it, darling? Except children can be cruel, too, can't they? So you got this—creature for yourself." She looked at me in the rear-view mirror again as she slowed down a little and for a moment I was afraid she'd seen what I was doing with the silvery stuff still pouring out of the Angel. It was starting to slow now. There wasn't much time left. I wanted to scream but the Angel was calming me for what was coming next. "What happened to you, anyway?"

Tell her, said the Angel. To stall for time, I knew, keep her occupied.

I was born funny, I said. I had both sexes.

"A hermaphrodite!" she exclaimed with real delight.

She loves freaks, the Angel said but she didn't pay any attention.

There was an operation but things went wrong. They kept trying to fix it as I got older but my body didn't have the right kind of chemistry or something. My parents were ashamed. I left after awhile.

"You poor thing," she said, not meaning anything like that. "You were just what darling, here, needed, weren't you? Just a little nothing, no demands, no desires. For anything." Her voice got all hard. "They could probably fix you up now, you know." I don't want it. I left all that behind a long time ago, I don't need it. "Just the sort of little pet that would be perfect for you," she said to the Angel. "Sorry I have to tear you away. But I can't get along without you now. Life is so boring. And empty. And—" She sounded puzzled. "And like there's nothing more to live for since you left me." That's not me, said the Angel. That's you. "No, it's a lot of you, too, and you know it. You know you're addictive to human beings, you knew that when you came here—when they *sent* you here. Hey, you, pet, do you know what his crime was, why they sent him to this little backwater penal colony of a planet?" Yeah, I know, I said. I really didn't, but I wasn't going to tell her that.

"What do you think about that, little pet neuter?" she said gleefully, hitting the accelerator pedal and speeding up. "What do you think of the crime of refusing to mate?"

The Angel made a sort of an out-loud groan and lunged at the steering wheel. The car swerved wildly and I fell backwards, the silvery stuff from the Angel going all over me. I tried to keep scooping it into my mouth the way I'd been doing but it was flying all over the place now. I heard the crunch as the tires left the road and went onto the shoulder. Something struck the side of the car, probably the guard rail, and made it fishtail, throwing me down on the floor. Up front the woman was screaming and cursing and the Angel wasn't making a sound but in my head, I could hear him sort of keening. Whatever happened, this would be it. The Angel had told me all that time ago after I'd taken him home that they didn't last long after they got here, the exiles from his world and other worlds. Things tended to happen to them, even if they latched on to someone like me or the woman. They'd be in accidents or the people here would kill them. Like antibodies in a human rejecting something or fighting a disease. At least I belonged here, but it looked like I was going to die in a car accident with the Angel and the woman both. I didn't care.

The car swerved back onto the highway for a few seconds and then pitched to the right again. Suddenly there was nothing under us and then we thumped down on something, not road but dirt or grass or something, bombing madly up and down. I pulled myself up on the back of the seat just in time to see the sign coming at us at an angle. The corner of it started to go through the windshield on the woman's side and then all I saw for a long time was the biggest display of silver fireworks ever.

It was hard to be gentle with him. Every move hurt but I didn't want to leave him sitting in the car next to her, even if she was dead. Being in the back seat had kept most of the glass from flying into me but I was still shaking some out of my hair and the impact hadn't done much for my back.

I laid the Angel out on the lumpy grass a little ways from the car and looked around. We were maybe a hundred yards from the highway, near a road that ran parallel to it. It was dark but I could still read the sign that had come through the windshield and split the woman's head in half. It said, CONSTRUCTION AHEAD REDUCE SPEED. Far off on the other road, I could see a flashing yellow light and at first I was afraid it was the police or something but it stayed where it was and I realised that must be the construction.

"Friend," whispered the Angel, startling me. He'd never spoken aloud to me, not directly.

Don't talk, I said, bending over him, trying to figure out some way I could touch him, just for comfort. There wasn't anything else I could do now.

"I have to," he said, still whispering. "It's almost all gone. Did you get it?"

Mostly, I said. Not all.

"I meant for you to have it."

I know.

"I don't know that it will really do you any good." His breath kind of bubbled in his throat. I could see something wet and shiny on his mouth but it wasn't silver fireworks. "But it's yours. You can do as you like with it. Live on it the way I did. Get what you need when you need it. But you can live as a human, too. Eat. Work. However, whatever."

I'm not human, I said. I'm not any more human than you, even if I do belong here.

"Yes you are, little friend. I haven't made you any less human," he said, and coughed some. "I'm not sorry I wouldn't mate. I couldn't mate with my own. It was too, I don't know, too little of me, too much of them, something. I couldn't bond, it would have been nothing but emptiness. The Great Sin, to be unable to give, because the universe knows only less or more and I insisted that it would be good or bad. So they sent me here. But in the end, you know, they got their way, little friend." I felt his hand on me for a moment before it fell away. "I did it after all. Even if it wasn't with my own."

The bubbling in his throat stopped. I sat next to him for awhile in the dark. Finally I felt it, the Angel stuff. It was kind of fluttery-churny, like too much coffee on an empty stomach. I closed my eyes and lay down on the grass, shivering. Maybe some of it was shock but I don't think so. The silver fireworks started, in my head this time, and with them came a lot of pictures I couldn't understand. Stuff about the Angel and where he'd come from and the way they mated. It was a lot like how we'd been together, the Angel and me. They looked a lot like us but there were a lot of differences, too, things I couldn't make out. I couldn't make out how they'd sent him here, either—by light, in, like, little bundles or something. It didn't make any sense to me but I guessed an Angel could be light. Silver fireworks.

I must have passed out or something because when I opened my eyes, it felt like I'd been laying there a long time. It was still dark, though. I sat up and reached for the Angel, thinking I ought to hide his body.

He was gone. There was just a sort of wet sandy stuff where he'd been.

I looked at the car and her. All that was still there. Somebody was going to see it soon. I didn't want to be around for that.

Everything still hurt but I managed to get to the other road and start walking back toward the city. It was like I could feel it now, the way the Angel must have, as though it were vibrating like a drum or ringing like a bell with all kinds of stuff, people laughing and crying and loving and hating and being afraid and everything else that happens to people. The stuff that the Angel took in, energy, that I could take in now if I wanted.

And I knew that taking it in that way, it would be bigger than anything all those people had, bigger than anything I could have had if things hadn't gone wrong with me all those years ago.

I wasn't so sure I wanted it. Like the Angel, refusing to mate back where he'd come from. He wouldn't, there, and I couldn't, here. Except now I could do something else.

I wasn't so sure I wanted it. But I didn't think I'd be able to stop it, either, any more than I could stop my heart from beating. Maybe it wasn't really such a good thing or a right thing. But it was like the Angel said: the universe doesn't know good or bad, only less or more.

Yeah. I heard *that*.

I thought about the waitress with no face. I could find them all now, all the ones from the other places, other worlds that sent them away for some kind of alien crimes nobody would have understood. I could find them all. They threw away their outcasts, I'd tell them, but here, we kept ours. And here's how. Here's how you live in a universe that only knows less or more.

I kept walking toward the city.

Cassandra

by C.J. Cherryh

One of the most popular writers in science fiction, C.J. Cherryh has published more than sixty novels since DAW released her first in 1975. Her debut was so impressive that she won the John W. Campbell Award for Best New Writer in 1977, something only writers with an instantly high visibility in the field manage to do.

She has been nominated for the Hugo Award six times, winning it three times. She's also been nominated for the Nebula, the Philip K. Dick Award, the British Science Fiction Award, among many others. She's received at least (by my count) fifteen Locus *Award nominations, winning it with* Cyteen *(also one of her Hugo-winning novels). In 2016, the Science Fiction Writers of America named her a Grand Master for her contributions to the literature of science fiction and fantasy.*

Like Anne McCaffrey, C.J. writes both fantasy and science fiction in many different series. She has translated four books from French into English. She has also edited several shared world anthologies in the world of Merovin in her Alliance-Union universe.

She's still publishing at least one new novel per year, as well as a wide variety other material.

It's hard to find a representative C.J. Cherryh story because she writes so many different things. She explains why on her website, cherryh.com:

I cross [genre] lines myself, and don't like this specialization in which one side sniffs at the other as if they were some other species. No, no, no. We started out one creature. I don't care if "they" have spots. We're still the same breed of cat.

If you want to explore the worlds of C.J. Cherryh, there's no better place to start than The Collected Short Fiction of C.J. Cherryh. *After you read the Hugo-award winning "Cassandra," that is.*

❁ ❁ ❁

FIRES.

They grew unbearable here.

Alis felt for the door of the flat and knew that it would be solid. She could feel the cool metal of the knob amid the flames . . . saw the shadow-stairs through the roiling smoke outside, clearly enough to feel her way down them, convincing her senses that they would bear her weight.

Crazy Alis. She made no haste. The fires burned steadily. She passed through them, descended the insubstantial steps to the solid ground— she could not abide the elevator, that closed space with the shadow-floor, that plummeted down and down; she made the ground floor, averted her eyes from the red, heatless flames.

A ghost said good morning to her . . . old man Willis, thin and transparent against the leaping flames. She blinked, bade it good morning in return—did not miss old Willis's shake of the head as she opened the door and left. Noon traffic passed, heedless of the flames, the hulks that blazed in the street, the tumbling brick.

The apartment caved in—black bricks falling into the inferno, Hell amid the green, ghostly trees. Old Willis fled, burning, fell—turned to jerking, blackened flesh—died, daily. Alis no longer cried, hardly flinched. She ignored the horror spilling about her, forced her way through crumbling brick that held no substance, past busy ghosts that could not be troubled in their haste.

Kingsley's Cafe stood, whole, more so than the rest. It was refuge for the afternoon, a feeling of safety. She pushed open the door, heard the tinkle of a lost bell. Shadowy patrons looked, whispered.

Crazy Alis.

The whispers troubled her. She avoided their eyes and their presence, settled in a booth in the corner that bore only traces of the fire.

WAR, the headline in the vendor said in heavy type. She shivered, looked up into Sam Kingsley's wraithlike face.

"Coffee," she said. "Ham sandwich." It was constantly the same. She varied not even the order. Mad Alis. Her affliction supported her. A check came each month, since the hospital had turned her out. Weekly she returned to the clinic, to doctors who now faded like the others. The building burned about them. Smoke rolled down the blue, antiseptic halls. Last week a patient ran—burning—

A rattle of china. Sam set the coffee on the table, came back shortly and brought the sandwich. She bent her head and ate, transparent food on half-broken china, a cracked, fire-smudged cup with a transparent handle. She ate, hungry enough to overcome the horror that had become ordinary. A hundred times seen, the most terrible sights lost their power over her: she no longer cried at shadows. She talked to ghosts and touched them, ate the food that somehow stilled the ache in her belly, wore the same too-large black sweater and worn blue shirt and gray slacks because they were all she had that seemed solid. Nightly she washed them and dried them and put them on the next day, letting others hang in the closet. They were the only solid ones.

She did not tell the doctors these things. A lifetime in and out of hospitals had made her wary of confidences. She knew what to say. Her half-vision let her smile at ghost-faces, cannily manipulate their charts and cards, sitting in the ruins that had begun to smolder by late afternoon. A blackened corpse lay in the hall. She did not flinch when she smiled good naturedly at the doctor.

They gave her medicines. The medicines stopped the dreams, the siren screams, the running steps in the night past her apartment. They let her sleep in the ghostly bed, high above ruin, with the flames crackling and the voices screaming. She did not speak of these things. Years in hospitals had taught her. She complained only of nightmares, and restlessness, and they let her have more of the red pills.

WAR, the headline blazoned.

The cup rattled and trembled against the saucer as she picked it up. She swallowed the last bit of bread and washed it down with coffee, tried not to look beyond the broken front window, where twisted metal hulks smoked on the street. She stayed, as she did each day, and Sam grudgingly refilled her cup, which she would nurse as far as she could and then she would order another one. She lifted it, savoring the feeling of it, stopping the trembling of her hands.

The bell jingled faintly. A man closed the door, settled at the counter.

Whole, clear in her eyes. She stared at him, startled, heart pounding. He ordered coffee, moved to buy a paper from the vendor, settled again and let the coffee grow cold while he read the news. She had view only of his back while he read—scuffed brown leather coat, brown hair a little over his collar. At last he drank the cooled coffee all at one draught, shoved money onto the counter and left the paper lying, headlines turned face down.

A young face, flesh and bone among the ghosts. He ignored them all and went for the door.

Alis thrust herself from her booth.

"Hey!" Sam called at her.

She rummaged in her purse as the bell jingled, flung a bill onto the counter, heedless that it was a five. Fear was coppery in her mouth; he was gone. She fled the cafe, edged round debris without thinking of it, saw his back disappearing among the ghosts.

She ran, shouldering them, braving the flames—cried out as debris showered painlessly on her, and kept running.

Ghosts turned and stared, shocked—*he* did likewise, and she ran to him, stunned to see the same shock on his face, regarding her.

"What is it?" he asked.

She blinked, dazed to realize he saw her no differently than the others. She could not answer. In irritation he started walking again, and she followed. Tears slid down her face, her breath hard in her throat. People stared. He noticed her presence and walked faster, through debris, through fires. A wall began to fall and she cried out despite herself.

He jerked about. The dust and the soot rose up as a cloud behind him. His face was distraught and angry. He stared at her as the others did. Mothers drew children away from the scene. A band of youths stared, cold-eyed and laughing.

"Wait," she said. He opened his mouth as if he would curse her; she flinched, and the tears were cold in the heatless wind of the fires. His face twisted in an embarrassed pity. He thrust a hand into his pocket and began to pull out money, hastily, tried to give it to her. She shook her head furiously, trying to stop the tears—stared upward, flinching, as another building fell into flames.

"What's wrong?" he asked her. "What's wrong with you?"

"Please," she said. He looked about at the staring ghosts, then began to walk slowly. She walked with him, nerving herself not to cry out at the ruin, the pale moving figures that wandered through burned shells of buildings, the twisted corpses in the street, where traffic moved.

"What's your name?" he asked. She told him. He gazed at her from time to time as they walked, a frown creasing his brow. He had a face well-worn for youth, a tiny scar beside the mouth. He looked older than she. She felt uncomfortable in the way his eyes traveled over her: she decided to accept it—to bear with anything that gave her this one solid presence. Against every inclination she reached her hand into the bend of his arm, tightened her fingers on the worn leather. He accepted it.

And after a time he slid his arm behind her and about her waist, and they walked like lovers.

WAR, the headline at the newsstand cried.

He started to turn into a street by Tenn's Hardware. She balked at what she saw there. He paused when he felt it, faced her with his back to the fires of that burning.

"Don't go," she said.

"Where do you want to go?"

She shrugged helplessly, indicated the main street, the other direction.

He talked to her then, as he might talk to a child, humoring her fear. It was pity. Some treated her that way. She recognized it, and took even that.

His name was Jim. He had come into the city yesterday, hitched rides. He was looking for work. He knew no one in the city. She listened to his rambling awkwardness, reading through it. When he was done, she stared at him still, and saw his face contract in dismay at her.

"I'm not crazy," she told him, which was a lie that everyone in Sudbury would have known, only *he* would not, knowing no one. His face was true and solid, and the tiny scar by the mouth made it hard when he was thinking; at another time she would have been terrified of him. Now she was terrified of losing him amid the ghosts.

"It's the war," he said.

She nodded, trying to look at him and not at the fires. His fingers touched her arm, gently. "It's the war," he said again. "It's all crazy. Everyone's crazy."

And then he put his hand on her shoulder and turned her back the other way, toward the park, where green leaves waved over black, skeletal limbs. They walked along the lake, and for the first time in a long time she drew breath and felt a whole, sane presence beside her.

They bought corn, and sat on the grass by the lake, and flung it to the spectral swans. Wraiths of passersby were few, only enough to keep a feeling of occupancy about the place—old people, mostly, tottering about the deliberate tranquillity of their routine despite the headlines.

"Do you see them," she ventured to ask him finally, "all thin and gray?"

He did not understand, did not take her literally, only shrugged. Warily, she abandoned that questioning at once. She rose to her feet and stared at the horizon, where the smoke bannered on the wind.

"Buy you supper?" he asked.

She turned, prepared for this, and managed a shy, desperate smile. "Yes," she said, knowing what else he reckoned to buy with that— willing, and hating herself, and desperately afraid that he would walk away, tonight, tomorrow. She did not know men. She had no idea what she could say or do to prevent his leaving, only that he would when someday he recognized her madness.

Even her parents had not been able to bear with that—visited her only at first in the hospitals, and then only on holidays, and then not at all. She did not know where they were.

There was a neighbor boy who drowned. She had said he would. She had cried for it. All the town said it was she who pushed him.

Crazy Alis.

Fantasizes, the doctors said. Not dangerous.

They let her out. There were special schools, state schools.

And from time to time—hospitals.

Tranquilizers.

She had left the red pills at home. The realization brought sweat to her palms. They gave sleep. They stopped the dreams. She clamped her lips against the panic and made up her mind that she would not need them—not while she was not alone. She slipped her hand into his arm and walked with him, secure and strange, up the steps from the park to the streets.

And stopped.

The fires were out.

Ghost-buildings rose above their jagged and windowless shells. Wraiths moved through masses of debris, almost obscured at times. He tugged her on, but her step faltered, made him look at her strangely and put his arm about her.

"You're shivering," he said. "Cold?"

She shook her head, tried to smile. The fires were out. She tried to take it for a good omen. The nightmare was over. She looked up into his solid, concerned face, and her smile almost became a wild laugh.

"I'm hungry," she said.

They lingered over a dinner in Graben's—he in his battered jacket, she in her sweater that hung at the tails and elbows: the spectral patrons were in far better clothes, and stared at them, and they were set in a corner nearest the door, where they would be less visible. There was cracked crystal and broken china on insubstantial tables, and the stars winked coldly in gaping ruin above the wan glittering of the broken chandeliers.

Ruins, cold, peaceful ruins.

Alis looked about her calmly. One could live in ruins, only so the fires were gone.

And there was Jim, who smiled at her without any touch of pity, only a wild, fey desperation that she understood—who spent more than he could afford in Graben's, the inside of which she had never hoped to see—and told her—predictably—that she was beautiful. Others had said it. Vaguely she resented such triteness from him, from him whom she had decided to trust. She smiled sadly when he said it; and gave it up for a frown; and, fearful of offending him with her melancholies, made it a smile again.

Crazy Alis. He would learn and leave tonight if she were not careful. She tried to put on gaiety, tried to laugh.

And then the music stopped in the restaurant, and the noise of the other diners went dead, and the speaker was giving an inane announcement.

Shelters . . . shelters . . . shelters.

Screams broke out. Chairs overturned. Alis went limp in her chair, felt Jim's cold, solid hand tugging at hers, saw his frightened face mouthing her name as he took her up into his arms, pulled her with him, started running.

The cold air outside hit her, shocked her into sight of the ruins again, wraith figures pelting toward that chaos where the fires had been worst. And she knew.

"No!" she cried, pulling at his arm. "No!" she insisted, and bodies half-seen buffeted them in a rush to destruction. He yielded to her sudden certainty, gripped her hand and fled with her against the crowds as the sirens wailed madness through the night—fled with her as she ran her sighted way through the ruin.

And into Kingsley's, where cafe tables stood abandoned with food still on them, doors ajar, chairs overturned. Back they went into the kitchens and down and down into the cellar, the dark, the cold safety from the flames.

No others found them there. At last the earth shook, too deep for sound. The sirens ceased and did not come on again.

They lay in the dark and clutched each other and shivered, and above them for hours raged the sound of fire, smoke sometimes drifting in to sting their eyes and noses. There was the distant crash of brick, rumblings that shook the ground, that came near, but never touched their refuge.

And in the morning, with the scent of fire still in the air, they crept up into the murky daylight.

The ruins were still and hushed. The ghost-buildings were solid now, mere shells. The wraiths were gone. It was the fires themselves that were strange, some true, some not, playing above dark, cold brick, and most were fading.

Jim swore softly, over and over again, and wept.

When she looked at him she was dry-eyed, for she had done her crying already.

And she listened as he began to talk about food, about leaving the city, the two of them. "All right," she said.

Then clamped her lips, shut her eyes against what she saw in his face. When she opened them it was still true, the sudden transparency, the wash of blood. She trembled, and he shook at her, his ghost-face distraught.

"What's wrong?" he asked. "What's wrong?"

She could not tell him, would not. She remembered the boy who had drowned, remembered the other ghosts. Of a sudden she tore from his hands and ran, dodging the maze of debris that, this morning, was solid.

"Alis!" he cried and came after her.

"No!" she cried suddenly, turning, seeing the unstable wall, the cascading brick. She started back and stopped, unable to force herself. She held out her hands to warn him back, saw them solid.

The brick rumbled, fell. Dust came up, thick for a moment, obscuring everything.

She stood still, hands at her sides, then wiped her sooty face and turned and started walking, keeping to the center of the dead streets.

Overhead, clouds gathered, heavy with rain.

She wandered at peace now, seeing the rain spot the pavement, not yet feeling it.

In time the rain did fall, and the ruins became chill and cold. She visited the dead lake and the burned trees, the ruin of Graben's, out of which she gathered a string of crystal to wear.

She smiled when, a day later, a looter drove her from her food supply. He had a wraith's look, and she laughed from a place he did not dare to climb and told him so.

And recovered her cache later when it came true, and settled among the ruined shells that held no further threat, no other nightmares, with her crystal necklace and tomorrows that were the same as today.

One could live in ruins, only so the fires were gone.

And the ghosts were all in the past, invisible.

Shambleau

by C.L. Moore

And now, we ease into the myth-busting part of our anthology.

Some women writers are better known in 2015 for the myth of their history as women in the field than they are for the actual writing. One of those women is C.L. Moore. Articles on discrimination against women in science fiction consistently cite Catherine Lucille Moore's 1933 decision to use her initials as a byline as proof that she was afraid she would be discriminated against for her gender.

Nothing could be farther from the truth. C.L. Moore told Marion Zimmer Bradley (another influential female writer I couldn't find room for in this anthology) that she used her initials because writing for the pulp magazines was a disreputable thing to do—for men and women— in the 1930s, and she was afraid of losing her job in the depths of the Depression. [Davin, page 114]. Moore alludes to that in her essay "Footnote to Shambleau . . . and others," in The Best of C.L. Moore. *[Ballantine Books, 1975, page 365]:*

> By incredible good fortune, before I'd finished [a shorthand and typing] course, a job opening in a large bank loomed up and I leaped at it, unprepared but eager. (In those days, you didn't mess around. You bluffed, prayed, and grabbed.)

She also corrects another record in that essay—she sent her first short story Weird Tales, *to only one market, "because that was the only magazine of its type I knew well," where it was purchased immediately.*

That story was "Shambleau."

Moore went from being an unknown to being one of the most recognizable writers of her generation. She continued to write science fiction for another thirty years. She also wrote mystery novels and screenplays for many popular television shows, like Maverick *and* 77 Sunset Strip. *Sadly, most of her work is out of print now, although you can find her two most famous characters in the* C.L. Moore SF Gateway Omnibus.

After she met and married her husband, the writer Henry Kuttner, she wrote a lot of stories in collaboration with him, including the classic time travel tale, "A Vintage Season." She was so prolific under many names, with Kuttner and on her own, that Connie Willis writes in "The Women SF Doesn't See:"

> There were all these women [writing science fiction], and I know because I was reading them. They're women like Mildred Clingerman and Shirley Jackson and Zenna Henderson and Margaret St. Clair and Carol Emshwiller, and a whole bunch I didn't know about because they were all really C.L. Moore.

The moment Moore appeared on the scene, she changed science fiction—and not because she was a woman. She changed it because of the way she wrote. In 1975, Lester Del Rey tried to explain how she changed the field in his introduction to The Best of C.L. Moore:

> It's probably impossible to explain to modern readers how great an impact that first C.L. Moore story had. Science fiction has learned a great deal from her many examples. But if you go back to the old science fiction magazines of the time and read a few issues, and then turn to "Shambleau" for the first time, you might begin to understand. The influences of that story were and are tremendous.
>
> Here, for the first time in the field, we find mood, feeling, and color. Here is an alien who is truly alien—far different from the crude monsters and slightly altered humans found in other stories. Here are rounded and well-developed characters.

Northwest Smith, for instance, is neither a good guy nor a bad guy—he may be slightly larger than life, but he displays all aspects of humanity. In "Shambleau" we also experience as never before both the horror at what we may find in space and the romance of space itself. And—certainly for the first time that I can remember in the field—this story presents the sexual drive of humanity in all of its complexity. [Best of C.L. Moore, page ix]

Many of the gender-focused anthologies that have appeared in the last several decades ignored the powerful "Shambleau" because its protagonist is male and because of the negative portrayal of a creature that might or might not be female.

That means one of the great science fiction stories of all time, one of the triumphs by the field's most important early women, nearly vanished.

"Shambleau" does a few other things that have echoed through the science fiction field for more than eighty years. Its Martian setting influenced many other writers, including Leigh Brackett and Ray Bradbury. But the story also introduces Northwest Smith, a spaceship pilot and a smuggler, a rogue with a heart of gold, just like a certain Han Solo would be more than forty years later.

To my great relief as an editor and fan, "Shambleau" holds up. I read it late one night, with one eye closed and the book extended as far from me as possible, entranced and terrified by the writing of the marvelous C.L. Moore.

☸ ☸ ☸

Man has conquered Space before. You may be sure of that. Somewhere beyond the Egyptians, in that dimness out of which come echoes of half-mythical names—Atlantis, Mu—somewhere back of history's first beginnings there must have been an age when mankind, like us today, built cities of steel to house its star-roving ships and knew the names of the planets in their own native tongues—heard Venus' people call their wet world "Sha-ardol" in that soft, sweet, slurring speech and mimicked Mars' guttural "Lakkdiz" from the harsh tongues of Mars' dryland dwellers. You may be sure of it. Man has conquered Space before, and out of that conquest faint, faint echoes run still through a world that has forgotten the very fact of a civilization which must have been as mighty as our own. There have been too many myths and legends for us to doubt it. The myth of the Medusa, for instance, and never have had its roots in the soil of Earth. That tale of the snake-haired Gorgon whose gaze turned the gaze to stone never originated about any creature that Earth nourished. And those ancient Greeks who told the story must have remembered, dimly and half believing, a tale of antiquity about some strange being from one of the outlying planets their remotest ancestors once trod.

"SHAMBLEAU! Ha . . . Shambleau!" The wild hysteria of the mob rocketed from wall to wall of Lakkdarol's narrow streets and the storming of heavy boots over the slag-red pavement made an ominous undernote to that swelling bay, "Shambleau! Shambleau!"

Northwest Smith heard it coming and stepped into the nearest doorway, laying a wary hand on his heat-gun's grip, and his colorless eyes narrowed. Strange sounds were common enough in the streets of Earth's latest colony on Mars—a raw, red little town where anything might happen, and very often did. But Northwest Smith, whose name is known and respected in every dive and wild outpost on a dozen wild planets, was a cautious man, despite his reputation. He set his back against the wall and gripped his pistol, and heard the rising shout come nearer and nearer.

Then into his range of vision flashed a red running figure, dodging like a hunted hare from shelter to shelter in the narrow street. It was a girl—a berry-brown girl in a single tattered garment whose scarlet burnt the eyes with its brilliance. She ran wearily, and he could hear her gasping breath from where he stood. As she came into view he saw her hesitate and lean one hand against the wall for support, and glance wildly around for shelter. She must not have seen him in the depths of the doorway, for as the bay of the mob grew louder and the pounding of feet sounded almost at the corner she gave a despairing little moan and dodged into the recess at his very side.

When she saw him standing there, tall and leather-brown, hand on his heat-gun, she sobbed once, inarticulately, and collapsed at his feet, a huddle of burning scarlet and bare, brown limbs.

Smith had not seen her face, but she was a girl, and sweetly made and in danger; and though he had not the reputation of a chivalrous man, something in her hopeless huddle at his feet touched that chord of sympathy for the underdog that stirs in every Earthman, and he pushed her gently into the corner behind him and jerked out his gun, just as the first of the running mob rounded the corner.

It was a motley crowd, Earthmen and Martians and a sprinkling of Venusian swampmen and strange, nameless denizens of unnamed planets—a typical Lakkdarol mob. When the first of them turned the corner and saw the empty street before them there was a faltering in the rush and the foremost spread out and began to search the doorways on both sides of the street.

"Looking for something?" Smith's sardonic call sounded clear above the clamor of the mob.

They turned. The shouting died for a moment as they took in the scene before them—tall Earthman in the space-explorer's leathern garb, all one color from the burning of savage suns save for the sinister pallor of his no-colored eyes in a scarred and resolute face, gun in his steady hand and the scarlet girl crouched behind him, panting.

The foremost of the crowd—a burly Earthman in tattered leather from which the Patrol insignia had been ripped away—stared for a moment with a strange expression of incredulity on his face overspreading the savage exultation of the chase. Then he let loose a deep-throated bellow, "Shambleau!" and lunged forward. Behind him the mob took up the cry again. "Shambleau! Shambleau! Shambleau!" and surged after.

Smith, lounging negligently against the wall, arms folded and gun-hand draped over his left forearm, looked incapable of swift motion, but at the leader's first forward step the pistol swept in a practised half-circle and the dazzle of blue-white heat leaping from its muzzle seared an arc in the slag pavement at his feet. It was an old gesture, and not a man in the crowd understood it. The foremost recoiled swiftly against the surge of those in the rear, and for a moment there was confusion as the two tides met and struggled. Smith's mouth curled into a grim curve as he watched. The man in the mutilated Patrol uniform lifted a threatening fist and stepped to the very edge of the deadline, while the crowd rocked to and fro behind him.

"Are you crossing that line?" queried Smith in an ominously gentle voice.

"We want that girl!"

"Come and get her!" Recklessly Smith grinned into his face. He saw danger there, but his defiance was not the foolhardy gesture it seemed. An expert psychologist of mobs from long experience, he sensed no murder here. Not a gun had appeared in any hand in the crowd. They desired the girl with an inexplicable bloodthirstiness he was at a loss to understand, but toward himself he sensed no such fury. A mauling he might expect, but his life was in no danger. Guns would have appeared before now if they were coming out at all. So he grinned in the man's angry face and leaned lazily against the wall.

Behind their self-appointed leader the crowd milled impatiently, and threatening voices began to rise again. Smith heard the girl moan at his feet.

"What do you want with her?" he demanded.

"She's Shambleau! Shambleau, you fool! Kick her out of there—we'll take care of her!"

"I'm taking care of her," drawled Smith.

"She's Shambleau, I tell you! Damn your hide, man, we never let those things live! Kick her out here!"

The repeated name had no meaning to him, but Smith's innate stubbornness rose defiantly as the crowd surged forward to the very edge of the arc, their clamor growing louder. "Shambleau! Kick her out here! Give us Shambleau! Shambleau!"

Smith dropped his indolent pose like a cloak and planted both feet wide, swinging up his gun threateningly. "Keep back!" he yelled. "She's mine! Keep back!"

He had no intention of using that heat-beam. He knew by now that they would not kill him unless he started the gunplay himself, and he did not mean to give up his life for any girl alive. But a severe mauling he expected, and he braced himself instinctively as the mob heaved within itself.

To his astonishment a thing happened then that he had never known to happen before. At his shouted defiance the foremost of the mob—those who had heard him clearly—drew back a little, not in alarm but evidently surprised. The ex-Patrolman said, "Yours! She's *yours?*" in a voice from which puzzlement crowded out the anger.

Smith spread his booted legs wide before the crouching figure and flourished his gun.

"Yes," he said. "And I'm keeping her! Stand back there!"

The man stared at him wordlessly, and horror and disgust and incredulity mingled on his weather-beaten face. The incredulity triumphed for a moment and he said again,

"Yours!"

Smith nodded defiance.

The man stepped back suddenly, unutterable contempt in his very pose. He waved an arm to the crowd and said loudly, "It's—his!" and the press melted away, gone silent, too, and the look of contempt spread from face to face.

The ex-Patrolman spat on the slag-paved street and turned his back indifferently. "Keep her, then," he advised briefly over one shoulder. "But don't let her out again in this town!"

Smith stared in perplexity almost open-mouthed as the suddenly scornful mob began to break up. His mind was in a whirl. That such bloodthirsty animosity should vanish in a breath he could not believe. And the curious mingling of contempt and disgust on the faces he saw baffled him even more. Lakkdarol was anything but a puritan town— it did not enter his head for a moment that his claiming the brown girl as his own had caused that strangely shocked revulsion to spread through the crowd. No, it was something deeper-rooted than that. Instinctive, instant disgust had been in the faces he saw—they would have looked less so if he had admitted cannibalism or *Pharol*-worship.

And they were leaving his vicinity as swiftly as if whatever unknowing sin he had committed were contagious. The street was emptying as rapidly as it had filled. He saw a sleek Venusian glance back over his shoulder as he turned the corner and sneer, "Shambleau!" and the word awoke a new line of speculation in Smith's mind. Shambleau! Vaguely of French origin, it must be. And strange enough to hear it from the lips of Venusian and Martian drylanders, but it was their use of it that puzzled him more. "We never let those things live," the ex-Patrolman had said. It reminded him dimly of something . . . an ancient line from some writing in his own tongue. . . . "Thou shalt not suffer a witch to live." He smiled to himself at the similarity, and simultaneously was aware of the girl at his elbow.

She had risen soundlessly. He turned to face her, sheathing his gun and stared at first with curiosity and then in the entirely frank openness with which men regard that which is not wholly human. For she was not. He knew it at a glance, though the brown, sweet body was shaped like a woman's and she wore the garment of scarlet—he saw it was leather—with an ease that few unhuman beings achieve toward clothing. He knew it from the moment he looked into her eyes, and a shiver of unrest went over him as he met them. They were frankly green as young grass, with slit-like, feline pupils that pulsed unceasingly, and there was a look of dark, animal wisdom in their depths—that look of the beast which sees more than man.

There was no hair upon her face—neither brows nor lashes, and he would have sworn that the tight scarlet turban bound around her head covered baldness. She had three fingers and a thumb, and her feet had four digits apiece too, and all sixteen of them were tipped with round claws that sheathed back into the flesh like a cat's. She ran her tongue over her lips—a thin, pink, flat tongue as feline as her eyes—and spoke with difficulty. He felt that that throat and tongue had never been shaped for human speech.

"Not—afraid now," she said softly, and her little teeth were white and polished as a kitten's.

"What did they want you for?" he asked her curiously. "What have you done? Shambleau . . . is that your name?"

"I—not talk your—speech," she demurred hesitantly.

"Well, try to—I want to know. Why were they chasing you? Will you be safe on the street now, or hadn't you better get indoors somewhere? They looked dangerous."

"I—go with you." She brought it out with difficulty.

"Say you!" Smith grinned. "What are you, anyhow? You look like a kitten to me."

"Shambleau." She said it somberly.

"Where d'you live? Are you a Martian?"

"I come from—from far—from long ago—far country—"

"Wait!" laughed Smith. "You're getting your wires crossed. You're not a Martian?"

She drew herself up very straight beside him, lifting the turbaned head, and there was something queenly in the pose of her.

"Martian?" she said scornfully. "My people—are—are—you have no word. Your speech—hard for me."

"What's yours? I might know it—try me."

She lifted her head and met his eyes squarely, and there was in hers a subtle amusement—he could have sworn it.

"Some day I—speak to you in—my own language," she promised, and the pink tongue flicked out over her lips, swiftly, hungrily.

Approaching footsteps on the red pavement interrupted Smith's reply. A dryland Martian came past, reeling a little and exuding an aroma of *segir*-whisky, the Venusian brand. When he caught the red flash of the girl's tatters he turned his head sharply, and as his *segir*-steeped brain took in the fact of her presence he lurched toward the recess unsteadily, bawling, "Shambleau, by *Pharol!* Shambleau!" and reached out a clutching hand.

Smith struck it aside contemptuously.

"On your way, drylander," he advised.

The man drew back and stared, bleary-eyed.

"Yours, eh?" he croaked. "*Zut!* You're welcome to it!" And like the ex-Patrolman before him he spat on the pavement and turned away, muttering harshly in the blasphemous tongue of the drylands.

Smith watched him shuffle off, and there was a crease between his colorless eyes, a nameless unease rising within him.

"Come on," he said abruptly to the girl. "If this sort of thing is going to happen we'd better get indoors. Where shall I take you?"

"With—you," she murmured.

He stared down into the flat green eyes. Those ceaselessly pulsing pupils disturbed him, but it seemed to him, vaguely, that behind the animal shallows of her gaze was a shutter—a closed barrier that might at any moment open to reveal the very deeps of that dark knowledge he sensed there.

Roughly he said again, "Come on, then," and stepped down into the street.

She pattered along a pace or two behind him, making no effort to keep up with his long strides, and though Smith—as men know from Venus to Jupiter's moons—walks as softly as a cat, even in spacemen's boots, the girl at his heels slid like a shadow over the rough pavement, making so little sound that even the lightness of his footsteps was loud in the empty street.

Smith chose the less frequented ways of Lakkdarol, and somewhat shamefacedly thanked his nameless gods that his lodgings were not far away, for the few pedestrians he met turned and stared after the two with that by now familiar mingling of horror and contempt which he was as far as ever from understanding.

The room he had engaged was a single cubicle in a lodging-house on the edge of the city. Lakkdarol, raw camptown that it was in those days, could have furnished little better anywhere within its limits, and Smith's errand there was not one he wished to advertise. He had slept in worse places than this before, and knew that he would do so again.

There was no one in sight when he entered, and the girl slipped up the stairs at his heels and vanished through the door, shadowy, unseen by anyone in the house. Smith closed the door and leaned his broad shoulders against the panels, regarding her speculatively.

She took in what little the room had to offer in a glance—frowsy bed, rickety table, mirror hanging unevenly and cracked against the wall, unpainted chairs—a typical camptown room in an Earth settlement abroad. She accepted its poverty in that single glance, dismissed it, then crossed to the window and leaned out for a moment, gazing across the low roof-tops toward the barren countryside beyond, red slag under the late afternoon sun.

"You can stay here," said Smith abruptly, "until I leave town. I'm waiting here for a friend to come in from Venus. Have you eaten?"

"Yes," said the girl quickly. "I shall—need no—food for—a while."

"Well—" Smith glanced around the room. "I'll be in sometime tonight. You can go or stay just as you please. Better lock the door behind me."

With no more formality than that he left her. The door closed and he heard the key turn, and smiled to himself. He did not expect, then, ever to see her again.

He went down the steps and out into the late-slanting sunlight with a mind so full of other matters that the brown girl receded very quickly into the background. Smith's errand in Lakkdarol, like most of his errands, is better not spoken of. Man lives as he must, and Smith's living was a perilous affair outside the law and ruled by the ray-gun only. It is enough to say that the shipping-port and its cargoes outbound interested him deeply just now, and that the friend he awaited was Yarol the Venusian, in that swift little Edsel ship the *Maid* that can flash from world to world with a derisive speed that laughs at Patrol boats and leaves pursuers floundering in the ether far behind.

Smith and Yarol and the *Maid* were a trinity that had caused Patrol leaders much worry and many gray hairs in the past, and the future looked very bright to Smith himself that evening as he left his lodging-house.

Lakkdarol roars by night, as Earthmen's camp-towns have a way of doing on every planet where Earth's outposts are, and it was beginning lustily as Smith went down among the awakening lights toward the center of town. His business there does not concern us. He mingled with the crowds where the lights were brightest, and there was the click of ivory counters and the jingle of silver, and red *segir* gurgled invitingly from black Venusian bottles, and much later Smith strolled homeward under the moving moons of Mars, and if the street wavered a little under his feet now and then—why, that is only understandable. Not even Smith could drink red *segir* at every bar from the *Martian Lamb* to the *New Chicago* and remain entirely steady on his feet. But he found his way back with very little difficulty—considering—and spent a good five minutes hunting for his key before he remembered he had left it in the inner lock for the girl.

He knocked then, and there was no sound of footsteps from within, but in a few moments the latch clicked and the door swung open. She retreated soundlessly before him as he entered, and took up her favorite place against the window, leaning back on the sill and outlined against the starry sky beyond. The room was in darkness.

Smith flipped the switch by the door and then leaned back against the panels, steadying himself. The cool night air had sobered him a little and his head was clear enough—liquor went to Smith's feet, not his head, or he would never have come this far along the lawless way he had chosen. He lounged against the door now and regarded the girl in the sudden glare of the bulbs, blindking a little as much at the scarlet of her clothing as at the light.

"So you stayed," he said.

"I—waited," she answered softly, leaning farther back against the sill and clasping the rough wood with slim, three-fingered hands, pale brown against the darkness.

"Why?"

She did not answer that, but her mouth curved into a slow smile. On a woman it would have been reply enough—provocative, daring.

On Shambleau there was something pitiful and horrible in it—so human on the face of one half-animal. And yet . . . that sweet brown body curving so softly from the tatters of scarlet leather—the velvety texture of that brownness—the white-flashing smile. . . . Smith was aware of a stirring excitement within him. After all—time would be hanging heavy now until Yarol came. . . . Speculatively he allowed the steel-pale eyes to wander over her, with a slow regard that missed nothing. And when he spoke he was aware that his voice had deepened a little. . . .

"Come here," he said.

She came forward slowly, on bare clawed feet that made no slightest sound on the floor, and stood before him with downcast eyes and mouth trembling in that pitifully human smile. He took her by the shoulders—velvety soft shoulders, of a creamy smoothness that was not the texture of human flesh. A little tremor went over her, perceptibly, at the contact of his hands. Northwest Smith caught his breath suddenly and dragged her to him . . . sweet yielding brownness in the circle of his arms . . . heard her own breath catch and quicken as her velvety arms closed about his neck. And then he was looking down into her face, very near, and the green animal eyes met his with the pulsing pupils and the flicker of—something—deep behind their shallows—and through the rising clamor of his blood, even as he stooped his lips to hers, Smith felt something deep within him shudder away—inexplicable, instinctive, revolted. What it might be he had no words to tell, but the very touch of her was suddenly loathsome—so soft and velvet and unhuman—and it might have been an animal's face that lifted itself to his mouth—the dark knowledge looked hungrily from the darkness of those slit pupils— and for a mad instant he knew that same wild, feverish revulsion he had seen in the faces of the mob . . .

"God!" he gasped, a far more ancient invocation against evil than he realized, then or ever, and he ripped her arms from his neck, swung her away with such a force that she reeled half-across the room. Smith fell back against the door, breathing heavily, and stared at her while the wild revolt died slowly within him.

She had fallen to the floor beneath the window, and as she lay there against the wall with bent head he saw, curiously, that her turban had slipped—the turban that he had been so sure covered baldness—and a lock of scarlet hair fell below the binding leather, hair as scarlet as her garment, as unhumanly red as her eyes were unhumanly green. He stared, and shook his head dizzily and stared again, for it seemed to him that the thick lock of crimson had moved, *squirmed* of itself against her cheek.

At the contact of it her hands flew up and she tucked it away with a very human gesture and then dropped her head again into her hands. And from the deep shadow of her fingers he thought she was staring up at him covertly.

Smith drew a deep breath and passed a hand across his forehead. The inexplicable moment had gone as quickly as it came—too swiftly for him to understand or analyze it. "Got to lay off the *segir*," he told himself unsteadily. Had he imagined that scarlet hair? After all, she was no more than a pretty brown girl-creature from one of the many half-human races peopling the planets. No more than that, after all. A pretty little thing, but animal . . . . He laughed, a little shakily.

"No more of that," he said. "God knows I'm no angel, but there's got to be a limit somewhere. Here." He crossed to the bed and sorted out a pair of blankets from the untidy heap, tossing them to the far corner of the room. "You can sleep there."

Wordlessly she rose from the floor and began to rearrange the blankets, the uncomprehending resignation of the animal eloquent in every line of her.

Smith had a strange dream that night. He thought he had awakened to a room full of darkness and moonlight and moving shadows, for the nearer moon of Mars was racing through the sky and everything on the planet below her was endued with a restless life in the dark. And something . . . some nameless, unthinkable *thing* . . . was coiled about his throat . . . something like a soft snake, wet and warm. It lay loose and light about his neck . . . and it was moving gently, very gently, with a soft, caressive pressure that sent little thrills of delight through every nerve and fiber of him, a perilous delight—beyond physical pleasure, deeper than joy of the mind. That warm softness was caressing the very roots of his soul and with a terrible intimacy. The ecstasy of it left him weak, and yet he knew—in a flash of knowledge born of this impossible dream—that the soul should not be handled. . . . And with that knowledge a horror broke upon him, turning the pleasure into a rapture of revulsion, hateful, horrible—but still most foully sweet. He tried to lift his hands and tear the dream-monstrosity from his throat—tired but half-heartedly; for though his soul was revolted to its very deeps, yet the delight of his body was so great that his hands all but refused the attempt. But when at last he tried to lift his arms a cold shock went over him and he found that he could not stir . . . his body lay stony as marble beneath the blankets, a living marble that shuddered with a dreadful delight through every rigid vein.

The revulsion grew strong upon him as he struggled against the paralyzing dream—a struggle of soul against sluggish body—titanically, until the moving dark was streaked with blankness that clouded and closed about him at last and he sank back into the oblivion from which he had awakened.

Next morning, when the bright sunlight shining through Mars' clear thin air awakened him, Smith lay for a while trying to remember. The dream had been more vivid than reality, but he could not now quite recall . . . only that it had been more sweet and horrible than anything else in life. He lay puzzling for a while, until a soft sound from the corner aroused him from his thoughts and he sat up to see the girl lying in a cat-like coil on her blankets, watching him with round, grave eyes. He regarded her somewhat ruefully.

"Morning," he said. "I've just had the devil of a dream . . . Well, hungry?"

She shook her head silently, and he could have sworn there was a covert gleam of strange amusement in her eyes.

He stretched and yawned, dismissing the nightmare temporarily from his mind.

"What am I going to do with you?" he inquired, turning to more immediate matters. "I'm leaving here in a day or two and I can't take you along, you know. Where'd you come from in the first place?"

Again she shook her head.

"Not telling? Well, it's your business. You can stay here until I give up the room. From then on you'll have to do your own worrying."

He swung his feet to the floor and reached for his clothes.

Ten minutes later, slipping the heat-gun into its holster at his thigh, Smith turned to the girl. "There's food-concentrate in that box on the table. It ought to hold you until I get back. And you'd better lock the door again after I've gone."

Her wide, unwavering stare was his only answer, and he was not sure she had understood, but at any rate the lock clicked after him as before, and he went down the steps with a faint grin on his lips.

The memory of last night's extraordinary dream was slipping from him, as such memories do, and by the time he had reached the street the girl and the dream and all of yesterday's happenings were blotted out by the sharp necessities of the present.

Again the intricate business that had brought him here claimed his attention. He went about it to the exclusion of all else, and there was a good reason behind everything he did from the moment he stepped out into the street until the time when he turned back again at evening; though had one chosen to follow him during the day his apparently aimless rambling through Lakkdarol would have seemed very pointless.

He must have spent two hours at the least idling by the space-port, watching with sleepy, colorless eyes the ships that came and went, the passengers, the vessels lying at wait, the cargoes—particularly the cargoes. He made the rounds of the town's saloons once more, consuming many glasses of varied liquors in the course of the day and engaging in idle conversation with men of all races and worlds, usually in their own languages, for Smith was a linguist of repute among his contemporaries. He heard the gossip of the spaceways, news from a dozen planets of a thousand different events. He heard the latest joke about the Venusian Emperor and the latest report on the Chino-Aryan war and the latest song hot from the lips of Rose Robertson, whom every man on the civilized planets adored as "the Georgia Rose." He passed the day quite profitably, for his own purposes, which do not concern us now, and it was not until late evening, when he turned homeward again, that the thought of the brown girl in his room took definite shape in his mind, though it had been lurking there, formless and submerged, all day.

He had no idea what comprised her usual diet, but he bought a can of New York roast beef and one of Venusian frog-broth and a dozen fresh canal-apples and two pounds of that Earth lettuce that grows so vigorously in the fertile canal-soil of Mars. He felt that she must surely find something to her liking in this broad variety of edibles, and—for his day had been very satisfactory—he hummed *The Green Hills of Earth* to himself in a surprisingly good baritone as he climbed the stairs.

The door was locked, as before, and he was reduced to kicking the lower panels gently with his boot, for his arms were full. She opened the door with that softness that was characteristic of her and stood regarding him in the semidarkness as he stumbled to the table with his load. The room was unlit again.

"Why don't you turn on the lights?" he demanded irritably after he had barked his shin on the chair by the table in an effort to deposit his burden there.

"Light and—dark—they are alike—to me," she murmured.

"Cat eyes, eh? Well, you look the part. Here, I've brought you some dinner. Take your choice. Fond of roast beef? Or how about a little frog-broth?"

She shook her head and backed away a step.

"No," she said. "I cannot—eat your food."

Smith's brows wrinkled. "Didn't you have any of the food-tablets?"

Again the red turban shook negatively.

"Then you haven't had anything for—why, more than twenty-four hours! You must be starved."

"Not hungry," she denied.

"What can I find for you to eat, then? There's time yet if I hurry. You've got to eat, child."

"I shall—eat," she said softly. "Before long—I shall—feed. Have no—worry."

She turned away then and stood at the window, looking out over the moonlit landscape as if to end the conversation. Smith cast her a puzzled glance as he opened the can of roast beef. There had been an odd undernote in that assurance that, undefinably, he did not like. And the girl had teeth and tongue and presumably a fairly human digestive system, to judge from her human form. It was nonsense for her to pretend that he could find nothing that she could eat. She must have had some of the food concentrate after all, he decided, prying up the thermos lid of the inner container to release the long-sealed savor of the hot meat inside.

"Well, if you won't eat you won't," he observed philosophically as he poured hot broth and diced beef into the dish-like lid of the thermos can and extracted the spoon from its hiding-place between the inner and outer receptacles. She turned a little to watch him as he pulled up a rickety chair and sat down to the food, and after a while the realization that her green gaze was fixed so unwinkingly upon him made the man nervous, and he said between bites of creamy canal-apple, "Why don't you try a little of this? It's good."

"The food—I eat is—better," her soft voice told him in its hesitant murmur, and again he felt rather than heard a faint undernote of unpleasantness in the words. A sudden suspicion struck him as he pondered on that last remark—some vague memory of horror-tales told about campfires in the past—and he swung round in the chair to look at her, a tiny, creeping fear unaccountably arising. There had been that in her words—in her unspoken words, that menaced . . .

She stood up beneath his gaze demurely, wide green eyes with their pulsing pupils meeting his without a falter. But her mouth was scarlet and her teeth were sharp. . . .

"What food do you eat?" he demanded. And then, after a pause, very softly, "Blood?"

She stared at him for a moment, uncomprehending; then something like amusement curled her lips and she said scornfully, "You think me—vampire, eh? No—I am Shambleau!"

Unmistakably there were scorn and amusement in her voice at the suggestion, but as unmistakably she knew what he meant—accepted it as a logical suspicion—vampires! Fairy-tales—but fairy-tales this unhuman, outland creature was most familiar with. Smith was not a credulous man, nor a superstitious one, but he had seen too many strange things himself to doubt that the wildest legend might have a basis of fact. And there was something namelessly strange about her. . . .

He puzzled over it for a while between deep bites of the canal-apple. And though he wanted to question her about a great many things, he did not, for he knew how futile it would be.

He said nothing more until the meat was finished and another canal-apple had followed the first, and he had cleared away the meal by the simple expedient of tossing the empty can out of the window. Then he lay back in the chair and surveyed her from half-closed eyes, colorless in a face tanned like saddle-leather. And again he was conscious of the brown, soft curves of her, velvety—subtle arcs and planes of smooth flesh under the tatters of scarlet leather. Vampire she might be, unhuman she certainly was, but desirable beyond words as she sat submissive beneath his low regard, her red-turbaned head bent, her clawed fingers lying in her lap. They sat very still for a while, and the silence throbbed between them.

She was so like a woman—an Earth woman—sweet and submissive and demure, and softer than soft fur, if he could forget the three-fingered claws and the pulsing eyes—and that deeper strangeness beyond words. . . . (Had he dreamed that red lock of hair that moved? Had it been *segir* that woke the wild revulsion he knew when he held her in his arms? Why had the mob so thirsted for her?) He sat and stared, and despite the mystery of her and the half-suspicions that thronged his mind—for she was so beautifully soft and curved under those revealing tatters—he slowly realized that his pulses were mounting, became aware of a kindling within . . . brown girl-creature with downcast eyes . . . and then the lids lifted and the green flatness of a cat's gaze met his, and last night's revulsion woke swiftly again, like a warning bell that clanged as their eyes met—animal, after all, too sleek and soft for humanity, and that inner strangeness . . .

Smith shrugged and sat up. His failings were legion, but the weakness of the flesh was not among the major ones. He motioned the girl to her pallet of blankets in the corner and turned to his own bed.

From deeps of sound sleep he awoke much later. He awoke suddenly and completely, and with that inner excitement that presages something momentous. He awoke to brilliant moonlight, turning the room so bright that he could see the scarlet of the girl's rags as she sat up on her pallet. She was awake, she was sitting with her shoulder half turned to him and her head bent, and some warning instinct crawled coldly up his spine as he watched what she was doing. And yet it was a very ordinary thing for a girl to do—any girl, anywhere. She was unbinding her turban . . .

He watched, not breathing, a presentiment of something horrible stirring in his brain, inexplicably. . . . The red folds loosened, and—he knew then that he had not dreamed—again a scarlet lock swung down against her cheek . . . a hair, was it? a lock of hair? . . . thick as a thick worm it fell, plumply, against that smooth cheek . . . more scarlet than blood and thick as a crawling worm . . . and like a worm it crawled.

Smith rose on an elbow, not realizing the motion, and fixed an unwinking stare, with a sort of sick, fascinated incredulity, on that—that lock of hair. He had not dreamed. Until now he had taken it for granted that it was the *segir* which had made it seem to move on that evening before. But now . . . it was lengthening, stretching, moving of itself. It must be hair, but it *crawled*; with a sickening life of its own it squirmed down against her cheek, caressingly, revoltingly, impossibly. . . . Wet, it was, and round and thick and shining. . . .

She unfastened the last fold and whipped the turban off. From what he saw then Smith would have turned his eyes away—and he had looked on dreadful things before, without flinching—but he could not stir. He could only lie there on elbow staring at the mass of scarlet, squirming—worms, hairs, what?—that writhed over her head in a dreadful mockery of ringlets. And it was lengthening, falling, somehow growing before his eyes, down over her shoulders in a spilling cascade, a mass that even at the beginning could never have been hidden under the skull-tight turban she had worn. He was beyond wondering, but he realized that. And still it squirmed and lengthened and fell, and she shook it out in a horrible travesty of a woman shaking out her unbound hair—until the unspeakable tangle of it—twisting, writhing, obscenely scarlet—hung to her waist and beyond, and still lengthened, an endless mass of crawling horror that until now, somehow, impossibly, had been hidden under the tight-bound turban. It was like a nest of blind, restless red worms . . . it was—it was like naked entrails endowed with an unnatural aliveness, terrible beyond words.

Smith lay in the shadows, frozen without and within in a sick numbness that came of utter shock and revulsion.

She shook out the obscene, unspeakable tangle over her shoulders, and somehow he knew that she was going to turn in a moment and that he must meet her eyes. The thought of that meeting stopped his heart with dread, more awfully than anything else in this nightmare horror; for nightmare it must be, surely. But he knew without trying that he could not wrench his eyes away—the sickened fascination of that sight held him motionless, and somehow there was a certain beauty. . . .

Her head was turning. The crawling awfulness rippled and squirmed at the motion, writhing thick and wet and shining over the soft brown shoulders about which they fell now in obscene cascades that all but hid her body. Her head was turning. Smith lay numb. And very slowly he saw the round of her cheek foreshorten and her profile come into view, all the scarlet horrors twisting ominously, and the profile shortened in turn and her full face came slowly round toward the bed—moonlight shining brilliantly as day on the pretty girl-face, demure and sweet, framed in tangled obscenity that crawled. . . .

The green eyes met his. He felt a perceptible shock, and a shudder rippled down his paralyzed spine, leaving an icy numbness in its wake. He felt the goose-flesh rising. But that numbness and cold horror he scarcely realized, for the green eyes were locked with his in a long, long look that somehow presaged nameless things—not altogether unpleasant things—the voiceless voice of her mind assailing him with little murmurous promises. . . .

For a moment he went down into a blind abyss of submission; and then somehow the very sight of that obscenity in eyes that did not then realize they saw it, was dreadful enough to draw him out of the seductive darkness . . . the sight of her crawling and alive with unnamable horror.

She rose, and down about her in a cascade fell the squirming scarlet of—of what grew upon her head. It fell in a long, alive cloak to her bare feet on the floor, hiding her in a wave of dreadful, wet, writhing life. She put up her hands and like a swimmer she parted the waterfall of it, tossing the masses back over her shoulders to reveal her own brown body, sweetly curved. She smiled exquisitely, and in starting waves back from her forehead and down about her in a hideous background writhed the snaky wetness of her living tresses. And Smith knew that he looked upon Medusa.

The knowledge of that—the realization of vast backgrounds reaching into misted history—shook him out of his frozen horror for a moment, and in that moment he met her eyes again, smiling, green as glass in the moonlight, half hooded under drooping lids. Through the twisting scarlet she held out her arms. And there was something soul shakingly desirable about her, so that all the blood surged to his head suddenly and he stumbled to his feet like a sleeper in a dream as she swayed toward him, infinitely graceful, infinitely sweet in her cloak of living horror.

And somehow there was beauty in it, the wet scarlet writhings with moonlight sliding and shining along the thick, worm-round tresses and losing itself in the masses only to glint again and move silvery along writhing tendrils—an awful, shuddering beauty more dreadful than any ugliness could be.

But all this, again, he but half realized, for the insidious murmur was coiling again through his brain, promising, caressing, alluring, sweeter than honey; and the green eyes that held his were clear and burning like the depths of a jewel, and behind the pulsing slits of darkness he was staring into a greater dark that held all things. . . . He had known—dimly he had known when he first gazed into those flat animal shallows that behind them lay this—all beauty and terror, all horror and delight, in the infinite darkness upon which her eyes opened like windows, paned with emerald glass.

Her lips moved, and in a murmur that blended indistinguishably with the silence and the sway of her body and the dreadful sway of her—her hair—she whispered—very softly, very passionately, "I shall—speak to you now—in my own tongue—oh, beloved!"

And in her living cloak she swayed to him, the murmur swelling seductive and caressing in his innermost brain—promising, compelling, sweeter than sweet. His flesh crawled to the horror of her, but it was a perverted revulsion that clasped what it loathed. His arms slid round her under the sliding cloak, wet, wet and warm and hideously alive—and the sweet velvet body was clinging to his, her arms locked about his neck—and with a whisper and a rush the unspeakable horror closed about them both.

In nightmares until he died he remembered that moment when the living tresses of Shambleau first folded him in their embrace. A nauseous, smothering odor as the wetness shut around him—thick, pulsing worms clasping every inch of his body, sliding, writhing, their wetness and warmth striking through his garments as if he stood naked to their embrace.

All this in a graven instant—and after that a tangled flash of conflicting sensation before oblivion closed over him for he remembered the dream—and knew it for nightmare reality now, and the sliding, gently moving caresses of those wet, warm worms upon his flesh was an ecstasy above words—that deeper ecstasy that strikes beyond the body and beyond the mind and tickles the very roots of soul with unnatural delight. So he stood, rigid as marble, as helplessly stony as any of Medusa's victims in ancient legends were, while the terrible pleasure of Shambleau thrilled and shuddered through every fiber of him; through every atom of his body and the intangible atoms of what men call the soul, through all that was Smith the dreadful pleasure ran. And it was truly dreadful. Dimly he knew it, even as his body answered to the root-deep ecstasy, a foul and dreadful wooing from which his very soul shuddered away—and yet in the innermost depths of that soul some grinning traitor shivered with delight. But deeply, behind all this, he knew horror and revulsion and despair beyond telling, while the intimate caresses crawled obscenely in the secret places of his soul—knew that the soul should not be handled— and shook with the perilous pleasure through it all.

And this conflict and knowledge, this mingling of rapture and revulsion all took place in the flashing of a moment while the scarlet worms coiled and crawled upon him, sending deep, obscene tremors of that infinite pleasure into every atom that made up Smith. And he could not stir in that slimy, ecstatic embrace—and a weakness was flooding that grew deeper after each succeeding wave of intense delight, and the traitor in his soul strengthened and drowned out the revulsion—and something within him ceased to struggle as he sank wholly into a blazing darkness that was oblivion to all else but that devouring rapture. . . .

The young Venusian climbing the stairs to his friend's lodging room pulled out his key absent mindedly, a pucker forming between his fine brows. He was slim, as all Venusians are, as fair and sleek as any of them, and as with most of his countrymen the look of cherubic innocence on his face was wholly deceptive. He had the face of a fallen angel, without Lucifer's majesty to redeem it; for a black devil grinned in his eyes and there were faint lines of ruthlessness and dissipation about his mouth to tell of the long years behind him that had run the gamut of experiences and made his name, next to Smith's, the most hated and the most respected in the records of the Patrol.

He mounted the stairs now with a puzzled frown between his eyes. He had come into Lakkdarol on the noon liner—the *Maid* in her hold very skillfully disguised with paint and otherwise—to find in lamentable disorder the affairs he had expected to be settled. And cautious inquiry elicited the information that Smith had not been seen for three days. That was not like his friend—he had never failed before, and the two stood to lose not only a large sum of money but also their personal safety by the inexplicable lapse on the part of Smith. Yarol could think of one solution only: fate had at last caught up with his friend. Nothing but physical disability could explain it.

Still puzzling, he fitted his key in the lock and swung the door open.

In that first moment, as the door opened, he sensed something very wrong. . . . The room was darkened, and for a while he could see nothing, but at the first breath he scented a strange, unnamable odor, half-sickening, half-sweet. And deep stirrings of ancestral memory awoke within him—ancient swamp-born memories from Venusian ancestors far away and long ago. . . .

Yarol laid his hand on his gun, lightly, and opened the door wider. In the dimness all he could see at first was a curious mound in the far corner. . . . Then his eyes grew accustomed to the dark, and he saw it more clearly, a mound that somehow heaved and stirred within itself. . . . A mound of—he caught his breath sharply—a mound like a mass of entrails, living, moving, writhing with an unspeakable aliveness. Then a hot Venusian oath broke from his lips and he cleared the door-sill in a swift stride, slammed the door and set his back against it, gun ready in his hand, although his flesh crawled—for he *knew* . . .

"Smith!" he said softly, in a voice thick with horror.

The moving mass stirred—shuddered—sank back into crawling quiescence again.

"Smith! Smith!" The Venusian's voice was gentle and insistent, and it quivered a little with terror.

An impatient ripple went over the whole mass of aliveness in the corner. It stirred again, reluctantly, and then tendril by writhing tendril it began to part itself and fall aside, and very slowly the brown of a spaceman's leather appeared beneath it, all slimed and shining.

"Smith! Northwest!" Yarol's persistent whisper came again, urgently, and with a dream-like slowness the leather garments moved . . . a man sat up in the midst of the writhing worms, a man who once, long ago, might have been Northwest Smith. From head to foot he was slimy from the embrace of the crawling horror about him. His face was that of some creature beyond humanity—dead-alive, fixed in a gray stare, and the look of terrible ecstasy that overspread it seemed to come from somewhere far within, a faint reflection from immeasurable distances beyond the flesh. And as there is mystery and magic in the moonlight which is after all but a reflection of the everyday sun, so in that gray face turned to the door was a terror unnamable and sweet, a reflection of ecstasy beyond the understanding of any who had known only earthly ecstasy themselves. And as he sat there turning a blank, eyeless face to Yarol the red worms writhed ceaselessly about him, very gently, with a soft, caressive motion that never slacked.

"Smith . . . come here! Smith . . . get up . . . Smith, Smith!" Yarol's whisper hissed in the silence, commanding, urgent—but he made no move to leave the door.

And with a dreadful slowness, like a dead man rising, Smith stood up in the nest of slimy scarlet. He swayed drunkenly on his feet, and two or three crimson tendrils came writhing up his legs to the knees and wound themselves there, supportingly, moving with a ceaseless caress that seemed to give him some hidden strength, for he said then, without inflection.

"Go away. Go away. Leave me alone." And the dead ecstatic face never changed.

"Smith!" Yarol's voice was desperate. "Smith, listen! Smith, can't you hear me?"

"Go away," the monotonous voice said. "Go away. Go away. Go—"

"Not unless you come too. Can't you hear? Smith! Smith! I'll—"

He hushed in mid-phrase, and once more the ancestral prickle of race-memory shivered down his back, for the scarlet mass was moving again, violently, rising . . .

Yarol pressed back against the door and gripped his gun, and the name of a god he had forgotten years ago rose to his lips unbidden. For he knew what was coming next, and the knowledge was more dreadful than any ignorance could have been.

The red, writhing mass rose higher, and the tendrils parted and a human face looked out—no, half-human, with green cat-eyes that shone in that dimness like lighted jewels, compellingly. . . .

Yarol breathed, "Shar!" again, and flung up an arm across his face, and the tingle of meeting that green gaze for even an instant went thrilling through him perilously.

"Smith!" he called in despair. "Smith, can't you hear me?"

"Go away," said that voice that was not Smith's. "Go away."

And somehow, although he dared not look, Yarol knew that the—the other—had parted those worm-thick tresses and stood there in all the human sweetness of the brown, curved woman's body, cloaked in living horror. And he felt the eyes upon him, and something was crying insistently in his brain to lower that shielding arm. . . . He was lost—he knew it, and the knowledge gave him that courage which comes from despair. The voice in his brain was growing, swelling, deafening him with a roaring command that all but swept him before it—command to lower that arm—to meet the eyes that opened upon darkness—to submit—and a promise, murmurous and sweet and evil beyond words, of pleasure to come. . . .

But somehow he kept his head—somehow, dizzily, he was gripping his gun in his upflung hand—somehow, incredibly, crossing the narrow room with averted face, groping for Smith's shoulder. There was a moment of blind fumbling in emptiness, and then he found it, and gripped the leather that was slimy and dreadful and wet—and simultaneously he felt something loop gently about his ankle and a shock of repulsive pleasure went through him, and then another coil, and another, wound about his feet. . . .

Yarol set his teeth and gripped the shoulder hard, and his hand shuddered of itself, for the feel of that leather was slimy as the worms about his ankles, and a faint tingle of obscene delight went through him from the contact.

That caressive pressure on his legs was all he could feel, and the voice in his brain drowned out all other sounds, and his body obeyed him reluctantly—but somehow he gave one heave of tremendous effort and swung Smith, stumbling, out of that nest of horror. The twining tendrils ripped loose with a little sucking sound, and the whole mass quivered and reached after, and then Yarol forgot his friend utterly and turned his whole being to the hopeless task of freeing himself. For only a part of him was fighting, now—only a part of him struggled against the twining obscenities, and in his innermost brain the sweet, seductive murmur sounded, and his body clamored to surrender. . . .

"*Shar! Shar y'danis . . . Shar mor'la-rol*—" prayed Yarol, gasping and half-unconscious that he spoke, boy's prayers that he had forgotten years ago, and with his back half turned to the central mass he kicked desperately with his heavy boots at the red, writhing worms about him.

They gave back before him, quivering and curling themselves out of reach, and though he knew that more were reaching for his throat from behind, at least he could go on struggling until he was forced to meet those eyes. . . .

He stamped and kicked and stamped again, and for one instant he was free of the slimy grip as the bruised worms curled back from his heavy feet, and he lurched away dizzily, sick with revulsion and despair as he fought off the coils, and then he lifted his eyes and saw the cracked mirror on the wall. Dimly in its reflection he could see the writhing scarlet horror behind him, cat face peering out with its demure girl-smile, dreadfully human, and all the red tendrils reaching after him. And remembrance of something he had read long ago swept incongruously over him, and the gasp of relief and hope that he gave shook for a moment the grip of the command in his brain.

Without pausing for a breath he swung the gun over his shoulder, the reflected barrel in line with the reflected horror in the mirror, and flicked the catch.

In the mirror he saw its blue flame leap in a dazzling spate across the dimness, full into the midst of that squirming, reaching mass behind him. There was a hiss and a blaze and a high, thin scream of inhuman malice and despair—the flame cut a wide arc and went out as the gun fell from his hand, and Yarol pitched forward to the floor.

Northwest Smith opened his eyes to Martian sunlight streaming thinly through the dingy window. Something wet and cold was slapping his face, and the familiar fiery sting of *segir*-whiskey burnt his throat.

"Smith!" Yarol's voice was saying from far away. "N.W.! Wake up, damn you! Wake up!"

"I'm—awake," Smith managed to articulate thickly. "Wha's matter?"

Then a cup-rim was thrust against his teeth and Yarol said irritably, "Drink it, you fool!"

Smith swallowed obediently and more of the fire-hot *segir* flowed down his grateful throat. It spread a warmth through his body that awakened him from the numbness that had gripped him until now, and helped a little toward driving out the all-devouring weakness he was becoming aware of slowly. He lay still for a few minutes while the warmth of the whisky went through him, and memory sluggishly began to permeate his brain with the spread of the *segir*. Nightmare memories . . . sweet and terrible . . . memories of—

"God!" gasped Smith suddenly, and tried to sit up. Weakness smote him like a blow, and for an instant the room wheeled as he fell back against something firm and warm—Yarol's shoulder. The Venusian's arm supported him while the room steadied, and after a while he twisted a little and stared into the other's black gaze.

Yarol was holding him with one arm and finishing the mug of *segir* himself, and the black eyes met his over the rim and crinkled into sudden laughter, half-hysterical after that terror that was passed.

"By *Pharol*!" gasped Yarol, choking into his mug. "By *Pharol*, N.W.! I'm never gonna let you forget this! Next time you have to drag me out of a mess I'll say—"

"Let it go," said Smith. "What's been going on? How—"

"Shambleau," Yarol's laughter died. "Shambleau! What were you doing with a thing like that?"

"What was it?" Smith asked soberly.

"Mean to say you didn't know? But where'd you find it? How—"

"Suppose you tell me first what you know," said Smith firmly. "And another swig of that *segir*, too. I need it."

"Can you hold the mug now? Feel better?"

"Yeah—some. I can hold it—thanks. Now go on."

"Well—I don't know just where to start. They call them Shambleau—"

"Good God, is there more than one?"

"It's a—a sort of race, I think, one of the very oldest. Where they come from nobody knows. The name sounds a little French, doesn't it? But it goes back beyond the start of history. There have always been Shambleau."

"I never heard of 'em."

"Not many people have. And those who know don't care to talk about it much."

"Well, half this town knows. I hadn't any idea what they were talking about, then. And I still don't understand—"

"Yes, it happens like this, sometimes. They'll appear, and the news will spread and the town will get together and hunt them down, and after that—well, the story doesn't get around very far. It's too—too unbelievable."

"But—my God, Yarol!—what was it? Where'd it come from? How—"

"Nobody knows just where they come from. Another planet— maybe some undiscovered one. Some say Venus—I know there are some rather awful legends of them handed down in our family—that's how I've heard about it. And the minute I opened that door, awhile back—I—I think I knew that smell. . . ."

"But—what *are* they?"

"God knows. Not human, though they have the human form. Or that may be only an illusion . . . or maybe I'm crazy. I don't know. They're a species of the vampire—or maybe the vampire is a species of—of them. Their normal form must be that—that mass, and in that form they draw nourishment from the—I suppose the life-forces of men. And they take some form—usually a woman form, I think, and key you up to the highest pitch of emotion before they—begin. That's to work the life-force up to intensity so it'll be easier. . . . And they give, always, that horrible, foul pleasure as they—feed. There are some men who, if they survive the first experience, take to it like a drug—can't give it up—keep the thing with them all their lives—which isn't long— feeding it for that ghastly satisfaction. Worse than smoking *ming* or—or 'praying to *Pharol.*'"

"Yes," said Smith. "I'm beginning to understand why that crowd was so surprised and—and disgusted when I said—well, never mind. Go on."

"Did you get to talk to—to it?" asked Yarol.

"I tried to. It couldn't speak very well. I asked it where it came from and it said—'from far away and long ago'—something like that."

"I wonder. Possibly some unknown planet—but I think not. You know there are so many wild stories with some basis of fact to start from, that I've sometimes wondered—mightn't there be a lot more of even worse and wilder superstitions we've never even heard of? Things like this, blasphemous and foul, that those who know have to keep still about? Awful, fantastic things running around loose that we never hear rumors of at all!

"These things—they've been in existence for countless ages. No one knows when or where they first appeared. Those who've seen them, as we saw this one, don't talk about it. It's just one of those vague, misty rumors you find half-hinted at in old books sometimes. . . . I believe they are an older race than man, spawned from ancient seed in times before ours, perhaps on planets that have gone to dust, and so horrible to man that when they are discovered the discoverers keep still about it—forget them again as quickly as they can.

"And they go back to time immemorial. I suppose you recognized the legend of Medusa? There isn't any question that the ancient Greeks knew of them. Does it mean that there have been civilizations before yours that set out from Earth and explored other planets? Or did one of the Shambleau somehow make its way into Greece three thousand years ago? If you think about it long enough you'll go off your head! I wonder how many other legends are based on things like this—things we don't suspect, things we'll never know.

"The Gorgon, Medusa, a beautiful woman with—with snakes for hair, and a gaze that turned men to stone, and Perseus finally killed her—I remembered this just by accident, N.W., and it saved your life and mine—Perseus killed her by using a mirror as he fought to reflect what he dared not look at directly. I wonder what the old Greek who first started that legend would have thought if he'd known that three thousand years later his story would save the lives of two men on another planet. I wonder what that Greek's own story was, and how he met the thing, and what happened. . . .

"Well, there's a lot we'll never know. Wouldn't the records of that race of—of *things*, whatever they are, be worth reading! Records of other planets and other ages and all the beginnings of mankind! But I don't suppose they've kept any records. I don't suppose they've even any place to keep them—from what little I know, or anyone knows about it, they're like the Wandering Jew, just bobbing up here and there at long intervals, and where they stay in the meantime I'd give my eyes to know! But I don't believe that terribly hypnotic power they have indicates any superhuman intelligence. It's their means of getting food—just like a frog's long tongue or a carnivorous flower's odor. Those are physical because the frog and the flower eat physical food. The Shambleau uses a—a mental reach to get mental food. I don't quite know how to put it. And just as a beast that eats the bodies of other animals acquires with each meal greater power over the bodies of the rest, so the Shambleau, stoking itself up with the life-forces of men, increases its power over the minds and souls of other men. But I'm talking about things I can't define—things I'm not sure exist.

"I only know that when I felt—when those tentacles closed around my legs—I didn't want to pull loose, I felt sensations that—that—oh, I'm fouled and filthy to the very deepest part of me by that—pleasure—and yet—"

"I know," said Smith slowly. The effect of the *segir* was beginning to wear off, and weakness was washing back over him in waves, and when he spoke he was half meditating in a lower voice, scarcely realizing that Yarol listened. "I know it—much better than you do—and there's something so indescribably awful that the thing emanates, something so utterly at odds with everything human—there aren't any words to say it. For a while I was a part of it, literally, sharing its thoughts and memories and emotions and hungers, and—well, it's over now and I don't remember very clearly, but the only part left free was that part of me that was all but insane from the—the obscenity of the thing. And yet it was a pleasure so sweet—I think there must be some nucleus of utter evil in me—in everyone—that needs only the proper stimulus to get complete control; because even while I was sick all through from the touch of those—things—there was something in me that was—was simply gibbering with delight. . . . Because of that I saw things—and knew things—horrible, wild things I can't quite remember—visited unbelievable places, looked backward through the memory of that—creature—I was one with, and saw—God, I wish I could remember!"

"You ought to thank your God you can't," said Yarol soberly.

His voice roused Smith from the half-trance he had fallen into, and he rose on his elbow, swaying a little from weakness. The room was wavering before him, and he closed his eyes, not to see it, but he asked, "You say they—they don't turn up again? No way of finding—another?"

Yarol did not answer for a moment. He laid his hands on the other man's shoulders and pressed him back, and then sat staring down into the dark, ravaged face with a new, strange, undefinable look upon it that he had never seen there before—whose meaning he knew, too well.

"Smith," he said finally, and his black eyes for once were steady and serious, and the little grinning devil had vanished from behind them, "Smith, I've never asked your word on anything before, but I've—I've earned the right to do it now, and I'm asking you to promise me one thing."

Smith's colorless eyes met the black gaze unsteadily. Irresolution was in them, and a little fear of what that promise might be. And for just a moment Yarol was looking, not into his friend's familiar eyes, but into a wide gray blankness that held all horror and delight—a pale sea with unspeakable pleasures sunk beneath it. Then the wide stare focused again and Smith's eyes met his squarely and Smith's voice said, "Go ahead. I'll promise."

"That if you ever should meet a Shambleau again—ever, anywhere—you'll draw your gun and burn it to hell the instant you realize what it is. Will you promise me that?"

There was a long silence. Yarol's somber black eyes bored relentlessly into the colorless ones of Smith, not wavering. And the veins stood out on Smith's tanned forehead. He never broke his word— he had given it perhaps half a dozen times in his life, but once he had given it, he was incapable of breaking it. And once more the gray seas flooded in a dim tide of memories, sweet and horrible beyond dreams. Once more Yarol was staring into blankness that hid nameless things. The room was very still.

The gray tide ebbed. Smith's eyes, pale and resolute as steel, met Yarol's levelly.

"I'll—try," he said. And his voice wavered.

The Last Days of Shandakor

⚙

by Leigh Brackett

One of the most popular writers in mid twentieth century science fiction, Leigh Brackett, started publishing science fiction long before the science fiction field developed awards for fiction. She eventually got a Hugo, but it was a posthumous one, given in 1981 for Best Dramatic Presentation, an award she shared with Irvin Kershner, Lawrence Kasdan and George Lucas, for the movie The Empire Strikes Back.

By then, science fiction fans already knew that Star Wars *would not have existed without Leigh Brackett, not because she co-wrote the best of all the* Star Wars *movies, but because George Lucas had liberally borrowed from tropes that Leigh Brackett sprinkled all over the genre with unconscious ease.*

If C.L. Moore's Northwest Smith provided some of Han Solo's DNA, Brackett's Eric John Stark more or less fathered him. In his introduction to Martian Quest, *Haffner Press's 2002 collection of Brackett's Mars stories, Michael Moorcock called her work on that screenplay "self-imitation." If you read a lot of Brackett, you see his point.*

Tough women, battles between the sexes, sharp witty dialogue all mark much of Brackett's work. And she wrote a lot of it, not just in science fiction, but in western and detective fiction as well. She also wrote the screenplays for many of the classics of the silver screen, including The Big Sleep *and* Rio Bravo.

But she always said her favorite genre was science fiction. In her Afterword to The Best of Leigh Brackett, *published in 1977, she wrote:*

Aside from the pleasure of congenial work and the making of a living, science fiction has given me much that is beyond price: life-long friends, a worldwide family, and a marriage that has lasted almost thirty years to date. [page 362]

In his introduction to the same book, her husband, science fiction writer Edmond Hamilton, says her sharp eye and even sharper pen improved his own writing. [page xiii]. In his foreword to Lorelei of The Red Mist, *Haffner Press's 2007 collection of Brackett's planetary romances, Ray Bradbury says Brackett improved his writing as well. He writes "She kicked me on to doing better" and called her a teacher as well as a dear friend. [page x]*

But Brackett didn't just influence writers whose work she saw in draft form. She influenced generations of writers. Michael Moorcock, in his introduction, lists some of them who claimed that Brackett's writing influenced their own. In addition to himself, he listed Andre Norton, John Brunner, Jack Vance, Samuel R. Delany, Roger Zelazny, Harlan Ellison, Philip Jose Farmer, Marian Zimmer Bradley, Gene Wolfe, Tanith Lee, and many more.

Which makes it all the more upsetting that Brackett fell out of favor with the literary police in the late 1950s, so much so that Hamilton had to defend her (as we saw in the introduction). Because her work fell out of print, her Martian worlds—which informed Bradbury and so many others—do not get listed among the great space fantasy stories.

She claimed inspiration from Edgar Rice Burroughs, but she improved on his work greatly. As Moorcock writes, "Burroughs lacked her poetic vision, her specific, characteristic talent, and in my view her finest Martian adventure stories remain superior to all others." [page xiii]

I agree. When Brackett's powerful stories fell out of print, we lost one of the beating hearts of the field.

My biggest problem in choosing a Brackett story was stopping at just one. She had lots of great stories at the proper length. Some are hard science fiction stories (still!). Others fit in beautifully with Zenna Henderson's the People stories (and probably inspired them). Still others are shocking sf horror stories that make "Shambleau" seem tame. She wrote science fiction adventure, science fiction mystery, science fiction romance—

If there's a subgenre of science fiction that Leigh Brackett missed, I haven't found it. I wrote on my blog after I finished one of her collections that I believed that all of us who write science fiction owe our biggest debt to Leigh Brackett, and I got email after email from writers and readers who agreed.

For this volume, I finally settled on "The Last Days of Shandakor" because it brings something to the anthology that we haven't seen yet— a lost world story.

✹ ✹ ✹

1

HE CAME alone into the wineshop, wrapped in a dark red cloak, with the cowl drawn over his head. He stood for a moment by the doorway and one of the slim dark predatory women who live in those places went to him, with a silvery chiming from the little bells that were almost all she wore.

I saw her smile up at him. And then, suddenly, the smile became fixed and something happened to her eyes. She was no longer looking at the cloaked man but through him. In the oddest fashion—it was as though he had become invisible.

She went by him. Whether she passed some word along or not I couldn't tell but an empty space widened around the stranger. And no one looked at him. They did not avoid looking at him. They simply refused to see him.

He began to walk slowly across the crowded room. He was very tall and he moved with a fluid, powerful grace that was beautiful to watch. People drifted out of his way, not seeming to, but doing it. The air was thick with nameless smells, shrill with the laughter of women.

Two tall barbarians, far gone in wine, were carrying on some intertribal feud and the yelling crowd had made room for them to fight. There was a silver pipe and a drum and a double-banked harp making old wild music. Lithe brown bodies leaped and whirled through the laughter and the shouting and the smoke.

The stranger walked through all this, alone, untouched, unseen.

He passed close to where I sat. Perhaps because I, of all the people in that place, not only saw him but stared at him, he gave me a glance of black eyes from under the shadow of his cowl—eyes like blown coals, bright with suffering and rage.

I caught only a glimpse of his muffled face. The merest glimpse but that was enough. *Why did he have to show his face to me in that wineshop in Barrakesh?*

He passed on. There was no space in the shadowy corner where he went but space was made, a circle of it, a moat between the stranger and the crowd. He sat down. I saw him lay a coin on the outer edge of the table. Presently a serving wench came up, picked up the coin and set down a cup of wine. But it was as if she waited on an empty table.

I turned to Kardak, my head drover, a Shunni with massive shoulders and uncut hair braided in an intricate tribal knot. "What's all that about?" I asked.

Kardak shrugged. "Who knows?" He started to rise. "Come, JonRoss. It is time we got back to the serai."

"We're not leaving for hours yet. And don't lie to me, I've been on Mars a long time. What is that man? Where does he come from?"

Barrakesh is the gateway between north and south. Long ago, when there were oceans in equatorial and southern Mars, when Valkis and Jekkara were proud seats of empire and not thieves' dens, here on the edge of the northern Drylands the great caravans had come and gone to Barrakesh for a thousand thousand years. It is a place of strangers.

In the time-eaten streets of rock you see tall Keshi hillmen, nomads from the high plains of Upper Shun, lean dark men from the south who barter away the loot of forgotten tombs and temples, cosmopolitan sophisticates up from Kahora and the trade cities, where there are spaceports and all the appurtenances of modern civilization.

The red-cloaked stranger was none of these.

A glimpse of a face—I am a planetary anthropologist. I was supposed to be charting Martian ethnology and I was doing it on a fellowship grant I had wangled from a Terran university too ignorant to know that the vastness of Martian history makes such a project hopeless.

I was in Barrakesh, gathering an outfit preparatory to a year's study of the tribes of Upper Shun. And suddenly there had passed close by me a man with golden skin and un-Martian black eyes and a facial structure that belonged to no race I knew. I have seen the carven faces of fauns that were a little like it.

Kardak said again, "It is time to go, JonRoss!"

I looked at the stranger, drinking his wine in silence and alone. "Very well, I'll ask him."

Kardak sighed. "Earthmen," he said, "are not given much to wisdom." He turned and left me.

I crossed the room and stood beside the stranger. In the old courteous High Martian they speak in all the Low-Canal towns I asked permission to sit.

Those raging, suffering eyes met mine. There was hatred in them, and scorn, and shame. "What breed of human are you?"

"I am an Earthman."

He said the name over as though he had heard it before and was trying to remember. "Earthman. Then it is as the winds have said, blowing across the desert—that Mars is dead and men from other worlds defile her dust." He looked out over the wineshop and all the people who would not admit his presence. "Change," he whispered. "Death and change and the passing away of things."

The muscles of his face drew tight. He drank and I could see now that he had been drinking for a long time, for days, perhaps for weeks. There was a quiet madness on him.

"Why do the people shun you?"

"Only a man of Earth would need to ask," he said and made a sound of laughter, very dry and bitter.

I was thinking, *A new race, an unknown race!* I was thinking of the fame that sometimes comes to men who discover a new thing, and of a Chair I might sit in at the University if I added one bright unheard-of piece of the shadowy mosaic of Martian history. I had had my share of wine and a bit more. That Chair looked a mile high and made of gold.

The stranger said softly, "I go from place to place in this wallow of Barrakesh and everywhere it is the same. I have ceased to be." His white teeth glittered for an instant in the shadow of the cowl. "They were wiser than I, my people. When Shandakor is dead, we are dead also, whether our bodies live or not."

"Shandakor?" I said. It had a sound of distant bells.

"How should an Earthman know? Yes, Shandakor! Ask of the men of Kesh and the men of Shun! Ask the kings of Mekh, who are half around the world! Ask of all the men of Mars—they have not forgotten Shandakor! But they will not tell you. It is a bitter shame to them, the memory and the name."

He stared out across the turbulent throng that filled the room and flowed over to the noisy street outside. "And I am here among them—lost."

"Shandakor is dead?"

"Dying. There were three of us who did not want to die. We came south across the desert—one turned back, one perished in the sand, I am here in Barrakesh." The metal of the wine-cup bent between his hands.

I said, "And you regret your coming."

"I should have stayed and died with Shandakor. I know that now. But I cannot go back."

"Why not?" I was thinking how the name John Ross would look, inscribed in golden letters on the scroll of the discoverers.

"The desert is wide, Earthman. Too wide for one alone."

And I said, "I have a caravan. I am going north tonight."

A light came into his eyes, so strange and deadly that I was afraid. "No," he whispered. "No!"

I sat in silence, looking out across the crowd that had forgotten me as well, because I sat with the stranger. *A new race, an unknown city. And I was drunk.*

After a long while the stranger asked me, "What does an Earthman want in Shandakor?"

I told him. He laughed. "You study men," he said and laughed again, so that the red cloak rippled.

"If you want to go back, I'll take you. If you don't, tell me where the city lies and I'll find it. Your race, your city, should have their place in history."

He said nothing but the wine had made me very shrewd and I could guess at what was going on in the stranger's mind. I got up.

"Consider it," I told him. "You can find me at the serai by the northern gate until the lesser moon is up. Then I'll be gone."

"Wait." His fingers fastened on my wrist. They hurt. I looked into his face and I did not like what I saw there. But, as Kardak had mentioned, I was not given much to wisdom.

The stranger said, "Your men will not go beyond the Wells of Karthedon."

"Then we'll go without them."

A long long silence. Then he said, "So be it."

I knew what he was thinking as plainly as though he had spoken the words. He was thinking that I was only an Earthman and that he would kill me when we came in sight of Shandakor.

2

THE CARAVAN TRACKS branch off at the Wells of Karthedon. One goes westward into Shun and one goes north through the passes of Outer Kesh. But there is a third one, more ancient than the others. It goes toward the east and it is never used. The deep rock wells are dry and the stone-built shelters have vanished under the rolling dunes. It is not until the track begins to climb the mountains that there are even memories.

Kardak refused politely to go beyond the Wells. He would wait for me, he said, a certain length of time, and if I came back we would go on into Shun. If I didn't—well, his full pay was left in charge of the local headman. He would collect it and go home. He had not liked having the stranger with us. He had doubled his price.

In all that long march up from Barrakesh I had not been able to get a word out of Kardak or the men concerning Shandakor. The stranger had not spoken either. He had told me his name—Corin—and nothing more. Cloaked and cowled he rode alone and brooded. His private devils were still with him and he had a new one now—impatience. He would have ridden us all to death if I had let him.

So Corin and I went east alone from Karthedon, with two led animals and all the water we could carry. And now I could not hold him back.

"There is no time to stop," he said. "The days are running out. There—is no time!"

When we reached the mountains we had only three animals left and when we crossed the first ridge we were afoot and leading the one remaining beast which carried the dwindling water skins.

We were following a road now. Partly hewn and partly worn it led up and over the mountains, those naked leaning mountains that were full of silence and peopled only with the shapes of red rock that the wind had carved.

"Armies used to come this way," said Corin. "Kings and caravans and beggars and human slaves, singers and dancing girls and the embassies of princes. This was the road to Shandakor."

And we went along it at a madman's pace.

The beast fell in a slide of rock and broke its neck and we carried the last water skin between us. It was not a heavy burden. It grew lighter and then was almost gone.

One afternoon, long before sunset, Corin said abruptly, "We will stop here."

The road went steeply up before us. There was nothing to be seen or heard. Corin sat down in the drifted dust. I crouched down too, a little distance from him. I watched him. His face was hidden and he did not speak.

The shadows thickened in that deep and narrow way. Overhead the strip of sky flared saffron and then red—and then the bright cruel stars came out. The wind worked at its cutting and polishing of stone, muttering to itself, an old and senile wind full of dissatisfaction and complaint. There was the dry faint click of falling pebbles.

The gun felt cold in my hand, covered with my cloak. I did not want to use it. But I did not want to die here on this silent pathway of vanished armies and caravans and kings.

A shaft of greenish moonlight crept down between the walls. Corin stood up.

"Twice now I have followed lies. Here I am met at last by truth."

I said, "I don't understand you."

"I thought I could escape the destruction. That was a lie. Then I thought I could return to share it. That too was a lie. Now I see the truth. Shandakor is dying. I fled from that dying, which is the end of the city and the end of my race. The shame of flight is on me and I can never go back."

"What will you do?"

"I will die here."

"And I?"

"Did you think," asked Corin softly, "that I would bring an alien creature in to watch the end of Shandakor?"

I moved first. I didn't know what weapons he might have, hidden under that dark red cloak. I threw myself over on the dusty rock. Something went past my head with a hiss and a rattle and a flame of light and then I cut the legs from under him and he fell down forward and I got on top of him, very fast.

He had vitality. I had to hit his head twice against the rock before I could take out of his hands the vicious little instrument of metal rods. I threw it far away. I could not feel any other weapons on him except a knife and I took that, too. Then I got up.

I said, "I will carry you to Shandakor."

He lay still, draped in the tumbled folds of his cloak. His breath made a harsh sighing in his throat. "So be it." And then he asked for water.

I went to where the skin lay and picked it up, thinking that there was perhaps a cupful left. I didn't hear him move. What he did was done very silently with a sharp-edged ornament. I brought him the water and it was already over. I tried to lift him up. His eyes looked at me with a curiously brilliant look. Then he whispered three words, in a language I didn't know, and died. I let him down again.

His blood had poured out across the dust. And even in the moonlight I could see that it was not the color of human blood.

I crouched there for a long while, overcome with a strange sickness. Then I reached out and pushed that red cowl back to bare his head. It was a beautiful head. I had never seen it. If I had, I would not have gone alone with Corin into the mountains. I would have understood many things if I had seen it and not for fame nor money would I have gone to Shandakor.

His skull was narrow and arched and the shaping of the bones was very fine. On that skull was a covering of short curling fibers that had an almost metallic luster in the moonlight, silvery and bright. They stirred under my hand, soft silken wires responding of themselves to an alien touch. And even as I took my hand away the luster faded from them and the texture changed.

When I touched them again they did not stir. Corin's ears were pointed and there were silvery tufts on the tips of them. On them and on his forearms and his breast were the faint, faint memories of scales, a powdering of shining dust across the golden skin. I looked at his teeth and they were not human either.

I know now why Corin had laughed when I told him that I studied men.

It was very still. I could hear the falling of pebbles and the little stones that rolled all lonely down the cliffs and the shift and whisper of dust in the settling cracks. The Wells of Karthedon were far away. Too far by several lifetimes for one man on foot with a cup of water.

I looked at the road that went steep and narrow on ahead. I looked at Corin. The wind was cold and the shaft of moonlight was growing thin. I did not want to stay alone in the dark with Corin.

I rose and went on along the road that led to Shandakor.

It was a long climb but not a long way. The road came out between two pinnacles of rock. Below that gateway, far below in the light of the little low moons that pass so swiftly over Mars, there was a mountain valley.

Once around that valley there were great peaks crowned with snow and crags of black and crimson where the flying lizards nested, the hawk-lizards with the red eyes. Below the crags there were forests, purple and green and gold, and a black tarn deep on the valley floor. But when I saw it it was dead. The peaks had fallen away and the forests were gone and the tarn was only a pit in the naked rock.

In the midst of that desolation stood a fortress city.

There were lights in it, soft lights of many colors. The outer walls stood up, black and massive, a barrier against the creeping dust, and within them was an island of life. The high towers were not ruined. The lights burned among them and there was movement in the streets.

A living city—and Corin had said that Shandakor was almost dead.

A rich and living city. I did not understand. But I knew one thing. Those who moved along the distant streets of Shandakor were not human.

I stood shivering in that windy pass. The bright towers of the city beckoned and there was something unnatural about all light-life in the deathly valley. And then I thought that human or not the people of Shandakor might sell me water and a beast to carry it and I could get away out of these mountains, back to the Wells.

The road broadened, winding down the slope. I walked in the middle of it, not expecting anything. And suddenly two men came out of nowhere and barred the way.

I yelled. I jumped backward with my heart pounding and the sweat pouring off me. I saw their broadswords glitter in the moonlight. And they laughed.

They were human. One was a tall red barbarian from Mekh, which lay to the east half around Mars. The other was a leaner browner man from Taarak, which was farther still. I was scared and angry and astonished and I asked a foolish question.

"What are you doing *here?*"

"We wait," said the man of Taarak. He made a circle with his arm to take in all the darkling slopes around the valley. "From Kesh and Shun, from all the countries of the Norlands and the Marches men have come, to wait. And you?"

"I'm lost," I said. "I'm an Earthman and I have no quarrel with anyone." I was still shaking but now it was with relief. I would not have to go to Shandakor. If there was a barbarian army gathered here it must have supplies and I could deal with them.

I told them what I needed. "I can pay for them, pay well."

They looked at each other.

"Very well. Come and you can bargain with the chief."

They fell in on either side of me. We walked three paces and then I was on my face in the dirt and they were all over me like two great wildcats. When they were finished they had everything I owned except the few articles of clothing for which they had no use. I got up again, wiping the blood from my mouth.

"For an outlander," said the man of Mekh, "you fight well." He chinked my money-bag up and down in his palm, feeling the weight of it, and then he handed me the leather bottle that hung at his side. "Drink," he told me. "That much I can't deny you. But our water must be carried a long way across these mountains and we have none to waste on Earthmen."

I was not proud. I emptied his bottle for him. And the man of Taarak said, smiling, "Go on to Shandakor. Perhaps they will give you water."

"But you've taken all my money!"

"They are rich in Shandakor. They don't need money. Go ask them for water."

They stood there, laughing at some secret joke of their own, and I did not like the sound of it. I could have killed them both and danced on their bodies but they had left me nothing but my bare hands to fight with. So presently I turned and went on and left them grinning in the dark behind me.

The road led down and out across the plain. I could feel eyes watching me, the eyes of the sentinels on the rounding slopes, piercing the dim moonlight. The walls of the city began to rise higher and higher. They hid everything but the top of one tall tower that had a queer squat globe on top of it. Rods of crystal projected from the globe. It revolved slowly and the rods sparkled with a sort of white fire that was just on the edge of seeing.

A causeway lifted toward the Western Gate. I mounted it, going very slowly, not wanting to go at all. And now I could see that the gate was open. Open—and this was a city under siege!

I stood still for some time, trying to puzzle out what meaning this might have—an army that did not attack and a city with open gates. I could not find a meaning. There were soldiers on the walls but they were lounging at their ease under the bright banners. Beyond the gate many people moved about but they were intent on their own affairs. I could not hear their voices.

I crept closer, closer still. Nothing happened. The sentries did not challenge me and no one spoke.

You know how necessity can force a man against his judgment and against his will?

I entered Shandakor.

3

THERE WAS an open space beyond the gate, a square large enough to hold an army. Around its edges were the stalls of merchants. Their canopies were of rich woven stuffs and the wares they sold were such things as have not been seen on Mars for more centuries than men can remember.

There were fruits and rare furs, the long-lost dyes that never fade, furnishings carved from vanished woods. There were spices and wines and exquisite cloths. In one place a merchant from the far south offered a ceremonial rug woven from the long bright hair of virgins. And it was new.

These merchants were all human. The nationalities of some of them I knew. Others I could guess at from traditional accounts. Some were utterly unknown.

Of the throngs that moved about among the stalls, quite a number were human also. There were merchant princes come to barter and there were companies of slaves on their way to the auction block. But the others . . .

I stayed where I was, pressed into a shadowy corner by the gate, and the chill that was on me was not all from the night wind.

The golden-skinned silver-crested lords of Shandakor I knew well enough from Corin. I say lords because that is how they bore themselves, walking proudly in their own place, attended by human slaves. And the humans who were not slaves made way for them and were most deferential as though they knew that they were greatly favored to be allowed inside the city at all. The women of Shandakor were very beautiful, slim golden sprites with their bright eyes and pointed ears.

And there were others. Slender creatures with great wings, some who were lithe and furred, some who were hairless and ugly and moved with a sinuous gliding, some so strangely shaped and colored that I could not even guess at their possible evolution.

The lost races of Mars. The ancient races, of whose pride and power nothing was left but the half-forgotten tales of old men in the farthest corners of the planet. Even I, who had made the anthropological history of Mars my business, had never heard of them except as the distorted shapes of legend, as satyrs and giants used to be known on Earth.

Yet here they were in gorgeous trappings, served by naked humans whose fetters were made of precious metals. And before them too the merchants drew aside and bowed.

The lights burned, many-colored—not the torches and cressets of the Mars I knew but cool radiances that fell from crystal globes. The walls of the buildings that rose around the market-place were faced with rare veined marbles and the fluted towers that crowned them were inlaid with turquoise and cinnabar, with amber and jade and the wonderful corals of the southern oceans.

The splendid robes and the naked bodies moved in a swirling pattern about the square. There was buying and selling and I could see the mouths of the people open and shut. The mouths of the women laughed. But in all that crowded place there was no sound. No voice, no scuff of sandal, no chink of mail. There was only silence, the utter stillness of deserted places.

I began to understand why there was no need to shut the gates. No superstitious barbarian would venture himself into a city peopled by living phantoms.

And I—I was civilized. I was, in my non-mechanical way, a scientist. And had I not been trapped by my need for water and supplies I would have run away right out of the valley. But I had no place to run to and so I stayed and sweated and gagged on the acrid taste of fear.

What were these creatures that made no sound? Ghosts-images—dreams? The human and the non-human, the ancient, the proud, the lost and forgotten who were so insanely present—did they have some subtle form of life I knew nothing about? Could they see me as I saw them? Did they have thought and volition of their own?

It was the solidity of them, the intense and perfectly prosaic business in which they were engaged. Ghosts do not barter. They do not hang jeweled necklets upon their women nor argue about the price of a studded harness.

The solidity and the silence—that was the worst of it. If there had been one small living sound . . .

A dying city, Corin had said. *The days are running out.* What if they had run out? What if I were here in this massive pile of stone with all its countless rooms and streets and galleries and hidden ways, alone with the lights and the soundless phantoms?

Pure terror is a nasty thing. I had it then.

I began to move, very cautiously, along the wall. I wanted to get away from that market-place. One of the hairless gliding non-humans was bartering for a female slave. The girl was shrieking. I could see every drawn muscle in her face, the spasmodic working of her throat. Not the faintest sound came out.

I found a street that paralleled the wall. I went along it, catching glimpses of people—human people—inside the lighted buildings. Now and then men passed me and I hid from them. There was still no sound. I was careful how I set my feet. Somehow I had the idea that if I made a noise something terrible would happen.

A group of merchants came toward me. I stepped back into an

archway and suddenly from behind me there came three spangled women of the serais. I was caught.

I did not want those silent laughing women to touch me. I leaped back toward the street and the merchants paused, turning their heads. I thought that they had seen me. I hesitated and the women came on. Their painted eyes shone and their red lips glistened. The ornaments on their bodies flashed. They walked straight into me.

I made noise then, all I had in my lungs. And the women passed through me. They spoke to the merchants and the merchants laughed. They went off together down the street. They hadn't seen me. They hadn't heard me. And when I got in their way I was no more than a shadow. They passed through me.

I sat down on the stones of the street and tried to think. I sat for a long time. Men and women walked through me as through the empty air. I sought to remember any sudden pain, as of an arrow in the back that might have killed me between two seconds, so that I hadn't known about it. It seemed more likely that I should be the ghost than the other way around.

I couldn't remember. My body felt solid to my hands as did the stones I sat on. They were cold and finally the cold got me up and sent me on again. There was no reason to hide any more. I walked down the middle of the street and I got used to not turning aside.

I came to another wall, running at right angles back into the city. I followed that and it curved around gradually until I found myself back at the market-place, at the inner end of it. There was a gateway, with the main part of the city beyond it, and the wall continued. The non-humans passed back and forth through the gate but no human did except the slaves. I realized then that all this section was a ghetto for the humans who came to Shandakor with the caravans.

I remembered how Corin had felt about me. And I wondered— granted that I were still alive and that some of the people of Shandakor were still on the same plane as myself—how they would feel about me if I trespassed in their city.

There was a fountain in the market-place. The water sprang up sparkling in the colored light and filled a wide basin of carved stone. Men and women were drinking from it. I went to the fountain but when I put my hands in it all I felt was a dry basin filled with dust. I lifted my hands and let the dust trickle from them. I could see it clearly.

But I saw the water too. A child leaned over and splashed it and it wetted the garments of the people. They struck the child and he cried and there was no sound.

I went on through the gate that was forbidden to the human race.

The avenues were wide. There were trees and flowers, wide parks and garden villas, great buildings as graceful as they were tall. A wise proud city, ancient in culture but not decayed, as beautiful as Athens but rich and strange, with a touch of the alien in every line of it. Can you think what it was like to walk in that city, among the silent throngs that were not human—to see the glory of it, that was not human either?

The towers of jade and cinnabar, the golden minarets, the lights and the colored silks, the enjoyment and the strength. And the people of Shandakor! No matter how far their souls have gone they will never forgive me.

How long I wandered I don't know. I had almost lost my fear in wonder at what I saw. And then, all at once in that deathly stillness, I heard a sound—the quick, soft scuffing of sandaled feet.

4

I STOPPED where I was, in the middle of a plaza. The tall silver-crested ones drank wine under canopies of dusky blooms and in the center a score of winged girls as lovely as swans danced a slow strange measure that was more like flight than dancing. I looked all around. There were many people. How could you tell which one had made a noise?

Silence.

I turned and ran across the marble paving. I ran hard and then suddenly I stopped again, listening. *Scuff-scuff*—no more than a whisper, very light and swift. I spun around but it was gone. The soundless people walked and the dancers wove and shifted, spreading their white wings.

Someone was watching me. Some one of those indifferent shadow was not a shadow.

I went on. Wide streets led off from the plaza. I took one of them. I tried the trick of shifting pace and two or three times I caught the echo of other steps than mine. Once I knew it was deliberate. Whoever followed me slipped silently among the noiseless crowd, blending with them, protected by them, only making a show of footsteps now and then to goad me.

I spoke to that mocking presence. I talked to it and listened to my own voice ringing hollow from the walls. The groups of people ebbed and flowed around me and there was no answer.

I tried making sudden leaps here and there among the passersby with my arms outspread. But all I caught was empty air. I wanted a place to hide and there was none.

The street was long. I went its length and the someone followed me. There were many buildings, all lighted and populous and deathly still. I thought of trying to hide in the buildings but I could not bear to be closed in between walls with those people who were not people.

I came into a great circle, where a number of avenues met around the very tall tower I had seen with the revolving globe on top of it. I hesitated, not knowing which way to go. Someone was sobbing and I realized that it was myself, laboring to breathe. Sweat ran into the corners of my mouth and it was cold, and bitter.

A pebble dropped at my feet with a brittle *click*.

I bolted out across the square. Four or five times, without reason, like a rabbit caught in the open, I changed course and fetched up with my back against an ornamental pillar. From somewhere there came a sound of laughter.

I began to yell. I don't know what I said. Finally I stopped and there was only the silence and the passing throngs, who did not see nor hear me. And now it seemed to me that the silence was full of whispers just below the threshold of hearing.

A second pebble clattered off the pillar above my head. Another stung my body. I sprang away from the pillar. There was laughter and I ran.

There were infinities of streets, all glowing with color. There were many faces, strange faces, and robes blown out on a night wind, litters with scarlet curtains and beautiful cars like chariots drawn by beasts. They flowed past me like smoke, without sound, without substance, and the laughter pursued me, and I ran.

Four men of Shandakor came toward me. I plunged through them *but their bodies opposed mine, their hands caught me and I could see their eyes, their black shining eyes, looking at me. . . .*

I struggled briefly and then it was suddenly very dark.

The darkness caught me up and took me somewhere. Voices talked far away. One of them was a light young shiny sort of voice. It matched the laughter that had haunted me down the streets. I hated it.

I hated it so much that I fought to get free of the black river that was carrying me. There was a vertiginous whirling of light and sound and stubborn shadow and then things steadied down and I was ashamed of myself for having passed out.

I was in a room. It was fairly large, very beautiful, very old, the first place I had seen in Shandakor that showed real age—Martian age, that runs back before history had begun on Earth. The floor, of some magnificent somber stone the color of a moonless night, and the pale slim pillars that upheld the arching roof all showed the hollowings and smoothnesses of centuries. The wall paintings had dimmed and softened and the rugs that burned in pools of color on that dusky floor were worn as thin as silk.

There were men and women in that room, the alien folk of Shandakor. But these breathed and spoke and were alive. One of them, a girl-child with slender thighs and little pointed breasts, leaned against a pillar close beside me. Her black eyes watched me, full of dancing lights. When she saw that I was awake again she smiled and flicked a pebble at my feet.

I got up. I wanted to get that golden body between my hands and make it scream. And she said in High Martian, "Are you a human? I have never seen one before close to."

A man in a dark robe said, "Be still, Duani." He came and stood before me. He did not seem to be armed but others were and I remembered Corin's little weapon. I got hold of myself and did none of the things I wanted to do.

"What are you doing here?" asked the man in the dark robe.

I told him about myself and Corin, omitting only the fight that he and I had had before be died, and I told him how the hillmen had robbed me.

"They sent me here," I finished, "to ask for water."

Someone made a harsh humorless sound. The man before me said, "They were in a jesting mood."

"Surely you can spare some water and a beast!"

"Our beasts were slaughtered long ago. And as for water . . ."

He paused, then asked bitterly, "Don't you understand? We are dying here of thirst!"

I looked at him and at the she-imp called Duani and the others. "You don't show any signs of it," I said.

"You saw how the human tribes have gathered like wolves upon the hills. What do you think they wait for? A year ago they found and cut the buried aqueduct that brought water into Shandakor from the polar cap. All they needed then was patience. And their time is very near. The store we had in the cisterns is almost gone."

A certain anger at their submissiveness made me say, "Why do you stay here and die like mice bottled up in a jar? You could have fought your way out. I've seen your weapons.

"Our weapons are old and we are very few. And suppose that some of us did survive—tell me again, Earthman, how did Corin fare in the world of men?" He shook his head. "Once we were great and Shandakor was mighty. The human tribes of half a world paid tribute to us. We are only the last poor shadow of our race but we will not beg from men!"

"Besides," said Duani softly, "where else could we live but in Shandakor?"

"What about the others?" I asked. "The silent ones."

"They are the past," said the dark-robed man and his voice rang like a distant flare of trumpets.

Still I did not understand. I did not understand at all. But before I could ask more questions a man came up and said, "Rhul, he will have to die."

The tufted tips of Duani's ears quivered and her crest of silver curls came almost erect.

"No, Rhul!" she cried. "At least not right away."

There was a clamor from the others, chiefly in a rapid angular speech that must have predated all the syllables of men. And the one who had spoken before to Rhul repeated, "He will have to die! He has no place here. And we can't spare water."

"I'll share mine with him," said Duani, "for a while."

I didn't want any favors from her and said so. "I came here after supplies. You haven't any, so I'll go away again. It's as simple as that." I couldn't buy from the barbarians, but I might make shift to steal.

Rhul shook his head. "I'm afraid not. We are only a handful. For years our single defense has been the living ghosts of our past who walk the streets, the shadows who man the walls. The barbarians believe in enchantments. If you were to enter Shandakor and leave it again alive the barbarians would know that the enchantment cannot kill. They would not wait any longer."

Angrily, because I was afraid, I said, "I can't see what difference that would make. You're going to die in a short while anyway."

"But in our own way, Earthman, and in our own time. Perhaps, being human, you can't understand that. It is a question of pride. The oldest race of Mars will end well, as it began."

He turned away with a small nod of the head that said *kill him*—as easily as that. And I saw the ugly little weapons rise.

5

THERE WAS a split second then that seemed like a year. I thought of many things but none of them were any good. It was a devil of a place to die without even a human hand to help me under. And then Duani flung her arms around me.

"You're all so full of dying and big thoughts!" she yelled at them. "And you're all paired off or so old you can't do anything but think! What about *me*? I don't have anyone to talk to and I'm sick of wandering alone, thinking how I'm going to die! Let me have him just for a little while? I told you I'd share my water."

On Earth a child might talk that way about a stray dog. And it is written in an old Book that a live dog is better than a dead lion. I hoped they would let her keep me.

They did. Rhul looked at Duani with a sort of weary compassion and lifted his hand. "Wait," he said to the men with the weapons. I have thought how this human may be useful to us. We have so little time left now that it is a pity to waste any of it, yet much of it must be used up in tending the machine. He could do that labor—and a man can keep alive on very little water."

The others thought that over. Some of them dissented violently, not so much on the grounds of water as that it was unthinkable that a human should intrude on the last days of Shandakor. Corin had said the same thing. But Rhul was an old man. The tufts of his pointed ears were colorless as glass and his face was graven deep with years and wisdom had distilled in him its bitter brew.

"A human of our own world, yes. But this man is of Earth and the men of Earth will come to be the new rulers of Mars as we were the old. And Mars will love them no better than she did us because they are as alien as we. So it is not unfitting that he should see us out."

They had to be content with that. I think they were already so close to the end that they did not really care. By ones and twos they left as though already they had wasted too much time away from the wonders that there were in the streets outside. Some of the men still held the weapons on me and others went and brought precious chains such as the human slaves had worn—shackles, so that I should not escape. They put them on me and Duani laughed.

"Come," said Rhul, "and I will show you the machine."

He led me from the room and up a winding stair. There were tall embrasures and looking through them I discovered that we were in the base of the very high tower with the globe. They must have carried me back to it after Duani had chased me with her laughter and her pebbles. I looked out over the glowing streets, so full of splendor and of silence, and asked Rhul why there were no ghosts inside the tower.

"You have seen the globe with the crystal rods?"

"Yes."

"We are under the shadow of its core. There had to be some retreat for us into reality. Otherwise we would lose the meaning of the dream."

The winding stair went up and up. The chain between my ankles clattered musically. Several times I tripped on it and fell.

"Never mind," Duani said. "You'll grow used to it."

We came at last into a circular room high in the tower. And I stopped and stared.

Most of the space in that room was occupied by a web of metal girders that supported a great gleaming shaft. The shaft disappeared upward through the roof. It was not tall but very massive, revolving slowly and quietly. There were traps, presumably for access to the offset shaft and the cogs that turned it. A ladder led to a trap in the roof.

All the visible metal was sound with only a little surface corrosion. What the alloy was I don't know and when I asked Rhul he only smiled rather sadly. "Knowledge is found," he said, "only to be lost again. Even we of Shandakor forget."

Every bit of that enormous structure had been shaped and polished and fitted into place by hand. Nearly all the Martian peoples work in metal. They seem to have a genius for it and while they are not and apparently never have been mechanical, as some of our races are on Earth, they find many uses for metal that we have never thought of.

But this before me was certainly the high point of the metal-workers' craft. When I saw what was down below, the beautifully simple power plant and the rotary drive set-up with fewer moving parts than I would have thought possible, I was even more respectful. "How old is it?" I asked and again Rhul shook his head.

"Several thousand years ago there is a record of the yearly Hosting of the Shadows and it was not the first." He motioned me to follow him up the ladder, bidding Duani sternly to remain where she was. She came anyway.

There was a railed platform open to the universe and directly above it swung the mighty globe with its crystal rods that gleamed so strangely. Shandakor lay beneath us, a tapestry of many colors, bright and still, and out along the dark sides of the valley the tribesmen waited for the light to die.

"When there is no one left to tend the machine it will stop in time and then the men who have hated us so long will take what they want of Shandakor. Only fear has kept them out this long. The riches of half a world flowed through these streets and much of it remained."

He looked up at the globe. "Yes," he said, "we had knowledge. More, I think, than any other race of Mars."

"But you wouldn't share it with the humans."

Rhul smiled. "Would you give little children weapons to destroy you? We gave men better ploughshares and brighter ornaments and if they invented a machine we did not take it from them. But we did not tempt and burden them with knowledge that was not their own. They were content to make war with sword and spear and so they had more pleasure and less killing and the world was not torn apart."

"And you—how did you make war?"

"We defended our city. The human tribes had nothing that we coveted, so there was no reason to fight them except in self-defense. When we did we won." He paused. "The other non-human races were more stupid or less fortunate. They perished long ago."

He turned again to his explanations of the machine. "It draws its power directly from the sun. Some of the solar energy is converted and stored within the globe to serve as the light-source. Some is sent down to turn the shaft."

"What if it should stop," Duani said, "while we're still alive?" She shivered, looking out over the beautiful streets.

"It won't—not if the Earthman wishes to live."

"What would I have to gain by stopping it?" I demanded.

"Nothing. And that," said Rhul, "is why I trust you. As long as the globe turns you are safe from the barbarians. After we are gone you will have the pick of the loot of Shandakor."

How I was going to get away with it afterward he did not tell me.

He motioned me down the ladder again but I asked him, "What is the globe, Rhul? How does it make the—the Shadows?"

He frowned. "I can only tell you what has become, I'm afraid, mere traditional knowledge. Our wise men studied deeply into the properties of light. They learned that light has a definite effect upon solid matter and they believed, because of that effect, that stone and metal and crystalline things retain a 'memory' of all that they have 'seen.' Why this should be I do not know."

I didn't try to explain to him the quantum theory and the photoelectric effect nor the various experiments of Einstein and Millikan and the men who followed them. I didn't know them well enough myself and the old High Martian is deficient in such terminology.

I only said, "The wise men of my world also know that the impact of light tears away tiny particles from the substance it strikes."

I was beginning to get a glimmering of the truth. Light-patterns "cut" in the electrons of metal and stone—sound-patterns cut in unlikely looking mediums of plastic, each needing only the proper "needle" to recreate the recorded melody or the recorded picture.

"They constructed the globe," said Rhul. "I do not know how many generations that required nor how many failures they must have had. But they found at last the invisible light that makes the stones give up their memories."

In other words they had found their needle. What wave-length or combination of wave-lengths in the electromagnetic spectrum flowed out from those crystal rods, there was no way for me to know. But where they probed the walls and the paving blocks of Shandakor they scanned the hidden patterns that were buried in them and brought them forth again in form and color—as the electron needle brings forth whole symphonies from a little ridged disc.

How they had achieved sequence and selectivity was another matter. Rhul said something about the "memories" having different lengths. Perhaps he meant depth of penetration. The stones of Shandakor were ages old and the outer surfaces would have worn away. The earliest impressions would be gone altogether or at least have become fragmentary and extremely shallow.

Perhaps the scanning beams could differentiate between the overlapping layers of impressions by that fraction of a micron difference in depth. Photons only penetrate so far into any given substance but if that substance is constantly growing less in thickness the photons would have the effect of going deeper. I imagine the globe was accurate in centuries or numbers of centuries, not in years.

However it was, the Shadows of a golden past walked the streets of Shandakor and the last men of the race waited quietly for death, remembering their glory.

Rhul took me below again and showed me what my tasks would be, chiefly involving a queer sort of lubricant and a careful watch over the power leads. I would have to spend most of my time there but not all of it. During the free periods, Duani might take me where she would.

The old man went away. Duani leaned herself against a girder and studied me with intense interest. "How are you called?" she asked.

"John Ross."

"JonRoss," she repeated and smiled. She began to walk around me, touching my hair, inspecting my arms and chest, taking a child's delight in discovering all the differences there were between herself and what we call a human. And that was the beginning of my captivity.

6

THERE WERE days and nights, scant food and scanter water. There was Duani. And there was Shandakor. I lost my fear. And whether I lived to occupy the Chair or not, this was something to have seen.

Duani was my guide. I was tender of my duties because my neck depended on them but there was time to wander in the streets, to watch the crowded pageant that was not and sense the stillness and the desolation that were so cruelly real.

I began to get the feel of what this alien culture had been like and how it had dominated half a world without the need of conquest.

In a Hall of Government, built of white marble and decorated with wall friezes of austere magnificence, I watched the careful choosing and the crowning of a king. I saw the places of learning. I saw the young men trained for war as fully as they were instructed in the arts of peace. I saw the pleasure gardens, the theaters, the forums, the sporting fields—and I saw the places of work, where the men and women of Shandakor coaxed beauty from their looms and forges to trade for the things they wanted from the human world.

The human slaves were brought by their own kind to be sold, and they seemed to be well treated, as one treats a useful animal in which one has invested money. They had their work to do but it was only a small part of the work of the city.

The things that could be had nowhere else on Mars—the tools, the textiles, the fine work in metal and precious stones, the glass and porcelain—were fashioned by the people of Shandakor and they were proud of their skill. Their scientific knowledge they kept entirely to themselves, except what concerned agriculture or medicine or better ways of building drains and houses.

They were the lawgivers, the teachers. And the humans took all they would give and hated them for it. How long it had taken these people to attain such a degree of civilization Duani could not tell me. Neither could old Rhul.

"It is certain that we lived in communities, had a form of civil government, a system of numbers and written speech, before the human tribes. There are traditions of an earlier race than ours, from whom we learned these things. Whether or not this is true I do not know."

In its prime Shandakor had been a vast and flourishing city with countless thousands of inhabitants. Yet I could see no signs of poverty or crime. I couldn't even find a prison.

"Murder was punishable by death," said Rhul, "but it was most infrequent. Theft was for slaves. We did not stoop to it." He watched my face, smiling a little acid smile. "That startles you—a great city without suffering or crime or places of punishment."

I had to admit that it did. "Elder race or not, how did you manage to do it? I'm a student of cultures, both here and on my own world. I know all the usual patterns of development and I've read all the theories about them—but Shandakor doesn't fit any of them."

Rhul's smile deepened. "You are human," he said. "Do you wish the truth?"

"Of course."

"Then I will tell you. We developed the faculty of reason."

For a moment I thought he was joking. "Come," I said, "man is a reasoning being—on Earth the only reasoning being."

"I do not know of Earth," he answered courteously. "But on Mars man has always said, 'I reason, I am above the beasts because I reason.' And he has been very proud of himself because he could reason. It is the mark of his humanity. Being convinced that reason operates automatically within him he orders his life and his government upon emotion and superstition.

"He hates and fears and believes, not with reason but because he is told to by other men or by tradition. He does one thing and says another and his reason teaches him no difference between fact and falsehood. His bloodiest wars are fought for the merest whim—and that is why we did not give him weapons. His greatest follies appear to him the highest wisdom, his basest betrayals become noble acts—and that is why we could not teach him justice. We learned to reason. Man only learned to talk."

I understood then why the human tribes had hated the men of Shandakor. I said angrily, "Perhaps that is so on Mars. But only reasoning minds can develop great technologies and we humans of Earth have outstripped yours a million times. All right, you know or knew some things we haven't learned yet, in optics and some branches of electronics and perhaps in metallurgy. But . . ."

I went on to tell him all the things we had that Shandakor did not. "You never went beyond the beast of burden and the simple wheel. We achieved flight long ago. We have conquered space and the planets. We'll go on to conquer the stars!"

Rhul nodded. "Perhaps we were wrong. We remained here and conquered ourselves." He looked out toward the slopes where the barbarian army waited and he sighed. "In the end it is all the same."

Days and nights and Duani, bringing me food, sharing her water, asking questions, taking me through the city. The only thing she would not show me was something they called the Place of Sleep. "I shall be there soon enough," she said and shivered.

"How long?" I asked. It was an ugly thing to say.

"We are not told. Rhul watches the level in the cisterns and when it's time . . ." She made a gesture with her hands. "Let us go up on the wall."

We went up among the ghostly soldiery and the phantom banners. Outside there were darkness and death and the coming of death. Inside there were light and beauty, the last proud blaze of Shandakor under the shadow of its doom. There was an eerie magic in it that had begun to tell on me. I watched Duani. She leaned against the parapet, looking outward. The wind ruffled her silver crest, pressed her garments close against her body. Her eyes were full of moonlight and I could not read them. Then I saw that there were tears.

I put my arm around her shoulders. She was only a child, an alien child, not of my race or breed.

"JonRoss."

"Yes?"

"There are so many things I will never know."

It was the first time I had touched her. Those curious curls stirred under my fingers, warm and alive. The tips of her pointed ears were soft as a kitten's.

"Duani."

"What?"

"I don't know . . ."

I kissed her. She drew back and gave me a startled look from those black brilliant eyes and suddenly I stopped thinking that she was a child and I forgot that she was not human and—I didn't care.

"Duani, listen. You don't have to go to the Place of Sleep."

She looked at me, her cloak spread out upon the night wind, her hands against my chest.

"There's a whole world out there to live in. And if you aren't happy there I'll take you to my world, to Earth. There isn't any reason why you have to die!"

Still she looked at me and did not speak. In the streets below the silent throngs went by and the towers glowed with many colors. Duani's gaze moved slowly to the darkness beyond the wall, to the barren valley and the hostile rocks.

"No."

"Why not? Because of Rhul, because of all this talk of pride and race?"

"Because of truth. Corin learned it."

I didn't want to think about Corin. "He was alone. You're not. You'd never be alone."

She brought her hands up and laid them on my cheeks very gently. "That green star, that is your world. Suppose it were to vanish and you were the last of all the men of Earth. Suppose you lived with me in Shandakor forever—would you not be alone?"

"It wouldn't matter if I had you."

She shook her bead. "It would matter. And our two races are as far apart as the stars. We would have nothing to share between us."

Remembering what Rhul had told me I flared up and said some angry things. She let me say them and then she smiled. "It is none of that, JonRoss." She turned to look out over the city. "This is my place and no other. When it is gone I must be gone too."

Quite suddenly I hated Shandakor.

I didn't sleep much after that. Every time Duani left me I was afraid she might never come back. Rhul would tell me nothing and I didn't dare to question him too much. The hours rushed by like seconds and Duani was happy and I was not. My shackles had magnetic locks. I couldn't break them and I couldn't cut the chains.

One evening Duani came to me with something in her face and in the way she moved that told me the truth long before I could make her put it into words. She clung to me, not wanting to talk, but at last she said, "Today there was a casting of lots and the first hundred have gone to the Place of Sleep."

"It is the beginning, then."

She nodded. "Every day there will be another hundred until all are gone."

I couldn't stand it any longer. I thrust her away and stood up. "You know where the 'keys' are. Get these chains off me!"

She shook her head. "Let us not quarrel now, JonRoss. Come. I want to walk in the city."

We had quarreled more than once, and fiercely. She would not leave Shandakor and I couldn't take her out by force as long as I was chained. And I was not to be released until everyone but Rhul had entered the Place of Sleep and the last page of that long history had been written.

I walked with her among the dancers and the slaves and the bright-cloaked princes. There were no temples in Shandakor. If they worshipped anything it was beauty and to that their whole city was a shrine. Duani's eyes were rapt and there was a remoteness on her now.

I held her hand and looked at the towers of turquoise and cinnabar, the pavings of rose quartz and marble, the walls of pink and white and deep red coral, and to me they were hideous. The ghostly crowds, the mockery of life, the phantom splendors of the past were hideous, a drug, a snare.

"The faculty of reason!" I thought and saw no reason in any of it.

I looked up to where the great globe turned and turned against the sky, keeping these mockeries alive. "Have you ever seen the city as it is—without the Shadows?"

"No. I think only Rhul, who is the oldest, remembers it that way. I think it must have been very lonely. Even then there were less than three thousand of us left."

It must indeed have been lonely. They must have wanted the Shadows as much to people the empty streets as to fend off the enemies who believed in magic.

I kept looking at the globe. We walked for a long time. And then I said, "I must go back to the tower."

She smiled at me very tenderly. "Soon you will be free of the tower—and of these." She touched the chains. "No, don't be sad, JonRoss. You will remember me and Shandakor as one remembers a dream." She held up her face, that was so lovely and so unlike the meaty faces of human women, and her eyes were full of somber lights. I kissed her and then I caught her up in my arms and carried her back to the tower.

In that room, where the great shaft turned, I told her, "I have to tend the things below. Go up onto the platform, Duani, where you can see all Shandakor. I'll be with you soon."

I don't know whether she had some hint of what was in my mind or whether it was only the imminence of parting that made her look at me as she did. I thought she was going to speak but she did not, climbing the ladder obediently. I watched her slender golden body vanish upward. Then I went into the chamber below.

There was a heavy metal bar there that was part of a manual control for regulating the rate of turn. I took it off its pin. Then I closed the simple switches on the power plant. I tore out all the leads and smashed the connections with the bar. I did what damage I could to the cogs and the offset shaft. I worked very fast. Then I went up into the main chamber again. The great shaft was still turning but slowly, ever more slowly.

There was a cry from above me and I saw Duani. I sprang up the ladder, thrusting her back onto the platform. The globe moved heavily of its own momentum. Soon it would stop but the white fires still flickered in the crystal rods. I climbed up onto the railing, clinging to a strut. The chains on my wrists and ankles made it hard but I could reach. Duani tried to pull me down. I think she was screaming. I hung on and smashed the crystal rods with the bar, as many as I could.

There was no more motion, no more light. I got down on the platform again and dropped the bar. Duani had forgotten me. She was looking at the city.

The lights of many colors that had burned there were burning still but they were old and dim, cold embers without radiance. The towers of jade and turquoise rose up against the little moons and they were broken and cracked with time and there was no glory in them. They were desolate and very sad. The night lay clotted around their feet. The streets, the plazas and the market-squares were empty, their marble paving blank and bare. The soldiers had gone from the walls of Shandakor, with their banners and their bright mail, and there was no longer any movement anywhere within the gates.

Duani let out one small voiceless cry. And as though in answer to it, suddenly from the darkness of the valley and the slopes beyond there rose a thin fierce howling as of wolves.

"Why?" she whispered. "*Why?*" She turned to me. Her face was pitiful. I caught her to me.

"I couldn't let you die! Not for dreams and visions, nothing. Look, Duani. Look at Shandakor." I wanted to force her to understand. "Shandakor is broken and ugly and forlorn. It is a dead city—but you're alive. There are many cities but only one life for you."

Still she looked at me and it was hard to meet her eyes. She said, "We knew all that, JonRoss."

"Duani, you're a child, you've only a child's way of thought. Forget the past and think of tomorrow. We can get through the barbarians. Corin did. And after that . . ."

"And after that you would still be human—and I would not."

From below us in the dim and empty streets there came a sound of lamentation. I tried to hold her but she slipped out from between my hands. "And I am glad that you are human," she whispered. "You will never understand what you have done."

And she was gone before I could stop her, down into the tower.

I went after her. Down the endless winding stairs with my chains clattering between my feet, out into the streets, the dark and broken and deserted streets of Shandakor. I called her name and her golden body went before me, fleet and slender, distant and more distant. The chains dragged upon my feet and the night took her away from me.

I stopped. The whelming silence rushed smoothly over me and I was bitterly afraid of this dark dead Shandakor that I did not know. I called again to Duani and then I began to search for her in the shattered shadowed streets. I know now how long it must have been before I found her.

For when I found her, she was with the others. The last people of Shandakor, the men and the women, the women first, were walking silently in a long line toward a low flat-roofed building that I knew without telling was the Place of Sleep.

They were going to die and there was no pride in their faces now. There was a sickness in them, a sickness and a hurt in their eyes as they moved heavily forward, not looking, not wanting to look at the sordid ancient streets that I had stripped of glory.

"Duani!" I called, and ran forward but she did not turn in her place in the line. And I saw that she was weeping.

Rhul turned toward me, and his look had a weary contempt that was bitterer than a curse. "Of what use, after all, to kill you now?"

"But I did this thing! *I* did it!"

"You are only human."

The long line shuffled on and Duani's little feet were closer to that final doorway. Rhul looked upward at the sky. "There is still time before the sunrise. The women at least will be spared the indignity of spears."

"Let me go with her!"

I tried to follow her, to take my place in line. And the weapon in

Rhul's hand moved and there was the pain and I lay as Corin had lain while they went silently on into the Place of Sleep.

The barbarians found me when they came, still half doubtful, into the city after dawn. I think they were afraid of me. I think they feared me as a wizard who had somehow destroyed all the folk of Shandakor.

For they broke my chains and healed my wounds and later they even gave me out of the loot of Shandakor the only thing I wanted—a bit of porcelain, shaped like the head of a young girl.

I sit in the Chair that I craved at the University and my name is written on the roll of the discoverers. I am eminent, I am respectable—I, who murdered the glory of a race.

Why didn't I go after Duani into the Place of Sleep? I could have crawled! I could have dragged myself across those stones. And I wish to God I had. I wish that I had died with Shandakor!

All Cats Are Gray

by Andre Norton

Andre Norton is one of two of our contributors who has had an award named after her. The Science Fiction Writers of America started giving the Andre Norton Award for outstanding young adult and middle grade fiction that includes speculative content. The award, the brainchild of another wonderful female science fiction writer, Catherine Asaro, came into existence in 2006, a year after Norton's death at the age of ninety-three. The award's website states the reason that SFWA named the award for Norton:

> Ms. Norton's work shaped generations of young science fiction and fantasy fans, setting a high standard for excellence in young adult fiction.

In cold hard print, that seems like such an understatement. Scratch most modern science fiction writers, you'll find that Andre Norton inspired them. I spent my twelfth summer reading everything that my small town library had by her. I was not alone. Other contributors to this anthology, including C.J. Cherryh and Lois McMaster Bujold, cite her as a major influence. As do Mercedes Lackey, Joan D. Vinge, Tanya Huff, Charles de Lint and countless others.

I deliberately put Andre Norton's story after Leigh Brackett's. Andre Norton cited Leigh Brackett as a major influence. Lois McMaster Bujold, whose story follows this one, cites Andre Norton as a major influence. The generations influence each other, and as long as a writer's work remains in print, her work will continue to inspire young writers.

Even though later readers remember Andre Norton for her fantasy, I read her science fiction. I particularly loved The Time Traders *series. Like so many others, I thought she was a male writer, and did not discover she was female until I saw a picture of her on the back cover of an edition of* Witch World. *(Yes, it was a surprise. That's why I remember it.)*

She was born Alice Mary Norton in 1912, but in 1934, legally changed her name to Andre Alice Norton. She mentioned several reasons for the name change over her long life, but the main one seems to be that she wanted to write boys adventure fiction, and in 1934, she believed it would be easier to sell to that market if she had a male name. She did not become a science fiction writer for nearly twenty years after the 1934 publication of her first novel.

In her lifetime, she published more than three hundred novels in multiple genres and under several pen names. She also published at least one hundred short stories. She became the first woman named Grand Master by SFWA, the first woman named the Gandalf Grand Master of Fantasy, and the first woman inducted into The Science Fiction and Fantasy Hall of Fame. Her awards and award nominations are too numerous to mention in this short introduction.

"All Cats Are Gray" is one of my favorite Andre Norton short stories. It works well here, being space opera as well as a delightful tale that wouldn't be out of place in a young adult anthology.

❉ ❉ ❉

STEENA OF THE SPACEWAYS—that sounds just like a corny title for one of the Stellar-Vedo spreads. I ought to know, I've tried my hand at writing enough of them. Only this Steena was no glamour babe. She was as colorless as a Lunar plant—even the hair netted down to her skull had a sort of grayish cast and I never saw her but once draped in anything but a shapeless and baggy gray space-all.

Steena was strictly background stuff and that is where she mostly spent her free hours—in the smelly smoky background corners of any stellar-port dive frequented by free spacers. If you really looked for her you could spot her—just sitting there listening to the talk—listening and remembering. She didn't open her own mouth often. But when she did spacers had learned to listen. And the lucky few who heard her rare spoken words—these will never forget Steena.

She drifted from port to port. Being an expert operator on the big calculators she found jobs wherever she cared to stay for a time. And she came to be something like the master-minded machines she tended—smooth, gray, without much personality of her own.

But it was Steena who told Bub Nelson about the Jovan moon-rites—and her warning saved Bub's life six months later. It was Steena who identified the piece of stone Keene Clark was passing around a table one night, rightly calling it unworked Slitite. That started a rush that made ten fortunes overnight for men who were down to their last jets. And, last of all, she cracked the case of the Empress of Mars.

All the boys who had profited by her queer store of knowledge and her photographic memory tried at one time or another to balance the scales. But she wouldn't take so much as a cup of Canal water at their expense, let alone the credits they tried to push on her. Bub Nelson was the only one who got around her refusal. It was he who brought her Bat.

About a year after the Jovan affair he walked into the Free Fall one night and dumped Bat down on her table. Bat looked at Steena and growled. She looked calmly back at him and nodded once. From then on they traveled together—the thin gray woman and the big gray tom-cat. Bat learned to know the inside of more stellar bars than even most spacers visit in their lifetimes. He developed a liking for Vernal juice, drank it neat and quick, right out of a glass. And he was always at home on any table where Steena elected to drop him.

This is really the story of Steena, Bat, Cliff Moran and the Empress of Mars, a story which is already a legend of the spaceways. And it's a damn good story too. I ought to know, having framed the first version of it myself.

For I was there, right in the Rigel Royal, when it all began on the night that Cliff Moran blew in, looking lower than an antman's belly and twice as nasty. He'd had a spell of luck foul enough to twist a man into a slug-snake and we all knew that there was an attachment out for his ship. Cliff had fought his way up from the back courts of

Venaport. Lose his ship and he'd slip back there—to rot. He was at the snarling stage that night when he picked out a table for himself and set out to drink away his troubles.

However, just as the first bottle arrived, so did a visitor. Steena came out of her corner, Bat curled around her shoulders stole-wise, his favorite mode of travel. She crossed over and dropped down without invitation at Cliff's side. That shook him out of his sulks. Because Steena never chose company when she could be alone. If one of the man-stones on Ganymede had come stumping in, it wouldn't have made more of us look out of the corners of our eyes.

She stretched out one long-fingered hand and set aside the bottle he had ordered and said only one thing, "It's about time for the Empress of Mars to appear again."

Cliff scowled and bit his lip. He was tough, tough as jet lining—you have to be granite inside and out to struggle up from Venaport to a ship command. But we could guess what was running through his mind at that moment. The Empress of Mars was just about the biggest prize a spacer could aim for. But in the fifty years she had been following her queer derelict orbit through space many men had tried to bring her in—and none had succeeded.

A pleasure-ship carrying untold wealth, she had been mysteriously abandoned in space by passengers and crew, none of whom had ever been seen or heard of again. At intervals thereafter she had been sighted, even boarded. Those who ventured into her either vanished or returned swiftly without any believable explanation of what they had seen—wanting only to get away from her as quickly as possible. But the man who could bring her in—or even strip her clean in space—that man would win the jackpot.

"All right!" Cliff slammed his fist down on the table. "I'll try even that!"

Steena looked at him, much as she must have looked at Bat the day Bub Nelson brought him to her, and nodded. That was all I saw. The rest of the story came to me in pieces, months later and in another port half the System away.

Cliff took off that night. He was afraid to risk waiting—with a writ out that could pull the ship from under him. And it wasn't until he was in space that he discovered his passengers—Steena and Bat. We'll never know what happened then. I'm betting that Steena made no explanation at all. She wouldn't.

It was the first time she had decided to cash in on her own tip and she was there—that was all. Maybe that point weighed with Cliff, maybe he just didn't care. Anyway the three were together when they sighted the Empress riding, her dead-lights gleaming, a ghost ship in night space.

She must have been an eerie sight because her other lights were on too, in addition to the red warnings at her nose. She seemed alive, a Flying Dutchman of space. Cliff worked his ship skillfully alongside and had no trouble in snapping magnetic lines to her lock. Some minutes later the three of them passed into her. There was still air in her cabins and corridors. Air that bore a faint corrupt taint which set Bat to sniffing greedily and could be picked up even by the less sensitive human nostrils.

Cliff headed straight for the control cabin but Steena and Bat went prowling. Closed doors were a challenge to both of them and Steena opened each as she passed, taking a quick look at what lay within. The fifth door opened on a room which no woman could leave without further investigation.

I don't know who had been housed there when the Empress left port on her last lengthy cruise. Anyone really curious can check back on the old photo-reg cards. But there was a lavish display of silks trailing out of two travel kits on the floor, a dressing table crowded with crystal and jeweled containers, along with other lures for the female which drew Steena in. She was standing in front of the dressing table when she glanced into the mirror—glanced into it and froze.

Over her right shoulder she could see the spider-silk cover on the bed. Right in the middle of that sheer, gossamer expanse was a sparkling heap of gems, the dumped contents of some jewel case. Bat had jumped to the foot of the bed and flattened out as cats will, watching those gems, watching them and—something else!

Steena put out her hand blindly and caught up the nearest bottle. As she unstoppered it she watched the mirrored bed. A gemmed bracelet rose from the pile, rose in the air and tinkled its siren song. It was as if an idle hand played . . . . Bat spat almost noiselessly. But he did not retreat. Bat had not yet decided his course.

She put down the bottle. Then she did something that perhaps few of the men she had listened to through the years could have done. She moved without hurry or sign of disturbance on a tour about the room. And although she approached the bed, she did not touch the jewels. She could not force herself to that. It took her five minutes to play out her innocence and unconcern. Then it was Bat who decided the issue.

He leaped from the bed and escorted something to the door, remaining a careful distance behind. Then he mewed loudly twice. Steena followed him and opened the door wider.

Bat went straight on down the corridor, as intent as a hound on the warmest of scents. Steena strolled behind him, holding her pace to the unhurried gait of an explorer. What sped before them both was invisible to her but Bat was never baffled by it.

They must have gone into the control cabin almost on the heels of the unseen—if the unseen had heels, which there was good reason to doubt—for Bat crouched just within the doorway and refused to move on. Steena looked down the length of the instrument panels and officers' station-seats to where Cliff Moran worked. On the heavy carpet her boots made no sound and he did not glance up but sat humming through set teeth as he tested the tardy and reluctant responses to buttons that had not been pushed in years.

To human eyes they were alone in the cabin. But Bat still followed a moving something with his gaze. And it was something that he had at last made up his mind to distrust and dislike. For now he took a step or two forward and spat—his loathing made plain by every raised hair along his spine. And in that same moment Steena saw a flicker—a flicker of vague outline against Cliff's hunched shoulders as if the invisible one had crossed the space between them.

But why had it been revealed against Cliff and not against the back of one of the seats or against the panels, the walls of the corridor or the cover of the bed where it had reclined and played with its loot? What could Bat see?

The storehouse memory that had served Steena so well through the years clicked open a half-forgotten door. With one swift motion she tore loose her spaceall and flung the baggy garment across the back of the nearest seat.

Bat was snarling now, emitting the throaty rising cry that was his hunting song. But he was edging back, back toward Steena's feet, shrinking from something he could not fight but which he faced defiantly. If he could draw it after him, past that dangling spaceall . . . . He had to—it was their only chance.

"What the . . . ." Cliff had come out of his seat and was staring at them.

What he saw must have been weird enough. Steena, bare-armed and shouldered, her usually stiffly netted hair falling wildly down her back, Steena watching empty space with narrowed eyes and set mouth, calculating a single wild chance. Bat, crouched on his belly, retreating from thin air step by step and wailing like a demon.

"Toss me your blaster." Steena gave the order calmly—as if they still sat at their table in the Rigel Royal.

And as quietly Cliff obeyed. She caught the small weapon out of the air with a steady hand—caught and leveled it.

"Stay just where you are!" she warned. "Back, Bat, bring it back!"

With a last throat-splitting screech of rage and hate, Bat twisted to safety between her boots. She pressed with thumb and forefinger, firing at the spacealls. The material turned to powdery flakes of ash— except for certain bits which still flapped from the scorched seat—as if something had protected them from the force of the blast. Bat sprang straight up in the air with a scream that tore their ears.

"What . . . ?" began Cliff again.

Steena made a warning motion with her left hand. "Wait!"

She was still tense, still watching Bat. The cat dashed madly around the cabin twice, running crazily with white-ringed eyes and flecks of foam on his muzzle. Then he stopped abruptly in the doorway, stopped and looked back over his shoulder for a long silent moment. He sniffed delicately.

Steena and Cliff could smell it too now, a thick oily stench which was not the usual odor left by an exploding blaster-shell.

Bat came back, treading daintily across the carpet, almost on the tips of his paws. He raised his head as he passed Steena and then he went confidently beyond to sniff, to sniff and spit twice at the unburned strips of the spaceall. Having thus paid his respects to the late enemy he sat down calmly and set to washing his fur with deliberation. Steena sighed once and dropped into the navigator's seat.

"Maybe now you'll tell me what in the hell's happened?" Cliff exploded as he took the blaster out of her hand.

"Gray," she said dazedly, "it must have been gray—or I couldn't have seen it like that. I'm colorblind, you see. I can see only shades of gray—my whole world is gray. Like Bat's—his world is gray too—all gray. But he's been compensated for he can see above and below our range of color vibrations and—apparently—so can I!"

Her voice quavered and she raised her chin with a new air Cliff had never seen before—a sort of proud acceptance. She pushed back her wandering hair, but she made no move to imprison it under the heavy net again.

"That is why I saw the thing when it crossed between us. Against your spaceall it was another shade of gray—an outline. So I put out mine and waited for it to show against that—it was our only chance, Cliff.

"It was curious at first, I think, and it knew we couldn't see it—which is why it waited to attack. But when Bat's actions gave it away it moved. So I waited to see that flicker against the spaceall and then I let him have it. It's really very simple . . . ."

Cliff laughed a bit shakily. "But what was this gray thing? I don't get it."

"I think it was what made the Empress a derelict. Something out of space, maybe, or from another world somewhere." She waved her hands. "It's invisible because it's a color beyond our range of sight. It must have stayed in here all these years. And it kills—it must—when its curiosity is satisfied." Swiftly she described the scene in the cabin and the strange behavior of the gem pile which had betrayed the creature to her.

Cliff did not return his blaster to its holder. "Any more of them on board, d'you think?" He didn't look pleased at the prospect.

Steena turned to Bat. He was paying particular attention to the space between two front toes in the process of a complete bath. "I don't think so. But Bat will tell us if there are. He can see them clearly, I believe."

But there weren't any more and two weeks later Cliff, Steena and Bat brought the Empress into the Lunar quarantine station. And that is the end of Steena's story because, as we have been told, happy marriages need no chronicles. And Steena had found someone who knew of her gray world and did not find it too hard to share with her—someone besides Bat. It turned out to be a real love match.

The last time I saw her she was wrapped in a flame-red cloak from the looms of Rigel and wore a fortune in Jovan rubies blazing on her wrists. Cliff was flipping a three-figure credit bill to a waiter. And Bat had a row of Vernal juice glasses set up before him. Just a little family party out on the town.

Aftermaths

✦

by Lois McMaster Bujold

One of the most popular and decorated writers in science fiction, New York Times *bestseller Lois McMaster Bujold, still flies under the radar in discussions of women who write science fiction. Perhaps that's because her best known works, while often about gender issues, fall into the subgenre of military science fiction, a subgenre that the literary branch of sf has often scorned.*

The fans haven't scorned it, however. They've given Lois five Hugo Awards, four of them for best novel, placing her alongside Robert Heinlein as the only two people to ever win four Hugos in that category. She has won three Nebula Awards, and several other awards, including the Edward E. Smith Memorial Award for Imaginative Fiction, aka the "Skylark," for lifetime contribution to the field of science fiction.

The fans don't just give her awards, however. They buy her books in record numbers and, despite the harsh publishing climate of the past two decades, have not allowed any of those books to go out of print. In 2010, her publisher Baen Books said it had sold more than two million copies of her books.

In fact, 2016 marks the thirtieth anniversary of the publication of the first three novels in her most popular series, the Miles Vorkosigan Saga: Shards of Honor, The Warrior's Apprentice, *and* Ethan of Athos. *The latest book in that series,* Gentleman Jole and the Red Queen, *just appeared in February.*

Clarkesworld Magazine, *in its November 2010 edition, paid her the* high compliment by labeling her "*a fan's writer, a reader's writer.*" Perhaps that's because, like so many writers in this book, she started in science fiction fandom. Or perhaps its because she has interacted with and nurtured her fans for three full decades.

Or, perhaps, it is simply what Anne McCaffrey once said about Lois, "*Boy, can she write!*"

Oh, boy, can she. The story that follows, "Aftermaths," is a standalone in the Vorkosigan universe, and shows just how powerful a Lois McMaster Bujold story can be.

🐢 🐢 🐢

THE SHATTERED SHIP hung in space, hung in space, a black bulk in the darkness. It still turned, imperceptibly slowly; one edge eclipsed and swallowed the bright point of a star. The lights of the salvage crew arced over the skeleton. *Ants, ripping up a dead moth*, Ferrell thought. *Scavengers* . . .

He sighed dismay into his forward observation screen, and pictured the ship as it had been, scant weeks before. The wreckage untwisted in his mind—a cruiser, alive with patterns of gaudy lights that always made him think of a party seen across night waters. Responsive as a mirror to the mind under its pilot's headset, where man and machine penetrated the interface and became one. Swift, gleaming, functional . . . no more. He glanced to his right and cleared his throat self-consciously.

"Well, Medtech," he spoke to the woman who stood beside his station, staring into the screen as silently and long as he had. "There's our starting point. Might as well go ahead and begin the pattern sweep now, I suppose.

"Yes, please do, Pilot Officer." She had a gravelly alto voice, suitable for her age, which Ferrell judged to be about forty-five. The collection of thin silver five-year service chevrons on her left sleeve made an impressive glitter against the dark red uniform of the Escobaran military medical service. Dark hair shot with gray, cut short for ease of maintenance, not style; a matronly heaviness to her hips. A veteran, it appeared. Ferrell's sleeve had yet to sprout even his first-year stripe, and his hips, and the rest of his body, still maintained an unfilled adolescent stringiness.

But she was only a tech, he reminded himself, not even a physician. He was a full-fledged pilot officer. His neurological implants and biofeedback training were all complete. He was certified, licensed, and graduated—just three frustrating days too late to participate in what was now being dubbed the 120-Day War. Although in fact it had only been 118 days and part of an hour between the time the spearhead of the Barrayaran invasion fleet penetrated Escobaran local space, and the time the last survivors fled the counterattack, piling through the wormhole exit for home as though scuttling for a burrow.

"Do you wish to stand by?" he asked her.

She shook her head. "Not yet. This inner area has been pretty well worked over in the last three weeks. I wouldn't expect to find anything on the first four turns, although it's good to be thorough. I've a few things to arrange yet in my work area, and then I think I'll get a catnap. My department has been awfully busy the last few months," she added apologetically. "Understaffed, you know. Please call me if you do spot anything, though—I prefer to handle the tractor myself, whenever possible."

"Fine by me." He swung about in his chair to his comconsole. "What minimum mass do you want a bleep for? About forty kilos, say?"

"One kilo is the standard I prefer."

"One kilo!" He stared. "Are you joking?"

"Joking?" She stared back, then seemed to arrive at enlightenment. "Oh, I see. You were thinking in terms of whole—I can make positive identification with quite small pieces, you see. I wouldn't even mind picking up smaller bits than that, but if you go much under a kilo you spend too much time on false alarms from micrometeors and other rubbish. One kilo seems to be the best practical compromise."

"Bleh." But he obediently set his probes for a mass of one kilo, minimum, and finished programming the search sweep.

She gave him a brief nod and withdrew from the closet-sized Navigation and Control Room. The obsolete courier ship had been pulled from junkyard orbit and hastily overhauled with some notion first of converting it into a personnel carrier for middle brass—top brass in a hurry having a monopoly on the new ships—but like Ferrell himself, it had graduated too late to participate. So they both had been rerouted together, he and his first command, to the dull duties he privately thought on a par with sanitation engineering, or worse.

He gazed one last moment at the relic of battle in the forward screen, its structural girdering poking up like bones through sloughing skin, and shook his head at the waste of it all. Then, with a little sigh of pleasure, he pulled his headset down into contact with the silvery circles on his temples and midforehead, closed his eyes, and slid into control of his own ship.

Space seemed to spread itself all around him, buoyant as a sea. He was the ship, he was a fish, he was a merman; unbreathing, limitless, and without pain. He fired his engines as though flame leapt from his fingertips, and began the slow rolling spiral of the search pattern.

"Medtech Boni?" He keyed the intercom to her cabin. "I believe I have something for you here."

She rubbed sleep from her face, framed in the intercom screen. "Already? What time—oh. I must have been tireder than I realized. I'll be right up, Pilot Officer."

Ferrell stretched, and began an automatic series of isometrics in his chair. It had been a long and uneventful watch. He would have been hungry, but what he contemplated now through the viewscreens subdued his appetite.

Boni appeared, sliding into the seat beside him. "Oh, quite right, Pilot Officer." She unshipped the controls to the exterior tractor beam, and flexed her fingers before taking a delicate hold.

"Yeah, there wasn't much doubt about that one," he agreed, leaning back and watching her work. "Why so tender with the tractors?" he asked in curiosity, noting the low power level she was using.

"Well, they're frozen right through, you know," she replied, not taking her eyes from her readouts. "Brittle. If you play hotshot and bang them around, they can shatter. Let's stop that nasty spin, first," she added, half to herself. "A slow spin is all right. Seemly. But that fast spinning you get sometimes—it must be very unrestful for them, don't you think?"

His attention was pulled from the thing in the screen, and he stared at her. "They're *dead*, lady!"

She smiled slowly as the corpse, bloated from decompression, limbs twisted as though frozen in a strobe-flash of convulsion, was drawn gently toward the cargo bay. "Well, that's not their fault, is it?—one of our fellows, I see by the uniform."

"Bleh!" he repeated himself, then gave vent to an embarrassed laugh. "You act like you enjoy it."

"Enjoy? No . . . But I've been in Personnel Retrieval and Identification for nine years, now. I don't mind. And of course, vacuum work is always a little nicer than planetary work."

"Nicer? With that godawful decompression?"

"Yes, but there are the temperature effects to consider. No decomposition."

He took a breath, and let it out carefully. "I see. I guess you would get—pretty hardened, after a while. Is it true you guys call them corpse-sicles?"

"Some do," she admitted. "I don't."

She maneuvered the twisted thing carefully through the cargo bay doors and keyed them shut. "Temperature set for a slow thaw and he'll be ready to handle in a few hours," she murmured.

"What do you call them?" he asked as she rose.

"People."

She awarded his bewilderment a small smile, like a salute, and withdrew to the temporary mortuary set up next to the cargo bay.

On his next scheduled break he went down himself, drawn by morbid curiosity. He poked his nose around the doorframe. She was seated at her desk. The table in the center of the room was yet unoccupied.

"Uh—hello."

She looked up with her quick smile. "Hello, Pilot Officer. Come on in."

"Uh, thank you. You know, you don't really have to be so formal. Call me Falco, if you want," he said, entering.

"Certainly, if you wish. My first name is Tersa."

"Oh, yeah? I have a cousin named Tersa."

"It's a popular name. There were always at least three in my classes at school." She rose and checked a gauge by the door to the cargo bay. "He should be just about ready to take care of, now. Pulled to shore, so to speak."

Ferrell sniffed, and cleared his throat, wondering whether to stay or excuse himself. "Grotesque sort of fishing." *Excuse myself, I think.*

She picked up the control lead to the float pallet, trailing it after her into the cargo bay. There were some thumping noises, and she returned, the pallet drifting behind her. The corpse was in the dark blue of a deck officer, and covered thickly with frost, which flaked and dripped upon the floor as the medtech slid it onto the examining table. Ferrell shivered with disgust.

Definitely excuse myself. But he lingered, leaning against the doorframe at a safe distance.

She pulled an instrument, trailing its lead to the computers, from the crowded rack above the table. It was the size of a pencil, and emitted a thin blue beam of light when aligned with the corpse's eyes.

"Retinal identification," Tersa explained. She pulled down a pad-like object, similarly connected, and pressed it to each of the monstrosity's hands. "And fingerprints," she went on. "I always do both, and cross-match. The eyes can get awfully distorted. Errors in identification can be brutal for the families. Hm. Hm." She checked her readout screen. "Lieutenant Marco Deleo. Age twenty-nine. Well, Lieutenant," she went on chattily, "let's see what I can do for you."

She applied an instrument to its joints, which loosened them, and began removing its clothes.

"Do you often talk to—them?" inquired Ferrell, unnerved.

"Always. It's a courtesy, you see. Some of the things I have to do for them are rather undignified, but they can still be done with courtesy."

Ferrell shook his head. "I think it's obscene, myself."

"Obscene?"

"All this horsing around with dead bodies. All the trouble and expense we go to collecting them. I mean, what do they care? Fifty or a hundred kilos of rotting meat. It'd be cleaner to leave them in space."

She shrugged, unoffended, undiverted from her task. She folded the clothes and inventoried the pockets, laying out their contents in a row.

"I rather like going through the pockets," she remarked. "It reminds me of when I was a little girl, visiting in someone else's home. When I went upstairs by myself, to go to the bathroom or whatever, it was always a kind of pleasure to peek into the other rooms, and see what kind of things they had, and how they kept them. If they were very neat, I was always very impressed—I've never been able to keep my own things neat. If it was a mess, I felt I'd found a secret kindred spirit. A person's things can be a kind of exterior morphology of their mind—like a snail's shell, or something. I like to imagine what kind of person they were, from what's in the pockets. Neat, or messy. Very regulation, or full of personal things . . . Take Lieutenant Deleo, here. He must have been very conscientious. Everything regulation, except this little vid disc from home. From his wife, I'd imagine. I think he must have been a very nice person to know."

She placed the collection of objects into its labeled bag.

"Aren't you going to listen to it?" asked Ferrell.

"Oh, no. That would be prying."

He barked a laugh. "I fail to see the distinction."

"Ah." She completed the medical examination, readied the plastic body bag, and began to wash the corpse. When she worked her way down to the careful cleaning around the genital area, necessary because of sphincter relaxation, Ferrell fled at last.

That woman is nuts, he thought. *I wonder if it's the cause of her choice of work, or the effect?*

It was another full day before they hooked their next fish. Ferrell had a dream, during his sleep cycle, about being on a deep-sea boat, and hauling up nets full of corpses to be dumped, wet and shining as though with iridescent scales, in a huge pile in the hold. He awoke from it sweating, but with very cold feet. It was with profound relief that he returned to the pilot's station and slid into the skin of his ship. The ship was clean, mechanical and pure, immortal as a god; one could forget one had ever owned a sphincter muscle.

"Odd trajectory," he remarked, as the medtech again took her place at the tractor controls.

"Yes . . . Oh, I see. He's a Barrayaran. He's a long way from home."

"Oh, bleh. Throw him back."

"Oh, no. We have identification files for all their missing. Part of the peace settlement, you know, along with prisoner exchange."

"Considering what they did to our people as prisoners, I don't think we owe them a thing."

She shrugged.

※ ※ ※

The Barrayaran officer had been a tall, broad-shouldered man, a commander by the rank on his collar tabs. The medtech treated him with the same care she had expended on Lieutenant Deleo, and more. She went to considerable trouble to smooth and straighten him, and massage the mottled face back into some semblance of manhood with her fingertips, a process Ferrell watched with a rising gorge.

"I wish his lips wouldn't curl back *quite* so much," she remarked, while at this task. "Gives him what I imagine to be an uncharacteristically snarly look. I think he must have been rather handsome."

One of the objects in his pockets was a little locket. It held a tiny glass bubble filled with a clear liquid. The inside of its gold cover was densely engraved with the elaborate curlicues of the Barrayaran alphabet.

"What is it?" asked Ferrell curiously.

She held it pensively to the light. "It's a sort of charm, or memento. I've learned a lot about the Barrayarans in the last three months. Turn ten of them upside down and you'll find some kind of good luck charm or amulet or medallion or something in the pockets of nine of them. The high-ranking officers are just as bad as the enlisted people."

"Silly superstition."

"I'm not sure if it's superstition or just custom. We treated an injured prisoner once—he claimed it was just custom. People gave them to the soldiers as presents, and that nobody really believes in them. But when we took his away from him, when we were undressing him for surgery, he tried to fight us for it. It took three of us to hold him down for the anesthetic. I thought it a rather remarkable performance for a man whose legs had been blown away. He wept . . . Of course, he was in shock."

Ferrell dangled the locket on the end of its short chain, intrigued in spite of himself. It hung with a companion piece, a curl of hair embedded in a plastic pendant.

"Some sort of holy water, is it?" he inquired.

"Almost. It's a very common design. It's called a mother's tears charm. Let me see if I can make out—he's had it a while, it seems. From the inscription—I think that says 'ensign,' and the date—it must have been given him on the occasion of his commission."

"It's not really his mother's tears, is it?"

"Oh, yes. That's what's supposed to make it work, as a protection."

"Doesn't seem to be very effective."

"No, well . . . no."

Ferrell snorted ironically. "I hate those guys—but I do guess I feel sort of sorry for his mother."

Boni retrieved the chain and its pendants, holding the curl in plastic to the light and reading its inscription. "No, not at all. She's a fortunate woman."

"How so?"

"This is her death lock. She died three years ago, by this."

"Is that supposed to be lucky, too?"

"No, not necessarily. Just a remembrance, as far as I know. Kind of a nice one, really. The nastiest charm I ever ran across, and the most unique, was this little leather bag hung around a fellow's neck. It was filled with dirt and leaves, and what I took at first to be some sort of little frog-like animal skeleton, about ten centimeters long. But when I looked at it more closely, it turned out to be the skeleton of a human fetus. Very strange. I suppose it was some sort of black magic. Seemed an odd thing to find on an engineering officer."

"Doesn't seem to work for any of them, does it?"

She smiled wryly. "Well, if there are any that work, I wouldn't see them, would I?"

She took the processing one step further, by cleaning the Barrayaran's clothes and carefully re-dressing him, before bagging him and returning him to the freeze.

"The Barrayarans are all so army-mad," she explained. "I always like to put them back in their uniforms. They mean so much to them, I'm sure they're more comfortable with them on."

Ferrell frowned in unease. "I still think he ought to be dumped with the rest of the garbage."

"Not at all," said the medtech. "Think of all the work he represents on somebody's part. Nine months of pregnancy, childbirth, two years of diapering, and that's just the beginning. Tens of thousands of meals, thousands of bedtime stories, years of school. Dozens of teachers. And all that military training, too. A lot of people went into making him."

She smoothed a strand of the corpse's hair into place. "That head held the universe, once. He had a good rank for his age," she added, rechecking her monitor. "Thirty-two. Commander Aristede

Vorkalloner. It has a kind of nice ethnic ring. Very Barrayaranish, that name. Vor, too, one of those warrior-class fellows."

"Homicidal-class loonies. Or worse," Ferrell said automatically. But his vehemence had lost momentum, somehow.

Boni shrugged. "Well, he's joined the great democracy now. And he had nice pockets."

Three full days went by with no further alarms but a rare scattering of mechanical debris. Ferrell began to hope the Barrayaran was the last pickup they would have to make. They were nearing the end of their search pattern. Besides, he thought resentfully, this duty was sabotaging the efficiency of his sleep cycle. But the medtech made a request.

"If you don't mind, Falco," she said, "I'd greatly appreciate it if we could run the pattern out just a few extra turns. The original orders are based on this average estimated trajectory speed, you see, and if someone just happened to get a bit of extra kick when the ship split, they could well be beyond it by now."

Ferrell was less than thrilled, but the prospect of an extra day of piloting had its attractions, and he gave a grudging consent. Her reasoning proved itself; before the day was half done, they turned up another gruesome relic.

"Oh," muttered Ferrell, when they got a close look. It had been a female officer. Boni reeled her in with enormous tenderness. He didn't really want to go watch, this time, but the medtech seemed to have come to expect him.

"I—don't really want to look at a woman blown up," he tried to excuse himself.

"Mm," said Tersa. "Is it fair, though, to reject a person just because they're dead? You wouldn't have minded her body a bit when she was alive."

He laughed a little, macabrely. "Equal rights for the dead?"

Her smile twisted. "Why not? Some of my best friends are corpses."

He snorted.

She grew more serious. "I'd—sort of like the company, on this one." So he took up his usual station by the door.

The medtech laid out the thing that had been a woman upon her table, undressed, inventoried, washed, and straightened it. When she finished, she kissed the dead lips.

"Oh, God," cried Ferrell, shocked and nauseated. "You *are* crazy! You're a damn, damn necrophiliac! A *lesbian* necrophiliac, at that!" He turned to go.

"Is that what it looks like, to you?" Her voice was soft, and still unoffended. It stopped him, and he looked over his shoulder. She was looking at him as gently as if he had been one of her precious corpses. "What a strange world you must live in, inside your head."

She opened a suitcase, and shook out a dress, fine underwear, and a pair of white embroidered slippers. A wedding dress, Ferrell realized. This woman was a bona fide *psychopath* . . .

She dressed the corpse, arranging its soft dark hair with great delicacy, before bagging it.

"I believe I shall place her next to that nice tall Barrayaran," she said. "I think they would have liked each other very well, if they could have met in another place and time. And Lieutenant Deleo was married, after all."

She completed the label. Ferrell's battered mind was sending him little subliminal messages; he struggled to overcome his shock and bemusement, and pay attention. It tumbled into the open day of his consciousness with a start.

She had not run an identification check on this one.

Out the door, he told himself, *is the way you want to walk. I guarantee it*. Instead, timorously, he went over to the corpse and checked its label.

Ensign Sylva Boni, it said. *Age twenty*. His own age . . .

He was trembling, as if with cold. It *was* cold, in that room. Tersa Boni finished packing up the suitcase, and turned back with the float pallet.

"Daughter?" he asked. It was all he could ask.

She pursed her lips, and nodded.

"It's—a helluva coincidence."

"No coincidence at all. I asked for this sector."

"Oh." He swallowed, turned away, turned back, face flaming. "I'm sorry I said—"

She smiled her slow sad smile. "Never mind."

They found yet one more bit of mechanical debris, so agreed to run another cycle of the search spiral, to be sure that all possible trajectories had been outdistanced. And yes, they found another; a nasty one, spinning fiercely, guts split open from some great blow and hanging out in a frozen cascade.

The acolyte of death did her dirty work without once so much as wrinkling her nose. When it came to the washing, the least technical of the tasks, Ferrell said suddenly, "May I help?"

"Certainly," said the medtech, moving aside. "An honor is not diminished for being shared."

And so he did, as shy as an apprentice saint washing his first leper.

"Don't be afraid," she said. "The dead cannot hurt you. They give you no pain, except that of seeing your own death in their faces. And one can face that, I find."

Yes, he thought, *the good face pain. But the great—they embrace it.*

The Last Flight
of Doctor Ain

※

by James Tiptree, Jr.

I approached this introduction to James Tiptree, Jr.'s story, "The Last Flight of Doctor Ain," with more than a little trepidation. James Tiptree, Jr., is the pen name of Alice B. Sheldon who deliberately tried to protect her privacy with a nom de plum from the moment she submitted her first short story.

Almost immediately, though, the power of her work got the entire field asking who this Tiptree guy was. As Tiptree published more and more stories, many about gender issues, some suspected he wasn't male at all, leading poor Robert Silverberg to famously write that it was absurd to think Tiptree was a woman because Tiptree's writing was so masculine.

That statement, then the big reveal that Tiptree was female, combined with the stories that Sheldon wrote—particularly "The Women That Men Don't See"—led most everything written about this very private woman to be more about her than it was about her fiction. (Including the first three paragraphs of this introduction.)

It also means that the stories we read of Sheldon's are her most overtly feminist tales, generally "The Women That Men Don't See," "The Screwfly Solution," and "Houston, Houston, Do You Read?" She wrote so much more than those stories, other stories that had little to do with gender issues.

She had a writing career before she wrote science fiction. Her first short story, "The Lucky Ones," was published in the November 16, 1946, issue of The New Yorker, *under her real name, Alice Bradley Sheldon. She used a pen name in the 1960s to protect her academic reputation after she had gotten her doctorate at George Washington University.*

She's the other contributor to this book to have an award named after her, the James Tiptree Jr. award, which I discussed in the introduction. She won her fair share of awards in her lifetime, including two Hugo Awards and two Nebula awards. She wrote two novels, but she's best known for her short fiction. Eighteen of her most famous tales are collected in Her Smoke Rose Up Forever.

More than anything else, Sheldon tended to write science fiction horror stories with a lot of social commentary. Some of that commentary seems dated forty years after its first publication.

But "The Last Flight of Doctor Ain," which first appeared in 1968 and received a Nebula nomination, reads (with the exception of one or two details) like it was written last week. A terrifying little story told in the cold language of the bureaucratic reports Sheldon used to write when she worked in military intelligence and for the CIA, "The Last Flight of Doctor Ain" convinced the entire science fiction field that this Tiptree guy was someone to watch.

❁ ❁ ❁

DR. AIN WAS RECOGNIZED on the Omaha-Chicago flight. A biologist colleague from Pasadena came out of the toilet and saw Ain in an aisle seat. Five years before, this man had been jealous of Ain's huge grants. Now he nodded coldly and was surprised at the intensity of Ain's response. He almost turned back to speak, but he felt too tired; like nearly everyone, he was fighting the flu.

The stewardess handing out coats after they landed remembered Ain too: a tall thin nondescript man with rusty hair. He held up the line staring at her; since he already had his raincoat with him she decided it was some kooky kind of pass and waved him on.

She saw Ain shamble off into the airport smog, apparently alone. Despite the big Civil Defense signs, O'Hare was late getting underground. No one noticed the woman.

The wounded, dying woman.

Ain was not identified en route to New York, but a 2:40 jet carried an "Ames" on the checklist, which was thought to be a misspelling of Ain. It was. The plane had circled for an hour while Ain watched the smoky seaboard monotonously tilt, straighten, and tilt again.

The woman was weaker now. She coughed, picking weakly at the scabs on her face half-hidden behind her long hair. Her hair, Ain saw, that great mane which had been so splendid, was drabbed and thinning now. He looked to seaward, willing himself to think of cold, clean breakers. On the horizon he saw a vast black rug: somewhere a tanker had opened its vents. The woman coughed again. Ain closed his eyes. Smog shrouded the plane.

He was picked up next while checking in for the BOAC flight to Glasgow. Kennedy Underground was a boiling stew of people, the air system unequal to the hot September afternoon. The check-in line swayed and sweated, staring dully at the newscast. SAVE THE LAST GREEN MANSIONS—a conservation group was protesting the defoliation and drainage of the Amazon basin. Several people recalled the beautifully colored shots of the new clean bomb. The line squeezed together to let a band of uniformed men go by. They were wearing buttons inscribed: WHO'S AFRAID?

That was when a woman noticed Ain. He was holding a newssheet, and she heard it rattling in his hand. Her family hadn't caught the flu, so she looked at him sharply. Sure enough, his forehead was sweaty. She herded her kids to the side away from Ain.

He was using *Instac* throat spray, she remembered. She didn't think much of *Instac;* her family used *Kleer*. While she was looking at him, Ain suddenly turned his head and stared into her face, with the spray still floating down. Such inconsiderateness! She turned her back. She didn't recall his talking to any woman, but she perked up her ears when the clerk read off Ain's destination. Moscow!

The clerk recalled that too, with disapproval. Ain checked in alone, he reported. No woman had been ticketed for Moscow, but it would have been easy enough to split up her tickets. (By that time they were sure she was with him.)

Ain's flight went via Iceland with an hour's delay at Keflavik. Ain walked over to the airport park, gratefully breathing the sea-filled air. Every few breaths he shuddered. Under the whine of bulldozers the sea could be heard running its huge paws up and down the keyboard of the land. The little park had a grove of yellowed birches, and a flock of wheatears foraged by the path. Next month they would be in North Africa, Ain thought. Two thousand miles of tiny wing-beats. He threw them some crumbs from a packet in his pocket.

The woman seemed stronger here. She was panting in the sea wind, her large eyes fixed on Ain. Above her the birches were as gold as those where he had first seen her, the day his life began. . . . Squatting under a stump to watch a shrewmouse he had been, when he caught a falling ripple of green and recognized the shocking girl-flesh, creamy, pink-tipped—coming toward him among the golden bracken! Young Ain held his breath, his nose in the sweet moss and his heart going *crash— crash*. And then he was staring at the outrageous fall of that hair down her narrow back, watching it dance around her heart-shaped buttocks, while the shrewmouse ran over his paralyzed hand. The lake was utterly still, dusty silver under the misty sky, and she made no more than a muskrat's ripple to rock the floating golden leaves. The silence closed back, the trees burning like torches where the naked girl had walked the wild wood, reflected in Ain's shining eyes. For a time he believed he had seen an oread.

Ain was last on board for the Glasgow leg. The stewardess recalled dimly that he seemed restless. She could not identify the woman. There were a lot of women on board, and babies. Her passenger list had had several errors.

At Glasgow airport a waiter remembered that a man like Ain had called for Scottish oatmeal, and eaten two bowls, although of course it wasn't really oatmeal. A young mother with a pram saw him tossing crumbs to the birds.

When he checked in at the BOAC desk, he was hailed by a Glasgow professor who was going to the same conference at Moscow. This man had been one of Ain's teachers. (It was now known that Ain had done his postgraduate work in Europe.) They chatted all the way across the North Sea.

"I wondered about that," the professor said later. "Why have you come round about? I asked him. He told me the direct flights were booked up." (This was found to be untrue: Ain had, apparently, avoided the Moscow jet to escape attention.)

The professor spoke with relish of Ain's work.

"Brilliant? Oh, aye. And stubborn, too; very very stubborn. It was as though a concept—often the simplest relation, mind you—would stop him in his tracks, and fascinate him. He would hunt all round it instead of going on to the next thing as a more docile mind would. Truthfully, I wondered at first if he could be just a bit thick. But you recall who it was said that the capacity for wonder at matters of common acceptance occurs in the superior mind? And, of course, so it proved when he shook us all up over that enzyme conversion business. A pity your government took him away from his line, there. No, he said nothing of this, I say it to you, young man. We spoke in fact largely of my work. I was surprised to find he'd kept up. He asked me what my *sentiments* about it were, which surprised me again. Now, understand, I'd not seen the man for five years, but he seemed—well, perhaps just tired, as who is not? I'm sure he was glad to have a change; he jumped out for a legstretch wherever we came down. At Oslo, even Bonn. Oh, yes, he did feed the birds, but that was nothing new for Ain. His social life when I knew him? Radical causes? Young man, I've said what I've said because of who it was that introduced you, but I'll have you know it is an impertinence in you to think ill of Charles Ain, or that he could do a harmful deed. Good evening."

The professor said nothing of the woman in Ain's life.

Nor could he have, although Ain had been intimately with her in the university time. He had let no one see how he was obsessed with her, with the miracle, the wealth of her body, her inexhaustibility. They met at his every spare moment; sometimes in public pretending to be casual strangers under his friends' noses, pointing out a pleasing view to each other with grave formality. And later in their privacies—what doubled intensity of love! He reveled in her, possessed her, allowed her no secrets. His dreams were of her sweet springs and shadowed places and her white rounded glory in the moonlight, finding always more, always new dimensions of his joy.

The danger of her frailty was far off then in the rush of birdsong and the springing leverets of the meadow. On dark days she might cough a bit, but so did he. . . . In those years he had had no thought to the urgent study of disease.

At the Moscow conference nearly everyone noticed Ain at some point or another, which was to be expected in view of his professional stature. It was a small, high-caliber meeting. Ain was late in; a day's reports were over, and his was to be on the third and last.

Many people spoke with Ain, and several sat with him at meals. No one was surprised that he spoke little; he was a retiring man except on a few memorable occasions of argument. He did strike some of his friends as a bit tired and jerky.

An Indian molecular engineer who saw him with the throat spray kidded him about bringing over Asian flu. A Swedish colleague recalled that Ain had been called away to the transatlantic phone at lunch; and when he returned Ain volunteered the information that something had turned up missing in his home lab. There was another joke, and Ain said cheerfully, "Oh, yes, quite active."

At that point one of the Chicom biologists swung into his daily propaganda chores about bacteriological warfare and accused Ain of manufacturing biotic weapons. Ain took the wind out of his sails by saying: "You're perfectly right." By tacit consent, there was very little talk about military applications, industrial dusting, or subjects of that type. And nobody recalled seeing Ain with any woman other than old Madame Vialche, who could scarcely have subverted anyone from her wheelchair.

Ain's one speech was bad, even for him. He always had a poor public voice, but his ideas were usually expressed with the lucidity so typical of the first-rate mind. This time he seemed muddled, with little new to say. His audience excused this as the muffling effects of security. Ain then got into a tangled point about the course of evolution in which he seemed to be trying to show that something was very wrong indeed. When he wound up with a reference to Hudson's bellbird "singing for a later race," several listeners wondered if he could be drunk.

The big security break came right at the end, when he suddenly began to describe the methods he had used to mutate and redesign a leukemia virus. He explained the procedure with admirable clarity in four sentences and paused. Then gave a terse description of the effects of the mutated strain, which were maximal only in the higher primates. Recovery rate among the lower mammals and other orders was close to ninety percent. As to vectors, he went on, any warm-blooded animal served. In addition, the virus retained its viability in most environmental media and performed very well airborne. Contagion rate was extremely high. Almost offhand, Ain added that no test primate or accidentally exposed human had survived beyond the twenty-second day.

These words fell into a silence broken only by the running feet of the Egyptian delegate making for the door. Then a gilt chair went over as an American bolted after him.

Ain seemed unaware that his audience was in a state of unbelieving paralysis. It had all come so fast: a man who had been blowing his nose was staring pop-eyed around his handkerchief. Another who had been lighting a pipe grunted as his fingers singed. Two men chatting by the door missed his words entirely, and their laughter chimed info a dead silence in which echoed Ain's words: "—really no point in attempting."

Later they found he had been explaining that the virus utilized the body's own immunomechanisms, and so defense was by definition hopeless.

That was all. Ain looked around vaguely for questions and then started down the aisle. By the time he got to the door, people were swarming after him. He wheeled about and said rather crossly, "Yes, of course it is very wrong. I told you that. We are all wrong. Now it's over."

An hour later they found he had gone, having apparently reserved a Sinair flight to Karachi.

The security men caught up with him at Hong Kong. By then he seemed really very ill, and went with them peacefully. They started back to the States via Hawaii.

His captors were civilized types; they saw he was gentle and treated him accordingly. He had no weapons or drugs on him. They took him out handcuffed for a stroll at Osaka, let him feed his crumbs to the birds, and they listened with interest to his account of the migration routes of the common brown sandpiper. He was very hoarse. At that point, he was wanted only for the security thing. There was no question of a woman at all.

He dozed most of the way to the islands, but when they came in sight he pressed to the window and began to mutter. The security man behind him got the first inkling that there was a woman in it, and turned on his recorder.

". . . Blue, blue and green until you see the wounds. O my girl, O beautiful, you won't die. I won't let you die. I tell you girl, it's over. . . . Lustrous eyes, look at me, let me see you now alive! Great queen, my sweet body, my girl, have I saved you? . . . O terrible to know, and noble, Chaos's child green-robed in blue and golden light . . . the thrown and spinning ball of life alone in space . . . Have I saved you?"

On the last leg, he was obviously feverish.

"She may have tricked me, you know," he said confidentially to the government man. "You have to be prepared for that, of course. I know her!" He chuckled confidentially. "She's no small thing. But wring your heart out –"

Coming over San Francisco he was merry. "Don't you know the otters will go back in there? I'm certain of it. That fill won't last; there'll be a bay there again."

They got him on a stretcher at Hamilton Air Base, and he went unconscious shortly after takeoff. Before he collapsed, he'd insisted on throwing the last of his birdseed on the field.

"Birds are, you know, warm-blooded," he confided to the agent who was handcuffing him to the stretcher. Then Ain smiled gently and lapsed into inertness. He stayed that way almost all the remaining ten days of his life. By then, of course, no one really cared. Both the government men had died quite early, after they finished analyzing the birdseed and throat spray. The woman at Kennedy had just started feeling sick.

The tape recorder they put by his bed functioned right on through, but if anybody had been around to replay it they would have found little but babbling. "Gaea Gloriatrix," he crooned, "Gaea girl, queen . . ." At times he was grandiose and tormented. "Our life, your death!" he yelled. "Our death would have been your death too, no need for that, no need."

At other times he was accusing. "What did you do about the dinosaurs?" he demanded. "Did they annoy you? How did you fix *them*? Cold. Queen, you're too cold! You came close to it this time, my girl," he raved. And then he wept and caressed the bedclothes and was maudlin.

Only at the end, lying in his filth and thirst, still chained where they had forgotten him, he was suddenly coherent. In the light clear voice of a lover planning a summer picnic he asked the recorder happily:

"Have you ever thought about bears? They have so much . . . funny they never came along further. By any chance were you saving them, girl?" And he chuckled in his ruined throat, and later, died.

Sur

A SUMMARY REPORT OF THE *YELCHO* EXPEDITION TO THE ANTARCTIC, 1909-1910

❖

by Ursula K. Le Guin

In 2014, Ursula K. Le Guin received The National Book Foundation Medal for Distinguished Contribution to American Letters. She shares that honor with such writers as Eudora Welty, Toni Morrison, Judy Blume, Stephen King, Ray Bradbury, Arthur Miller, and Gwendolyn Brooks.

That isn't the first such major literary award Ursula has won. The Library of Congress honored her with its Living Legend designation. She has won the PEN/Malamud Award for excellence in short fiction, the Margaret A. Edwards Award for her contributions to young adult literature, and a slew of lifetime achievement awards. She's been shortlisted for the Pulitzer Prize. She's won a Newberry Award, and a National Book Award.

In the science fiction and fantasy genre, she has received SFWA's Grand Master Award, and the Gandalf Award. She was inducted into the Science Fiction Hall of Fame. Over her long career, she has won five Nebula awards and six Hugos. I did not look to see how many times she's been nominated.

If I were to continue listing just her awards and honors, I would use up the remaining word count for this introduction, and I wouldn't even make it to a discussion of the fiction.

When she won the Margaret A. Edwards Award, the award committee chair noted in the press release accompanying the announcement:

A fantasy writer and social activist since her youth, [Ursula K. Le Guin] has inspired four generations of young adults to read beautifully constructed language, visit fantasy worlds that inform them about their own lives, and think about their ideas that are neither easy nor inconsequential.

That award focused on Le Guin's fantasy series Earthsea. *But she's equally important to science fiction. Her novel,* The Left Hand of Darkness, *continually makes lists of the best science fiction novels of all time. It certainly inspired and challenged me, just as Ursula's short stories and essays have.*

Initially, I planned to use one of Ursula's early short stories, a personal favorite of mine called "Semley's Necklace," which fits into the universe of the technological Hainish Cycle. The story proved longer than I remembered. Then I read "Sur" for the first time, and realized it's alternate history, a subgenre I didn't have yet in this anthology.

"Sur" is a sly tale of nine women who arrive at the South Pole over a year before Roald Amundsen's all-male team reached the Pole on 14 December, 1911. "Sur" has a richness and a depth that marks the best Le Guin stories. It also, in its own way, speaks to the theme of this entire anthology.

☀ ☀ ☀

SUR

The Map in the Attic

ALTHOUGH I HAVE NO INTENTION of publishing this report, I think it would be nice if a grandchild of mine, or somebody's grandchild, happened to find it some day; so I shall keep it in the leather trunk in the attic, along with Rosita's christening dress and Juanito's silver rattle and my wedding shoes and finneskos.

The first requisite for mounting an expedition—money—is normally the hardest to come by. I grieve that even in a report destined for a trunk in the attic of a house in a very quiet suburb of Lima I dare not write the name of the generous benefactor, the great soul without whose unstinting liberality the *Yelcho* Expedition would never have been more than the idlest excursion into daydream. That our equipment was the best and most modern—that our provisions were plentiful and fine—that a ship of the Chilean Government, with her brave officers and gallant crew, was twice sent halfway round the world for our convenience: all this is due to that benefactor whose name, alas! I must not say, but whose happiest debtor I shall be till death.

When I was little more than a child my imagination was caught by a newspaper account of the voyage of the *Belgica,* which, sailing south from Tierra del Fuego, became beset by ice in the Bellingshausen Sea and drifted a whole year with the floe, the men aboard her suffering a great deal from want of food and from the terror of the unending winter darkness. I read and reread that account, and later followed with excitement the reports of the rescue of Dr. Nordenskjold from the South Shetland Isles by the dashing Captain Irizar of the *Uruguay,* and the adventures of the *Scotia* in the Weddell Sea. But all these exploits were to me but forerunners of the British National Antarctic Expedition of 1902-1904, in the *Discovery,* and the wonderful account of that expedition by Captain Scott. This book, which I ordered from London and reread a thousand times, filled me with longing to see with my own eyes that strange continent, last Thule of the South, which lies on our maps and globes like a white cloud, a void, fringed here and there with scraps of coastline, dubious capes, supposititious islands, headlands that may or may not be there: Antarctica. And the desire was as pure as the polar snows: to go, to see—no more, no less. I deeply respect the scientific accomplishments of Captain Scott's expedition, and have read with passionate interest the findings of physicists, meteorologists, biologists, etc.; but having had no training in any science, nor any opportunity for such training, my ignorance obliged me to forego any thought of adding to the body of scientific knowledge concerning Antarctica; and the same is true for all the members of my expedition. It seems a pity; but there was nothing we could do about it. Our goal was limited to observation and exploration. We hoped to go a little farther, perhaps, and see a little more; if not, simply to go and to see. A simple ambition, I think, and essentially a modest one.

Yet it would have remained less than an ambition, no more than a longing, but for the support and encouragement of my dear cousin and friend Juana —————. (I use no surnames, lest this report fall into strangers' hands at last, and embarrassment or unpleasant notoriety thus be brought upon unsuspecting husbands, sons, etc.) I had lent Juana my copy of *The Voyage of the Discovery,* and it was she who, as we strolled beneath our parasols across the Plaza de Armas after Mass one Sunday in 1908, said, "Well, if Captain Scott can do it, why can't we?"

It was Juana who proposed that we write Carlotta ——— in Valparaiso. Through Carlota we met our benefactor, and so obtained our money, our ship, and even the plausible pretext of going on retreat in a Bolivian convent, which some of us were forced to employ (while the rest of us said we were going to Paris for the winter season). And it was my Juana who in the darkest moments remained resolute, unshaken in her determination to achieve our goal.

And there were dark moments, especially in the early months of 1909—times when I did not see how the Expedition would ever become more than a quarter ton of pemmican gone to waste and a lifelong regret. It was so very hard to gather our expeditionary force together! So few of those we asked even knew what we were talking about—so many thought we were mad, or wicked, or both! And of those few who shared our folly, still fewer were able, when it came to the point, to leave their daily duties and commit themselves to a voyage of at least six months, attended with not inconsiderable uncertainty and danger. An ailing parent; an anxious husband beset by business cares; a child at home with only ignorant or incompetent servants to look after it: these are not responsibilities lightly to be set aside. And those who wished to evade such claims were not the companions we wanted in hard work, risk, and privation.

But since success crowned our efforts, why dwell on the setbacks and delays, or the wretched contrivances and downright lies that we all had to employ? I look back with regret only to those friends who wished to come with us but could not, by any contrivance, get free—those we had to leave behind to a life without danger, without uncertainty, without hope.

On the seventeenth of August, 1909, in Punta Arenas, Chile, all the members of the Expedition met for the first time: Juana and I, the two Peruvians; from Argentina, Zoe, Berta, and Teresa; and our Chileans, Carlota and her friends Eva, Pepita, and Dolores. At the last moment 1 had received word that Maria's husband, in Quito, was ill, and she must stay to nurse him, so we were nine, not ten. Indeed, we had resigned ourselves to being but eight, when, just as night fell, the indomitable Zoe arrived in a tiny pirogue manned by Indians, her yacht having sprung a leak just as it entered the Strait of Magellan.

That night before we sailed we began to get to know one another; and we agreed, as we enjoyed our abominable supper in the abominable seaport inn of Punta Arenas, that if a situation arose of such urgent danger that one voice must be obeyed without present question, the unenviable honor of speaking with that voice should fall first upon myself; if I were incapacitated, upon Carlota; if she, then upon Berta. We three were then toasted as "Supreme Inca," "La Araucana," and "The Third Mate" among a lot of laughter and cheering. As it came out, to my very great pleasure and relief, my qualities as a "leader" were never tested; the nine of us worked things out amongst us from beginning to end without any orders being given by anybody, and only two or three times with recourse to a vote by voice or show of hands. To be sure, we argued a good deal. But then, we had time to argue. And one way or another the arguments always ended up in a decision, upon which action could be taken. Usually at least one person grumbled about the decision, sometimes bitterly. But what is life without grumbling, and the occasional opportunity to say, "I told you so"? How could one bear housework, or looking after babies, let alone the rigors of sledge-hauling in Antarctica, without grumbling? Officers—as we came to understand aboard the *Yelcho*—are forbidden to grumble; but we nine were, and are, by birth and upbringing, unequivocally and irrevocably, all crew.

Though our shortest course to the southern continent, and that originally urged upon us by the captain of our good ship, was to the

South Shetlands and the Bellingshausen Sea, or else by the South Orkneys into the Weddell Sea, we planned to sail west to the Ross Sea, which Captain Scott had explored and described, and from which the brave Ernest Shackleton had returned only the previous autumn. More was known about this region than any other portion of the coast of Antarctica, and though that more was not much, yet it served as some insurance of the safety of the ship, which we felt we had no right to imperil. Captain Pardo had fully agreed with us after studying the charts and our planned itinerary; and so it was westward that we took our course out of the Strait next morning.

Our journey half round the globe was attended by fortune. The little *Yelcho* steamed cheerily along through gale and gleam, climbing up and down those seas of the Southern Ocean that run unbroken round the world. Juana, who had fought bulls and the far more dangerous cows on her family's *estancia,* called the ship "*la vaca valiente,*" because she always returned to the charge. Once we got over being seasick we all enjoyed the sea voyage, though oppressed at times by the kindly but officious protectiveness of the captain and his officers, who felt that we were only "safe" when huddled up in the three tiny cabins which they had chivalrously vacated for our use.

We saw our first iceberg much farther south than we had looked for it, and saluted it with Veuve Clicquot at dinner. The next day we entered the ice pack, the belt of floes and bergs, broken loose from the land ice and winter-frozen seas of Antarctica, which drifts northward in the spring. Fortune still smiled on us: our little steamer, incapable, with her unreinforced metal hull, of forcing a way into the ice, picked her way from lane to lane without hesitation, and on the third day we were through the pack, in which ships have sometimes struggled for weeks and been obliged to turn back at last. Ahead of us now lay the dark grey waters of the Ross Sea, and beyond that, on the horizon, the remote glimmer, the cloud-reflected whiteness of the Great Ice Barrier.

Entering the Ross Sea a little east of Longitude West 160°, we came in sight of the Barrier at the place where Captain Scott's party, finding a bight in the vast wall of ice, had gone ashore and sent up their hydrogen-gas balloon for reconnaissance and photography. The towering face of the Barrier, its sheer cliffs and azure and violet water-worn caves, all were as described, but the location had changed:

instead of a narrow bight there was a considerable bay, full of the beautiful and terrific orca whales playing and spouting in the sunshine of that brilliant southern spring.

Evidently masses of ice many acres in extent had broken away from the Barrier (which—at least for most of its vast extent—does not rest on land but floats on water) since the *Discovery*'s passage in 1902. This put our plan to set up camp on the Barrier itself in a new light; and while we were discussing alternatives, we asked Captain Pardo to take the ship west along the Barrier face towards Ross Island and McMurdo Sound. As the sea was clear of ice and quite calm, he was happy to do so, and, when we sighted the smoke plume of Mount Erebus, to share in our celebration—another half case of Veuve Clicquot.

The *Yelcho* anchored in Arrival Bay, and we went ashore in the ship's boat. I cannot describe my emotions when I set foot on the earth, on that earth, the barren, cold gravel at the foot of the long volcanic slope. I felt elation, impatience, gratitude, awe, familiarity. I felt that I was home at last. Eight Addlie penguins immediately came to greet us with many exclamations of interest not unmixed with disapproval. "Where on earth have you been? What took you so long? The Hut is around this way. Please come this way. Mind the rocks!" They insisted on our going to visit Hut Point, where the large structure built by Captain Scott's party stood, looking just as in the photographs and drawings that illustrate his book. The area about it, however, was disgusting—a kind of graveyard of seal skins, seal bones, penguin bones, and rubbish, presided over by the mad, screaming skua gulls. Our escorts waddled past the slaughterhouse in all tranquillity, and one showed me personally to the door, though it would not go in.

The interior of the hut was less offensive, but very dreary. Boxes of supplies had been stacked up into a kind of room within the room; it did not look as I had imagined it when the *Discovery* party put on their melodramas and minstrel shows in the long winter night. (Much later, we learned that Sir Ernest had rearranged it a good deal when he was there just a year before us.) It was dirty, and had about it a mean disorder. A pound tin of tea was standing open. Empty meat tins lay about; biscuits were spilled on the floor; a lot of dog turds were underfoot—frozen, of course, but not a great deal improved by that. No doubt the last occupants had had to leave in a hurry, perhaps even in a blizzard. All the same, they could have closed the tea tin. But housekeeping, the art of the infinite, is no game for amateurs.

Teresa proposed that we use the hut as our camp. Zoe counter-proposed that we set fire to it. We finally shut the door and left it as we had found it. The penguins appeared to approve, and cheered us all the way to the boat.

McMurdo Sound was free of ice, and Captain Pardo now proposed to take us off Ross Island and across to Victoria Land, where we might camp at the foot of the Western Mountains, on dry and solid earth. But those mountains, with their storm-darkened peaks and hanging cirques and glaciers, looked as awful as Captain Scott had found them on his western journey, and none of us felt much inclined to seek shelter among them.

Aboard the ship that night we decided to go back and set up our base as we had originally planned, on the Barrier itself. For all available reports indicated that the clear way south was across the level Barrier surface until one could ascend one of the confluent glaciers to the high plateau which appears to form the whole interior of the continent. Captain Pardo argued strongly against this plan, asking what would become of us if the Barrier "calved"—if our particular acre of ice broke away and started to drift northward. "Well," said Zoe, "then you won't have to come so far to meet us." But he was so persuasive on this theme that he persuaded himself into leaving one of the *Yelcho*'s boats with us when we camped, as a means of escape. We found it useful for fishing, later on.

My first steps on Antarctic soil, my only visit to Ross Island, had not been pleasure unalloyed. I thought of the words of the English poet:

Though every prospect pleases,
And only Man is vile.

But then, the backside of heroism is often rather sad; women and servants know that. They know also that the heroism may be no less real for that. But achievement is smaller than men think. What is large is the sky, the earth, the sea, the soul I looked back as the ship sailed east again that evening. We were well into September now, with ten hours or more of daylight The spring sunset lingered on the twelve-thousand-foot peak of Erebus and shone rosy gold on her long plume of steam. The steam from our own small funnel faded blue on the twilit water as we crept along under the towering pale wall of ice.

On our return to "Orca Bay"—Sir Ernest, we learned years later, had named it the Bay of Whales—we found a sheltered nook where the Barrier edge was low enough to provide fairly easy access from the ship. The *Yelcho* put out her ice anchor, and the next long, hard days were spent in unloading our supplies and setting up our camp on the ice, a half kilometer in from the edge: a task in which the *Yelcho*'s crew lent us invaluable aid and interminable advice. We took all the aid gratefully, and most of the advice with salt.

The weather so far had been extraordinarily mild for spring in this latitude; the temperature had not yet gone below -20° Fahrenheit, and there was only one blizzard while we were setting up camp. But Captain Scott had spoken feelingly of the bitter south winds on the Barrier, and we had planned accordingly. Exposed as our camp was to every wind, we built no rigid structures above ground. We set up tents to shelter in while we dug out a series of cubicles in the ice itself, lined them with hay insulation and pine boarding, and roofed them with canvas over bamboo poles, covered with snow for weight and insulation. The big central room was instantly named Buenos Aires by our Argentineans, to whom the center, wherever one is, is always Buenos Aires. The heating and cooking stove was in Buenos Aires. The storage tunnels and the privy (called Punta Arenas) got some back heat from the stove. The sleeping cubicles opened off Buenos Aires, and were very small, mere tubes into which one crawled feet first; they were lined deeply with hay and soon warmed by one's body warmth. The sailors called them "coffins" and "wormholes," and looked with horror on our burrows in the ice. But our little warren or prairie-dog village served us well, permitting us as much warmth and privacy as one could reasonably expect under the circumstances. If the *Yelcho* was unable to get through the ice in February, and we had to spend the winter in Antarctica, we certainly could do so, though on very limited rations. For this coming summer, our base—Sudamérica del Sur, South South America, but we generally called it the Base—was intended merely as a place to sleep, to store our provisions, and to give shelter from blizzards.

To Berta and Eva, however, it was more than that. They were its chief architect-designers, its most ingenious builder-excavators, and its most diligent and contented occupants, forever inventing an improvement in ventilation, or learning how to make skylights, or revealing to us a new addition to our suite of rooms, dug in the living ice. It was thanks to them that our stores were stowed so handily, that our stove drew and heated so efficiently, and that Buenos Aires, where nine people cooked, ate, worked, conversed, argued, grumbled, painted, played the guitar and banjo, and kept the Expedition's library of books and maps, was a marvel of comfort and convenience. We lived there in real amity; and if you simply had to be alone for a while, you crawled into your sleeping hole head first.

Berta went a little farther. When she had done all she could to make South South America livable, she dug out one more cell just under the ice surface, leaving a nearly transparent sheet of ice like a greenhouse roof; and there, alone, she worked at sculptures. They were beautiful forms, some like a blending of the reclining human figure with the subtle curves and volumes of the Weddell seal, others like the fantastic shapes of ice cornices and ice caves. Perhaps they are there still, under the snow, in the bubble in the Great Barrier. There where she made them they might last as long as stone. But she could not bring them north. That is the penalty for carving in water.

Captain Pardo was reluctant to leave us, but his orders did not permit him to hang about the Ross Sea indefinitely, and so at last, with many earnest injunctions to us to stay put—make no journeys—take no risks—beware of frostbite—don't use edge tools—look out for cracks in the ice—and a heartfelt promise to return to Orca Bay on the twentieth of February, or as near that date as wind and ice would permit, the good man bade us farewell, and his crew shouted us a great goodbye cheer as they weighed anchor. That evening, in the long orange twilight of October, we saw the topmast of the Yelcho go down the north horizon, over the edge of the world, leaving us to ice, and silence, and the Pole.

That night we began to plan the Southern Journey.

The ensuing month passed in short practice trips and depot-laying. The life we had led at home, though in its own way strenuous, had not fitted any of us for the kind of strain met in sledge-hauling at ten or twenty degrees below freezing. We all needed as much working out as possible before we dared undertake a long haul.

My longest exploratory trip, made with Dolores and Carlota, was southwest towards Mount Markham, and it was a nightmare—blizzards and pressure ice all the way out, crevasses and no view of the mountains when we got there, and white weather and sastrugi all the way back. The trip was useful, however, in that we could begin to estimate our capacities; and also in that we had started out with a very heavy load of provisions, which we depoted at 100 and 130 miles SSW of Base. Thereafter other parties pushed on farther, till we had a line of snow cairns and depots right down to Latitude 83° 43' where Juana and Zoe, on an exploring trip, had found a kind of stone gateway opening on a great glacier leading south. We established these depots to avoid, if possible, the hunger that had bedevilled Captain Scott's Southern Party, and the consequent misery and weakness. And we also established to our own satisfaction—intense satisfaction—that we were sledgehaulers at least as good as Captain Scott's husky dogs. Of course we could not have expected to pull as much or as fast as his men. That we did so was because we were favored by much better weather than Captain Scott's party ever met on the Barrier; and also the quantity and quality of our food made a very considerable difference. I am sure that the fifteen percent of dried fruits in our pemmican helped prevent scurvy; and the potatoes, frozen and dried according to an ancient Andean Indian method, were very nourishing yet very light and compact—perfect sledging rations. In any case, it was with considerable confidence in our capacities that we made ready at last for the Southern Journey.

The Southern Party consisted of two sledge teams: Juana, Dolores, and myself; Carlota, Pepita, and Zoe. The support team of Berta, Eva, and Teresa set out before us with a heavy load of supplies, going right up onto the glacier to prospect routes and leave depots of supplies for our return journey. We followed five days behind them, and met them returning between Depot Ercilla and Depot Miranda (see map). That "night"—of course there was no real darkness—we were all nine together in the heart of the level plain of ice. It was the fifteenth of November, Dolores's birthday. We celebrated by putting eight ounces of pisco in the hot chocolate, and became very merry. We sang. It is strange now to remember how thin our voices sounded in that great silence. It was overcast, white weather, without shadows and without visible horizon or any feature to break the level; there was nothing to see at all. We had come to that white place on the map, that void, and there we flew and sang like sparrows.

After sleep and a good breakfast the Base Party continued north, and the Southern Party sledged on. The sky cleared presently. High up, thin clouds passed over very rapidly from southwest to northeast, but down on the Barrier it was calm and just cold enough, five or ten degrees below freezing, to give a firm surface for hauling.

On the level ice we never pulled less than eleven miles, seventeen kilometers, a day, and generally fifteen or sixteen miles, twenty-five kilometers. (Our instruments, being British made, were calibrated in feet, miles, degrees Fahrenheit, etc., but we often converted miles to kilometers because the larger numbers sounded more encouraging.) At the Jime we left South America, we knew only that Mr. Shackleton had mounted another expedition to the Antarctic in 1908, had tried to attain the Pole but failed, and had returned to England in June of the current year, 1909. No coherent report of his explorations had yet reached South America when we left; we did not know what route he had gone, or how far he had got. But we were not altogether taken by surprise when, far across the featureless white plain, tiny beneath the mountain peaks and the strange silent flight of the rainbow-fringed cloud wisps, we saw a fluttering dot of black. We turned west from our course to visit it: a snow heap nearly buried by the winter's storms—a flag on a bamboo pole, a mere shred of threadbare cloth—an empty oilcan—and a few footprints standing some inches above the ice. In some conditions of weather the snow compressed under one's weight remains when the surrounding soft snow melts or is scoured away by the wind; and so these reversed footprints had been left standing all these months, like rows of cobbler's lasts—a queer sight.

We met no other such traces on our way. In general I believe our course was somewhat east of Mr. Shackleton's. Juana, our surveyor, had trained herself well and was faithful and methodical in her sightings and readings, but our equipment was minimal—a theodolite on tripod legs, a sextant with artificial horizon, two compasses, and chronometers. We had only the wheel meter on the sledge to give distance actually travelled.

In any case, it was the day after passing Mr. Shackleton's waymark that I first saw clearly the great glacier among the mountains to the southwest, which was to give us a pathway from the sea level of the Barrier up to the altiplano, ten thousand feet above. The approach was magnificent a gateway formed by immense vertical domes and pillars of rock. Zoe and Juana had called the vast ice river that flowed through that gateway the Florence Nightingale Glacier, wishing to honor the British, who had been the inspiration and guide of our expedition; that very brave and very peculiar lady seemed to represent so much that is best and strangest, in the island race. On maps, of course, this glacier bears the name Mr. Shackleton gave it, the Beardmore.

The ascent of the Nightingale was not easy. The way was open at first, and well marked by our support party, but after some days we came among terrible crevasses, a maze of hidden cracks, from a foot to thirty feet wide and from thirty to a thousand feet deep. Step by step we went, and step by step, and the way always upward now. We were fifteen days on the glacier. At first the weather was hot, up to 20° Fahrenheit, and the hot nights without darkness were wretchedly uncomfortable in our small tents. And all of us suffered more or less from snowblindness just at the time when we wanted clear eyesight to pick our way among the ridges and crevasses of the tortured ice, and to see the wonders about and before us. For at every day's advance more great, nameless peaks came into view in the west and southwest, summit beyond summit, range beyond range, stark rock and snow in the unending noon.

We gave names to these peaks, not very seriously, since we did not expect our discoveries to come to the attention of geographers. Zoe had gift for naming, and it is thanks to her that certain sketch maps in various suburban South American attics bear such curious features as "Bolivar's Big Nose," "I Am General Rosas," "The Cloudmaker," "Whose Toe?" and "Throne of Our Lady of the Southern Cross." And when at last we got up onto the altiplano, the great interior plateau, it was Zoe who called it the pampa, and maintained that we walked there among vast herds of invisible cattle, transparent cattle pastured on the spindrift snow, their gauchos the restless, merciless winds. We were by then all a little crazy with exhaustion and the great altitude—twelve thousand feet—and the cold and the wind blowing and the luminous circles and crosses surrounding the suns, for often there were three or four suns in the sky, up there.

That is not a place where people have any business to be. We should have turned back; but since we had worked so hard to get there, it seemed that we should go on, at least for a while.

A blizzard came with very low temperatures, so we had to stay in the tents, in our sleeping bags, for thirty hours, a rest we all needed;

though it was warmth we needed most, and there was no warmth on that terrible plain anywhere at all but in our veins. We huddled close together all that time. The ice we lay on is two miles thick.

It cleared suddenly and became, for the plateau, good weather: twelve below zero and the wind not very strong. We three crawled out of our tent and met the others crawling out of theirs. Carlota told us then that her group wished to turn back. Pepita had been feeling very ill; even after the rest during the blizzard, her temperature would not rise above 94°. Carlota was having trouble breathing. Zoe was perfectly fit, but much preferred staying with her friends and lending them a hand in difficulties to pushing on towards the Pole. So we put the four ounces of pisco which we had been keeping for Christmas into the breakfast cocoa, and dug out our tents, and loaded our sledges, and parted there in the white daylight on the bitter plain.

Our sledge was fairly light by now. We pulled on to the south. Juana calculated our position daily. On the twenty-second of December, 1909, we reached the South Pole. The weather was, as always, very cruel. Nothing of any kind marked the dreary whiteness. We discussed leaving some kind of mark or monument, a snow cairn, a tent pole and flag; but there seemed no particular reason to do so. Anything we could do, anything we were, was insignificant, in that awful place. We put up the tent for shelter for an hour and made a cup of tea, and then struck "90° Camp." Dolores, standing patient as ever in her sledging harness, looked at the snow; it was so hard frozen that it showed no trace of our footprints coming, and she said, "Which way?"

"North," said Juana.

It was a joke, because at that particular place there is no other direction. But we did not laugh. Our lips were cracked with frostbite and hurt too much to let us laugh. So we started back, and the wind at our backs pushed us along, and dulled the knife edges of the waves of frozen snow.

All that week the blizzard wind pursued us like a pack of mad dogs. I cannot describe it. I wished we had not gone to the Pole. I think I wish it even now. But I was glad even then that we had left no sign there, for some man longing to be first might come some day, and find it, and know then what a fool he had been, and break his heart.

We talked, when we could talk, of catching up to Carlota's party, since they might be going slower than we. In fact they had used their tent as a sail to catch the following wind and had got far ahead of us. But in many places they had built snow cairns or left some sign for us; once Zoe had written on the lee side of a ten-foot sastrugi, just as children write on the sand of the beach at Miraflores, "This Way Out!" The wind blowing over the frozen ridge had left the words perfectly distinct.

In the very hour that we began to descend the glacier, the weather turned warmer, and the mad dogs were left to howl forever tethered to the Pole. The distance that had taken us fifteen days going up we covered in only eight days going down. But the good weather that had aided us descending the Nightingale became a curse down on the Barrier ice, where we had looked forward to a kind of royal progress from depot to depot, eating our fill and taking our time for the last three hundred-odd miles. In a tight place on the glacier I lost my goggles—I was swinging from my harness at the time in a crevasse— and then Juana had broken hers when we had to do some rock climbing coming down to the Gateway. After two days in bright sunlight with only one pair of snow goggles to pass amongst us, we were all suffering badly from snowblindness. It became acutely painful to keep lookout for landmarks or depot flags, to take sightings, even to study the compass, which had to be laid down on the snow to steady the needle. At Concolorcorvo Depot, where there was a particularly good supply of food and fuel, we gave up, crawled into our sleeping bags with bandaged eyes, and slowly boiled alive like lobsters in the tent exposed to the relentless sun. The voices of Berta and Zoe were the sweetest sound I ever heard. A little concerned about us, they had skied south to meet us. They led us home to Base.

We recovered quite swiftly, but the altiplano left its mark. When she was very little, Rosita asked if a dog "had bitted Mama's toes." I told her, Yes, a great, white, mad dog named Blizzard! My Rosita and my Juanito heard many stories when they were little, about that fearful dog and how it howled, and the transparent cattle of the invisible gauchos, and a river of ice eight thousand feet high called Nightingale, and how Cousin Juana drank a cup of tea standing on the bottom of the world under seven suns, and other fairy tales.

We were in for one severe shock when we reached Base at last. Teresa was pregnant. I must admit that my first response to the poor girl's big belly and sheepish look was anger—rage—fury. That one of us should have concealed anything, and such a thing, from the others! But Teresa had done nothing of the sort. Only those who had concealed from her what she most needed to know were to blame. Brought up by servants, with four years' schooling in a convent, and married at sixteen, the poor girl was still so ignorant at twenty years of age that she had thought it was "the cold weather" that made her miss her periods. Even this was not entirely stupid, for all of us on the Southern Journey had seen our periods change or stop altogether as we experienced increasing cold, hunger, and fatigue. Teresa's appetite had begun to draw general attention; and then she had begun, as she said pathetically, "to get fat." The others were worried at the thought of all the sledge-hauling she had done, but she flourished, and the only problem was her positively insatiable appetite. As well as could be determined from her shy references to her last night on the hacienda with her husband, the baby was due at just about the same time as the *Yelcho,* the twentieth of February. But we had not been back from the Southern Journey two weeks when, on February 14, she went into labor.

Several of us had borne children and had helped with deliveries, and anyhow most of what needs to be done is fairly self-evident; but a first labor can be long and trying, and we were all anxious, while Teresa was frightened out of her wits. She kept calling for her José till she was as hoarse as a skua. Zoe lost all patience at last and said, "By God, Teresa, if you say 'José!' once more I hope you have a penguin!" But what she had, after twenty long hours, was a pretty little red-faced girl.

Many were the suggestions for that child's name from her eight proud midwife-aunts: Polita, Penguina, McMurdo, Victoria . . . But Teresa announced, after she had had a good sleep and a large serving of pemmican, "I shall name her Rosa—Rosa del Sur," Rose of the South. That night we drank the last two bottles of Veuve Clicquot (having finished the pisco at 88° 30' South) in toasts to our little Rose.

On the nineteenth of February, a day early, my Juana came down into Buenos Aires in a hurry. "The ship," she said, "the ship has come," and she burst into tears—she who had never wept in all our weeks of pain and weariness on the long haul.

Of the return voyage there is nothing to tell. We came back safe.

In 1912 all the world learned that the brave Norwegian Amundsen had reached the South Pole; and then, much later, came the accounts of how Captain Scott and his men had come there after him, but did not come home again.

Just this year, Juana and I wrote to the captain of the *Yelcho,* for the newspapers have been full of the story of his gallant dash to rescue Sir Ernest Shackleton's men from Elephant Island, and we wished to congratulate him, and once more to thank him. Never one word has he breathed of our secret. He is a man of honor, Luis Pardo.

I add this last note in 1929. Over the years we have lost touch with one another. It is very difficult for women to meet, when they live so far apart as we do. Since Juana died, I have seen none of my old sledge-mates, though sometimes we write. Our little Rosa del Sur died of the scarlet fever when she was five years old. Teresa had many other children. Carlota took the veil in Santiago ten years ago. We are old women now, with old husbands, and grown children, and grandchildren who might someday like to read about the Expedition. Even if they are rather ashamed of having such a crazy grandmother, they may enjoy sharing in the secret. But they must not let Mr. Amundsen know! He would be terribly embarrassed and disappointed. There is no need for him or anyone else outside the family to know. We left no footprints, even.

Fire Watch

۞

by Connie Willis

I am consistently stunned that anthology after anthology purporting to be about women in science fiction ignores Connie Willis. If a story of hers is included, it's generally "Even The Queen," which even Connie admits is not representative of her work.

Connie Willis's eleven Hugo Awards mark her as the person in the science fiction field who has won the most Hugo Awards for fiction. Hands down. Her closest competitor is Harlan Ellison, who won eight, if you count the one he won for his script for Star Trek's *"City on The Edge of Forever" episode.*

Most of Connie's nominations have been for short fiction. Even when she doesn't win, she still makes the record books. For example, in 1992, she was nominated in all three short fiction categories. She has also won seven Nebula Awards, two Arthur C. Clarke Awards, and has been chosen as a Grand Master of science fiction by SFWA.

She's as adept as a novelist as she is as a short fiction writer. Her books Blackout *and* All Clear *are the best time travel novel I've read in years. (And yes, I mean* novel, *singular. Her publisher couldn't figure out how to publish that long work in one volume, one of the many marketing mistakes that have hampered her popular appeal at the novel length.)*

To fail to include Connie Willis in any anthology claiming to publish classic works of science fiction by women and *men is just plain astonishing. To limit her short work to one short story is just as astonishing. If this is your introduction to Connie's short fiction, pick up* The Best of Connie Willis, *and disappear into some marvelous fiction.*

We close the volume with Connie's "Fire Watch." The story won the Hugo and Nebula for Best Novelette in 1982. "Fire Watch" features the timetraveling historians from Oxford University who later appear in Connie's award-winning novels, Doomsday Book, To Say Nothing of The Dog, Blackout *and* All Clear. *"Fire Watch" brings the Blitz in London in 1940 into full and dramatic life—fictional time travel at its finest.*

❁ ❁ ❁

> *History hath triumphed over time, which besides it*
> *nothing but eternity hath triumphed over.*
> — Sir Walter Raleigh

September 20—Of course the first thing I looked for was the fire watch stone. And of course it wasn't there yet. It wasn't dedicated until 1951, accompanying speech by the Very Reverend Dean Walter Matthews, and this is only 1940. I knew that. I went to see the fire watch stone only yesterday, with some kind of misplaced notion that seeing the scene of the crime would somehow help. It didn't.

The only things that would have helped were a crash course in "London during the Blitz" and a little more time. I had not gotten either.

"Traveling in time is not like taking the Tube, Mr. Bartholomew," the esteemed Dunworthy had said, blinking at me through those antique spectacles of his. "Either you report on the twentieth or you don't go at all."

"But I'm not ready," I'd said. "Look, it took me four years to get ready to travel with St. Paul. *St. Paul.* Not St. Paul's. You can't expect me to get ready for London in the Blitz in two days."

"Yes," Dunworthy had said. "We can." End of conversation.

"Two days!" I had shouted at my roommate Kivrin. "All because some computer adds an 's.'"

"And the esteemed Dunworthy doesn't even bat an eye when I tell him. 'Time travel is not like taking the tube, young man,' he says. 'I'd suggest you get ready. You're leaving the day after tomorrow.' The man's a total incompetent."

"No," she said. "He isn't. He's the best there is. He wrote the book on St. Paul's. Maybe you should listen to what he says."

I had expected Kivrin to be at least a little sympathetic. She had been practically hysterical when her practicum got changed from fifteenth- to fourteenth-century England, and how did either century qualify as a practicum? Even counting infectious diseases, they couldn't have been more than a five. The Blitz is an eight, and St. Paul's itself is, with my luck, a ten.

"You think I should go see Dunworthy again?" I said.

"Yes."

"And then what? I've got two days. I don't know the money, the language, the history. Nothing."

"He's a good man," Kivrin said. "I think you'd better listen to him while you can." Good old Kivrin. Always the sympathetic ear.

The good man was responsible for my standing just inside the propped-open west doors, gawking like the country boy I was supposed to be, looking for a stone that wasn't there. Thanks to the good man, I was about as unprepared for my practicum as it was possible for him to make me.

I couldn't see more than a few feet into the church. I could see a candle gleaming feebly a long way off and a closer blur of white moving toward me. A verger, or possibly the Very Reverend Dean himself. I pulled out the letter from my clergyman uncle in Wales that was supposed to gain me access to the Dean, and patted my back pocket to make sure I hadn't lost the microfiche *Oxford English Dictionary, Revised, with Historical Supplements* I'd smuggled out of the Bodleian. I couldn't pull it out in the middle of the conversation, but with luck I could muddle through the first encounter by context and look up the words I didn't know later.

"Are you from the ayarpee?" he said. He was no older than I am, a head shorter and much thinner. Almost ascetic-looking. He reminded me of Kivrin. He was not wearing white, but clutching it to his chest. In other circumstances I would have thought it was a pillow. In other circumstances I wouldn't know what was being said to me, but there had been no time to unlearn sub-Mediterranean Latin and Jewish law and learn Cockney and air raid procedures.

Two days, and the esteemed Dunworthy, who wanted to talk about the sacred burdens of the historian instead of telling me what the ayarpee was.

"Are you?" he demanded again.

I considered whipping out the OED after all on the grounds that Wales was a foreign country, but I didn't think they had microfiche in 1940. Ayarpee. It could be anything, including a nickname for the fire watch, in which case the impulse to say no was not safe at all. "No," I said.

He lunged suddenly toward and past me and peered out the open doors. "Damn," he said, coming back to me. "Where are they then? Bunch of lazy bourgeois tarts!" And so much for getting by on context.

He looked at me closely, suspiciously, as if he thought I was only pretending not to be with the ayarpee. "The church is closed," he said finally.

I held up the envelope and said, "My name's Bartholomew. Is Dean Matthews in?"

He looked out the door a moment longer as if he expected the lazy bourgeois tarts at any moment and intended to attack them with the white bundle; then he turned and said, as if he were guiding a tour, "This way, please," and took off into the gloom.

He led me to the right and down the south aisle of the nave. Thank God I had memorized the floor plan or, at that moment, heading into total darkness, led by a raving verger, the whole bizarre metaphor of my situation would have been enough to send me out the west doors and back to St. John's Wood. It helped a little to know where I was. We should have been passing number twenty-six: Hunt's painting of *The Light of the World*—Jesus with his lantern—but it was too dark to see it. We could have used the lantern ourselves.

He stopped abruptly ahead of me, still raving. "We weren't asking for the bloody savoy, just a few cots. Nelson's better off than we are— at least he's got a pillow provided." He brandished the white bundle like a torch in the darkness. It was a pillow after all. "We asked for them over a fortnight ago, and here we still are, sleeping on the bleeding generals from Trafalgar because those bitches want to play tea and crumpets with the tommies at victoria and the hell with us!"

He didn't seem to expect me to answer his outburst, which was good, because I had understood perhaps one key word in three. He stomped on ahead, moving out of sight of the one pathetic altar candle and stopping again at a black hole. Number twenty-five: stairs to the Whispering Gallery, the dome, the library (not open to the public).

Up the stairs, down a hall, stop again at a medieval door and knock. "I've got to go wait for them," he said. "If I'm not there they'll likely take them over to the abbey. Tell the Dean to ring them up again, will you?" and he took off down the stone steps, still holding his pillow like a shield against him.

He had knocked, but the door was at least a foot of solid oak, and it was obvious the Very Reverend Dean had not heard. I was going to have to knock again. Yes, well, and the man holding the pinpoint had to let go of it, too, but even knowing it will all be over in a moment and you won't feel a thing doesn't make it any easier to say, "Now!"

So I stood in front of the door, cursing the history department and the esteemed Dunworthy and the computer that had made the mistake and brought me here to this dark door with only a letter from a fictitious uncle whom I trusted no more than I trusted the rest of them.

Even the old reliable Bodleian had let me down. The batch of research stuff I'd cross-ordered through Balliol and the main terminal is probably sitting in my room right now, a century out of reach. And Kivrin, who had already done her practicum and should have been bursting with advice, walked around as silent as a saint until I begged her to help me.

"Did you go to see Dunworthy?" she said.

"Yes. You want to know what priceless bit of information he had for me? 'Silence and humility are the sacred burdens of the historian.' He also told me I would love St. Paul's. Golden gems from the Master. Unfortunately, what I need to know are the times and places of the bombs so one doesn't fall on me." I flopped down on the bed. "Any suggestions?"

"How good are you at memory retrieval?" she said.

I sat up. "I'm pretty good. You think I should assimilate?"

"There isn't time for that," she said. "I think you should put everything you can directly into long-term."

"You mean endorphins?" I said.

The biggest problem with using memory-assistance drugs to put information into your long-term memory is that it never sits, even for a microsecond, in your short-term memory, and that makes retrieval complicated, not to mention unnerving. It gives you the most unsettling sense of déjà vu to suddenly know something you're positive you've never seen or heard before.

The main problem, though, is not eerie sensations but retrieval. Nobody knows exactly how the brain gets what it wants out of storage, but short-term is definitely involved. That brief, sometimes microscopic, time information spends in short-term is apparently used for something besides tip-of-the-tongue availability. The whole complex sort-and-file process of retrieval is apparently centered in the short-term, and without it, and without the help of the drugs that put it there or artificial substitutes, information can be impossible to retrieve. I'd used endorphins for examinations and never had any difficulty with retrieval, and it looked like it was the only way to store all the information I needed in anything approaching the time I had left, but it also meant that I would *never* have known any of the things I needed to know, even for long enough to have forgotten them. If and when I could retrieve the information, I would know it. Till then I was as ignorant of it as if it were not stored in some cobwebbed corner of my mind at all.

"You can retrieve without artificials, can't you?" Kivrin said, looking skeptical.

"I guess I'll have to."

"Under stress? Without sleep? Low body endorphin levels?" What exactly had her practicum been? She had never said a word about it, and undergraduates are not supposed to ask. Stress factors in the Middle Ages? I thought everybody slept through them.

"I hope so," I said. "Anyway, I'm willing to try this idea if you think it will help."

She looked at me with that martyred expression and said, "Nothing will help." Thank you, St. Kivrin of Balliol.

But I tried it anyway. It was better than sitting in Dunworthy's rooms having him blink at me through his historically accurate eyeglasses and tell me I was going to love St. Paul's. When my Bodleian requests didn't come, I overloaded my credit and bought out Blackwell's. Tapes on World War II, Celtic literature, history of mass transit, tourist guidebooks, everything I could think of. Then I rented a high-speed recorder and shot up. When I came out of it, I was so panicked by the feeling of not knowing any more than I had when I started that I took the Tube to London and raced up Ludgate Hill to see if the fire watch stone would trigger any memories.

It didn't.

"Your endorphin levels aren't back to normal yet," I told myself and tried to relax, but that was impossible with the prospect of the practicum looming up before me. And those are real bullets, kid. Just because you're a history major doing his practicum doesn't mean you can't get killed.

I read history books all the way home on the Tube and right up until Dunworthy's flunkies came to take me to St. John's Wood this morning. Then I jammed the microfiche OED in my back pocket and went off feeling as if I would have to survive by my native wit and hoping I could get hold of artificials in 1940. Surely I could get through the first day without mishap, I thought, and now here I was, stopped cold by almost the first word that was spoken to me.

Well, not quite. In spite of Kivrin's advice that I not put anything in short-term, I'd memorized the British money, a map of the tube system, a map of my own Oxford. It had gotten me this far. Surely I would be able to deal with the Dean.

Just as I had almost gotten up the courage to knock, he opened the door, and as with the pinpoint, it really was over quickly and without pain. I handed him my letter and he shook my hand and said something understandable like, "Glad to have another man, Bartholomew."

He looked strained and tired and as if he might collapse if I told him the Blitz had just started. I know, I know: Keep your mouth shut. The sacred silence, etc.

He said, "We'll get Langby to show you round, shall we?" I assumed that was my Verger of the Pillow, and I was right. He met us at the foot of the stairs, puffing a little but jubilant.

"The cots came," he said to Dean Matthews. "You'd have thought they were doing us a favor. All high heels and hoity-toity. 'You made us miss our tea, luv,' one of them said to me. 'Yes, well, and a good thing, too,' I said. 'You look as if you could stand to lose a stone or two.'"

Even Dean Matthews looked as though he did not completely understand him. He said, "Did you set them up in the crypt?" and then introduced us. "Mr. Bartholomew's just got in from Wales," he said. "He's come to join our volunteers." Volunteers, not fire watch.

Langby showed me around, pointing out various dimnesses in the general gloom, and then dragged me down to see the ten folding canvas cots set up among the tombs in the crypt, also in passing, Lord Nelson's black marble sarcophagus. He told me I don't have to stand a watch the first night and suggested I go to bed, since sleep is the most precious commodity in the raids. I could well believe it. He was clutching that silly pillow to his breast like his beloved.

"Do you hear the sirens down here?" I asked, wondering if he buried his head in it.

He looked round at the low stone ceilings. "Some do, some don't. Brinton has to have his Horlich's. Bence-Jones would sleep if the roof fell in on him. I must have a pillow. The important thing is to get your eight in no matter what. If you don't, you turn into one of the walking dead. And then you get killed."

On that cheering note he went off to post the watches for tonight, leaving his pillow on one of the cots with orders for me to let nobody touch it. So here I sit, waiting for my first air raid siren and trying to get all this down before I turn into one of the walking or non-walking dead.

I've used the stolen OED to decipher a little Langby. Middling success. A tart is either a pastry or a prostitute (I assume the latter, although I was wrong about the pillow). "Bourgeois" is a catchall term for all the faults of the middle class. A Tommy's a soldier. Ayarpee I could not find under any spelling and I had nearly given up when something in long-term about the use of acronyms and abbreviations in wartime popped forward (bless you, St. Kivrin) and I realized it must be an abbreviation. ARP. Air Raid Precautions. Of course. Where else would you get the bleeding cots from?

September 21—Now that I'm past the first shock of being here, I realize that the history department neglected to tell me what I'm supposed to do in the three-odd months of this practicum. They handed me this journal, the letter from my uncle, and a ten-pound note and sent me packing into the past. The ten pounds (already depleted by train and tube fares) is supposed to last me until the end of December and get me back to St. John's Wood for pickup when the second letter calling me back to Wales to my ailing uncle's bedside comes.

Till then I live here in the crypt with Nelson, who, Langby tells me, is pickled in alcohol inside his coffin. If we take a direct hit, will he burn like a torch or simply trickle out in a decaying stream onto the crypt floor, I wonder. Board is provided by a gas ring, over which are cooked wretched tea and indescribable kippers. To pay for all this luxury I am to stand on the roofs of St. Paul's and put out incendiaries.

I must also accomplish the purpose of this practicum, whatever it may be. Right now the only purpose I care about is staying alive until the second letter from Uncle arrives and I can go home.

I am doing make-work until Langby has time to "show me the ropes". I've cleaned the skillet they cook the foul little fishes in, stacked wooden folding chairs at the altar end of the crypt (flat instead of standing because they tend to collapse like bombs in the middle of the night), and tried to sleep.

I am apparently not one of the lucky ones who can sleep through the raids. I spend most of the night wondering what St. Paul's risk rating is. Practica have to be at least a six. Last night I was convinced this was a ten, with the crypt as ground zero, and that I might as well have applied for Denver.

The most interesting thing that's happened so far is that I've seen a cat. I am fascinated, but trying not to appear so since they seem commonplace here.

September 22—Still in the crypt. Langby comes dashing through periodically cursing various government agencies (all abbreviated) and promising to take me up on the roofs. In the meantime, I've run out of make-work and taught myself to work a stirrup pump. Kivrin was overly concerned about my memory-retrieval abilities. I have not had any trouble so far. Quite the opposite. I called up firefighting information and got the whole manual with pictures, including instructions on the use of the stirrup pump. If the kippers set Lord Nelson on fire, I shall be a hero.

Excitement last night. The sirens went early and some of the chars who clean offices in the City sheltered in the crypt with us. One of them woke me out of a sound sleep, going like an air-raid siren. Seems she'd seen a mouse. We had to go whacking at tombs and under the cots with a rubber boot to persuade her it was gone. Obviously what the history department had in mind: murdering mice.

September 24—Langby took me on rounds. Into the choir, where I had to learn the stirrup pump all over again, assigned rubber boots and a tin helmet. Langby says Commander Allen is getting us asbestos firemen's coats, but hasn't yet, so it's my own wool coat and muffler and very cold on the roofs even in September. It feels like November and looks it, too, bleak and cheerless with no sun. Up to the dome and onto the roofs, which should be flat but in fact are littered with towers, pinnacles, gutters, statues, all designed expressly to catch and hold incendiaries out of reach. Shown how to smother an incendiary with sand before it burns through the roof and sets the church on fire. Shown the ropes (literally) lying in a heap at the base of the dome in case somebody has to go up one of the west towers or over the top of the dome. Back inside and down to the Whispering Gallery.

Langby kept up a running commentary through the whole tour, part practical instruction, part church history. Before we went up into the Gallery he dragged me over to the south door to tell me how Christopher Wren stood in the smoking rubble of Old St. Paul's and asked a workman to bring him a stone from the graveyard to mark the cornerstone. On the stone was written in Latin, "I shall rise again," and Wren was so impressed by the irony that he had the word inscribed above the door. Langby looked as smug as if he had not told me a story every first-year history student knows, but I suppose without the impact of the fire watch stone, the other is just a nice story.

Langby raced me up the steps and onto the narrow balcony circling the Whispering Gallery. He was already halfway round to the other side, shouting dimensions and acoustics at me. He stopped facing the wall opposite and said softly, "You can hear me whispering because of the shape of the dome. The sound waves are reinforced around the perimeter of the dome. It sounds like the very crack of doom up here during a raid. The dome is one hundred and seven feet across. It is eighty feet above the nave."

I looked down. The railing went out from under me and the black-and-white marble floor came up with dizzying speed. I hung onto something in front of me and dropped to my knees, staggered and sick at heart. The sun had come out, and all of St. Paul's seemed drenched in gold. Even the carved wood of the choir, the white stone pillars, the leaden pipes of the organ, all of it golden, golden.

Langby was beside me, trying to pull me free. "Bartholomew," he shouted, "what's wrong? For God's sake, man."

I knew I must tell him that if I let go, St. Paul's and all the past would fall in on me, and that I must not let that happen because I was an historian. I said something, but it was not what I intended because Langby merely tightened his grip. He hauled me violently free of the railing and back onto the stairway, then let me collapse limply on the steps and stood back from me, not speaking.

"I don't know what happened in there," I said. "I've never been afraid of heights before."

"You're shaking," he said sharply. "You'd better lie down." He led me back to the crypt.

September 25—Memory retrieval: ARP manual. Symptoms of bombing victims. Stage one—shock; stupefaction; unawareness of injuries; words may not make sense except to victim. Stage two—shivering; nightmares; nausea; injuries; losses felt; return to reality. Stage three—talkativeness that cannot be controlled; desire to explain shock behavior to rescuers.

Langby must surely recognize the symptoms, but how does he account for the fact there was no bomb? I can hardly explain my shock behavior to him, and it isn't just the sacred silence of the historian that stops me.

He has not said anything, in fact assigned me my first watches for tomorrow night as if nothing had happened, and he seems no more preoccupied than anyone else. Everyone I've met so far is jittery (one thing I had in short-term was how calm everyone was during the raids) and the raids have not come near us since I got here. They've been mostly over the East End and the docks.

There was reference tonight to a UXB, and I have been thinking about the Dean's manner and the church being closed, when I'm almost sure I remember reading it was open through the entire Blitz. As soon as I get a chance, I'll try to retrieve the events of September. As to retrieving anything else, I don't see how I can hope to remember the right information until I know what it is I am supposed to do here, if anything.

There are no guidelines for historians, and no restrictions, either. I could tell everyone I'm from the future if I thought they would believe me. I could murder Hitler if I could get to Germany. Or could I? Time paradox talk abounds in the history department, and the graduate students back from their practica don't say a word one way or the other. Is there a tough, immutable past? Or is there a new past every day and do we, the historians, make it? And what are the consequences of what we do, if there are consequences? And how do we dare do anything without knowing them? Must we interfere boldly, hoping we do not bring about all our downfalls? Or must we do nothing at all, not interfere, stand by and watch St. Paul's burn to the ground if need be so that we don't change the future?

All those are fine questions for a late-night study session. They do not matter here. I could no more let St. Paul's burn down than I could kill Hitler. No, that is not true. I found that out yesterday in the Whispering Gallery. I could kill Hitler if I caught him setting fire to St. Paul's.

September 26—I met a young woman today. Dean Matthews has opened the church, so the watch have been doing duties as chars and people have started coming in again. The young woman reminded me of Kivrin, though Kivrin is a good deal taller and would never frizz her hair like that. She looked as if she had been crying. Kivrin has looked like that since she got back from her practicum. The Middle Ages were too much for her. I wonder how she would have coped with this. By pouring out her fears to the local priest, no doubt, as I sincerely hoped her look-alike was not going to do.

"May I help you?" I said, not wanting in the least to help. "I'm a volunteer."

She looked distressed. "You're not paid?" she said, and wiped at her reddened nose with a handkerchief. "I read about St. Paul's and the fire watch and all, and I thought, perhaps there's a position there for me. In the canteen, like, or something. A paying position." There were tears in her red-rimmed eyes.

"I'm afraid we don't have a canteen," I said as kindly as I could, considering how impatient Kivrin always makes me, "and it's not actually a real shelter. Some of the watch sleep in the crypt. I'm afraid we're all volunteers, though."

"That won't do, then," she said. She dabbed at her eyes with the handkerchief. "I love St. Paul's, but I can't take on volunteer work, not with my little brother Tom back from the country."

I was not reading this situation properly. For all the outward signs of distress she sounded quite cheerful and no closer to tears than when she had come in.

"I've got to get us a proper place to stay. With Tom back, we can't go on sleeping in the Tube."

A sudden feeling of dread, the kind of sharp pain you get sometimes from involuntary retrieval, went over me. "The Tube?" I said, trying to get at the memory.

"Marble Arch, usually," she went on. "My brother Tom saves us a place early and I go . . ." She stopped, held the handkerchief close to her nose, and exploded into it. "I'm sorry," she said, "this awful cold!"

Red nose, watering eyes, sneezing. Respiratory infection. It was a wonder I hadn't told her not to cry. It's only by luck that I haven't made some unforgivable mistake so far, and this is not because I can't get at the long-term memory. I don't have half the information I need even stored: cats and colds and the way St. Paul's looks in full sun. It's only a matter of time before I am stopped cold by something I do not know. Nevertheless, I am going to try for retrieval tonight after I come off watch. At least I can find out whether and when something is going to fall on me.

I have seen the cat once or twice. He is coal-black with a white patch on h is throat that looks as if it were painted on for the blackout.

September 27—I have just come down from the roofs. I am still shaking.

Early in the raid the bombing was mostly over the East End. The view was incredible. Searchlights everywhere, the sky pink from the fires and reflecting in the Thames, the exploding shells sparkling like fireworks. There was a constant, deafening thunder broken by the occasional droning of the planes high overhead, then the repeating stutter of the ack-ack guns.

About midnight the bombs began falling quite near with a horrible sound like a train running over me. It took every bit of will I had to keep from flinging myself flat on the roof, but Langby was watching. I didn't want to give him the satisfaction of watching a repeat performance of my behavior in the dome. I kept my head up and my sand bucket firmly in hand and felt quite proud of myself.

The bombs stopped roaring past about three, and there was a lull of about half an hour, and then a clatter like hail on the roofs. Everybody except Langby dived for shovels and stirrup pumps. He was watching me. And I was watching the incendiary.

It had fallen only a few meters from me, behind the clock tower. It was much smaller than I had imagined, only about thirty centimeters long. It was sputtering violently, throwing greenish-white fire almost to where I was standing. In a minute it would simmer down into a molten mass and begin to burn through the roof. Flames and the frantic shouts of firemen, and then the white rubble stretching for miles and nothing, nothing left, not even the fire watch stone.

It was the Whispering Gallery all over again. I felt that I had said something, and when I looked at Langby's face he was smiling crookedly.

"St Paul's will burn down," I said. "There won't be anything left."

"Yes," Langby said. "That's the idea, isn't it? Burn St. Paul's to the ground? Isn't that the plan?"

"Whose plan?" I said stupidly.

"Hitler's, of course," Langby said. "Who did you think I meant?" and, almost casually, picked up his stirrup pump.

The page of the ARP manual flashed suddenly before me. I poured the bucket of sand around the still sputtering bomb, snatched up another bucket and dumped that on top of it. Black smoke billowed up in such a cloud that I could hardly find my shovel. I felt for the smothered bomb with the tip of it and scooped it into the empty bucket, then shoveled the sand in on top of it. Tears were streaming down my face from the acrid smoke. I turned to wipe them on my sleeve and saw Langby.

He had not made a move to help me. He smiled. "It's not a bad plan, actually. But of course we won't let it happen. That's what the fire watch is here for. To see that it doesn't happen. Right, Bartholomew?"

I know now what the purpose of my practicum is. I must stop Langby from burning down St. Paul's.

September 28—I try to tell myself I was mistaken about Langby last night, that I misunderstood what he said. Why would he want to burn down St. Paul's unless he is a Nazi spy? How can a Nazi spy have gotten on the fire watch? I think about my faked letter of introduction and shudder.

How can I find out? If I set him some test, some fatal thing that only a loyal Englishman in 1940 would know, I fear I am the one who would be caught out. I must get my retrieval working properly.

Until then, I shall watch Langby. For the time being at least, that should be easy. Langby has just posted the watches for the next two weeks. We stand every one together.

September 30—I know what happened in September. Langby told me.

Last night in the choir, putting on our coats and boots, he said, "They've already tried once, you know."

I had no idea what he meant. I felt as helpless as that first day when he asked me if I was from the ayarpee.

"The plan to destroy St. Paul's. They've already tried once. The tenth of September. A high-explosive bomb. But of course you didn't know about that. You were in Wales."

I was not even listening. The minute he had said "high-explosive bomb," I had remembered it all. It had burrowed in under the road and lodged on the foundations. The bomb squad had tried to defuse it, but there was a leaking gas main. They'd decided to evacuate St. Paul's, but Dean Matthews had refused to leave, and they'd got it out after all and exploded it in Barking Marshes. Instant and complete retrieval.

"The bomb squad saved her that time," Langby was saying. "It seems there's always somebody about."

"Yes," I said, "there is," and walked away from him.

October 1—I thought last night's retrieval of the events of September tenth meant some sort of breakthrough, but I have been lying here on my cot most of the night trying for Nazi spies in St. Paul's and getting nothing. Do I have to know exactly what I'm looking for before I can remember it? What good does that do me?

Maybe Langby is not a Nazi spy. Then what is he? An arsonist? A madman? The crypt is hardly conducive to thought, being not at all as silent as a tomb. The chars talk most of the night and the sound of the bombs is muffled, which somehow makes it worse. I find myself straining to hear them, When I did get to sleep this morning, I dreamed about one of the tube shelters being hit, broken mains, drowning people.

October 4—I tried to catch the cat today. I had some idea of persuading it to dispatch the mouse that has been terrifying the chars. I also wanted to see one up close. I took the water bucket I had used with the stirrup pump last night to put out some burning shrapnel from one of the antiaircraft guns. It still had a bit of water in it, but not enough to drown the cat, and my plan was to clamp the bucket over him, reach under, and pick him up, then carry him down to the crypt and point him at the mouse. I did not even come close to him.

I swung the bucket, and as I did so, perhaps an inch of water splashed out. I thought I remembered that the cat was a domesticated animal, but I must have been wrong about that. The cat's wide complacent face pulled back into a skull-like mask that was absolutely terrifying, vicious claws extended from what I had thought were harmless paws, and the cat let out a sound to top the chars.

In my surprise I dropped the bucket and it rolled against one of the pillars. The cat disappeared. Behind me, Langby said, "That's no way to catch a cat."

"Obviously," I said, and bent to retrieve the bucket.

"Cats hate water," he said, still in that expressionless voice.

"Oh," I said, and started in front of him to take the bucket back to the choir. "I didn't know that."

"Everybody knows it. Even the stupid Welsh."

October 8—We have been standing double watches for a week—bomber's moon. Langby didn't show up on the roofs, so I went looking for him in the church. I found him standing by the west doors talking to an old man. The man had a newspaper tucked under his arm and he handed it to Langby, but Langby gave it back to him. When the man saw me, he ducked out. Langby said, "Tourist. Wanted to know where the Windmill Theatre is. Read in the paper the girls are starkers."

I know I looked as if I didn't believe him because he said, "You look rotten, old man. Not getting enough sleep, are you? I'll get somebody to take the first watch for you tonight."

"No," I said coldly. "I'll stand my own watch. I like being on the roofs," and added silently, where I can watch you.

He shrugged and said, "I suppose it's better than being down in the crypt. At least on the roofs you can hear the one that gets you."

October 10—I thought the double watches might be good for me, take my mind off my inability to retrieve. The watched pot idea. Actually, it sometimes works. A few hours of thinking about something else, or a good night's sleep, and the fact pops forward without any prompting, without any artificials.

The good night's sleep is out of the question. Not only do the chars talk constantly, but the cat has moved into the crypt and sidles up to everyone, making siren noises and begging for kippers. I am moving my cot out of the transept and over by Nelson before I go on watch. He may be pickled, but he keeps his mouth shut.

October 11—I dreamed Trafalgar, ships' guns and smoke and falling plaster and Langby shouting my name. My first waking thought was that the folding chairs had gone off. I could not see for all the smoke.

"I'm coming," I said, limping toward Langby and pulling on my boots. There was a heap of plaster and tangled folding chairs in the transept. Langby was digging in it. "Bartholomew!" he shouted, flinging a chunk of plaster aside. "Bartholomew!"

I still had the idea it was smoke. I ran back for the stirrup pump and then knelt beside him and began pulling on a splintered chair back. It resisted, and it came to me suddenly, There is a body under here. I will reach for a piece of the ceiling and find it is a hand. I leaned back on my heels, determined not to be sick, then went at the pile again.

Langby was going far too fast, jabbing with a chair leg. I grabbed his hand to stop him, and he struggled against me as if I were a piece of rubble to be thrown aside. He picked up a large flat square of plaster, and under it was the floor. I turned and looked behind me. Both chars huddled in the recess by the altar. "Who are you looking for?" I said, keeping hold of Langby's arm.

"Bartholomew," he said, and swept the rubble aside, his hands bleeding through the coating of smoky dust.

"I'm here," I said. "I'm all right." I choked on the white dust. "I moved my cot out of the transept."

He turned sharply to the chars and then said quite calmly, "What's under here?"

"Only the gas ring," one of them said timidly from the shadowed recess, "and Mrs. Galbraith's pocketbook." He dug through the mess until he had found them both. The gas ring was leaking at a merry rate, though the flame had gone out.

"You've saved St. Paul's and me after all," I said, standing there in my underwear and boots and holding the useless stirrup pump. "We might all have been asphyxiated."

He stood up. "I shouldn't have saved you," he said.

Stage one: shock, stupefaction, unawareness of injuries, words may not make sense except to victim. He would not know his hand was bleeding yet. He would not remember what he had said. He had said he shouldn't have saved my life.

"I shouldn't have saved you," he repeated. "I have my duty to think of."

"You're bleeding," I said sharply. "You'd better lie down." I sounded just like Langby in the Gallery.

October 13—It was a high explosive bomb. It blew a hole in the choir roof, and some of the marble statuary is broken, but the ceiling of the crypt did not collapse, which is what I thought at first. It only jarred some plaster loose.

I do not think Langby has any idea what he said. That should give me some sort of advantage, now that I am sure where the danger lies, now that I am sure it will not come crashing down from some other direction. But what good is all this knowing, when I do not know what he will do? Or when?

Surely I have the facts of yesterday's bomb in long-term, but even falling plaster did not jar them loose this time. I am not even trying for retrieval now. I lie in the darkness waiting for the roof to fall in on me. And remembering how Langby saved my life.

October 15—The girl came in again today. She still has the cold, but she has gotten her paying position. It was a joy to see her. She was wearing a smart uniform and open-toed shoes, and her hair was in an elaborate frizz around her face. We are still cleaning up the mess from the bomb, and Langby was out with Allen getting wood to board up the choir, so I let the girl chatter at me while I swept. The dust made her sneeze, but at least this time I knew what she was doing.

She told me her name is Enola and that she's working for the WVS, running one of the mobile canteens that are sent to the fires. She came, of all things, to thank me for the job. She said that after she told the WVS that there was no proper shelter with a canteen for St. Paul's, they gave her a run in the City. "So I'll just pop in when I'm close and let you know how I'm making out, won't I just?"

She and her brother Tom are still sleeping in the Tube. I asked her if that was safe and she said probably not, but at least down there you couldn't hear the one that got you and that was a blessing.

October 18—I am so tired I can hardly write this. Nine incendiaries tonight and a land mine that looked as though it was going to catch on the dome till the wind drifted its parachute away from the church. I put out two of the incendiaries. I have done that at least twenty times since I got here and helped with dozens of others, and still it is not enough. One incendiary, one moment of not watching Langby, could undo it all.

I know that is partly why I feel so tired. I wear myself out every night trying to do my job and watch Langby, making sure none of the incendiaries falls without my seeing it. Then I go back to the crypt and wear myself out trying to retrieve something, anything, about spies, fires, St. Paul's in the fall of 1940, anything. It haunts me that I am not doing enough, but I do not know that else to do. Without the retrieval, I am as helpless as these poor people here, with no idea what will happen tomorrow.

If I have to, I will go on doing this till I am called home. He cannot burn down St. Paul's so long as I am here to put out the incendiaries.

"I have my duty," Langby said in the crypt.

And I have mine.

October 21—It's been nearly two weeks since the blast and I just now realized we haven't seen the cat since. He wasn't in the mess in the crypt. Even after Langby and I were sure there was no one in there, we sifted through the stuff twice more. He could have been in the choir, though.

Old Bence-Jones says not to worry. "He's all right," he said. "The jerries could bomb London right down to the ground and the cats would waltz out to greet them. You know why? They don't love anybody. That's what gets half of us killed. Old lady out in Stepney got killed the other night trying to save her cat. Bloody cat was in the Anderson."

"Then where is he?"

"Someplace safe, you can bet on that. If he's not around St. Paul's, it means we're for it. That old saw about the rats deserting a sinking ship, that's a mistake, that is. It's cats, not rats."

October 25—Langby's tourist showed up again. He cannot still be looking for the Windmill Theatre. He had a newspaper under his arm again today, and he asked for Langby, but Langby was across town with Allen, trying to get the asbestos firemen's coats. I saw the name of the paper. It was *The Worker*. A Nazi newspaper?

November 2—I've been up on the roofs for a week straight, helping some incompetent workmen patch the hole the bomb made. They're doing a terrible job. There's still a great gap on one side a man could fall into, but they insist it'll be all right because, after all, you wouldn't fall clear through but only as far as the ceiling, and "the fall can't kill you". They don't seem to understand it's a perfect hiding place for an incendiary.

And that is all Langby needs. He does not even have to set a fire to destroy St. Paul's. All he needs to do is let one burn uncaught until it is too late.

I could not get anywhere with the workmen. I went down into the church to complain to Matthews, and saw Langby and his tourist behind a pillar, close to one of the windows. Langby was holding a newspaper and talking to the man. When I came down from the library an hour later, they were still there. So is the gap. Matthews says we'll put planks across it and hope for the best.

November 5—I have given up trying to retrieve. I am so far behind on my sleep I can't even retrieve information on a newspaper whose name I already know. Double watches the permanent thing now. Our chars have abandoned us altogether (like the cat), so the crypt is quiet, but I cannot sleep.

If I do manage to doze off, I dream. Yesterday I dreamed Kivrin was on the roofs, dressed like a saint. "What was the secret of your practicum?" I said. "What were you supposed to find out?"

She wiped her nose with a handkerchief and said, "Two things. One, that silence and humility are the sacred burdens of the historian. Two"—she stopped and sneezed into the handkerchief—"don't sleep in the Tube."

My only hope is to get hold of an artificial and induce a trance. That's a problem. I'm positive it's too early for chemical endorphins and probably hallucinogens. Alcohol is definitely available, but I need something more concentrated than ale, the only alcohol I know by name. I do not dare ask the watch. Langby is suspicious enough of me already. It's back to the OED, to look up a word I don't know.

November 11—The cat's back. Langby was out with Allen again, still trying for the asbestos coats, so I thought it was safe to leave St. Paul's. I went to the grocer's for supplies, and hopefully, an artificial. It was late, and the sirens sounded before I had even gotten to Cheapside, but the raids do not usually start until after dark. It took awhile to get all the groceries and to get up my courage to ask whether he had any alcohol—he told me to go to a pub—and when I came out of the shop, it was as if I had pitched suddenly into a hole.

I had no idea where St. Paul's lay, or the street, or the shop I had just come from. I stood on what was no longer the sidewalk, clutching my brown-paper parcel of kippers and bread with a hand I could not have seen if I held it up before my face. I reached up to wrap my muffler closer about my neck and prayed for my eyes to adjust, but there was no reduced light to adjust to. I would have been glad of the moon, for all St. Paul's watch cursed it and called it a fifth columnist. Or a bus, with its shuttered headlights giving just enough light to orient myself by. Or a searchlight. Or the kickback flare of an ack-ack gun. Anything.

Just then I did see a bus, two narrow yellow slits a long way off. I started toward it and nearly pitched off the curb. Which meant the bus was sideways in the street, which meant it was not a bus. A cat meowed, quite near, and rubbed against my leg. I looked down into the yellow lights I had thought belonged to the bus. His eyes were picking up light from somewhere, though I would have sworn there was not a light for miles, and reflecting it flatly up at me.

"A warden'll get you for those lights, old tom," I said, and then as a plane droned overhead, "Or a jerry."

The world exploded suddenly into light, the searchlights and a glow along the Thames seeming to happen almost simultaneously, lighting my way home.

"Come to fetch me, did you, old tom?" I said gaily. "Where've you been? Knew we were out of kippers, didn't you? I call that loyalty." I talked to him all the way home and gave him half a tin of the kippers for saving my life. Bence-Jones said he smelled the milk at the grocer's.

November 13—I dreamed I was lost in the blackout. I could not see my hands in front of my face, and Dunworthy came and shone a pocket torch at me, but I could only see where I had come from and not where I was going.

"What good is that to them?" I said. "They need a light to show them where they're going."

"Even the light from the Thames? Even the light from the fires and the ack-ack guns?" Dunworthy said.

"Yes. Anything is better than this awful darkness." So he came closer to give me the pocket torch. It was not a pocket torch, after all, but Christ's lantern from the Hunt picture in the south nave. I shone it on the curb before me so I could find my way home, but it shone instead on the fire watch stone and I hastily put the light out.

November 20—I tried to talk to Langby today. "I've seen you talking to that old gentleman," I said. It sounded like an accusation. I meant it to. I wanted him to think it was and stop whatever he was planning.

"Reading," he said. "Not talking." He was putting things in order in the choir, piling up sandbags.

"I've seen you reading then," I said belligerently, and he dropped a sandbag and straightened.

"What of it?" he said. "It's a free country. I can read to an old man if I want, same as you can talk to that little WVS tart."

"What do you read?" I said.

"Whatever he wants. He's an old man. He used to come home from his job, have a bit of brandy and listen to his wife read the papers to him. She got killed in one of the raids. Now I read to him. I don't see what business it is of yours."

It sounded true. It didn't have the careful casualness of a lie, and I almost believed him, except that I had heard the tone of truth from him before. In the crypt. After the bomb.

"I thought he was a tourist looking for the Windmill," I said.

He looked blank only a second, and then he said, "Oh, yes, that. He came in with the paper and asked me to tell him where it was. I looked it up to find the address. Clever, that. I didn't guess he couldn't read it for himself." But it was enough. I knew that he was lying.

He heaved a sandbag almost at my feet. "Of course you wouldn't understand a thing like that, would you? A simple act of human kindness."

"No," I said coldly. "I wouldn't."

None of this proves anything. He gave away nothing, except perhaps the name of an artificial, and I can hardly go to Dean Matthews and accuse Langby of reading aloud.

I waited till he had finished in the choir and gone down to the crypt. Then I lugged one of the sandbags up to the roof and over to the chasm. The planking has held so far, but everyone walks gingerly around it, as if it were a grave. I cut the sandbag open and spilled the loose sand into the bottom. If it had occurred to Langby that this is the perfect spot for an incendiary, perhaps the sand will smother it.

November 21—I gave Enola some of "Uncle's" money today and asked her to get me the brandy. She was more reluctant than I thought she'd be, so there must be societal complications I am not aware of, but she agreed.

I don't know what she came for. She started to tell me about her brother and some prank he'd pulled in the Tube that got him in trouble with the guard, but after I asked her about the brandy, she left without finishing the story.

November 25—Enola came today, but without bringing the brandy. She is going to Bath for the holidays to see her aunt. At least she will be away from the raids for a while. I will not have to worry about her. She finished the story of her brother and told me she hopes to persuade this aunt to take Tom for the duration of the Blitz but is not at all sure the aunt will be willing.

Young Tom is apparently not so much an engaging scapegrace as a near-criminal. He has been caught twice picking pockets in the Bank tube shelter, and they have had to go back to Marble Arch. I comforted her as best I could, told her all boys were bad at one time or another. What I really wanted to say was that she needn't worry at all, that young Tom strikes me as a true survivor type, like my own tom, like Langby, totally unconcerned with anybody but himself, well-equipped to survive the Blitz and rise to prominence in the future.

Then I asked her whether she had gotten the brandy.

She looked down at her open-toed shoes and muttered unhappily, "I thought you'd forgotten all about that."

I made up some story about the watch taking turns buying a bottle, and she seemed less unhappy, but I am not convinced she will not use this trip to Bath as an excuse to do nothing. I will have to leave St. Paul's and buy it myself, and I don't dare leave Langby alone in the church. I made her promise to bring the brandy today before she leaves. But she is still not back, and the sirens have already gone.

November 26—No Enola, and she said their train left at noon. I suppose I should be grateful that at least she is safely out of London. Maybe in Bath she will be able to get over her cold.

Tonight one of the ARP girls breezed in to borrow half our cots and tell us about a mess over in the East End where a surface shelter was hit. Four dead, twelve wounded. "At least it wasn't one of the tube shelters!" she said. "Then you'd see a real mess, wouldn't you?"

November 30—I dreamed I took the cat to St. John's Wood. "Is this a rescue mission?" Dunworthy said.

"No, sir," I said proudly. "I know what I was supposed to find in my practicum. The perfect survivor. Tough and resourceful and selfish. This is the only one I could find. I had to kill Langby, you know, to keep him from burning down St. Paul's. Enola's brother has gone to Bath, and the others will never make it. Enola wears open-toed shoes in the winter and sleeps in the tubes and puts her hair up on metal pins so it will curl. She cannot possibly survive the Blitz."

Dunworthy said, "Perhaps you should have rescued her instead. What did you say her name was?"

"Kivrin," I said, and woke up cold and shivering.

December 5—I dreamed Langby had the pinpoint bomb. He carried it under his arm like a brown paper parcel, coming out of St. Paul's Station and up Ludgate Hill to the west doors.

"This is not fair," I said, barring his way with my arm. "There is no fire watch on duty."

He clutched the bomb to his chest like a pillow. "That is your fault," he said, and before I could get to my stirrup pump and bucket, he tossed it in the door.

The pinpoint was not even invented until the end of the twentieth century, and it was another ten years before the dispossessed communists got hold of it and turned it into something that could be carried under your arm. A parcel that could blow a quarter mile of the City into oblivion. Thank God that is one dream that cannot come true.

It was a sunlit morning in the dream, and this morning when I came off watch the sun was shining for the first time in weeks. I went down to the crypt and then came up again, making the rounds of the roofs twice more, then of the steps and the grounds and all the treacherous alleyways between where an incendiary could be missed. I felt better after that, but when I got to sleep I dreamed again, this time of fire and Langby watching it, smiling.

December 15—I found the cat this morning. Heavy raids last night, but most of them over toward Canning Town and nothing on the roofs to speak of. Nevertheless the cat was quite dead. I found him lying on the steps this morning when I made my own private rounds. Concussion. There was not a mark on him anywhere except the white blackout patch on his throat, but when I picked him up, he was all jelly under the skin.

I could not think what to do with him. I thought for one mad moment of asking Matthews if I could bury him in the crypt. Honorable death in war or something. Trafalgar, Waterloo, London, died in battle. I ended by wrapping him in my muffler and taking him down Ludgate Hill to a building that had been bombed out and burying him in the rubble. It will do no good. The rubble will be no protection from dogs or rats, and I shall never get another muffler. I have gone through nearly all of Uncle's money.

I should not be sitting here. I haven't checked the alleyways or the rest of the steps, and there might be a dud or a delayed incendiary or something that I missed.

When I came here, I thought of myself as the noble rescuer, the savior of the past. I am not doing very well at the job. At least Enola is out of it. I wish there were some way I could send St. Paul's to Bath for safekeeping. There were hardly any raids last night. Bence-Jones said cats can survive anything. What if he was coming to get me, to show me the way home? All the bombs were over Canning Town.

December 16—Enola has been back a week. Seeing her, standing on the west steps where I found the cat, sleeping in Marble Arch and not safe at all, was more than I could absorb. "I thought you were in Bath," I said stupidly.

"My aunt said she'd take Tom but not me as well. She's got a houseful of evacuation children, and what a noisy lot. Where is your muffler?" she said. "It's dreadful cold up here on the hill."

"I . . ." I said, unable to answer, "I lost it."

"You'll never get another one," she said. "They're going to start rationing clothes. And wool, too. You'll never get another one like that."

"I know," I said, blinking at her.

"Good things just thrown away," she said. "It's absolutely criminal, that's what it is."

I don't think I said anything to that, just turned and walked away with my head down, looking for bombs and dead animals.

December 20—Langby isn't a Nazi. He's a communist. I can hardly write this. A communist.

One of the chars found *The Worker* wedged behind a pillar and brought it down to the crypt as we were coming off the first watch.

"Bloody communists," Bence-Jones said. "Helping Hitler, they are. Talking against the king, stirring up trouble in the shelters. Traitors, that's what they are."

"They love England same as you," the char said.

"They don't love nobody but themselves, bloody selfish lot. I wouldn't be surprised to hear they were ringing Hitler up on the telephone," Bence-Jones said. "'Ello, Adolf, here's where to drop the bombs.'"

The kettle on the gas ring whistled. The char stood up and poured the hot water into a chipped teapot, then sat back down. "Just because they speak their minds don't mean they'd burn down old St. Paul's, does it now?"

"Of course not," Langby said, coming down the stairs. He sat down and pulled off his boots, stretching his feet in their wool socks. "Who wouldn't burn down St. Paul's?"

"The communists," Bence-Jones said, looking straight at him, and I wondered if he suspected Langby too.

Langby never batted an eye. "I wouldn't worry about them if I were you," he said. "It's the jerries that are doing their bloody best to burn her down tonight. Six incendiaries so far, and one almost went into that great hole over the choir." He held out his cup to the char, and she poured him a cup of tea.

I wanted to kill him, smashing him to dust and rubble on the floor of the crypt while Bence-Jones and the char looked on in helpless surprise, shouting warnings to them and the rest of the watch. "Do you know what the communists did?" I wanted to shout. "Do you? We have to stop him." I even stood up and started toward him as he sat with his feet stretched out before him and his asbestos coat still over his shoulders.

And then the thought of the Gallery drenched in gold, the communist coming out of the tube station with the package so casually under his arm, made me sick with the same staggering vertigo of guilt and helplessness, and I sat back down on the edge of my cot and tried to think what to do.

They do not realize the danger. Even Bence-Jones, for all his talk of traitors, thinks they are capable only of talking against the king. They do not know, cannot know, what the communists will become. Stalin is an ally. Communists mean Russia. They have never heard of the USSR or Karinsky or the New Russia or any of the things that will make "communist" into a synonym for "monster". They will never know it. By the time the communists become what they became, there will be no fire watch. Only I know what it means to hear the name "communist" uttered here, so carelessly, in St. Paul's.

A communist. I should have known. I should have known.

December 22—Double watches again. I have not had any sleep and I am getting very unsteady on my feet. I nearly pitched into the chasm this morning, only saved myself by dropping to my knees. My endorphin levels are fluctuating wildly, and I know I must get some sleep soon or I will become one of Langby's walking dead, but I am afraid to leave him alone on the roofs, alone in the church with his communist party leader, alone anywhere. I have taken to watching him when he sleeps.

If I could just get hold of an artificial, I think I could induce a trance, in spite of my poor condition. But I cannot even go out to a pub. Langby is on the roofs constantly, waiting for his chance. When

Enola comes again, I must convince her to get the brandy for me. There are only a few days left.

December 28—Enola came this morning while I was on the west porch, picking up the Christmas tree. It has been knocked over three nights running by concussion. I righted the tree and was bending down to pick up the scattered tinsel when Enola appeared suddenly out of the fog like some cheerful saint. She stooped quickly and kissed me on the cheek. Then she straightened up, her nose red from her perennial cold, and handed me a box wrapped in colored paper.

"Merry Christmas," she said. "Go on then, open it. It's a gift."

My reflexes are almost totally gone. I knew the box was far too shallow for a bottle of brandy. Nevertheless I believed she had remembered, had brought me my salvation. "You darling," I said, and tore it open.

It was a muffler. Gray wool. I stared at if for fully half a minute without realizing what it was. "Where's the brandy?" I said.

She looked shocked. Her nose got redder and her eyes started to blur. "You need this more. You haven't any clothing coupons and you have to be outside all the time. It's been so dreadful cold."

"I needed the brandy," I said angrily.

"I was only trying to be kind," she started, and I cut her off.

"Kind?" I said. "I asked you for brandy. I don't recall ever saying I needed a muffler. "I shoved it back at her and began untangling a string of colored lights that had shattered when the tree fell.

She got that same holy martyr look Kivrin is so wonderful at. "I worry about you all the time up here," she said in a rush. "They're *trying* for St. Paul's, you know. And it's so close to the river. I didn't think you should be drinking. I . . . it's a crime when they're trying so hard to kill us all that you won't take care of yourself. It's like you're in it with them. I worry someday I'll come up to St. Paul's and you won't be here."

"Well, and what exactly am I supposed to do with a muffler? Hold it over my head when they drop the bombs?"

She turned and ran, disappearing into the gray fog before she had gone down two steps. I started after her, still holding the string of broken lights, tripped over it, and fell almost all the way to the bottom of the steps.

Langby picked me up. "You're off watches," he said grimly.

"You can't do that," I said.

"Oh, yes, I can. I don't want any walking dead on the roofs with me."

I let him lead me down here to the crypt, make me a cup of tea, put me to bed, all very solicitous. No indication that this is what he has been waiting for. I will lie here till the sirens go. Once I am on the roofs he will not be able to send me back without seeming suspicious. Do you know what he said before he left, asbestos coat and rubber boots, the dedicated fire watcher? "I want you to get some sleep." As if I could sleep with Langby on the roofs. I would be burned alive.

December 30—The sirens woke me yesterday, and old Bence-Jones said, "That should have done you some good. You've slept the clock round."

"What day is it?" I said, going for my boots.

"The twenty-ninth," he said, and as I dived for the door, "No need to hurry. They're late tonight. Maybe they won't come at all. That'd be a blessing, that would. The tide's out."

I stopped by the door to the stairs, holding on to the cool stone. "Is St. Paul's all right?"

"She's still standing," he said. "Have a bad dream?"

"Yes," I said, remembering the bad dreams of all the past weeks—the dead cat in my arms in St. John's Wood, Langby with his parcel and his *Worker* under his arm, the fire watch stone garishly lit by Christ's lantern. Then I remembered I had not dreamed at all. I had slept the kind of sleep I had prayed for, the kind of sleep that would help me remember.

Then I remembered. Not St. Paul's, burned to the ground by the communists. A headline from the dailies. "Marble Arch hit. Eighteen killed by blast." The date was not clear except for the year. 1940. There were exactly two more days left in 1940. I grabbed my coat and muffler and ran up the stairs and across the marble floor.

"Where the hell do you think you're going?" Langby shouted to me. I couldn't see him.

"I have to save Enola," I said, and my voice echoed in the dark sanctuary. "They're going to bomb Marble Arch."

"You can't leave now," he shouted after me, standing where the fire watch stone would be. "The tide's out. You dirty . . ."

I didn't hear the rest of it. I had already flung myself down the steps and into a taxi. It took almost all the money I had, the money I had so carefully hoarded for the trip back to St. John's Wood. Shelling started while we were still in Oxford Street, and the driver refused to go any farther. He let me out into pitch blackness, and I saw I would never make it in time.

Blast. Enola crumpled on the stairway down to the Tube, her open-toed shoes still on her feet, not a mark on her. And when I try to lift her, jelly under the skin. I would have to wrap her in the muffler she gave me, because I was too late. I had gone back a hundred years to be too late to save her.

I ran the last blocks, guided by the gun emplacement that had to be in Hyde Park, and skidded down the steps into Marble Arch. The woman in the ticket booth took my last shilling for a ticket to St. Paul's Station. I stuck it in my pocket and raced toward the stairs.

"No running," she said placidly. "To your left, please." The door to the right was blocked off by wooden barricades, the metal gates beyond pulled to and chained. The board with names on it for the stations was X-ed with tape, and a new sign that read ALL TRAINS was nailed to the barricade, pointing left.

Enola was not on the stopped escalators or sitting against the wall in the hallway. I came to the first stairway and could not get through. A family had set out, just where I wanted to step, a communal tea of bread and butter, a little pot of jam sealed with waxed paper, and a kettle on a ring like the one Langby and I had rescued out of the rubble, all of it spread on a cloth embroidered at the corners with flowers. I stood staring down at the layered tea, spread like a waterfall down the steps.

"I . . . Marble Arch . . ." I said. Another twenty killed by flying tiles. "You shouldn't be here."

"We've as much right as anyone," the man said belligerently, "and who are you to tell us to move on?"

A woman lifting saucers out of a cardboard box looked up at me, frightened. The kettle began to whistle.

"It's you that should move on," the man said. "Go on then." He stood off to one side so I could pass. I edged past the embroidered cloth apologetically.

"I'm sorry," I said. "I'm looking for someone. On the platform."

"You'll never find her in there, mate," the man said, thumbing in that direction. I hurried past him, nearly stepping on the tea cloth, and rounded the corner into hell.

It was not hell. Shopgirls folded coats and leaned back against them, cheerful or sullen or disagreeable, but certainly not damned. Two boys scuffled for a shilling and lost it on the tracks. They bent over the edge, debating whether to go after it, and the station guard yelled to them to back away. A train rumbled through, full of people. A mosquito landed on the guard's hand and he reached out to slap it and missed. The boys laughed. And behind and before them, stretching in all directions down the deadly tile curves of the tunnel like casualties, backed into the entranceways and onto the stairs, were people. Hundreds and hundreds of people.

I stumbled back onto the stairs, knocking over a teacup. It spilled like a flood across the cloth.

"I told you, mate," the man said cheerfully. "It's hell in there, ain't it? And worse below."

"Hell," I said. "Yes." I would never find her. I would never save her. I looked at the woman mopping up the tea, and it came to me that I could not save her either. Enola or the cat or any of them, lost here in the endless stairways and cul-de-sacs of time. They were already dead a hundred years, past saving. The past is beyond saving. Surely that was the lesson the history department sent me all this way to learn. Well, fine, I've learned it. Can I go home now?

Of course not, dear boy. You have foolishly spent all your money on taxicabs and brandy, and tonight is the night the Germans burn the City. (Now it is too late, I remember it all. Twenty-eight incendiaries on the roofs.) Langby must have his chance, and you must learn the hardest lesson of all and the one you should have known from the beginning. You cannot save St. Paul's.

I went back out onto the platform and stood behind the yellow line until a train pulled up. I took my ticket out and held it in my hand all the way to St. Paul's Station. When I got there, smoke billowed toward me like an easy spray of water. I could not see St. Paul's.

"The tide's out," a woman said in a voice devoid of hope, and I went down in a snake pit of limp cloth hoses. My hands came up covered with rank-smelling mud, and I understood finally (and too late) the significance of the tide. There was no water to fight the fires.

A policeman barred my way and I stood helplessly before him with no idea what to say. "No civilians allowed up there," he said. "St Paul's is for it." The smoke billowed like a thundercloud, alive with sparks, and the dome rose golden above it.

"I'm fire watch," I said, and his arm fell away, and then I was on the roofs.

My endorphin levels must have been going up and down like an air raid siren—I do not have any short-term from then on, just moments that do not fit together: the people in the church when we brought Langby down, huddled in a corner playing cards, the whirlwind of burning scraps of wood in the dome, the ambulance driver who wore open-toed shoes like Enola and smeared salve on my burned hands. And in the center, the one clear moment when I went after Langby on a rope and saved his life.

I stood by the dome, blinking against the smoke. The City was on fire and it seemed as if St. Paul's would ignite from the heat, would crumble from the noise alone. Bence-Jones was by the northwest tower, hitting at an incendiary with a spade. Langby was too close to the patched place where the bomb had gone through, looking toward me. An incendiary clattered behind him. I turned to grab a shovel, and when I turned back, he was gone.

"Langby!" I shouted, and could not hear my own voice. He had fallen into the chasm and nobody saw him or the incendiary. Except me. I do not remember how I got across the roof. I think I called for a rope. I got a rope. I tied it around my waist, gave the ends of it into the hands of the fire watch, and went over the side. The fires lit the walls of the hole almost all the way to the bottom. Below me I could see a pile of whitish rubble. He's under there, I thought, and jumped free of the wall. The space was so narrow there was nowhere to throw the rubble. I was afraid I would inadvertently stone him, and I tried to toss the pieces of planking and plaster over my shoulder, but there was barely room to turn.

For one awful moment I thought he might not be there at all, that the pieces of splintered wood would brush away to reveal empty pavement, as they had in the crypt.

I was numbed by the indignity of crawling over him. If he was dead I did not think I could bear the shame of stepping on his helpless body. Then his hand came up like a ghost's and grabbed my ankle, and within seconds I had whirled and had his head free.

He was the ghastly white that no longer frightens me. "I put the bomb out," he said. I stared at him, so overwhelmed with relief I could not speak. For one hysterical moment I thought I would even laugh, I was so glad to see him. I finally realized what it was I was supposed to say.

"Are you all right?" I said.

"Yes," he said, and tried to raise himself on one elbow. "So much the worse for you."

He could not get up. He grunted with pain when he tried to shift his weight to his right side and lay back, the uneven rubble crunching sickeningly under him. I tried to lift him gently so I could see where he was hurt. He must have fallen on something.

"It's no use," he said, breathing hard. "I put it out."

I spared him a startled glance, afraid that he was delirious and went back to rolling him onto his side.

"I know you were counting on this one," he went on, not resisting me at all. "It was bound to happen sooner or later with all these roofs. Only I went after it. What'll you tell your friends?"

His asbestos coat was torn down the back in a long gash. Under it his back was charred and smoking. He had fallen on the incendiary. "Oh, my God," I said, trying frantically to see how badly he was burned without touching him. I had no way of knowing how deep the burns went, but they seemed to extend only in the narrow space where the coat had torn. I tried to pull the bomb out from under him, but the casing was as hot as a stove. It was not melting, though. My sand and Langby's body had smothered it. I had no idea if it would start up again when it was exposed to the air. I looked around, a little wildly, for the bucket and stirrup pump Langby must have dropped when he fell.

"Looking for a weapon?" Langby said, so clearly it was hard to believe he was hurt at all. "Why not just leave me here? A bit of overexposure and I'd be done for by morning. Or would you rather do your dirty work in private?"

I stood up and yelled to the men on the roof above us. One of them shone a pocket torch down at us, but its light didn't reach.

"Is he dead?" somebody shouted down to me.

"Send for an ambulance," I said. "He's been burned."

I helped Langby up, trying to support his back without touching the burn. He staggered a little and then leaned against the wall, watching me as I tried to bury the incendiary, using a piece of the planking as a scoop. The rope came down and I tied Langby to it. He had not spoken since I helped him up. He let me tie the rope around his waist, still looking steadily at me. "I should have let you smother in the crypt," he said.

He stood leaning easily, almost relaxed against the wooden supports, his hands holding him up. I put his hands on the slack rope and wrapped it once around them for the grip I knew he didn't have. "I've been onto you since that day in the Gallery. I knew you weren't afraid of heights. You came down here without any fear of heights when you thought I'd ruined your precious plans. What was it? An attack of conscience? Kneeling there like a baby, whining, "What have we done? What have we done?" You made me sick. But you know what gave you away first? The cat. Everybody knows cats hate water. Everybody but a dirty Nazi spy."

There was a tug on the rope. "Come ahead," I said, and the rope tautened.

"That WVS tart? Was she a spy, too? Supposed to meet you in Marble Arch? Telling me it was going to be bombed. You're a rotten spy, Bartholomew. Your friends already blew it up in September. It's open again."

The rope jerked suddenly and began to lift Langby. He twisted his hands to get a better grip. His right shoulder scraped the wall. I put my hands and pushed him gently so that his left side was to the wall. "You're making a big mistake, you know," he said. "You should have killed me. I'll tell."

I stood in the darkness, waiting for the rope. Langby was unconscious when he reached the roof. I walked past the fire watch to the dome and down to the crypt.

This morning the letter from my uncle came and with it a five-pound note.

December 31—Two of Dunworthy's flunkies met me in St. John's Wood to tell me I was late for my exams. I did not even protest. I shuffled obediently after them without even considering how unfair it was to give an exam to one of the walking dead. I had not slept in— how long? Since yesterday, when I went to find Enola. I had not slept in a hundred years.

Dunworthy was at his desk, blinking at me. One of the flunkies handed me a test paper and the other one called time. I turned the paper over and left an oily smudge from the ointment on my burns. I stared uncomprehendingly at them. I had grabbed at the incendiary when I turned Langby over, but these burns were on the backs of my hands. The answer came to me suddenly in Langby's unyielding voice. "They're rope burns, you fool. Don't they teach you Nazi spies the proper way to come down a rope?"

I looked down at the test. It read, "Number of incendiaries that fell on St. Paul's. Number of land mines. Number of high-explosive bombs. Method most commonly used for extinguishing incendiaries. Land mines. High-explosive bombs. Number of volunteers on first watch. Second watch. Casualties. Fatalities." The questions made no sense. There was only a short space, long enough for the writing of a number, after any of the questions. Method most commonly used for extinguishing incendiaries. How would I ever fit what I knew into that narrow space? Where were the questions about Enola and Langby and the cat?

I went up to Dunworthy's desk. "St. Paul's almost burned down last night," I said. "What kind of questions are these?"

"You should be answering questions, Mr. Bartholomew, not asking them."

"There aren't any questions about the people," I said. The outer casing of my anger began to melt.

"Of course there are," Dunworthy said, flipping to the second page of the test. "Number of casualties, 1940. Blast, shrapnel, other."

"Other?" I said. At any moment the roof would collapse on me in a shower of plaster dust and fury. "*Other*? Langby put out a fire with his own body. Enola has a cold that keeps getting worse. The cat . . ." I snatched the paper back from him and scrawled "one cat" in the narrow space next to "blast". "Don't you care about them at all?"

"They're important from a statistical point of view," he said, "but as individuals they are hardly relevant to the course of history."

My reflexes were shot. It was amazing to me that Dunworthy's were almost as slow. I grazed the side of his jaw and knocked his glasses off. "Of course they're relevant!" I shouted. "They *are* the history, not all these bloody numbers!"

The reflexes of the flunkies were very fast. They did not let me start another swing at him before they had me by both arms and were hauling me out of the room.

"They're back there in the past with nobody to save them," I shouted. They can't see their hands in front of their faces and there are bombs falling down on them and you tell me they aren't important? You call that being an historian?"

The flunkies dragged me out the door and down the hall. "Langby saved St. Paul's. How much more important can a person get? You're no historian! You're nothing but a . . ." I wanted to call him a terrible name, but the only curses I could summon up were Langby's. "You're nothing but a dirty Nazi spy!" I bellowed. "You're nothing but a lazy bourgeois tart!"

They dumped me on my hands and knees outside the door and slammed it in my face. "I wouldn't be an historian if you paid me!" I shouted, and went to see the fire watch stone.

December 31—I am having to write this in bits and pieces. My hands are in pretty bad shape, and Dunworthy's boys didn't help matters much. Kivrin comes in periodically, wearing her St. Joan look, and smears so much salve on my hands that I can't hold a pencil.

St Paul's Station is not there, of course, so I got out at Holborn and walked, thinking about my last meeting with Dean Matthews on the morning after the burning of the city. This morning.

"I understand you saved Langby's life," he said. "I also understand that between you, you saved St. Paul's last night."

I showed him the letter from my uncle and he stared at it as if he could not think what it was. "Nothing stays saved forever," he said, and for a terrible moment I thought he was going to tell me Langby had died. "We shall have to keep on saving St. Paul's until Hitler decides to bomb something else."

The raids on London are almost over, I wanted to tell him. He'll start bombing the countryside in a matter of weeks. Canterbury, Bath, aiming always at the cathedrals. You and St. Paul's will both outlast the war and live to dedicate the fire watch stone.

"I am hopeful, though," he said. "I think the worst is over."

"Yes, sir." I thought of the stone, its letters still readable after all this time. No sir, the worst is not over.

I managed to keep my bearings almost to the top of Ludgate Hill. Then I lost my way completely, wandering about like a man in a graveyard. I had not remembered that the rubble looked so much like the white plaster dust Langby had tried to dig me out of. I could not find the stone anywhere. In the end I nearly fell over it, jumping back as if I had stepped on a grave.

It is all that's left. Hiroshima is supposed to have had a handful of untouched trees at ground zero, Denver the capitol steps. Neither of them says, "Remember men and women of St. Paul's Watch who by the grace of God saved this cathedral." The grace of God.

Part of the stone is sheared off. Historians argue there was another line that said, "for all time," but I do not believe that, not if Dean Matthews had anything to do with it. And none of the watch it was dedicated to would have believed it for a minute. We saved St. Paul's every time we put out an incendiary, and only until the next one fell. Keeping watch on the danger spots, putting out the little fires with sand and stirrup pumps, the big ones with our bodies, in order to keep the whole vast complex structure from burning down. Which sounds to me like a course description for History Practicum 401. What a fine time to discover what historians are for when I have tossed my chance for being one out the windows as easily as they tossed the pinpoint bomb in! No, sir, the worst is not over.

There are flash burns on the stone, where legend says the Dean of St. Paul's was kneeling when the bomb went off. Totally apocryphal, of course, since the front door is hardly an appropriate place for prayers. It is more likely the shadow of a tourist who wandered in to ask the whereabouts of the Windmill Theatre, or the imprint of a girl bringing a volunteer his muffler. Or a cat.

Nothing is saved forever, Dean Matthews, and I knew that when I walked in the west doors that first day, blinking in the gloom, but it is pretty bad nevertheless. Standing here knee-deep in rubble out of which I will not be able to dig any folding chairs or friends, knowing that Langby died thinking I was a Nazi spy, knowing that Enola came one day and I wasn't there. It's pretty bad.

But it is not as bad as it could be. They are both dead, and Dean Matthews too, but they died without knowing what I knew all along, what sent me to my knees in the Whispering Gallery, sick with grief and guilt: that in the end none of us saved St. Paul's. And Langby cannot turn to me, stunned and sick at heart, and say, "Who did this? Your friends the Nazis?" And I would have to say, "No, the communists." That would be the worst.

I have come back to the room and let Kivrin smear more salve on my hands. She wants me to get some sleep. I know I should pack and get gone. It will be humiliating to have them come and throw me out, but I do not have the strength to fight her. She looks so much like Enola.

January 1—I have apparently slept not only through the night, but through the morning mail drop as well. When I woke up just now, I found Kivrin sitting on the end of the bed holding an envelope. "Your exam results came," she said.

I put my arm over my eyes. "They can be marvelously efficient when they want to, can't they?"

"Yes," Kivrin said.

"Well, let's see it," I said, sitting up. "How long do I have before they come and throw me out?"

She handed the flimsy computer envelope to me. I tore it along the perforation. "Wait," she said. "Before you open it, I want to say something." She put her hand gently on my burns. "You're wrong about the history department. They're very good."

It was not exactly what I expected her to say. "Good is not the word I'd use to describe Dunworthy," I said and yanked the inside slip free.

Kivrin's look did not change, not even when I sat there with the printout on my knees where she could surely see it.

"Well," I said.

The slip was hand-signed by the esteemed Dunworthy. I have taken a first. With honors.

January 2—Two things came in the mail today. One was Kivrin's assignment. The history department thinks of everything—even to keeping her here long enough to nursemaid me, even to coming up with a prefabricated trial by fire to send their history majors through.

I think I wanted to believe that was what they had done, Enola and Langby only hired actors, the cat a clever android with its clockwork innards taken out for the final effect, not so much because I wanted to believe Dunworthy was not good at all, but because then I would not have this nagging pain at not knowing what had happened to them.

"You said your practicum was England in 1300?" I said, watching her as suspiciously as I had watched Langby.

"1348," she said, and her face went slack with memory. "The plague year."

"My God," I said. "How could they do that? The plague's a ten."

"I have a natural immunity," she said, and looked at her hands.

Because I could not think of anything to say, I opened the other piece of mail. It was a report on Enola. Computer-printed, facts and dates and statistics, all the numbers the history department so dearly loves, but it told me what I thought I would have to go without knowing: that she had gotten over her cold and survived the Blitz. Young Tom had been killed in the Baedeker raids on Bath, but Enola had lived until 2015, the year before they blew up St. Paul's.

I don't know whether I believe the report or not, but it does not matter. It is, like Langby's reading aloud to the old man, a simple act of human kindness. They think of everything.

Not quite. They did not tell me what happened to Langby. But I find as I write this that I already know: I saved his life. It does not seem to matter that he might have died in hospital next day, and I find, in spite of all the hard lessons the history department has tried to teach me, I do not quite believe this one: that nothing is saved forever. It seems to me that perhaps Langby is.

January 3—I went to see Dunworthy today. I don't know what I intended to say—some pompous drivel about my willingness to serve in the fire watch of history, standing guard against the falling incendiaries of the human heart, silent and saintly.

But he blinked at me nearsightedly across his desk, and it seemed to me that he was blinking at that last bright image of St. Paul's in sunlight before it was gone forever and that he knew better than anyone that the past cannot be saved, and I said instead, "I'm sorry that I broke your glasses, sir."

"How did you like St. Paul's?" he said, and like my first meeting with Enola, I felt I must be somehow reading the signals all wrong, that he was not feeling loss, but something quite different.

"I loved it, sir," I said.

"Yes," he said. "So do I."

Dean Matthews is wrong. I have fought with memory my whole practicum only to find that it is not the enemy at all, and being an historian is not some saintly burden after all. Because Dunworthy is not blinking against the fatal sunlight of the last morning, but into the bloom of that first afternoon, looking at the great west doors of St. Paul's at what is, like Langby, like all of it, every moment, in us, saved forever.

About the Editor

Award-winning editor Kristine Kathryn Rusch first retired from editing at the age of 37 when she stepped down as the first female editor of *The Magazine of Fantasy & Science Fiction* to pursue her writing career. She pursued that career with a vengeance, writing international best-selling books in science fiction, mystery, romance, and nonfiction. She has won awards in every genre. She returned to editing five years ago. She acts as series editor for *Fiction River,* a bimonthly multi-genre anthology series, occasionally editing one of the anthologies. She also works on other editing projects, including *The Best Mystery Fiction 2016* which she co-edited with John Helfers. She continues to write fiction as well. Her latest science fiction novel, *The Falls: A Diving Universe Novel,* will appear in October. For more on her various projects, head to her website at *kristinekathrynrusch.com.*